Coffee Mourning

Jennifer Betts

For my parents

Many thanks to my parents who inspired me to write this story. Thank you to my sisters Suzanne and Linda, brothers Paul and Gary, my sister in law Christine, my brother in law Alan and my nephews Adam, Darragh and Cian for their support and encouragement.

Thank you to Claire Voet and the team at Blossom Spring Publishing for believing in Coffee Mourning and giving me that break.

She walks like a timid schoolgirl, but is
fearsome when required
She's had so much hardship in her life, yet her
strength should be admired
She keeps a tight ship; you won't find dust
in her home
She always knows to call around when
you feel alone
She's funny without realising and easily teased
She only needs a chocolate cake to be easily pleased
She comes up to my shoulder, but to me
she's ten feet tall
And when life gets too much for me
she's there to catch me fall
There'll never be enough words to use,
nor paper to write upon
To sum up how empty this world would be
if she were gone
But I'm the lucky one; I've had a
relationship like no other
She's everything I want to be, she's a lady,
she's my mother

Chapter One

Mary's hair was washed and blow dried, but she nervously ran the hair straightener over it and combed out any loose ends. Her neat platinum blonde bob sat perfectly just above her shoulders. She didn't want to overdo it with the makeup, just her usual bit of black mascara and a thin layer of tinted moisturiser. A spritz of Lace perfume and her silk green scarf completed her casual yet smart outfit of black trousers and cowl-neck jumper. She wore the watch her daughter had bought her just that Christmas, but inside quibbled about wearing her wedding ring; her mother's wedding ring to be exact. She hated admitting to herself that she was separated, even the word made her shudder, as the word no longer made her part of an institution and at sixty-five—never would be again. She thought about her late mother at that moment and wondered aloud to herself whether she was being foolish in thinking that she could 'start over.' She took a long look in the mirror and was immediately shocked at how much she resembled her mother, wrinkles and all. Though she had a youthful fun look about her, that her mother never seemed to possess. Beautiful as her mother was, life had aged her quickly. She took one last deep breath and made her way to the bus stop, with exact change in her hand.

The weather was mild, especially for January in Dublin and a cool soothing breeze washed over her face. She checked her watch anxiously, even though she was too early for the bus. Then she noticed that her wedding ring had unconsciously made its way onto her ring finger. Shall I change fingers? She thought. But that would bring up even more questions than if she were to not wear it at all.

She nodded at passers-by who all knew her well, too

well at times. She was aware enough to know that they all wondered where she was going—all dressed up and alone. She had lived here all her life, yet sometimes would have preferred to live somewhere anonymously. Come to think of it, she'd never really had much choice about that, until now.

"Morning Mary, my God you're looking well today."

Mary's stomach lurched as the bus driver gave her some unwanted attention. She just nodded quietly and smiled, glad that an old woman behind her had no patience for morning pleasantries.

She sat at the back of the bus beside the window. She liked travelling, even though she had never managed to make it that far. As she neared her destination she thought about turning back around and heading home, but another thought of her mother entered her head and she kept on going. She twisted her wedding ring on her finger and quietly thanked her mother for the 'support.'

As she arrived at the building she'd expected it to be swarmed with people, but it was quiet. She looked around nervously and realised she had never been here before, even though it wasn't far from her house. Just then a young girl came up from behind her.

"Morning! I'm so sorry I don't usually leave the desk unmanned, but I was desperate if you know what I mean?"

Mary laughed knowingly. She knew only too well that in that condition when you had to go, you had to go. The young girl seemed sweet and immediately put her at ease.

"So, how can I help you, are you here for a class?"

"Well yes, well I don't know if you'd call it a class, but..."

"No problem, are you from the university?"

"Eh...the university? No I'm..."

"Oh God I'm so sorry, I think before I speak, I thought

you were a lecturer,"

"Oh no, I'm just a..."

"Doctor?"

"Hardly, unless you can become a doctor of house cleaning," Mary laughed nervously. The young girl looked confused, but her pleasant smile never left her face. Mary felt that foolish feeling coming back and wondered again what was she doing here? She also regretted her outfit, thinking she'd overdone it.

"I'm sorry, I should have given my name when I came in, I'm Mary Bannick, I'm starting a ladies' coffee morning here today,"

"Oooh right, great Mary, nice to meet you, I'm Charlotte. If you give me one minute I'll show you where to set up."

Mary looked around while she waited. There were pamphlets and posters everywhere, advertising everything from, Thai Boxing on a Wednesday night to Life Drawing on a Thursday afternoon. And something called Reiki, which Mary assumed was some sort of gardening class. As Charlotte led her down a long corridor to her room for the next few weeks, Mary looked left and right through the glass paned doors. There were women on floor mats, doing yoga or something, men and women sketching, children playing together, far from the quiet atmosphere of reception, the place was alive with activity. Her expression must have reflected her thoughts as Charlotte shot her a knowing look.

"Most people don't realise what goes on in a community centre these days. Do you know I have enrolled in a self-defence class? Well, it will have to wait for a few months I suppose."

Mary couldn't help but smile as the young Charlotte patted her belly.

"How far are you along?"

3

"Oh, five months, I'm going to try and work right up to the pregnancy to have more time to myself at the end of my leave, much to my husband's protests of course, he wants to do everything but have the baby for me!"

Mary smiled, kind of sadly, thinking how different things were these days. By the time she was thirty-five she already had three children and never contemplated any 'time' for herself after each was born. Nor did she ever indulge in any help from her husband. But that was the norm back then.

She arrived at her 'room' number 15B and Charlotte showed her in. It was small, but airy with about ten chairs in a circle in the centre of the room.

"Sorry," said Charlotte, "the last group must have left the chairs like that,"

"It's fine, I'm used to tidying up after people!" said Mary.

"Well there's a small kitchen behind that wall for making tea, there should be milk in the fridge but if not let me know and I'll get you some,"

Mary was a woman who always came prepared and gestured to her bag where she had picked up two litres of milk en route, along with a selection of her favourite biscuits.

"Right you are, so Mary, please open that window if it gets too hot and I'm just at reception if you need me. I'll direct the other women to the room as they arrive, byeee!" and Charlotte was gone, leaving Mary alone with her thoughts.

'Other women' the words echoed in Mary's head. She felt her stomach lurch again. It had been so long since she had met new people. Everyone thought of her as confident and outgoing, but inside there was always a girlish shyness about her. Being a housewife for over forty years hadn't helped that shyness much and now here she was again, nearly a pensioner, feeling like it was her first day at school.

Mary glanced around the room, not really knowing what to do. She started by locating the small kitchen and was glad when she opened the fridge that she had brought her own milk. Being the second week of January she suspected that the milk inside had been there since Christmas. She searched around for some cups and a plate to display her biscuits on and found some hidden away in a cupboard. Being a housewife from the old school Mary washed each cup out with washing up liquid and boiling hot water before she attempted to serve any tea in them. Not that she was snobbish, but when anyone came to her home they always got a spotlessly clean cup. Especially someone new, it made a good first impression. And although this wasn't her home, she would indeed be making a few first impressions today. She wondered how many of the women she would know and how many she wouldn't. She didn't know which was better. The people she knew may be people she disliked—the people she didn't know may in turn, not like her. She grappled with negative thoughts but abandoned them for a brief moment while she arranged the biscuits. She had been very careful in selecting her assortment. The last thing she needed was to be judged by her biscuit tastes. She thought about getting a large tin of USA biscuits, but thought them too 'naff' as her son would always say. Then she thought about millionaire shortcake from Marks and Spencer, but then it would look like she was trying too hard. She even thought about making them herself but thought that was better left to her chef daughter, Helen. In the end she opted for a mixture of Chocolate Kimberly, Fig rolls and Hobnobs. It didn't really matter to Mary, as long as they had lots of sugar in them, much to the dismay of her doctor. Her non-alcoholic, cigarette-free life had caught up with her in the area of her only vice—sweets! And it punished her with high cholesterol. But boy did she need her fix today, she would make up for it tomorrow.

Mary checked her watch again, 10.50am. She had put 11am on the flyer, but still felt nervous that no one had arrived yet. What if no one comes? She thought with utter dismay. She contemplated making a run for it, until she heard a voice behind her.

"Eh...scuse me, dis is coffee morning yes?"

A petite woman, about forty Mary guessed, stood in the doorway, peeking her head around the door. She had long jet-black hair and milky-white skin. Mary hadn't expected someone so young to show up, although the young woman dressed beyond her years and her eyes looked kind of tired.

"Yes, please come in, I'm Mary,"

The woman smiled and walked toward Mary. Mary berated herself in her mind for expecting only Irish women to turn up; she simply never thought. After a few awkward moments of showing her around, which took all of two minutes, the woman spoke to Mary, in good, but broken English, about how she too was nervous of coming along.

"My name is Rosa, I come from Poland. My husband he is working and I cannot because I have son. He is at school now. I try to make friends but it is hard. My English is not so good."

"Well I think you're doing a very good job," said Mary and Rosa smiled.

Mary surprised herself by putting Rosa at ease, even though she was nervous herself. The women chatted together as they made tea, in fact they were so engrossed in conversation that they hadn't noticed another woman enter the room.

She was full of energy and marched straight into the

room, hand extended.

"Hiya doing I'm Marjorie, Marji for short. God isn't it cold out? Glad Christmas is over."

Marji was a sight to behold, early fifties Mary assumed. Mary liked her instantly. She had never seen so many colours on one person. She wore a long pink woollen skirt, adorned with blue embroidered flowers, a mustard-coloured shirt and finished off with a green poncho. And her jewellery? It looked like she had worn every piece she had, not expensive, but your typical knick-knack kind of jewellery that you would pick up in George's Arcade. She had plum coloured hair to her shoulders and gave the biggest handshake, nearly crushing Mary's fingers. She spoke a mile a minute and for a moment Mary thought that Marjorie would have been a better candidate to host this coffee morning than she was. Marji helped herself to a cup of coffee with about five sugars and got acquainted with Rosa.

Another two women entered, one who Mary knew from the area, but just to say hello to and the other woman looked like she was from the nicer part of the neighbourhood, judging by her beautiful attire.

"Cathy with a C, so nice to meet you," she said in a drawn-out accent, offering her hand like the queen, putting emphasis on the word 'so.' Mary felt slightly intimidated and for a moment thought Cathy might be in the wrong place, until she made her way to the kitchen exclaiming, "Christ I need some caffeine." Cathy was stunning Mary had to admit. Golden blonde hair cut into a short bob, tall, figure to die for and immaculately presented, right down to her polished false nails. Mary couldn't take her eyes off her, until she was brought out of her daze.

"Hi! I'm Alice! You must be Mary," Alice beamed, her smile stretched across her face. She shook Mary's

7

hand vigorously and it made Mary want to laugh. She didn't of course, it was just that Alice seemed so eager, it was endearing. Alice was the youngest so far, early thirties Mary guessed, with long thick red hair and striking green eyes. Mary had seen her in the village a few times pushing a pram.

After the greetings the women were just getting ready to sit down and Mary, in her mind's absence had forgotten to rearrange the chairs, when the last of the 'desperate housewives' had arrived, an older woman of about seventy or older entered, her age was hard to tell. She had beautifully coiffed white hair and gripped her handbag fiercely. She made her way over to Mary and stretched out her hand.

"Good morning, I'm Brigid, so nice to meet you," she said in an articulate accent.

Mary smiled and shook her hand, "very nice to meet you Brigid, I'm Mary, welcome."

Brigid squeezed Mary's hand and smiled—for a moment Mary forgot her nerves. Brigid reminded her of her late mother, not in appearance, but she had that nurturing motherly air that gave Mary a warm, tender feeling.

As Mary composed herself, ready for the welcome speech, there was an interruption.

Another young woman knocked nervously on the glass panelled door and popped her head in. She scanned the room quickly.

"Oh, I'm sorry, I'm looking for Brigid Mannion, she's...oh Mum there you are."

"Claire!" Brigid exclaimed in embarrassment.

"Mum I'm sorry but you left your tablets in the car, thought you might need them."

"Yes, thank you love," Brigid said sheepishly.

"Ok then I'm off, bye ladies, Mum I'll be outside at

half twelve ok?"

Brigid's daughter spoke to her mother in a loving yet motherly way. As the group settled back down the chatting came to an uncomfortable end, they all averted their eyes from Brigid, to save her the embarrassment. But Brigid herself broke the ice.

"What is it when you get to a certain age, that your children think that they have to look after you?"

The women erupted into laughter at Brigid's all too familiar feeling and her comment immediately opened up a conversation that would run over their hour and a half slot.

By the time the first morning had ended, Mary had learned that Brigid had six grandchildren and was a retired school teacher, "I still see some of my students today, although it breaks my heart to see them pushing prams so young with cigarettes hanging out of the side of their mouths."

Rosa found Ireland to be as cold as Poland. "We come for my husband job, he is ah, how do you say? Um... bricks?"

"Brick layer," Marjorie interjected, "I should've been a brick layer, a humbler vocation than working in PR!" Marji had no children and loved her me time. Far from being jealous of her life of leisure, Mary found her fascinating.

Alice, a little bit ditsy but endearing, worked as a nanny, minding two small children, "I mean they're all rolled up, how do they get the fig into the tiny little slot? What are figs anyway?" Alice mused on the wonderment of Fig Rolls. Cathy had once been a model and had a slightly cynical view on life, "I'm so glad Christmas is over, thank God my child is out of that 'assemble my bike on Christmas Eve' phase!"

Mary's head was buzzing as she tidied up the empty

cups and saucers. The women were so unique to each other, and she was enthralled at the different personalities and the fact that she had brought them all together. She felt something she hadn't felt in a long time—satisfaction. A job well done. She wondered if she'd made a good impression, if she had much in common with the other women and most of all, had they noticed how nervous she was. Her insecurities calmed as she glanced over at the half eaten plate of biscuits and noticed that no one had taken a chocolate Kimberly biscuit. Nerves she thought, glad I'm not the only one.

***

Mary thought about ringing Helen when she got home but wanted to keep her little weekly outing to herself for the time being. The house felt cold when she got home and brought her back to her familiar lonely feeling. Although, on reflection she quickly reminded herself that she was just as lonely within her marriage as she was now that it was over. Her thoughts were interrupted by the ringing of the house phone and brought her out of her melancholy mood.

"Mum?"

"Hi Helen, how are you?"

"Mum where were you this morning? I called round and there was no one in!"

"Oh I was eh...in town I had to get a roast for the dinner,"

Mary immediately regretted what she'd said, not only because she lied to her daughter, but that she had announced Helen's favourite for dinner.

"Oh, ok, well I could have driven you, you should have said—did you say roast?"

"Ah sure I don't like to bother you, you've enough to

be keeping busy with, so how's the tummy?"

"Oh fine today I think I'm over the morning sickness,"

"That's good to hear love,"

"Yeah thank God, she doesn't seem to like chocolate,"

"She?"

"Yeah well I just have a feeling it's a girl, Gerry's convinced it's a boy of course, I don't think I could cope with three boys in the house, wee all over the toilet."

Mary was distracted, she loved talking to her daughter and hearing her excitement about the upcoming baby, but she felt away with the fairies today.

"Mum? Mum! Did you hear what I said?"

"Sorry love I'm not with it today,"

"Are you ok? You're not sick are you?"

"No, no of course not,"

"You sure?"

"Positive hun, now sorry what did you say?"

"Oh I was just thinking, that seeing as how Gerry's working late tonight and you have a big roast all to yourself, maybe me and Josh could come over and help you eat it?"

Mary laughed, she could practically hear her daughter's 'butter wouldn't melt' smile down the phone.

"Yes of course," Mary laughed, "why don't you come over at 6, see you then."

"Great! Bye Mum see ya later."

Mary was both pleased and perplexed by Helen dropping over for dinner. She didn't want to lie about her day, yet part of her wanted to tell everyone how amazing she was. But she felt silly, silly that organising a small women's group was something to shout about, when her daughter was a trained chef with a toddler and another baby on the way; her thirty year old son had taken a year out of university to work with Goal in the Far East—her daughter Lily, her eldest, moved all the way to Canada, and as for Frank? Frank could make working behind a bar seem like the most dazzling job in the world. She came back down to earth, reminded herself who she was and set off to get the now tainted roast. She'd just put her shopping down and the phone rang. Popular today she thought!

"Hello?"

"Mary?"

"Yes?"

"It's Frank, your husband,"

"Yes Frank, I figured that much,"

"Eh, are you ok?"

"Yes I'm ok why wouldn't I be?"

"Well I was talking to Helen earlier and she said you sounded a bit off,"

"Urgh...I swear I could murder her, I'm fine Frank, Helen's just Helen, but honestly I'm fine,"

"Are you sure? Because I can come over if you're sick?"

"No honestly Frank I'm fine, but thanks."

The conversation hit an awkward silence, neither knowing what to say.

"Ok then, I'll be over on Thursday to collect my post,"

"Frank I can drop it off at your place, it's no trou..."

"No, no I'll be over,"

"Ok then, look Frank I have to go I've got a roast to cook and Helen and Josh are coming over and.."

"Oh, ok then. Well enjoy your evening, bye."

Mary guffawed, Frank used any excuse to come over to the house. She saw more of him now than she did when they were married. Well, technically they were still married. Mary's Catholic upbringing would never allow her to go through the blasphemous ordeal of a divorce. She felt guilty though, for shooing him off the phone and then adding that their daughter and grandson were coming for tea, but the fact was that they were separated, so why did she feel guilty? No time for that now she thought.

***

Frank hung up the phone and looked around at the bedsit he currently called home. He would never have Mary leave the family home, still he hated the confinement of his digs. He liked the peace though, which Mary never gave him much of before their separation. He still pondered where it all went wrong though. What he had done, was it his fault? Was he such a terrible husband? He got ready for his shift at the Haven and put it out of his mind for the time being.

By the time he got there, the pub was in full swing; he'd already put on his perfected friendly grin. Greeting the locals, he cleared a few tables and chatted with the regulars. He knew they talked about the fact that he was now living in a room above the pub, but it didn't bother him that much. Not as much as how he missed his old life.

"Hi Frank,"

"Hiya Tony, usual is it?"

"Yeah please,"

"So how's things, see the football on Sunday?" Frank asked.

"I did alright, we were robbed!"

"Ah you always say that."

"It's true though,"

"Anyway," said Tony changing the subject of what was a sore point for Frank today, "any news?"

"Nothing much,"

"How's Mary? You two still eh..."

"Still what?"

Frank was in no mood to talk about his failed marriage today, but quickly realised that Tony was just being a mate.

"Oh sorry Frank, I was just asking you know? Thought maybe things had changed a bit."

"No, Mary's fine thanks, but no, nothing's changed, that'll be €4.70."

"Cheers,"

"Listen, me and a couple of the lads are planning on heading to Bojangles this Saturday if you fancy it?"

"Thanks Tony, but town is not really my scene, I am a bit older than the lot of you as well ye know?"

"Ah so what, who cares what age you are and besides, you're only as young as the woman you're feeling."

Frank laughed, he liked Tony, he was a good mate, even though he was twelve years younger than him, the gap didn't seem to make a difference, except when it came to Tony's ideas of socialising. Tony was and would always be a confirmed bachelor, gallivanting off to different pubs and clubs, whereas Frank liked the simplicity of his local pub.

"All the same mate, I think I'll give it a miss,"

"You're probably right, you'd ruin my style," joked Tony.

"Funny today aren't we?" laughed Frank as he cleared away some glasses.

"Sure you know me, what have I got to be miserable about, I've got my own pad, no wife to annoy me and a nice pint of Guinness in front of me."

Tony had a big silly grin on his face and Frank just rolled his eyes to heaven jokingly, just as a few more regulars came into the bar.

***

Mary and Helen cleared the plates and left Josh to play with his trucks in the living room. Mary knew that Helen was fishing for information about this mild change in her Mum and was expecting the third degree. Helen missed nothing.

"So, did you buy anything else in town today Mum? Besides that gorgeous roast?"

"Eh…No just a few tea cloths and groceries,"

"You and your tea cloths! Will you ever have enough? Sure you have the dishwasher me and Gerry bought you for Christmas, you don't need to be drying dishes."

"Old habits love I suppose,"

"I spoke to Dad today,"

"Oh?"

"Yeah he was ringing to see how Josh was after his cold last week,"

"Oh right yeah,"

"Yeah, he asked for you."

"That's nice,"

Mary tried her best to avoid Helen's face, which was hopeful for reconciliation.

"You should give him a call, see how he's doing,"

"He called today love, we spoke for a bit," Mary answered, still not looking at Helen.

Helen got a bit over enthusiastic.

"Oh GREAT! So what did you guys talk about?"

"Ah not much, do you want to take some roast home for Gerry's tea?"

"What? Eh no, so how was Dad?"

"Fine Helen!!"

"I was just asking Mum,"

"I know love I'm sorry, I'm just...I've just had a long day ok? I really don't want to talk about your father."

Helen looked despondent and Mary felt horrible for hurting her daughter's feelings.

"Look, why don't I take Josh one of these nights and you could pop over to the Haven with Gerry to see your Dad?"

Helen knew not to push it at that point, it was obvious her Mum had some stuff on her mind.

"Em, yeah that'll be great I'll say it to Gerry and we'll sort something out."

The conversation changed then to talk about the baby, whether Mary's eldest daughter Lily would make it home from Canada this year and both wondered where on earth Greg, Mary's baby, would send a postcard from this month. After neither could drink more tea and as Josh started to get tired, the evening came to an end.

Mary kissed Josh goodbye as Helen popped him into his car seat, "Nannie, I don't like patoes."

Helen and Mary both laughed, "Well that put me in my place didn't it! I'll remember next time love, no potatoes for Joshy."

***

While Josh sang all the way home, Helen smiled in the mirror at her beautiful son and looked forward to cuddling into Gerry when she got home. Then she thought about her Mum and Dad and a sadness came over her. Why can't they just work it out she thought? Josh must have sensed her quietness.

"Mummy ok?"

"Yes love Mummy's fine, just tired."

"You want Tigger he bounce?"

"Not while I'm driving lovey but thank you, maybe when we get home and see Daddy. Her mind quickly drifted back to her parents, life goes on she thought, I have my own family, still, when your parents split up it kind of ruins the fantasy of married life, no matter what age you are.

"You know what Joshy, I think we'll stop off and get Daddy some apple cake and custard for when he comes in what do you think?

"Yeaay cake and Daddy."

***

Mary tidied up the kitchen and felt a pang of guilt at keeping her new hobby from Helen. She was dying to tell her but wanted to see how it would pan out first. 'Don't count your chickens Maisy' her Dad's voice echoed in her head. He would call her Maisy if he had had a particular good win on the horses that day. Mary thought back for a minute about her childhood—for a moment thought how nice it would be to be a child again, sitting on her Dad's knee. But then she'd quickly be reminded of the endless fights between her mother and father. She would sit at the top of the stairs and listen, sometimes with her younger brothers and sisters.

'James that was all we had, how could you?'

'I'm sorry Sheila but it was a sure thing, easy money.'

'How can you say that?! We're broke! That money was to last until the end of the week and you just flutter it away like rubbish!'

Mary hated when they fought. She never understood at the time why her mother got so angry with her father. All she remembered was her father being the joker, lots of fun, with extra pocket money to give out when his horse came in. Overlooked were the days that she'd come home from school and there was beans on toast for dinner, or some days just toast. Days when the house felt colder and her mother looked older.

***

Frank made his way over to the family home by foot. It was cold today, but he still fancied a walk. He knew that he'd get a less than welcoming reception from Mary but, part of him still looked forward to seeing her. He thought about the last time he'd stayed overnight in the house. Admittedly he'd had a few pints on him, but that couldn't have been the reason.

The Haven was in full swing that night. Everywhere Frank looked he saw familiar faces. He'd finished his shift around 6pm that evening and everyone cajoled him into staying for one or two pints. Tony was there as usual, as was Mick, a friend he went to school with and Joe, an old neighbour from the flats where he grew up. The first round was on Tony and they all settled into the cubby at the back of the bar—their usual spot.

"Get them drinks down yer necks lads there's more on the way," winked Tony.

"Not for me Tony," said Frank, "have to get home to the missus."

"Ah what? You joined at the hip or something?"

All the men laughed, except Frank's was more of a nervous laugh because he knew he'd be in for it if he came home drunk again. Although he couldn't see the problem to be honest, it was only a harmless bit of fun and Mary was never interested in joining them anyway.

"Seriously lads, Mary will kill me, she's still reeling after last week when you all had to carry me home."

"That was a good night though," said Joe and Mick agreed. Against his better judgement, Frank couldn't help but laugh too. He thought about Mary at home that night, on her own. A pang of guilt crept into his stomach but was quickly replaced with the anticipation of his next pint. He loved Mary but had to live his life.

Drinks continued to flow and after a lock in with the lads Frank looked at the clock, 3am. Crikey! I'm in for it now, he thought. Tony had thought it was a good idea to get whiskey chasers. Then again, he didn't have anyone waiting for him at home. And the other lad's wives? Well they had their own friends to socialize with and didn't seem to mind as much. Why did it bother Mary so? Frank wished she had her own friends to take some of the heat off him. He had asked her to go out weeks ago, but she said no. Although he had left her alone in the house the night previous. The guilt washed over him once again, she had told him that she was lonely in the house, but he didn't listen. And now, here he was again, in a drunken stupor.

The lights in the house were off by the time he stumbled down the road, with the help of Joe and Tony. Both took turns in holding each arm up as Frank's jellified legs couldn't make the fifteen minute journey through the estate. Then he thought it would be a good time to start singing, much to the dismay of his neighbours.

"Show me de way te go home, I tired and wanna go de bed…"

"Remind me not to give him whiskey again," muttered Tony, as he struggled to keep Frank from falling flat on his face.

"Mary's gonna kill us," said a concerned and suddenly sober Joe.

They arrived up to the front gate; Joe and Tony were planning to quit while they were ahead and leave him there, but Frank's state left them no other option than to walk him up the garden path. They finally reached the door and Frank fumbled with his keys, missing the lock at every try and laughing to himself childishly. Joe and Tony became increasingly worried at the attention they were adding to themselves. Frank suddenly became aware of the two lads.

"Lads, yiz don't have to bring me home I'm a hic...hic...big boy,"

"Ah you're alright Frank we have to make sure you get home safely."

Frank suddenly came over all enamoured with his two buddies.

"Ah yiz are great mates, don't know what I do without yiz hic...hic."

After several failed attempts to open the door Frank thought it would be a great idea to ring the bell and did so before Joe and Tony could stop him.

"Ding dong," Frank repeated.

With that a light came on upstairs and the lads knew that trouble was brewing. They straightened themselves up like proper schoolboys waiting for a punishment.

The hall light came on and they could hear movement. Mary didn't have to ask who it was, even with the late hour. She knew it was Frank, in all his drunken glory. She opened the door with a stern grimace across her face. Tony and Joe stood to attention and greeted Mary with consternation. Frank was hanging now between the two lads, barely able to hold his head up.

"Evening Mary," said the two lads.

"Don't you mean morning?!" Mary shot back with venom.

Tony and Joe hung their heads in shame, not out of fear, but out of respect for Mary, whom they all liked.

As if he just realized where he was, Frank lifted his head.

"Mary! My wife! I'm home!" and then thud! Frank had passed out and fell to his knees before Tony or Joe could rescue him.

Mary just sighed and said, "you'd better bring him in lads."

They carried him leg and a duck style into the front

room and lay him on the sofa, just as Mary ordered, which was his bed for the night. He looked like a big child curled up into a ball and was already snoring. But he wasn't a child, he was a grown man, a grandfather, Mary's husband. She just sighed again.

"Thanks lads I'll take it from here," was all she could say.

The lads turned to walk out and Tony stopped Mary and touched her arm, "go easy on him Mary, he's not a mean drunk, he just overdoes it at times."

"No Tony he's not a mean drunk, but I will always play second fiddle to a session down the local."

Tony didn't know what to say, so he just nodded and left quietly to join Joe who was waiting outside.

Mary sat there watching Frank for a while as he slept soundly on the sofa. Even with his company in the house at that moment she never felt so alone. The man who had once been her friend barely had time for her anymore and it hurt, more than she cared to admit. The anger felt like bile in her throat, but she thought it pointless to spit it out, so she swallowed it down, turned off the light and headed upstairs for another sleepless night.

The next morning Mary was up early, quietly eating her porridge at the kitchen table. She couldn't even face background noise that morning so the television and radio stayed off. She had a nervous pang in her stomach at the thought of the conversation that lay ahead. Suddenly she heard Frank stir and the butterflies grew in her tummy. He rummaged around for his keys and change, did a quick check that his head was still on his shoulders—then made his way to the kitchen.

"Morning," he said to Mary without a care in the world or any recollection of last night's shenanigans.

Mary felt like throttling him there and then, but she simply said nothing. It was a Sunday and she knew that today's plan was to finish off his weekend back in the pub, without her. She hesitated for a moment and then spoke, "Frank, are you going to say anything about last night?"

"What about last night?"

"What do you mean 'what about last night?' The state you were in, the embarrassment of having you collapse on the porch, what will the neighbours say?"

"To hell with the neighbours!"

"That's all well and good for you to say but I'm the one who has to deal with the glares and the whispers!"

"So I had a few drinks, what's the harm?"

"A few drinks is fine, but you were locked. You barely even knew your own name!"

"Am I not entitled to let me hair down once in a while?"

"There's letting your hair down and there's making a holy show of yourself Frank!"

"Something that you've never done Mary am I right?"

"That's neither here nor there."

Mary was fuming, but it wasn't the right time to tell him how she was really feeling. That she felt lonely in the marriage, that Frank gave more of his time to the locals down the pub than to his own wife. That she felt, since her children had left home and grown up she had no purpose in life anymore. That she wanted her husband to pay attention to her wants and needs. But as usual, she said nothing and hid her emotions in a veil of anger and resentment.

Frank was banging about the place and still muttering as Mary composed her thoughts.

"Maybe a few pints down the local is not your cup of tea and maybe you don't like the company I keep, but it's my life!" Frank retorted.

Mary couldn't help but respond in a sarcastic tone.

"Oh of course it's your life Frank, why should you care about the woman who has stood by you through the constant mood swings and late nights, even your kids are sick of it?!" Mary knew that would hit a nerve, but she was hurting and said it anyway.

"Don't bring my kids into this, I'm a good father!"

"Yeah when you're sober!"

"Ah to hell with this I'm going for a pint."

"That's right, run off with your mates Frank!"

"I will!"

The door slammed shut and once again Mary was alone. She slumped down in the chair and dropped her face in her hands and cried.

***

The cold air brought Frank back to the present and he had reached the house, his old home. He fumbled around for his key, but then thought better of using it. He rang the doorbell and waited for Mary to answer. She came to the door and Frank thought he noticed an air of annoyance on her face at the sight of seeing him. Did she really hate him that much?

"Hi Mary."

"Hello Frank."

Mary ushered him in. The house was spotless, much cleaner than when he lived there. Frank had a habit of hanging his clothes over the kitchen chairs when he retired for bed, never understanding why it bothered Mary so. He felt uneasy for a bit, the two of them standing there in silence.

"Eh, I just eh, came for my post,"

"I could've dropped it into the Haven for you,"

"No need, I don't mind the walk, I need it these days,"

Frank patted his rounded belly. Mary just smiled. She felt

uneasy with her husband standing in their home—her home now and she knew that Frank knew it. She wasn't trying to be cruel, she was just scared of the emotions that him being there dredged up.

"So how are you keeping?" she asked, throwing him a lifeline.

"Good, good and how about yourself?"

It was the same conversation every time they were together.

"I believe Helen was here yesterday?"

"Yes it was a last minute visit," Mary wondered why she was explaining herself.

"Good, that's nice," Frank muttered, "I've been meaning to visit her myself."

"You should," Mary said, "I'm sure Josh would like to see his Grandad,"

"Yes well..."

Frank didn't finish, he knew he neglected his kids now that they were grown up. He just figured they didn't need him now that they had their own lives.

"Well I..." they both said at the same time and Mary continued, "I better get to Tesco, have nothing in."

"Right ye be," and Frank turned to walk to the door as Mary politely escorted him out.

"Oh, nearly forgot my post!"

Frank made his way back to the hall table, to find only one letter waiting for him.

"Probably junk," he said.

Mary thought about suggesting to him that he should change his postal address to his new abode, but then she retracted, knowing that it would hurt him.

"Well I'm off then, bye Mary."

"Goodbye Frank."

Frank zipped his coat all the way up and made his way down the garden path. He shivered at the harsh air and had only one thing on his mind, a pint of the black stuff. Although he didn't feel like company today, so he made his way up to the Village Inn, where no one knew him. He sat at the bar and ordered a pint of Guinness and took out the paper he had bought along the way. He went straight to the back page to check out the sport, but immediately lost interest. He couldn't help but think of Mary and where he went wrong. He thought of his own parents then and their marriage and compared the two. It was his mother who was the drinker in his family. Although a quiet drinker who spent most of her time in her room. She was sick a lot too and Frank soon became used to the fact that his mother could not be the nurturing parent that he craved so much. At eleven, Frank's mother's health had started to deteriorate. That was the point when he noticed that something was wrong. She would get confused and found it hard to recall what happened the day before yet, had a vivid memory of years gone by. Looking back now Frank realised that his mother had Alzheimer's, but this was a condition foreign to Irish medics at the time so she was labelled as mad or senile. Still, Frank loved his mother and never got angry at the fact that she couldn't always be a mother to him. His father did his best but became more of a friend to Frank than a father. Frank learned to become a man at a very young age; he had no choice. But without the presence and guidance of stable parenting, he often used his fists to communicate his emotions, something he was always proud of and which Mary never approved of.

Frank took a sip of his pint, which wasn't going down as well as he'd anticipated, and felt a lump in his throat. Even over thirty years later, losing his parents still devastated him, what he didn't realise, was that he really lost them all those years ago when he was still just a boy. That little boy in him was still present and longed to be tended to, whether it was a subconscious need or not; he thought he had found that in his wife. Like many of his generation, who came through rough times; leaving school to support your family, stealing and getting involved with unsavoury souls, he turned to alcohol. This pattern was alien to Frank as he could never see the harm in getting drunk. He always worked, so couldn't see a problem and he was always a doting father on his children. Like Mary, and unbeknownst to each other, he felt like there was no purpose to his life anymore now that the family had grown up and moved on. He reflected on that and for a moment nearly saw the light, but the negative feelings and lack of confidence in himself took hold—he ordered another pint to blur his thoughts.

Chapter Two

It was the second week of the coffee morning and Mary felt even more butterflies today. The first day was broken into hushed chats left and right with endless pleasantries about the weather. Mary herself got through it with pure adrenalin. Today, the women were struggling to talk as a group and Mary found herself under pressure. The 'what am I doing?' thoughts were still there, but she knew she had to take more action today and piped up, surprised at her boldness.

"Ok ladies, I can see we're all a bit shy today, so I'll start the ball rolling." What ball she thought nervously to herself. "As you know by now, I'm Mary, and er...I'll start today by telling you something about myself. I have three children, Lily is forty and lives in Canada with her husband Glenn, they have two boys, Cillian and Sean, I don't get to see them as much as I'd like to. Helen is thirty-six, pregnant on her second child and mother to my grandson Josh, who's a little dote. And Greg, he's my baby, is travelling the world. He'll be thirty-one next month."

Mary scanned the women's faces for boredom, thinking her short description about herself was just that, short, because in essence that was Mary's life. She didn't want to mention Frank and hoped no one would ask.

Second to take the stand was Brigid. Brigid seemed more relaxed talking about her five grown up children, six grandchildren and late husband Pat, who she had been married to for fifty-two years. "Although they fuss over me like doctors," Brigid said of her children, "they think I should move in with one of them, but I love my home, it's full of all my memories, why would I leave?" she smiled.

"Why indeed?" Mary said, returning the smile, hoping

that she would one day mirror Brigid's confidence in her twilight years.

"God I hope I'm like you when I'm old," piped Alice, speaking before thinking. Marji let out a snort and Alice took note.

"Oh I mean old-er! Sorry Brigid," said Alice, her face turning red.

Brigid laughed. "It's ok dear."

"Well I'm Marji, as you all know," not waiting for any encouragement, "I've no children, have a cat though, Jeepers, she's my baby. I like my nights out with the girls, trying new things, recently took up skiing. Oh and I've been told I'm a bit gabby, so shut me up anytime."

The other women laughed, Mary was pleased. Her plan had worked.

"Me and Stephen would like children," began Alice, "it's all that's missing really," she said, kind of sadly.

"Oh it's not all it's cracked up to be believe me," snorted Cathy, "My daughter Jade, she's eighteen—haaates me! I know she's only counting the days until she has enough money to get the hell out of the house." Cathy spat, not directing her conversation to anyone in particular, not caring for a reaction either. She had married Thomas when she was twenty-two and lived comfortably with no need to work. A sharp silence fell over the room after her statement, each silently making their own judgement on her sarcastic view, not realising that each felt kind of sorry for her.

"So Mary, tell us, what made you set up a coffee morning?" asked Marji, changing the tone of the atmosphere.

Mary was expecting the dreaded question, but still it hit her like a bombshell. And she knew that Marji would have no intention of making her feel uncomfortable had she known.

"Well, I suppose em..I suppose I just needed to get out of the house you know?"

No they didn't know, she thought. Let's face it, she was the only pathetic one here.

"I know what you mean," said Cathy, "my hubby drives me up the wall sometimes! I need somewhere I can moan all I want in peace and comfort."

Mary relaxed a bit, she wasn't used to admitting that she needed to get away from her family, even in the candid way she had.

"Well I've no kids or husband and I still find plenty to moan about!" The women knew that Marji was not having a sly dig at Cathy, it was simply the way she came out with words. They thought her hilarious.

"I agree about husbands," said Rosa, "my husband can be, how do you say in Ireland?"

"Lazy?"

"Annoying?"

"Eh..no he is...big eejit!"

The women gasped at Rosa's statement, then howled with laughter, much to Rosa's confusion.

"Did I say wrong?"

"No, no Rosa, you got it spot on!" cheered Cathy.

"Yes," said Alice, "we couldn't have put it better ourselves, about our husbands I mean."

"Yes Rosa, fair play to you," said Marji, "and kudos on your lingo."

Rosa looked even more confused by now, but Mary put her at ease.

"She means you understand how the Irish speak,"

"Oh."

The women were still laughing and Mary was glad that the attention had been taken away from her. She worried slightly if these women, including herself, had much in common? It was such a diverse group, but nonetheless, she found each of them very interesting. The after effects of Christmas became a hot topic and she was pleased that the conversation continued to flow.

"Well I don't do the whole turkey and ham dinner," said Cathy, "we ended up having sushi,"

"Wow!" said Alice, "I've never had sushi!"

"It's ok," said Cathy, very nonchalant, "least I didn't have to cook."

"Oh I love cooking," said Alice proudly, "I made a five-course meal this Christmas, with all the trimmings." Cathy looked scared and horrified at the prospect.

"We'd make a suitable pair then Alice," said Marji, "because I love eating," Marji patted her plump belly and the women laughed.

"I must say I had a lovely Christmas," said Brigid, "although my family insisted on my going to them, which of course I had to give in to."

"Same here," said Mary, hoping that her input would be enough. In truth she hadn't had the best Christmas. It was her first as a separated woman. Helen had pleaded with her to come to her house, but she insisted she was fine and that Helen should take up the offer of dinner at her in-laws, who she got on very well with. It had been a funny sort of day, quieter than previous years, although she hadn't had the aggravation of Frank getting drunk, endless dishes to clean up and silly family board games that she was never good at. Still, the complexities of Christmas day and all that came with it was something that she had missed this year and it made her stomach lurch a bit; that all too familiar empty feeling that seemed to rear its ugly head since the house had become so quiet.

It wasn't long before the coffee morning had come to an end.

"Well girls, that wraps it up for today, by the way Alice, can I get that recipe for your shortbread?" Mary thought about trying something new at home. Her mother was a great baker and she was ashamed to admit that she hadn't done much baking since her mother was alive.

"Course you can Mary, tell you what, I'll text it to you, that ok?"

"Eh, yeah sure."

Great, thought Mary, now I have to figure out how to use text on my phone.

***

Mary got home and prepared her dinner for one. She didn't mind so much eating by herself, but she did miss the busy atmosphere that once was the family home. Now it was only home to Mary, her son occasionally and some broken memories. She thought of her son then and wondered where he might be at that moment. Skydiving off some bridge maybe, or bungee jumping, whatever you call it. She admired his strong sense of adventure but was dumbfounded as to where he got it from! Neither Mary nor Frank possessed that yearn for fun and excitement, well at least not on that level. She looked over at the last postcard she'd got from Greg and smiled contently, with maybe a hint of jealousy. She'd gotten used to the quiet house, but always left the telly on in the background for 'company.' She rarely watched it these days, there was never anything on anyway. She was just about to tidy her plate away when the most deafening sound sent a bolt into her spine and shot her upright! She had no idea what it was and her heart thumped wildly. It was only then, did she notice that her mobile had lit up. She tried to make out why it suddenly appeared so alive and even put it up to her ear and said hello. But nothing. She then saw that something had appeared on the screen but, had to reach for her glasses. Then she saw it, message received. She felt so silly and for once was glad that she was alone. She rummaged awkwardly with a few buttons until she eventually saw that oddly enough it was a message. She scanned it furiously and could only make out a few words; sugar, flour, butter. Then the penny dropped. Alice! It was the recipe as promised. She thought better of it than to try and reply back, scared of the tiny piece of modern technology that mocked her. Still, she had received and opened her first text and that was enough excitement for one night. She smiled satisfyingly.

"Welcome to the 21st century Mary," she said aloud.

***

Cathy

Cathy came home to an empty house, Jade was out with her friends, indicated by her note on the fridge, and Thomas, well, Thomas was working as always. She surprised herself at how much she had enjoyed the coffee morning. She didn't bother to tell her husband about it, he was never interested in what her day consisted of anyway. He was an auctioneer and very into his work. 'I get paid big bucks so you can live a leisurely life babe, you want for nothing!'

Yeah except some company, thought Cathy. They used to be so into each other, so excited to be around one another, then again, part of the excitement was not getting caught. Thomas wasn't exactly single when they met. But once he laid eyes on model Cathy, he could barely remember his wife's name. Cathy never put herself down as a mistress, but there was just something about Thomas, something stirred inside her that night when they met at a club where she was hosting. She simply thought, what the hell, it's only for one night.

32

Little did she know, her 'one nighters' were about to come back and bite her on the ass. She still loved Thomas but missed the spark; these last few months he'd been working a lot later than before.

"Hey babe," Thomas strutted into the kitchen, brief case in hand, "what's for dinner?"

"Chinese, I couldn't be bothered cooking,"

"That's my lovely wife," he teased, patting her on the bum.

"Someone's in a good mood,"

"And why wouldn't I be, it's a lovely day, I've got a lovely family..."

"Before you sit down to dinner, will you take a look at these holiday brochures? We have to decide where we're going this year," Cathy said, handing him a pile.

"Another holiday already?"

"Tom I'd hardly call visiting your mother in Wexford a holiday, and besides, Jade is getting older, she doesn't want an embarrassing holiday in a caravan with us old fogies, we should look at somewhere more sophisticated this year I think,"

"Whoa Cath, slow down will you? We're not that long after Christmas you know."

"But we always book our holiday this time of year, I was thinking of Sorrento, quaint little shops, drive up the Amalfi Coast, boat trip to Capri," said Cathy dreamily.

"And how much is that going to cost?"

"What is it with you and money? It's never been a problem before!"

"Well maybe we should start tightening the purse strings, I mean, we spend more money on takeaways that we do on heating bills!"

Cathy was starting to boil.

"Well excuse me if I don't cook more, I'm not your mother Thomas Ryan!"

"I didn't mean that God do you always have to take everything so personally?"

"You're the one getting personal, all I did was suggest a holiday, I hardly see you these days as it is!"

"I've been busy ok!!"

Cathy wasn't used to her husband losing his cool and it only confirmed her suspicions even further.

"Don't you dare shout at me you arrogant bastard!"

"Arrogant? I'm not the one who splurges on ridiculous things we don't need!"

"Excuse me?"

"Come on Cath, every time I get the Visa bill there's a charge for some swanky store on it."

Cathy started to boil, her anger infused with an unfamiliar feeling of guilt. Sure, she'd bought a leather jacket just that week, but Thomas never questioned her before. The guilt quickly dissolved and her mean streak was back with a bang.

"You're the one who always tells me how good I look on your arm when we go out! Not that we do much of that anymore either!"

"What do you mean I don't take you out? We were out last week!"

"With your parents to a crappy little bistro!"

Cathy didn't mean to sound like a spoilt little princess, but it wasn't the company or lack of a five-star eatery, it was the fact that they'd had company at all. Thomas seemed to avoid socialising alone with his wife of late, but she wasn't about to let her guard down and tell him how she really felt, the truth was, she didn't really know how she felt.

Thomas was scratching his head with his two hands, the way he did when he was frustrated. But it was normally something to do with work. Cathy wasn't used to being the instigator in his foul mood—before he could respond to her comment the words vomited out of her mouth.

"Is something going on Thomas Ryan??!!"

"What?! What do you mean?"

"You know exactly what I mean!"

"But you just....oh to hell with this I'm going out!"

"Out? Where?"

"Just out!"

"But what about...?"

But it was too late, the door slammed behind Thomas. Cathy was only glad that Jade was out and didn't witness the fight. She didn't even know what they were fighting about, but all the pieces of the puzzle were adding up in her head and she couldn't bear to bring herself to look at the full picture. She sat down to a cold plate and cried for the first time in years—the tears wouldn't stop.

Rosa

Rosa got home to a cold house, it was still January and the house was like a fridge. She did everything she could to save money on heating and any other bills. She gazed at herself in the mirror, dark circles shadowed under her eyes and she had too many wrinkles, for a young woman of thirty-eight. She ran her fingers through her long jet black hair and picked at a few greys. Rosa was a beautiful woman, but life aged her beyond her years. She looked at her son playing on the floor and gently kissed his forehead. That too was cold and she decided that enough was enough so she put the heating on. The house heated up in minutes and she went about preparing dinner for herself and Peter. She went to the local Polish market to pick up some garlic sausage which Peter liked and decided to cook them with some Irish mashed potatoes. She liked many things about Ireland but, could not understand the attraction with potatoes for dinner every day like most households. She had everything on the hob, then turned her attention to tidying the already spotless house. As Filip played with his toys she smiled to herself at the moment's peace she was enjoying, a moment that she knew wouldn't last.

Just then she heard Peter coming in from work. He worked as a labourer on a nearby building site and always came home smelling of plaster and cement.

"Hello darling, how was work?" she asked attentively.

Rosa and Peter spoke Polish to each other at home. As much as he reaped the benefits of working in Ireland, his interest did not extend to using the native tongue.

Peter simply ignored Rosa's greeting and began to take his boots off.

"I have made dinner Peter, your favourite, Polish garlic sausage with potato,"

"Potato again? Are you trying to poison me with Irish tripe?"

Rosa ignored his comment and went about busying herself in the kitchen. She had the table laid just the way he liked it, with a bottle of Zywiec beer sitting next to his knife. Peter paid no notice of the effort Rosa had gone to and concentrated his energy on his son.

"Hello Filip, Dada is home, how is my boy?"

Filip responded by showing him a toy car he was playing with. Peter rubbed his hair affectionately and smiled. Rosa was happy to see her husband in good form and she relaxed a bit. She went back to plating up Peter's dinner and then he turned to her.

"Why is the heating on?"

Rosa's stomach lurched as she turned and caught her husband's gaze.

"I'm sorry Peter, but the house was cold and we..."

"No heating on, I do not work so hard so that you can

waste my money!"

"I'm sorry dear."

Peter just ignored her and sat down to his dinner. Rosa breathed a quiet sigh of relief as she sat down to join him for her dinner, while Filip sat obediently in his chair, oblivious to the tension in the room.

Marji

Marji sat down to a blank message screen on lifestooshort.com. She nervously lit a cigarette and took a large swill from her coffee cup. What to write, she thought, what to say? How do you sum yourself up in a few sentences? She was always a very honest person, much to some people's disdain. It simply never entered her head to be anything but straight. A typical Scorpio, brutal with the truth, but fiercely loyal. Marji would take secrets to her grave. She was always quite open about herself, but rarely let people see the real her. For fear of rejection? She contemplated that for a bit, for what she was about to do opened her up to all kinds of rejection and persecution. Maybe she was reading too much into this, she always made fun of people who did it, yet here she was, feeling judgment from a machine. Yet to her it wasn't just a machine, it was a link to the unknown, and she felt fifteen again. "Ok here goes nothing," she said to her cat; her only solace in her cold apartment. She hugged herself warm and maybe for a little comfort, rubbed her hands together and started typing.

My name is Marjorie and I am from Dublin. I'm forty-eight years old (ahem, fifty-two) and this is my first time. She read that back, feeling that she had just shouted out to the world that she was a single, forty something with only her cat for comfort and stuck on her computer late on a Saturday night. Then she got to the dreaded description part. Marji never saw herself as attractive and she had always been on the plump side, so steered clear of the athletic body description and stated that she was full bodied, God, I sound like a wine she thought! A vintage one at that. She did keep herself looking well though, if not a bit old fashioned. She preferred charity shops to the latest fashion and always coloured her hair the same deep plum. She didn't have many extravagances, maybe an expensive handbag or two, but preferred a constant bottle of wine in the fridge to new clothes.

"Oh how sad am I Jeepers?" Jeepers stretched out on the floor, blissfully unaware of her owners' anxiety. "Don't you just have the life, God to be a cat." Jeepers seemed to sniff at the notion, or maybe her paranoid mind was imagining it, after all, she was virtually talking to herself. "Well meow to you too spoilt muggy." Right she thought, back to the drawing board.

She read her last words again, first time, and changed it to 'I'm new here.' "That's better"

I am interested in getting to know someone who shares my interests of the Dublin nightlife, a good bottle of wine, Chinese food and—and what? What were her interests? She'd been around the world in her twenties and no longer desired to back pack through European hostels in search of herself. Then again, maybe a well-travelled person sounded more interesting, but she had to admit, she'd gotten used to her one bed apartment in Dublin 2. She loved the noise, always did. The hustle and bustle of the city streets. Marji was never going to settle down in a quiet cul-de-sac. Her mother was a fruit and veg seller in Moore Street and she was always fascinated by the activity on a Saturday morning's shopping in the Capital. The sounds, the smell of fruit and fresh fish. The haggling over a bunch of bananas. No day was the same and any day she felt like feeling her late Mum around she would pop along to Moore Street and just inhale the atmosphere. She started to make a list of her interests and found the most enjoyment she'd had in such a long time was the coffee morning she'd attended. So she put that in; I like to have a good old natter about everything and anything. I'm very open minded, no wait, that sounded like she was 'for hire.' I have many interests and spend many a morning discussing topical interests of today's society. There, that was better. Then she went on, I have never been married, no sounds desperate, I am very independent and have no ties, scratch that again, I love my free time. I previously worked in public relations and on occasions still plan the odd event or campaign; until her sweet Dad had left her his three bed, detached house in Donnybrook, she thought. If you would like a pen friend, oops wait, pen friends were something you had when you were twelve and your 'friends' usually came from the Saint Martin's magazine, which her mother, Dolly, insisted on buying fortnightly. I would like to meet someone who lives in Dublin with the possibility of....damn...possibility of? Sex? Dinner? Moonlight walks along the beach? No, that just wasn't her. I would like to meet someone who has the same lust for life as me and she signed it, marjibarji15. There, I'm done she thought. She took the biggest exhale and composed herself before she hit the 'submit details' button. "Well Jeeps, wish me luck." Click! You have now submitted your profile, please check back for upcoming messages. "Oh my God that was stressful, another drink Jeeps? Yes you're right, think I need something stronger myself!"

Alice

Alice Mulroney Stafford lived just outside the city

with her husband of five years. Stephen, five years her senior, worked as a landscape gardener. His age didn't seem that much of an issue now, but when Alice was sixteen it caused quite a stir amongst her family. But they'd since gotten used to the idea. She still remembered her Dad's initial reaction.

"That lad is way too old for you Alice!"

"But Da I like him,"

"I know you do, that's what worries me,"

"I don't know what you mean?"

"Exactly and that's the way it should stay!"

"Huh?"

Alice was bewildered and relieved that her mother interjected.

"Joe, stop joshing her, she likes the chap."

"I'm not joshing, I don't want her dating boys twice her age, they'll be getting up to all sorts!"

Alice was completely oblivious to what her father was on about. What she made up for in school studies, she lacked in street sense. Still, her mother had every faith in her to do the right thing and Alice knew that her mother ruled the roost in their house, as much as Joe insisted *he* was the one who wore the trousers. He was a big softie really.

Mid conversation the familiar sound of Stephen Stafford's motorbike screeched to a halt outside the Mulroney's house. Alice's eyes beamed and she leapt up with excitement. But not before her father tried to get the last word in.

"You make sure you use protection young lady!!"

Alice beamed back from the front door and yelled, "don't worry Daddy I always wear a helmet!"

If any of her other siblings had muttered a comment like that her parents would have assumed it was bear faced cheek. But not with Alice. She was, for want of a better word, naive.

Joe looked at his wife in shock and the two of them broke into a fit of giggles.

Stephen arrived home as Alice was making her famous Thai Green Curry. She sang as she stirred, happy with life. Happy, but with one absence. The kids she took care of had already been picked up. Stephen took his boots off in the hall as he always did, careful and considerate so as not to undo the housework that Alice took great pride over.

"Hey dude, how was work?" Alice asked, stirring away.

"Mucky, what a day! How was yours?"

"Ah grand. I went to a coffee morning today,"

"A coffee morning? What's that?"

Alice giggled.

"It's where you go and drink coffee and have a chat, with other women like,"

"Very good. Did ye talk about me for the whole time yeah?" Stephen loved to jibe his wife.

"Oh yeah, they couldn't get enough of ye, told them what a ride you were ha ha,"

Alice turned the cooker off and faced Stephen now, who was stuck into a packet of digestives.

"Hun?" said Alice.

"Yes love?"

Stephen looked at her now, at her tense eyes.

"I took another test today..."

"Ah babe, you told me you'd wait,"

"I know, I know and I should have,"

"Well?"

Alice just shook her head in defeat and tears welled up in her eyes. Stephen was at her side in an instant.

"It'll be alright pet you'll see, there's a little angel out there waiting for us to be their Mammy and Daddy, promise."

Alice just sobbed quietly for a moment and then carried on as her chirpy self. Stephen could never fathom how quickly she could put a good spin on things. "There's always someone worse off than us," she'd always say. He couldn't understand how someone so special was wasted on him.

Brigid

Claire waited patiently that day outside the community centre as her mother walked to the car. She thought better of meeting her at the door after the reception she got when she'd dropped her off. She listened to Spin on the radio but quickly changed it to Lyric Fm once she saw her mother approaching. She laughed to herself at the funny quips her mother would come out with. "I don't want to listen to a bunch of killers blasting electro guitars at me!"

Claire loved her mother, but she could see the years in her eyes. Brigid would never acquiesce to the passing of age, which was frustrating at times. All the family wanted to do was take care of her, especially since Dad died. But Brigid wouldn't hear of it. This coffee morning was the latest hobby she'd undertaken. The family had talked her out of Salsa dancing and for once she compromised, to line dancing! But that was Mum.

"Claire I told you not to pick me up, how embarrassing, I could have got the bus!"

"Aw, am I embarrassing you in front of your pals?"

"You'll hush if you know what's good for you girl," Brigid said, half-heartedly.

"Seriously Mum, you should take it easy,"

"And why should I? I'm eighty-three, not dead!"

"You know what I mean,"

Brigid paid no attention as usual.

"Can you drop me off at the shops love? I need new tights."

"Why didn't you say? I could have got them for you."

Claire retracted quickly and could sense another grilling coming.

"I mean, I'll come with you,"

"Don't you have to get home to the kids?"

"It's alright, James took them to the cinema, he's off today,"

Brigid seemed suspicious, she didn't like the thought of being babysat and Claire knew this only too well!

"Sure I need to get a new pair of work shoes anyway Mum."

"Well if you need to go yourself then we may as well go together."

Claire was pleased with herself. She knew what way her mother's mind worked. She would never agree to something, even as simple as bringing her mother to town, if she thought she was being minded. Brigid in turn was also pleased, she loved Claire's company. As much as Claire always thought she knew what was best for her Mum, Brigid gave her more leeway being the youngest. Most of the time Brigid still saw Claire as a toddler, playing with slugs in the back garden of the home where Brigid still lived. How did they grow up so fast? She started to quietly question herself about whether she was too hard on them growing up. Maybe it was the teacher in her, everything in its right place. So many times she wanted to tell them how proud she was of them, how happy they made her. But her self-sufficient attitude to life didn't allow for such raw emotions. They were raw to her. She'd had a dark period when her husband died and swore, for her family's sake that she would become stronger than ever before. The only regret now was that her strength had become her weakness; she now sought solace in the comfort of a small coffee morning with a group of sweet strangers. She suddenly felt old and was lost in thought when Claire gently took her arm.

"Mum?...Mum!"

"Oh…yes dear?"

"I said do you want to grab lunch in the tea rooms? My treat!"

"Yes dear that would be lovely,"

"Are you ok?"

"I'm fine dear!" Brigid said, with too much gusto. Nothing a cup of tea won't fix she thought.

***

It was nearing the end of January and it had started to snow. Mary, having never learned how to drive, liked the snow and never faced it with the sense of dread that most motorists did. It reminded her of being young, when the entire block of the flats where she lived would turn out in wellies, mostly hand me downs that were too big, and hand knitted scarves and hats. You were never without a friend back in those days and Mary relished the games of snowball fights and making snowmen. The fun seemed cut short though, with Mary, the eldest, leaving school at fourteen, having to take up work to provide for her large family of five brothers and two sisters. Maybe she did have it hard back then, but she didn't seem to mind and always thought that there were other people less fortunate than her.

Mary looked out at the snow. It was beautiful. The roofs on the houses in the avenue were becoming covered in a soft white blanket. The grotto with the statue of our lady turned it into a picture, as the snow fell silently on the casing protecting the blessed virgin. There wasn't a sinner about, most of the neighbours, being of retirement age were probably tucked up indoors, not wanting to take the risk of a fall. It was a quiet avenue, it felt safe, it had been Mary's neighbourhood for over forty years—she felt comfort living so close to where she grew up.

She grabbed her scarf and hat and wore her long grey coat today, to brave the elements. She decided to walk to the community centre because she loved to feel the crunch of the snow beneath her feet. As she walked she thought of the local children in school, longingly gazing out from their classroom windows at this amazing blank canvas on which to disrupt. How simple life was for them. Then she suddenly thought, what if no one turns up at the coffee morning today? What if the weather would keep them indoors? Well she knew that Alice worked in the afternoon, so she had no choice to come out at some stage and Rosa, the only other non-driver, would have to pick up Filip from playschool so maybe she wouldn't be alone today. She had brought with her some mince pies that were in her cupboard and picked up some fresh cream from the shop on the way. Maybe everyone would be sick of mince pies in January, but not Mary, they were a favourite among the many desserts that satisfied her very sweet palette.

Mary was heading in the door as she met Brigid.

"Oh hello Mary, good to see you,"

"Hi Brigid, you too, are you keeping well?"

"Yes not a bother, although my children seem to think I should be staying at home in this weather!"

"Hmm, bit cold I suppose,"

"Let me tell you something, I still have my original hips, how many women my age can say that eh?"

Mary smiled, "Not many I'd imagine," completely forgetting about the nerves she felt at the previous coffee mornings.

Mary and Brigid settled into their room as Mary put the kettle on.

"Is this month never ending or what?" asked Brigid.

"January always drags in," said Mary.

"Still, new year and all that malarkey," mused Brigid.

"Yes I suppose it is," said Mary, who had drifted away slightly. Had it really been a year since her and Frank had split? She didn't have time to think about that right now and hadn't noticed that Brigid was still talking.

"Have you?" Brigid was looking at Mary, eyebrow arched.

Mary was about to ask, had she what... before Cathy walked in.

"Hi girls, snow what? We got through the whole of Christmas without it and then it comes in January for god's sake!"

"I know," said Mary, not wanting to share her secret love of the snow just yet.

Brigid spoke then and Mary was suddenly aware of what she had been talking about before.

"We're talking about new year's resolutions, have you made any Cathy?"

"God, resolutions? Oh the usual, lose ten pounds!"

Both Mary and Brigid looked at each other, wondering where Cathy could possibly lose ten pounds from as she still maintained her model class figure.

"Cathy you've a beautiful figure you don't need to lose weight," piped Mary.

Cathy just grabbed a pinch of tiny skin from her waist and said, "look at that! I'm a disgrace!"

Just then, Rosa, Marji and Alice walked in together.

"Hi all, I'm telling ye, if one more kid throws a snowball at me they're dead!" said Marji.

The women laughed.

"At home in Poland, we have ten foot of snow now,"

her family, well at least from Peter. Even the thought of her husband caused her stomach to do somersaults lately. She was suddenly brought back down to earth by his arrival home from work and knew instantly that it hadn't been a good day.

"Hello Peter," Rosa whispered. But Peter just grunted, making his way to the fridge for a cold beer. Then he turned and looked around the kitchen.

"Where is Filip?" he asked.

"Um, he is on play date..." but Peter didn't let her finish.

"Play date? With whom?!" he asked vehemently, rage emerging in his eyes.

"With Conor from his school, he is nice boy Peter and..."

"You listen to me, my son is not to play with any children from school!"

"But..."

"No! He should have enough to do with his mother! That's why I work all day damn it!"

Rosa knew she should have left the conversation there, but the words just tumbled out.

"Conor is nice boy, he needs friends Peter," Rosa said defiantly, but it wasn't what Peter wanted to hear and in a rage he threw the ironing board aside, but the cord caught on Rosa's hand and ricocheted it back to her, scalding her arm. Rosa screamed in pain.

"That is your own fault woman!" Peter bellowed and he left the room, comforted by his lack of involvement in the 'accident' leaving a tearful Rosa with another scar.

***

Alice and Stephen made their way to the fertility clinic for their first appointment. Both nervous, both apprehensive, but they remained each other's rock. The clinic was nicely decorated, not like the normal sterile feeling from a doctor's office or hospital. They were welcomed by a friendly receptionist and guided to the waiting room, where they noticed hundreds of thank you cards adorning the walls and shelves.

"Wow look at those Ste," Alice set about reading the cards. 'Thank you for all your help and support, *blank* is celebrating his first birthday today.' 'Many thanks to you all, we welcomed baby *blank* into the world today and she is happy and healthy.' The messages went on and on.

"Why are the names of the babies covered over?" asked a clueless Stephen.

"Probably confidentiality I'd imagine," said Alice.

"Oh right yeah, makes sense....pretty cool though eh?"

"Yeah," Alice was miles away.

"You ok babe?"

"Yeah sorry, just feels like I'm not really here you know?"

"I know what you mean."

Stephen coupled his young wife's hand and gave it a gentle kiss. Alice smiled.

"Hey look at this one Ali, triplets!" Stephen handed the card to Alice.

"All I want is one," said a despondent Alice. As usual, Stephen tried to put a happy spin on things, ever full of jokes.

"Here, do ya reckon if we did it in a fertility clinic you'd get pregnant?"

"Stephen!!" Alice couldn't help but laugh and the two of them giggled together until they were interrupted by one of the doctors.

"Alice and Stephen Stafford?"

"Yes," they both answered.

When they were brought into the room the doctor made them feel at ease instantly.

said Rosa.

"Ten foot??!" gasped the women.

"Oh I mean ten inches," Rosa apologised.

Marji couldn't resist, "Rosa, you'll be a very disappointed woman if you keep confusing your inches with feet!"

The girls giggled as Rosa sat with a confused look on her face.

"Never mind Marji, Rosa," Mary said; she pat her on the back.

"Oh I love the snow," said Alice, "it's so magical and pretty, makes me wanna run out and do snow angels!"

The women couldn't help but smile at Alice's innocent outlook and the conversation reverted back to new year's resolutions.

"I would like to learn more English," said Rosa, "I know some but I get lost sometimes, Irish people they talk so fast,"

"Know what ya mean!" said Marji totally obliterating Rosa's comment, "I used to have this client from Cork, lovely woman ya know? But man could she talk! I mean the woman never stopped for air!"

The women smiled at each other.

"Well I probably shouldn't tempt fate," said a meek looking Alice, "but I'd like a baby this year."

All the women smiled at Alice, for her apologetic tone and the fact that she was the baby of the group.

"Wow that's great Alice, best of luck," said Mary and Brigid.

"Let me tell you," said Cathy, "kids are not all they're cracked up to be!"

Alice seemed unfazed, even though Cathy scared her a bit, "I don't mind," she smiled.

Cathy went on, "I mean, I only have the one and all she does is moan, the few times I do see her these days, myself and her Dad are not good company apparently!"

Alice winced, she couldn't imagine a child becoming a burden, at any stage of their life, terrible twos and terrible teens included. She wondered if she should have said anything at all in case she jinxed the whole process.

Brigid brought her thoughts back to the group, "well I'd like to get myself published this year,"

"Oh Brigid do you write?" Mary asked, impressed, writing had always fascinated her.

"A few short stories here and there and some poetry, nothing life altering," Brigid said, modestly.

"I'd love to read some," said Mary and suddenly Brigid's confidence wavered a little.

"Oh I doubt they'd interest any of you, probably all nonsense,"

"But you enjoy writing them?" asked Mary rhetorically, "and I'm sure you're a great story teller, we love listening to you, don't we girls," said Mary.

"Oh yes Brigid," all the girls resounded.

"I couldn't write a bloody shopping list," snorted Cathy.

"Oh me neither," giggled Alice.

"I used to spend my days writing press releases," said Marji, "not the same thing though, doesn't give you the chance to be creative,"

"I would like to read your story Brigid," said Rosa— Brigid suddenly felt enamoured at the encouragement from all the women.

"Well maybe I'll bring something along one day and you could all critique it for me," Brigid was warming to the idea.

"Well I'm going to have more sex this year!" Marji suddenly exclaimed and the women didn't know where to look, apart from Alice, they had all but given up on the pleasures of the flesh. Alice broke the silence by giggling but Marji hadn't noticed any sort of discomfort by her new year's revelation.

"Fair play to ye Marji," said Alice, acting like someone had just said sex in the classroom.

"Why not?!" said Marji, "I still have a few 'active' years left in me yet and I'm not giving up!"

Rosa remembered hearing something on the television and thought it was the right time to say it, "you um...you go girl!" Rosa was pleased she remembered and the women burst out in laughter.

"Did I say wrong?" said Rosa, feeling a bit foolish and the women felt guilty for laughing.

"No," said Mary, "I think you hit the nail on the head Rosa," and Rosa sat back, once again pleased with herself. It was the perfect response to something that was maybe too much information for a bunch of virtual strangers. Still, they were getting used to Marji and she simply became funnier as the mornings went on.

"What about you Mary?" asked Cathy, "any new year's resolutions for you?"

Mary was once again on the spot and squirmed in her seat, the way you did in school when you had to address the whole class. What would she say? These days she lived day to day, not wanting to think about a future alone, but she did have one burning desire and decided to share it with the group.

"Well," Mary said, clearing her throat, "I would like to visit my daughter Lily in Canada. I'd visit my son Greg but he moves that often it's hard to track him down,"

"Wow Canada!" said Alice, "I've never been,"

"I was in Niagara Falls once," said Cathy, "didn't see what the big deal was, I mean, it's water, big whoop."

Mary didn't take Cathy's comment as a negative jibe towards her, that was her way, but she did feel sorry for her right then. She couldn't imagine not being impressed by something as amazing as Niagara Falls. Then again, she rarely left home.

"What part of Canada Mary?" asked Brigid.

"Em…Quebec?"

The women had heard of it, but none had ever been.

"You should go," said Rosa, "travel is good and you see your daughter,"

"Yeah," said Alice, "sounds like the trip of a lifetime!"

"I'd have to learn French," Mary laughed at the notion of learning anything new at her age.

"I'm sure you'd get by," said Brigid, "they speak English too,"

"Thank God," said Mary, "Bonjour would be the extent of my French!"

Mary felt good for sharing with the women, even if it was still just a pipe dream in her mind, but getting such encouragement felt like the dream could one day become a reality. Lily was forever inviting her Mum over to stay, but Mary always made an excuse. It's too far, what would I pack etc. But then she realised that all those excuses weren't hers, they were Frank's.

The coffee morning came to a close and Mary felt exhilarated. She had no idea that one little decision to start a coffee morning would make such a difference to her daily life. If she had stayed at home that morning she would have cleaned, ironed, maybe watched some boring programme on the telly and made something for dinner. But here she was, actually contemplating travelling thousands of miles across the world. Could she really do it? She was still unsure, but it made her feel good just thinking about it. On her way home she decided she would treat herself to a coffee slice.

***

Frank had a rare day off and decided to make use of it. He got up, had a bit of toast and a sugary cup of tea, then selected his clothes for the day. Frank had a million shirts, more so now that he had to do his own washing. He was always flummoxed to understand how a person can look shoddy with the prices in Penneys and Dunnes. He ironed a shirt on a towel placed on his small table, in his small flat, he could never get the hang of using an ironing board; to be honest there wasn't much room for one. He was quite proud of the way the shirt turned out, months of practise he supposed, he got dressed, admiring his hair in the mirror. That was one thing the Bannicks never faltered on, they had good hair genes and even with speckled grey Frank always prided himself on his hair looking pristinely combed and lacquered. He thought he might take the car today so grabbed his keys off the television. Then a thought occurred to him, "where will I go?" he said aloud.

Frank slumped back down on the bed, still careful not to crease his freshly ironed grey trousers. For a moment he thought of visiting Helen, but then thought that she was probably busy. He thought of Lily in Canada and wondered what she was doing at that moment, but his curiosity wasn't strong enough to ring her to find out. Then he thought of Greg and chuckled, God knows where he was and what he was up to! Frank felt a sadness wash over him and without realising it shared an emotion that Mary had felt just before they broke up. It was loneliness. But Frank couldn't identify this feeling or maybe some part of him didn't want to, it just brought back familiar feelings of when he was a boy, feelings he had pushed so far down that the memories eluded him. He thought about using an excuse to pop over to the house, but knew Mary didn't want him there, then an idea sprang to his mind and he leapt up, grabbed his keys once again and made way for the door.

The snow from that morning had begun to turn to slush and the ice had started to drip from Frank's green Ford Fiesta. He thought about going back inside but he had quietly made a promise to himself, one he was going to keep. So he set off towards the south suburbs of the city. Traffic was slow but Frank didn't mind today, he was in no rush. As he travelled he admired the large houses along the tree lined streets. Houses that were always out of reach for him and Mary when they were first dating. This was the nicer part of the city, where everyone came from money. A concept alien to Frank— as he always struggled with his tiny wage packet. The funny thing was, Frank had more money now than he ever had; nothing but hangovers to show for it. Still, he admired the somewhat intimidating residences he passed, with their manicured gardens, tall steel gated driveways and more windows than the empire state building, or so he imagined. He was so lost in the thought about what kind of people lived in theses dwellings that he almost missed his turn. Carefully he took the turn through the gates and made his way up the small winding road, until he arrived at his destination. He turned off the car and got out, rubbing his hands together at the biting cold. He looked around, he didn't know why, after all he knew where it was and made the small walk up, hands in his pockets—his scarf tied tightly round his neck. He saw the name in the distance and approached it slowly. Then he knelt down. He wiped the snow away for a better view and then it stared back at him. BANNICK.

"Hi Mum," he said. He didn't know why but he always said hello to her first. Maybe because she went before his father, even though there were only six months between their passings. He ran his fingers over the embossed lettering, like he had done many times before and sighed as he read it in his head. 'Rose Bannick nee Weafer, Beloved wife, mother and grandmother, died April 22nd, 1978 and her husband William (Billy) Bannick who died October 15th, 1978 May They Rest in Peace.' Frank remembered their deaths like it was yesterday, especially as Mary was pregnant with Helen when his father had died. He thought about his children for the second time that day and wondered if it was the time to start making his own arrangements, for when the time came. Frank sat there for a few moments, until he could no longer stand the cold, blew a kiss to his parents and headed back to the car.

Chapter Three

Mary entered the community centre for the coffee morning and was instantly accosted by hearts, everywhere! Pink hearts, red hearts, streamers, balloons, the place looked like a Hallmark shop had vomited on it. Then it quickly hit her, Valentine's Day! Mary had completely forgotten that the dreaded day was almost upon them. Mary had never been a fan of Valentine's Day, truth be told she'd never experienced a good Valentine's Day in all the years she'd been with Frank. She did remember one time, when she was in school, that a young boy in her class, what was his name, snotser, no wait that was his nickname, Bob? No, Billy? Yes Billy, Billy Costigan, he gave her a Valentine's Card and told her that he wanted to be her 'fella.' Mary was abhorred by the notion. Billy was called snotser for a reason, he always seemed to have a runny nose and most girls were repulsed by him. From what she could remember, she thanked him for the card, so as not to hurt his feelings and quickly added that her father wouldn't allow her to have a boyfriend.

The last Mary heard, Billy got married to an English girl and later moved there. She wondered if he still had the snotty nose and quietly laughed to herself. She made her way into her room and set about what had quickly become, her Wednesday morning routine. By the time the girls had arrived Mary had the tea and coffee ready, just how everyone liked it and today it was accompanied by jam donuts.

Marji was the first in and burst in the door.

"Happy Valentine's Day! Thank you Saint Valentine for reminding me that I'm single and have no prospect at marriage for the foreseeable future!"

Mary laughed, relieved that someone else shared her

opinion on this horrid day.

"Morning Marji,"

"Morning Mary, any rude/romantic/sickly cards make their way into your letterbox this morning?"

"None, how about you?"

"What? Not even from your hubbie?"

My husband, damn, right, thought Mary, "ah we never really bother with that anymore, it's a day for the youngsters now,"

"True that Mary, it's gone ridiculous now I think,"

Mary felt like she had side stepped a mine field!

"Yes very expensive these days," quick save, thought Mary.

They were interrupted by Rosa and Brigid coming through the door.

"Hello Brigid, Rosa,"

"Oh hello Mary," beamed Brigid amid conversation with Rosa, "go on love, go ahead," encouraged Brigid to Rosa, who seemed to be struggling with something.

"Heppy Balantine's Day," said Rosa, awaiting a response.

"Well done Rosa, yes very good," replied Mary and Marji.

Rosa was very pleased with herself, as was Brigid, with the obvious tutoring on the way in.

"So what do you girls think of Valentine's Day then," Marji asked Rosa and Brigid, "myself and Mary were just saying how commercialised it's gotten,"

"Oh I couldn't agree more," said Brigid, "seems preposterous to me that you need to buy a card and flowers and chocolates, just to tell someone I love you!"

"I get no flowers and chocolates," whispered Rosa.

"Now that's lovely Rosa, see? This girl has sense," quipped Brigid, "no need for big displays of affection, if you're married, you know you love each other, that should be enough."

Rosa stayed silent, looking a little disappointed that Brigid missed her point completely, although maybe thankfully—she was interrupted by Cathy coming in.

"If I see one more stupid love heart hanging from something I'm gonna puke I swear! Morning girls, man I need a..."

"Coffee?" Mary quickly interjected, steaming hot cup of coffee in hand, just the way Cathy liked it.

"Oh my God Mary you're a saint!"

"So not a fan of Valentine's Day then Cathy?" asked an amused looking Marji.

"Pffft! Romance? Please, Thomas' idea of romance is giving me his driving licence to look at so I can see his face when we have sex!"

It took the girls a minute, but soon there were embarrassed giggles all round.

"Now Cathy, you're a young lady, there's no need to be crude," said Brigid, who was quickly becoming the voice of reason.

"Sorry Brigid," whispered Cathy, like one of Brigid's former students being chastised.

"I don't understand," said Rosa.

"It's best that you don't, trust me!" said Marji.

With that Alice burst in the door, full of the joys of impending Spring.

"Morning girls! Nearly Valentine's Day eek! Can't wait!"

Several guffaws reverberated around the room, coupled with looks of disgust.

"What's wrong? Does no one like Valentine's Day?" asked an innocent Alice.

Mary saw the doe eyed look in Alice's face and immediately felt guilty at her attitude towards a day that some still held dear and obviously Alice was one of them.

Oh to be young and in love she thought.

"Sorry Alice, we're all a bit cynical in our old age, we forget how young you are at times!" offered Mary.

"Oh to be young and in love," Brigid copied Mary's thoughts aloud.

"I don't mind the potentially 'in love' aspect to the day, it's the young part I can't escape from ha!" chided Marjorie.

"Love my arse," said Cathy, ever the cynic, "can anyone honestly remember the last decent Valentine's Day they had? Seriously?"

Quizzical faces mirrored around the room and Alice, clearly the winner, had a story to tell, but was hesitant, "em...I had a nice one...last year."

"Then do tell us love," said Brigid and everyone sat down to listen.

Alice, clearly relieved and excited, started to regale her story.

"Well, it's not that exciting really, but I knew Stephen was working late so we didn't get to book a meal, so I decided to cook him his favourite; chicken and spinach pie with gratin potatoes, nothing fancy really, he just likes that, then for dessert I made baileys cheesecake, it was lovely, and Stephen came home with a....em,"

"Hard on!" screeched Cathy.

"Cathy!" screeched Marji back.

Alice laughed and Brigid just rolled her eyes to heaven.

"Em...hee hee no, he made this um, heart thing, you know he's a landscape gardener? Well he made a heart from twigs and wild flowers," finished Alice.

"Twigs?" Cathy asked sarcastically and Marji shot her a look.

"It was really nice actually," said a meek Alice, looking down at the floor.

"Well it sounds lovely," said Mary, ignoring Cathy, who couldn't see the sweetness in Alice's husband's gesture. Far from being annoyed at Cathy, Mary felt sorry for her once again, that at such a young age, not as young as Alice, but to have lost the anticipation of romance so early in her marriage, was kind of, well, sad. Then why wasn't she sad at her own misgivings she thought?

"Anyone else have a nice story to share?" asked Brigid and they were surprised to hear Rosa speak up, who up until now, kept relatively quiet in the group, be it her lack of confidence in the command of her English or what— they didn't know, yet they all listened intently.

"When I grow up in Poland we don't really celebrate Valentine Day, but in Ireland I see candy and flowers everywhere,"

The girls waited for more to the conversation, but Rosa felt that her offering was substantial enough and she knew there wouldn't be flowers and chocolates waiting for her on Valentine's Day.

As the other women recovered from the expectation of Rosa's 'story' they turned to Mary, their so called 'leader' of the group.

"How about you Mary?" asked Marji, "will your husband be whisking you off to some fancy restaurant?"

Oh hell Mary thought, what do I say?

"Ha I doubt that—Frank isn't that kind of husband," Mary laughed and hoped that that was the end of the conversation, it wasn't, shit.

"Well, we've been married a long time so we don't really bother with it anymore, come to think of it, we never really did," Mary went on, to her surprise, no one aside from her children had been this interested in her in a long time, she didn't feel that she had enough going on in her life to talk about, yet the women listened, "he did buy me a mop one year," Mary laughed.

"A mop?!" shouted Marji.

"Yes a mop," Mary chuckled.

"Why on earth would he get you a mop for Valentine's Day?" asked Cathy.

"Well he said, and I quote, 'you said you needed one!'"

The women erupted with laughter and Mary was shocked at their reaction, had she become funny in her old age? She supposed it was a funny story, she just never realised.

The laughing came to a halt and Alice asked, "what did you do with it Mary? What did you say?"

"Well my first thought was to break it over his head, in the end I just gave it to my mother I think, God, that was a while ago now."

"Well I've heard it all now!" said Brigid.

The women went on to talk about presents they got over the years from their husbands, boyfriends, some good, some bad; everything from match tickets to 'be my valentine' mugs. Before they knew it, it was time to go home. The hour and a half long chat had lifted their spirits somewhat and as they bid each other goodbye they expressed their excitement about the following coffee morning.

Valentine's Day came around unavoidably and the women each had their own experience, to cherish and to forget.

***

"Hey sexy, open the door I forgot me keys!" Stephen Stafford banged on the door for his wife to let him in.

"Hang on!" Alice shouted back as she made her way to the front door, "I swear to God I'm going to get those keys pinned to your forehead you big eeji..." Alice stopped talking as she opened the door, for there before her was a massive bunch of flowers and hidden behind them, somewhere, was the man she loved; at this moment, adored.

"OH MY GOD STEPHEN!!" Alice's eyes were like saucers as she admired the beautiful bouquet of lilies and roses before her.

"Here can you take these off me they weigh a tonne!" said a dishevelled Stephen.

"Oops sorry yes, yes thank you thank you!!"

"No probs babe, love you," Stephen kissed his happy wife hard on the lips.

"I'll put these in some water, they're beautiful!"

"And speaking of beautiful, come here," Stephen grabbed his wife, dipped her down to the floor in a Hollywood style embrace and nuzzled her neck.

"Get off me you big muppet," Alice laughed and Stephen swooped her back up.

"Hey what's that I smell? It's not...? Is it? Is it?!" Stephen practically jumped with glee.

"Yep, chicken and spinach pie!"

"Aw what did I do to deserve you? Apart from your Dad paying me to marry you," teased Stephen.

"Oh shut up and sit down," Alice said playfully as Stephen cracked open a bottle of white wine.

**

Cathy's house was a different story. She thought a lot about Alice and how excited she was about celebrating Valentine's Day with her husband. She had that once. She remembered a time when Thomas whisked her away to Paris at a moment's notice and how during their entire time there—they never left the bedroom. She looked at the clock, Thomas would be home soon and Jade as usual was out. "Jesus, how did I get to this, sitting clock-watching waiting for a man to come home!" she said to no one in the kitchen. Just then she heard Thomas's key in the door. He had text her that day asking if she wanted to do anything for Valentine's Day, she had wanted to say yes, dinner in Shanahans followed by cocktails in Harry's Bar and then finish it off with a night of dancing, but she wanted him to suggest that, not to put the idea in his head first. She wanted him to surprise her, take control, but in the end she just text back, 'no would rather stay in and watch a movie.'

Thomas came into the kitchen where Cathy was half reading Image magazine, glancing at the fashion shoots, not recognising any of the young fresh faces. She looked up at Thomas, about to say there was a salad in the fridge but was stunned to silence as she saw what was in his hand.

"Happy Valentine's Day darling," said Thomas, as he handed her a half dead bunch of carnations.

"Happy Valentine's Day? Happy Valentine's Day?! This is what I get after twenty-three years of marriage, a bunch of ugly petrol station carnations?!"

"But you said you hated Valentine's Day?"

"I know what I said!"

"But..."

Cathy could feel the tears starting to burn in her eyes and she quickly turned away from Thomas. She abhorred her every reaction to the fights with Thomas lately. When had she become so overly sensitive? Was it all the talk from the women of their great expectations of the day? In truth, the only one who seemed to take pleasure in the day was Alice. Was she jealous of Alice? She nearly let out a 'pffft' breath at the mere idea. Thomas once bought her a mink coat for Valentine's Day. Top that Alice she thought to herself. But the lavish gifts had dried up and what was left was two strangers who didn't know how to be around each other anymore. Thomas was at Cathy's side, rubbing her back. She still couldn't bring herself to look at him. Then she heaved her shoulders once again ready for battle and shouted, "Why didn't you just make me a heart out of twigs?!"

"Twigs?"

"Although at least it would be handmade!" Cathy stormed out of the kitchen and headed for bed, leaving Thomas standing, dumfounded, holding the flowers.

***

Brigid sat in her armchair in her front room, sipping a glass of sherry, fiddling around with one of her hobbies. She was working on a new poem, which she wasn't sure what was about yet. Her dog, Charlie, who had been a so called present when her husband died lay at her feet close to the fire. She never wanted Charlie, thought it was ridiculous that her family felt the need to buy her a pet to replace her late husband, yet she warmed to the grey, wiry haired mongrel. In fact, neither left each other's side, especially on these cold wintery nights. It never entered Brigid's head to be lonely, even after Mr. Mannion's death, the notion was absurd to her, she never felt lonely, sad maybe but never lonely, she had always kept herself busy and even today would not change her opinion. She thought of her coffee morning ladies and regales of Valentine disasters they'd shared and she chuckled. Then in a moment, she thought of her late husband. She put down her pages and leaned back into her high backed chair and sighed

"Happy Valentine's Day Bruce," she whispered softly. Suddenly Charlie jumped up from his slumber, perched himself on her lap, barked once and began wagging his tail.

"Yes Charlie, I'm sure he can hear the both of us," she sang and she smiled, then went back to her poem.

***

Rosa had just put Filip to bed and en route downstairs she began picking up his toys, he'd had such a busy day at school and was asleep the minute he hit the pillow. She grabbed his clothes from the bathroom floor and dropped them into the clothes hamper and made her way down to the living room where her husband had also fallen asleep. She watched him snore, arms folded across his chest, as the glare from the TV flickered across his face. How did I get here? She thought sadly. She missed her family and thought about ringing them, but she knew how Peter would moan about the cost of the phone call. She tiptoed into the kitchen to make herself a cup of coffee, delicately opening the drawer for a spoon and flinching when the kettle clicked to indicate it had fully boiled. She threw one eye back out to the living room to check that her husband was still sleeping. He was, thankfully, she thought. She stirred her coffee with the upmost care not to make a sound and sat down at the kitchen table, in darkness, hugging her cup and basking in its warmth. She looked across to the fridge, where Filip had proudly hung his Valentine's card to her and she smiled. But her smile turned to angst as she imagined her little boy one day growing up. What did the future hold for him? Would he be happy? Her thoughts were quickly interrupted by a growling sound from the living room. He's awake.

"Bring me a beer Rosa!" Peter yelled, not caring if he woke his son.

It startled Rosa and she jumped, dropping the coffee cup where it smashed on the tiled floor.

"What have you done?" Peter shouted, now stood in

the doorway.

"It was accident, I jumped, I'm sorry," Rosa answered apologetically.

Peter just muttered something in Polish under his breath, took his beer and went back into the living room, leaving Rosa, on her knees, picking up pieces of broken delf, with tears in her eyes.

***

Marji took her 'meal for one' from Marks and Spencer out of the microwave. She thought about getting the meal deal for €12.50 which included a bottle of wine, but she couldn't bring herself to be a fraud in light of Valentine's Day. So she opted for a sausage and mash meal, a bottle of Merlot and a lemon cheesecake.

"This is our downfall Jeepers," she said to her cat as she licked her fingers.

Marji was never a stick insect, but even she had to admit she'd put on a fair bit of weight since working from home. Desserts and wine being her most costly vices. She thought about the women from the coffee morning and wondered what they'd be doing today. Cathy's husband probably brought her out for a meal, Rosa the same, Alice was no doubt being showered with homemade gifts, Brigid was probably long since passed with celebrating the day and Mary had her husband, she thought.

"Who have I got?" she said aloud, to which Jeepers replied with a soft meow.

"Oh I know I've got you Jeepers," she said as she stroked her feline friend.

As she munched through her dinner she thought of what she would do with her evening. Book? Movie? Predictable soaps? Oh when did my life get so boring?!

she mused.

When she finished her satisfying and pathetic dinner; all at once she thought about going online. Part of her got excited at the prospect and the other part of her dreaded discovering an empty inbox. Still, what had she got to lose? She opened up her laptop, signed into lifestooshort.com and to her surprise saw five messages in her inbox. Wow! She thought. Lessons were learned instantly when she received four 'intimate encounters' which she quickly deleted, but the last one? It was inoffensive, short and sweet. It simply read, hi, good to meet you, welcome.

"Maybe Saint Valentine is pointing his arrows at me Jeepers," she said with a slight buzz about her, as she tapped the keys with a reply.

***

Mary had just finished watching an explosive episode of her favourite soap and finished off her cup of tea. She'd completely forgotten it was Valentine's Day until she watched the soap, as every couple in it were celebrating with romantic gestures. That won't last she thought! Mary didn't feel particularly alone because of the day, she'd never been one for lavish romantic escapades anyway, so what she never had—wouldn't be missed. Her thoughts then suddenly and surprisingly turned to Frank. What would he be doing tonight? Most likely working she thought. Frank wasn't that big on romance either. Sometimes he bought gifts, usually three days late and bought from the back of a van, but she supposed it was the thought that counted. She wondered if Frank was lonely then and a small tug pulled at her heart. She knew she'd made the right decision in leaving him, but over forty years of marriage was hard to switch off from.

She got up to make another cup of tea and knocked a card from the mantel. When she picked it up she read the response and smiled. 'To Mary, with love' and on the front it said from your secret admirer. She laughed as she traced over the words with her finger, words that were written in Helen's handwriting.

***

Frank Bannick was a man of few words, but those words counted and always came straight from the heart. He rarely expressed himself without being straight to the point and honesty was always his best policy. He found it hard to talk with the lads when it came to his wife though, ex-wife he reminded himself. He thought about what he might say, who he would say it to and most of all the reaction he'd get. No doubt he would be chided for putting a damper on the usual banter consisting mainly of football, the old days and drinking.

He made his way over to the Haven, having come from the park where he'd taken a late afternoon stroll. Spring had hit the old Dublin town with a burst of panache and Frank took in every detail. The park was open much later, giving way to many more punters at the local football matches. Heavy coats were replaced with light jackets and the customary dark clothing had been replaced with bright pastel colours. People even seemed to look happier with the sun in the sky, a rarity in Ireland. The anticipation of Summer and the promise of a pending heat wave made it a day to bask in and take in the wonder of nature.

Frank felt good today, although Mary was never far from his mind. He wondered how she was spending her Saturday, cleaning probably, the woman never stopped!

Frank helped out with the cleaning when he wasn't working, but soon got the message that the best help he could give Mary was no help at all. That was a long time ago now. He thought of when Mary and he were courting, both seventeen, although he told Mary he was twenty-one, he also told her he was a carpenter, which in essence wasn't a complete lie, he was a carpenter's apprentice, but didn't have the wage packet to match that he bragged about. He remembered the first date he took Mary on, a dance in the local Dance Hall. He was so broke that he had to pawn his best and only suit to cover the costs. Always trying to impress back then. Little did he know that it wouldn't have taken much to impress Mary, all she wanted was a man who was good to her.

Frank was surprised when Mary finally agreed to go out with him. Technically they'd had many dates, unfortunately Frank never actually made it to them. He would stand her up so many times, so much so that the friend he sent to send his apologies asked Mary out himself. Mary, being the loyal soul that she was politely declined. Frank was more interested in playing football with his friends which really tried Mary's patience. Of course there were no mobile phones back then, so the only way Mary knew the date was off was when her hands turned blue from standing alone in the cold for so long. Frank was always a one woman guy, but in turn adopted the 'treat them mean keep them keen' method of dating. Frank thought himself a bit of a looker in his day, however, if he was brave enough to admit it to himself, felt that Mary was out of his league, but this insecurity of his just turned him into the bad boy in town. He was forever getting into fights and scuffles as he wasn't afraid to get a beating or give one. It was in fact one such brawl which led Mary to learn his real age, when the radio reported a story of a seventeen year old youth who was assaulted. Of course Frank couldn't wait to get out of hospital for payback time, no one got the better of Frank Bannick and everyone knew it. It was behaviour like this that incensed Mary, but she was young and in love and knew no better.

Oh what a looker she was, still is thought Frank. Maybe the Valentine's Card was childish, maybe it was romantic, but Frank had trouble differentiating the two. He didn't know what reaction to expect, none whatsoever maybe and he was right. He put Mary out of his mind then and made his way into the bar, where his friends were sitting waiting for them. He had little much else to do with his days and secretly dreaded going home to his flat, but in front of the lads it was his 'bachelor pad' with no nagging wife and kids. Truthfully, it was a constant reminder of how things went so wrong.

"Pint Frank?" asked his old school pal Mick.

"You read my mind," replied Frank with glee, as he sat down in his usual seat at the window. He thought maybe he should talk to Mick. But would he be ridiculed? Mick was happily married to Teresa for forty-five years and Frank wondered how he did it. Then again, Mick remembered to go home after too much to drink.

***

Mary was running late today and scolded herself for being so disorganised. She always liked to get to the coffee morning before the girls as she was the one who was, for want of a better word the 'hostess.' She realised then the importance of her little coffee morning and how with each week she looked forward to it even more.

She arrived at the community centre and could hear the girls from way down the hall. Charlotte, the kind receptionist saw Mary come in and greeted her, "Hi Mrs

Bannick, I opened the room for your ladies so they're all there, I think they were a bit parched for some caffeine ha ha."

"Oh thank you love," Mary replied and then corrected her, "and please love, call me Mary," Mary smiled and Charlotte was delighted.

As Mary entered the room the girls hadn't even noticed her arrival, which made her relax a little. They seemed to be talking about jobs and Mary was delighted that she didn't have to start the conversation today.

"Oh no there's no way I could work as a waitress," Cathy said as she addressed Rosa, "I'd spill everything and drop everything I'd be useless! Hi Mary," Cathy greeted Mary as if she had been there since the start of the conversation.

"Hi sorry I'm late," said a meek looking Mary with her apologetic face.

"No probs Mary!" beamed Alice as the girls carried on talking.

"Oh it was ok," continued Rosa, "I have steady hand hee hee."

"Well fair balls to you is all I can say!" said Cathy.

"Well my family had a sweet shop," began Brigid, "we sold practically everything I suppose, so that's where I started. I remember trying to stuff iced caramels into my mouth without anyone seeing as you were scolded for 'helping yourself to the profits' but of course I had to pick the biggest sweets we had and you couldn't exactly hide them discreetly in your mouth, so of course I was caught red handed!"

The women laughed.

"Oh my God what did you do?" screamed an over excited Alice.

"What could I do?" said Brigid, "I just kept on chewing while my mother berated me! Think I went to bed with no supper that night but let me tell you it was worth it."

The women laughed again.

"I think they still make those sweets Brigid," offered Marji, "I'll pick you up a bag next time I'm shopping."

"Oh thank you dear,"

"What are iced caramels?" asked Rosa.

"Oh they're these white and pink toffees that just melt in your mouth Rosa," said Marji.

"Mmm sound yummy," said Rosa, imagining having one right there and then. The conversation was still on jobs and Mary panicked slightly, she hadn't worked for over thirty years and doubted that they would be interested in the odd jobs she'd had in her teens and doubted she had the panache to tell a story like Brigid about something as trivial as working in a laundry factory.

"Well I worked on the farm with Daddy," said Marji, "shit up to your knees at cock crow, seven days a week—not much different than public relations really," the women continued to laugh and Mary saw an opportunity to tell a story about her first job that she would never forget.

"Well I was fourteen," she began, "and I'd been taken out of school to work, that was the norm back then, and my father got me a job in a laundry factory," the women hung on Mary's every word, "well the worst part was getting there, you took a small boat with a bunch of dockers, all bustling men with nicotine stained teeth and fingers," the women still listened. "well anyway, my mother insisted I look my best for my first day, so dressed me in a snow white, boiled washed dress and put pipe cleaners in my hair to give me ringlets.."

"I'm sorry Mary, ringlets?" Rosa asked.

"Sorry Rosa, curls," Mary answered making squiggle

motions with her hands and getting more and more excited that someone was actually interested in her story.

"So, I set off down the docks with my father and we had to climb down some steps covered in slimy seaweed..."

There was a collective ugh from the women.

"Well I was a bit nervous, what with my first day at a new job, the intimidating Dockers and trying to keep my dress pristine and as I stretched out my leg from the last step, to step onto the boat I..."

"No!" screamed Alice, "you didn't!"

"Yes I fell in!" laughed Mary.

"Oh my God!" shouted the women, mouths gaping, wondering whether to laugh or not.

"Yes," said Mary, "and one of the men had to pull me out by my hair, my now, curl less, seaweed tattered hair."

Mary couldn't help herself and burst out laughing, to which all the women joined in. They laughed for a good five minutes—picturing poor Mary.

"So what happened then?" asked Cathy.

"Well I was sent to work,"

"What? Soaking wet?" the women asked.

"Yep, soaking wet!" Mary said, still laughing, "they gave me a coat to put on, a white coat, I looked like a doctor, a very young, wet, unkempt doctor!"

"Jesus!" said Cathy, "talk about your worst first day on the job!"

"I know," snorted Mary.

"Well, I think we've found our winner ladies!" said Brigid, "congratulations Mary, you had the worse first day in the history of first days!"

All the women clapped and cheered and Mary took a playful bow.

By the time the coffee morning had ended Mary felt invigorated. She hadn't laughed so much or so hard in years. She left for home with a spring in her step and looked forward to the rest of the day.

***

Rosa hurried home from the coffee morning picking Filip up from the playschool en route. She had been surprised that Peter had even agreed to allowing his son to attend an Irish school. He took his Polish heritage very seriously and normally wouldn't want his son being 'tarnished' by the Irish way of life. But even he had to admit, having a second language would further his son's life. He has no problem taking an Irish job thought Rosa. The money aspect was what was driving him in Ireland. There was simply a better ratio of pay in Ireland, money which he planned to build a house with in Poland when he had saved enough. It had always been his plan, Rosa had never wanted to leave her family, but she tried to make the most of it in Ireland.

The coffee morning had turned out better than she had hoped. Speaking with Mary afterwards had delayed her and normally she watched the clock as she had so much to do before Peter came home. She thought about telling Peter about it, but then quickly dispelled any kind of enthusiasm on his part. As she and Filip took the bus ride home she thought about when her and Peter first got married. He treated her like a princess, bringing her to new restaurants and bars. Rosa was never much of a party animal, even as a teenager. She counted on one hand the number of times she'd been drunk. She'd had one boyfriend before Peter whom she adored, Stefan.

Rosa met Stefan in a hotel where she'd worked and she was instantly smitten. He was the first man she ever made love to and thought he would be her last. That wasn't his plan though. She soon found that out when there was talk of him being out with some of the other female workers. At first she dismissed the rumours, telling people that Stefan would never dishonour her that way and she even believed her own fantasy for a while. After six months together Rosa fell pregnant. Initially she felt joyous, thinking that this might be the turning point for their relationship and a reason for Stefan to cease his womanising ways. When she told him her condition he was cold and heartless. He even questioned her as to whether or not he was the father, accusing her of sleeping around and branding her a slut. Rosa was devastated. Stefan was all she had known about love and now she was faced with raising a child alone. Even in the first month of her pregnancy Stefan did little to hide to fact that he was seeing another girl. Eventually he stopped returning her calls and made up malicious rumours about Rosa trying to trap him. The stress was almost too much to bear so Rosa left the hotel and went to work for her parents' shipping company.

In the early stages she tried to hide her pregnancy from her parents. She knew that they never approved of Stefan, she felt ashamed that she let it carry on the way it did. Her parents loved her dearly but it would have broken their hearts to know that their nineteen year old daughter was faced with the prospect of raising a child alone—with a father that never once feigned interest in his unborn child. She was working alone in the office one day when she got a stabbing pain in her stomach. At first she put it down to her body adjusting but then the pains got worse. She looked down and saw a pool of blood on the floor. She cried out for help but there was no one there. In the end she called for an ambulance, but it was too late, she had lost the baby. A baby, that at that moment she'd just realised, she had wanted so much. Rosa never had much time to deal with her feelings. It was hard not having a partner to share her emotions with. Her parents did the best they could, but probably thought it was for the best in some way.

It was many years later that Rosa met Peter. She went back to the hospitality industry and worked in a hotel bar. That was as close she got to a social life. She never had many friends and lived quite a content but sheltered life, probably due to the fact that her parents had her late in life. When she saw Peter for the first time, having drinks with his friends she didn't pay him much attention, meeting someone new was the last thing on her mind. But Peter was nice, different to his loud obnoxious friends who were leering at everything in a skirt that walked by. Peter seemed kind and wasn't too persistent. He left a substantial tip for Rosa one night along with his phone number. Rosa had no intention of calling him, it wasn't her style, if she had one at all. And even after two weeks of resisting his chivalry advances he still left his tip, phone number included. Eventually she gave into charms, after he insisted on taking her out for a meal. At that point, Rosa was simply being polite, not wanting to hurt his feelings, but the way he talked about leaving Poland and starting a new life, ignited something in Rosa. She could run away with this man, he would open her eyes to a new way of living. Maybe it was the undivided attention he gave her, maybe not all men were bad news, maybe she wanted to leave the shame of her past behind her.

***

Alice and Stephen made their way to the doctor's office for the umpteenth time. They longed for a baby and thought of how simple it was for other couples to get pregnant by merely looking at each other. They sat down in the doctor's office and held hands tightly. Doctor Rutledge walked into the room with their file, which had become increasingly thicker since their first visit. He eyed the file through his thick glasses for what seemed like an eternity and then looked over his glasses at the couple he had become very fond of and who were in desperate need to start a family and wished he'd had better news.

"Now, Alice, Stephen..."

Alice knew by his tone that it was not the news she was hoping for. She squeezed her husband's hand but neither took their gaze off Doctor Rutledge.

"Ok so we've done some more tests and Alice you seem to be producing eggs while Stephen we have found no abnormalities in your sperm. I'm embarrassed to say that we have found no problem as such with your inability to conceive."

"Well, isn't that a good thing Doctor?" Stephen asked hopefully.

"Well, yes but..."

"Is there something you're not telling us Doctor?" Alice was becoming teary now.

"No, it's nothing we have not found,"

"I don't understand," Alice looked at Stephen.

"Frankly, by our tests it appears that there is nothing wrong. Honestly, I can't see a reason why you can't conceive," Doctor Rutledge looked puzzled, "sometimes modern medicine cannot determine the cause for a case like this, science can only take us so far, in the end we are left turning to our faith,"

Alice and Stephen knew that Doctor Rutledge himself was frustrated with the outcome and was doing his best to explain the situation not in medical terms but in his own personal beliefs.

"So are you saying that maybe we're not meant to

have a baby?" Alice sobbed.

"I'm saying that I would never give up, that a baby would be very lucky to have you both as parents."

Alice and Stephen sat there in silence, not knowing if they should be happy that there was nothing wrong with them, or unhappy that there wasn't a problem to which they could fix.

"Alice, Stephen, I wonder have you thought of the possibility of having children by other methods?"

"Like what?" they both said.

"Well, there is always adoption,"

"I don't know if I could raise another woman's baby," Alice felt selfish at what she had said, but she simply wanted to carry her own baby, feel it growing inside her, even the pain of labour was worth seeing her own baby come into the world.

"There is another option which has proved very successful,"

"What is it?" Stephen asked.

"In Vitro Fertilization, IVF."

"Isn't that for couples who are infertile?" Stephen asked.

"Yes, but couples like yourselves who have no obvious problems with conceiving have also tried this method. Maybe something to think about?"

Alice and Stephen contemplated this for a moment — then Alice and her 'speak before you think' attribute came out with "is that where they use a turkey baster to make you pregnant?"

Doctor Rutledge laughed, "em...yes Alice, something like that. Look, here is a leaflet and I'm popping a number on for the Fertility Clinic. I feel it only fair to warn you that it is an expensive procedure, but I would recommend you go home, have a good long talk about it and then decide if it's something you want to do."

Alice took the leaflet, with the picture of a family on the front and she smiled, in a tiny daydream. They thanked Doctor Rutledge and left the surgery, heading to Stephen's Green for a coffee.

Alice sat at a window seat in a café in Stephen's Green shopping centre while she waited for Stephen to come back with her coffee and 'something nice.' She looked out the window at all the passers-by, to-ing and fro-ing to work, meetings, dates and so on and wondered how many other people in the world were in the same predicament that faced her and Stephen. Alice loved to people watch, but today she felt jealous of everyone else, even though she knew everyone had their own problems to deal with. Stephen watched his wife as he approached the table, she looked angelic sitting there and for a moment he felt guilty at not being able to give her a baby. They'd been together nearly twenty years and always saw children in their lives, it seemed unfair.

"Ok, so I didn't know if you were in a chocolatey humour or a fruity humour so I got you chocolate cake and a fruit slice," Stephen said as he walked to their table with a tray of goodies. Alice smiled, she loved her husband, but felt like a failure because she couldn't conceive, couldn't give him what they both wanted so badly.

"Thanks dude," she said.

They sat there people watching together for a while and then Stephen took her hand.

"I love you, you know that?"

"I know, I love you too."

"I'm sorry," they both said at the same time.

"Why are you sorry?" It happened again.

Alice spoke, "I don't know, I feel like some sort of failure,"

"I do too hun, I'd love nothing better than to give you

a baby,"

"Me too and I feel selfish not wanting to adopt,"

"Ali, I understand, you want the whole experience of getting pregnant, giving birth, taking our baby home,"

"Is that selfish?"

"Selfish?! You haven't got a selfish bone in your body,"

"So that leaves us with IVF then," said Alice.

"Yep,"

"Stephen, I want to do it,"

"Well if that's what you want, then we'll do it,"

"But you have to want it too,"

"I do, more than anything,"

They pondered their decision for a moment, each feeling that it was an incredible pressure on the other, but they had made their decision, one that would hopefully change their lives forever.

"IVF it is then," Stephen said, smiling.

They both smiled then, feeling hopeful, slightly excited even and sat there, holding hands in silence, as the coffee lost its warmth and the cakes lost their interest.

***

Cathy decided to cook tonight. It had been a long time and she wasn't always this way, she just never saw the point in going to all that trouble of shopping, cooking and cleaning up, for Jade to take her dinner into the living room and Thomas to stand eating it at the sink after he'd arrive home three hours late from work. Today though, he was showing a house around the corner at 5pm so he promised he'd be home on time. Cathy took out her old reliable cook book and after dusting off some flour from its last escapade, she began flicking through the pages. She came across chicken breasts with tomato and basil sauce and mozzarella. It was simple enough, she would use passata sauce, add some chopped fresh basil, shallots, cherry tomatoes, salt and pepper and olive oil, then pour over the chicken before topping it with sliced buffalo mozzarella, breadcrumbs and parsley. She would serve it with baby potatoes and steamed asparagus. It wasn't rocket science, but it was gourmet compared to what her family were normally used to. She had everything ready to bung in the oven when Jade called.

"Mam, Shauna just got tickets to see Kodaline in Vicar Street so I won't be home till about 11 that ok?"

It wasn't really a question and this annoyed Cathy. More so that her eighteen-year-old daughter had a better social life than her. She wanted to tell her that she had prepared a lovely meal and that it would be nice if the three of them could sit down together at the dinner table for once, but she stopped herself and she knew why.

"No that's fine love, you enjoy yourself."

Cathy was lonely; she felt sad for craving her daughter's attention, but she remembered when she was eighteen and all she wanted to do was go out with her friends. That was just it though, Cathy didn't have friends anymore. Not that she missed her old life that much, oh maybe a party or two, but it was her choice to settle down with Thomas. The girls who she partied with in the past would laugh at her life now. Most of them ran modelling companies, PR companies or nightclubs. It was Thomas' idea for her to give up work and she didn't exactly argue. Even if she had wanted to go back to work now, who would hire a forty-five-year-old model? She felt old, as old as her mother was at sixty. She felt that she shared the same life as her now. Housewife. It felt like a dirty word. How could her mother be content with that title for so long? Sure Daddy kept them comfortable with the stud farm, but Cathy never wanted that life. As soon as she was sixteen she left home and headed for the bright lights of the capital. No sooner was she there when she was snapped up by Vision Modelling Agency. It was all photo shoots, parties and male attention from the word go. She thought about her old friends then. They all thought she was mad for settling down with Thomas. Not because he was married, but because of all the opportunities she'd be giving up.

She was headed for Japan when they met and Thomas Ryan was an up and coming real estate agent and had just reaped commission from a property on Ailesbury Road worth €7,000,000. It wasn't just the money she was attracted to, it was his confidence, his ruthless business sense and leg weakening good looks. Cathy was working her final weeks as a hostess in the VIP bar of an exclusive nightclub. Everyone who was anyone drank there and Cathy was past the feeling of being impressed by famous faces and the elite of Dublin city. Until she saw Thomas Ryan.

He walked in that night in a custom made suit, hair slicked back with hints of grey that made him looked distinguished. He was accompanied by a few colleagues and they made their way to a reserved table in a more intimate part of the nightclub. They ordered Cristal and it was obvious they were celebrating landing a big account. Cathy was looking pretty good and wore a short black dress that accentuated her long legs. Her long blonde hair was sleeked back into a tight pony tail and her flawless bone structure and 'don't mess with me' attitude made the men drool and the other girls want to be her. The usual punters were all ogling her. The kind that had beer breath and stomachs that seriously exceeded the weight limits of their belts. Most of them were married and looking for 'extra services' which Cathy never supplied. They repulsed her—that was the down side of the job.

She was twenty-four at the time and later learned that Thomas was thirty-seven. Thomas and his friends seemed to be enjoying themselves yet Thomas was the only one who seemed disinterested in the bevies of beauties that surrounded this new money. The owner of the club asked Cathy to tend to their table and keep their drinks flowing and tab up. So being the professional that she was Cathy walked confidently over to their table and asked was everything satisfactory.

A few of the older men patted her bum and winked with comments such as, 'how much for you honey?'

Cathy simply replied, "more than you could afford," and walked away. Thomas seemed intrigued by her attitude and later impressed. When she came back he reached out his hand to her, "I must apologise for my friends, they don't get out much," and he smiled, with dazzling white teeth. For a moment Cathy forgot her name and said, "oh that's ok, all in a day's work."

"Have you worked here long?"

"About two years,"

"So you're used to prats then?"

"I can handle myself,"

"I'm sure you can, um..?"

"Cathy, with a C." she replied coolly.

"Nice to meet you Cathy with a C, my name is Thomas Ryan."

Cathy didn't know how or why, but she began flirting, very discreetly. She didn't take to being chatted up in the club because she knew that most of them were about as sincere as the prices. But this guy was different. He gave you his full attention when he spoke. It was rare in her line of work.

She just smiled and tended to other customers. A few of her model friends came in late and asked her to go to a late bar when she'd finished. She didn't notice Thomas again that night as it got really busy in the club. She left at about 3am with the girls and they all headed to a late wine bar, where people went when they didn't want their night to end. For Cathy, it had just started. The girls were starving come 6am so someone suggested they go to Manhattan's for breakfast. Manhattan's was a quaint little café that you had to knock on the door to get service. It was filled with every Tom, Dick and Harry—from truckers, taxi drivers and early morning revellers. They sat down in a booth at the back and while the girls ordered, Cathy excused herself to go outside for a cigarette. She lit up a Marlboro Red and inhaled deeply. It was then that she noticed him beside her.

"Hello again,"

By this time he was alone and still devilishly handsome by the light of day.

"Oh hi,"

"Burning the midnight oil?" he asked, with a raised eyebrow.

"More like 6am,"

"Right," he smirked.

Cathy turned her attention back to her cigarette, purposely avoiding his gaze. Let him work she thought.

"Can I bum one of those?" he asked her.

Cathy almost laughed.

"I would have thought that you could afford your own," she sniggered. She had him dangling and she was enjoying it. She was more of a chase than a kill girl up until then. But when she looked at him, she felt sorry for him, it had started to rain and he looked a bit dishevelled, standing there, hangover setting in, rain dripping from his brow. But he still brandished a killer smile.

"I actually gave them up a year ago," he said, not giving up on this stunning beauty before him, "but you're right, smoking 'op's' is a definite no no."

Cathy laughed and threw her cigarette on the pavement, stubbing it out with her designer shoes and just when Thomas thought it was time to go home, she took another cigarette out of the box, lit it with ease and handed it to him, accompanied with a seductive, "they're bad for you you know." They locked eyes as Thomas took a deep drag.

"Sometimes it's good to be bad," he whispered and Cathy shivered.

Cathy never re-joined her friends. They saw her as 'clicked' and left her alone. For Cathy it was just a simple flirtatious chat, but they eventually made it back inside and talked all morning, sipping coffee, after coffee. She could see his wedding ring but he didn't mention his other half and at that point she didn't care. Cathy didn't have much of a conscience in her twenties, never thought of the repercussions that one night of passion may bring. She was young, foolish and lapped the attention. She spent the night with Thomas Ryan, he wasn't like any other lover she'd ever had. He was gentle, attentive and tender. Nothing Cathy had expected. They parted ways never expecting to see each other again. Leaving that one perfect night as a hazy fantasy.

Cathy got back to making dinner after her trip down memory lane. While dinner cooked she thumbed through her address book, just out of curiosity, to see would she be tempted to reconnect with her old friends. She came across Lacey Montgomery. She didn't have to wonder what Lacey was doing with herself. She was head of Montgomery PR and had several wealthy clients on her books including Vintage Designs and Purple nightclub. Before she realised it she was dialling her number and after several 'drawling' where have you been, it's sooooo good to hear from you, what are you doing with yourself they arranged lunch for the following Tuesday. Lacey was still in touch with all the girls and for a minute Cathy felt like one of them again.

She looked at the clock, 6.30pm, where the hell was he? The chicken was done, all she had to do was add the cheese and breadcrumbs just before serving. Eventually Thomas arrived at 7.30pm. Cathy's first reaction was to scream where the hell have you been? But it felt silly to get upset over chicken and asparagus. But she was upset.

"Hey babe, ooh something smells good, did you order from that new take out?"

"No, I cooked," she said it quieter than expected.

"What?"

"I said I cooked," then she started to cry.

"Hey wait what's up? What did I say?" Thomas was trying, a bit too hard in Cathy's opinion to smooth her over.

"I'm just, I'm just, I don't know.." she kept on crying and couldn't stop. She ran upstairs and buried her head in the pillow. Thomas followed his wife.

"Babe I'm sorry I was late, work you know? Caught up on me."

Cathy didn't have the will to fight with him that night. She just wanted him to hold her.

"Thomas, I love you and if you don't love me then…"

"Whoa whoa wait a minute, I'm late from work and you think I don't love you?"

She thought he was going to flip there and then, but he didn't.

"Of course I love you Cath," then he kissed her. She still didn't know if he was being unfaithful to her and at that moment it didn't matter. She just needed him at that moment and for that moment he was all hers.

***

As Marji poured herself a glass of wine she thought about her ad. If she was honest she would have put, fifty something, fat, retired PR hag, with no life but her cat seeks 'devil may care' individual with money to burn— lover of neurotic has been. Oh my God, was that really how she saw herself? She shuddered at the idea. There was so much she wanted to do with her life, being married was never one of them, she realised that early on. Yet she still wanted someone to share her life with. Was that too much to ask at her age? She could hear her mother's voice inside her head. "You'll never get a man with that attitude Marjorie Dawson." She hated when her mother full named her, it always made her feel like she was in trouble. It was probably one of the reasons why she now liked being called Marji, it was more fun, a no bullshit title—less to commit to, but at times her non-committal attitude about herself left her feeling lonely. She thought then of her new coffee morning friends. How a simple meeting for coffee each week had given her a blank canvas, to be herself or indeed a better version of herself. She often wondered what the other women thought of her and if they would judge her for venturing onto a dating web site. Surely that was an area for the Facebook nation of this age? Not for a woman uncomfortable in the emotional area of her life.

She looked back at her submission and hit the refresh button. YOU HAVE NO NEW MESSAGES. What did she expect? There were other far more interesting submissions than hers, who in their right mind would respond to such a drab ad so quickly? She wished she had more confidence in herself. She was always very outgoing, very animated in regaling stories of her youth, yet she craved the quiet inner confidence that left an empty hole in her existence. She really admired Brigid and Mary. Nothing seemed to faze them. Brigid, in her eighties—Mary in her sixties and deciding that they still need a simple gossipy morning in their lives every once in a while. It was like they were all kids once again, in those couple of heady hours where no one had kids to look after, houses to clean, husbands to take care of or emotions to agonise over. It was a selfish break, an escape from the dreary woes of life. Who would have thought that a coffee morning could do all that? She wondered how much the other women needed it and if they needed it as much as she did.

Her mother popped into her head again and it brought her back to when she last felt this way. Hidden away in a vagrant sea of popular girls at school. She always knew she was different and hated it. She just wanted to be normal. Then again, her idea of 'normal' took many shapes over the years. Her father always encouraged her rebellious attitude to growing up in Dublin in the seventies. Her mother, on the other hand, was a different story.

"Marjorie stand still for goodness sake."

Marjorie twisted and squirmed as her mother hemmed the hideous ensemble she called a dance dress, which resembled a lemon meringue pie.

"Mum I don't want to wear this, it's hideous!"

"Don't you want boys to like you?"

"No! I don't care!"

Her mother used her selective ear and carried on pinning and measuring.

"Now, you look beautiful, oh Maurice, doesn't she look a picture?"

Marji's Dad moved his paper down as he scanned his daughter from above his glasses.

"Yes love."

"Yes love what? Tell your daughter how beautiful she looks!"

"My daughter doesn't need a dress to look beautiful," Maurice beamed at his only girl.

"Well I spent enough time making it, you could be a little more supportive."

"Oh yes love, you did a fantastic job! Wonderful! Exquisite!"

Marji stifled a little snigger at her father's over enthusiastic sarcasm, while her mother grimaced, a pin hanging from her mouth.

"Honestly, I don't know who's worse, there's the pair of you in it!"

Maurice winked at Marji and she grinned back at her Dad.

"Right, I need more pins, Marjorie Dawson don't you dare move, I'll be back in a minute to hem that skirt."

The minute her Mum left the room Marji did her usual pose of defiance and stood there in front of her father with her two hands on her hips.

"Dad, you can't seriously let me leave the house in this?"

"What? I think you look like a princess!"

"Oh very funny, have you any idea how ridiculous I look? I don't know if people will want to marry me or eat me!"

"What?!"

"I'm a feckin meringue Daddy!"

Maurice chuckled heartily.

"Oh I'm glad you find this so amusing, you don't have to wear this monstrosity!"

"It's not that bad love and your mother worked so hard."

"I know but I'll be ridiculed!"

Maurice sympathised with his daughter, but secretly had never seen her so beautiful, but was all too aware that his daughter possessed the same strong willed personality as his own.

"Look love, can you do me a favour? Indulge your mother just this once,"

"But..."

"I know I know, you don't wear dresses and you're not a conformist, but please, it would break her heart if you backed out now. To be honest, you spend enough time with me as it is down at the garage, I think your mother may be feeling a bit left out,"

Marji's stomach lurched, she knew her father was right, it had been a long time since she let her mother sit on the cheering lines. And she could never say no to her Dad when he asked her a favour.

"For me pudding?"

"Oh alright, but I don't have to enjoy myself, you can't make me!"

"I wouldn't dream of it," he smiled.

When her father grinned, his whole face smiled, even his eyes, she loved her Dad. She was a total Daddy's girl, although he would tease her that sometimes it seemed he had four sons instead of three.

Marji poured herself another glass of wine as she thought about her Dad. He always made her feel special. Her Mum loved her of course, but she never let Marji's choice of partner go unnoticed or without some comment being made. Then she thought of the lemon dress. The dress of the night she'd never forget.

"Well, well look at Marjorie Dawson, all dressed up like a whore's handbag!"

Marjorie pretended not to hear the group of bitches that went to her school. She caught the eye of her cousin John, her only buddy and made her way across the dance floor.

"Wow Marji, you scrub up well!"

"Oh shut up not you as well, it's bad enough that those

bitches have something to say,"

"No seriously you look great, who'd have thought you had legs, and two of them, wow!"

Marjorie giggled, John always made her laugh, they'd hung around together since they were kids, she always felt she could be herself around him. Although the dress made her feel different.

"I see Kate O'Hara is here, I swear if she opens her mouth again I'll..."

"You'll what? Deck her? And ruin your dress?"

"With a bit of luck!"

"Come on Cinderella, let's get you a drink."

As John and Marji sipped their orange squash they knew that all eyes were on them. Well Marji to be exact. No one had ever seen her dressed up, she normally wore cut-off jeans and boy's shoes, she felt more comfortable that way. She hated the feeling of vulnerability of wearing a dress that made her stick out so much. Then again, she always did stick out, no matter what she wore. She just didn't like to dress and behave the way the rest of the girls did.

Kate O'Hara eyed up John. Everyone knew that she always fancied him and especially as he was a year older and wore a leather jacket, he was instantly cool.

"Watch out John, here's your stalker," Marjorie teased.

"Oh God don't remind me, oh shit here she comes."

"Hi John!"

"Hello Kate,"

"John you're looking great as usual,"

Kate O'Hara waited for John to return the compliment, the kind of compliment she was used to receiving.

"Yeah you too,"

"Me? Oh thanks, I just threw this on,"

"Won't be long before it's off," mumbled Marji.

Kate ignored Marji's comment and grabbed hold of John's arm, using every opportunity to touch him and it made Marji's skin crawl.

"John why don't you come over to me and the girls, you're wasted over here,"

She shot Marji a look as if she shouldn't be here.

"No I'm fine where I am thanks Kate,"

"Well if you change your mind, you know where I am,"

Kate winked and sashayed back to her posse.

"Honestly John, I don't know why you're so nice to her, she's such a cow,"

"Ah I couldn't be bothered being rude, I just play along because I know it winds her up, actually looking at you tonight, you probably belong over with them more than I do,"

Marji playfully hit John, "take that back John Dawson!"

"Ok ok let go!"

"Only if you take it back,"

"Right, right I'm sorry, please forgive me fair maiden,"

The two giggled together, sneering at Kate and her friends—making faces when they weren't looking.

"Fancy a dance Marji?"

"Get lost! I don't dance I told you, but you go, I know how much you love ELO."

As John bopped away to Mr Blue Sky, Marji scanned the room for someone else she knew and quickly realised that there was no one she could hang with. Most people steered clear of her because she was such a tomboy and didn't share the usual interests of boys and make up. And then she saw him, Jack Barrett, the most popular guy at school. He was so pretty for a boy, with chiselled features and long hair like John Lennon. Marji watched as he made his way over to Kate and her friends.

"Penny for them?"

John was back with more drinks and some crisps.

"No need to wonder who you're looking at then!"

Marji blushed, she knew she never stood a chance with someone like Jack Barrett, but hey, a girl can dream. As much as she fought the age of conformity she always wondered what it would be like to be popular. And dating Jack Barrett would be an instant connection.

"Why don't you ask him to dance?"

"Who?"

"Who! The guy you've been staring at for the last twenty minutes!"

"John don't start this again!"

"Come on Marji, you're ten times better than any of those lot,"

"I don't want to be anything like those girls and besides, I've got you and that's all I need!"

John shot his eyes up to heaven and nudged his cousin. The music was back in full swing again and as much as Marji wanted to get up and strut her stuff she fought the urge for sake of ridicule from Kate O'Hara. Then just as she was getting another drink someone came up behind her. She froze.

"Hi Marjorie,"

"Oh…hi,"

Oh my God she thought, what do I do, what do I say?!

"I'm Jack, I'm in your English class,"

"Yes I know who you are,"

Oh shit, why did I have to say that, now he knows I know his name.

"I almost didn't recognise you in your lovely dress,"

"Oh this thing? God I've had it for years," Marji lied, suddenly warming to the dress.

Double shit, why was she lying and acting all girly?

"Listen, do you fancy having a dance?"

"Oh, eh no thanks I don't dance,"

"Come on! Don't be a party pooper,"

"No, honestly, I really don't.."

"Nonsense, come on, I'll let you lead,"

Marjorie walked to the dance floor holding Jack's hand. She felt like a little school girl. She knew everyone was looking at her, but this time, for a different reason. She could feel Kate O'Hara's eyes burning into her back. She looked back quickly and caught John's eye and gave him a 'help me' look. He just smiled and raised his glass, urging her ahead.

Jack Barrett was an excellent dancer. He shook his hips as he ran his fingers through his hair.

"Great music eh?"

Marjorie felt like she wasn't moving.

"Yeah great!"

They twisted and jived together like in the movies. Jack took Marjorie in his arms and spun her around and back again. She actually started to enjoy it and couldn't understand how she allowed herself to miss out on something this fun. She never took her eyes off Jack. Oh how beautiful he was. He looked so sexy as beads of perspiration ran down his neck. Marjorie wanted to brush his hair away from his face but thought better of it.

"Hey you're a really good dancer," Jack said.

"Not as good as you,"

What am I doing? She thought. I don't normally flirt! But then again, I could always make an exception. The music started to dial down and before they knew it, the slow set had kicked in. Marji didn't know what to do next.

"Hey, I could get us some drinks if you're thirsty?" Marji asked.

Jack ignored Marji's offer and took her in his arms,

holding her close.

"Come here you,"

This was it Marjorie thought, all her birthdays had come at once. They slow danced together, her hands wrapped tightly round his neck, his arms around her waist as they danced to Goodbye Yellow Brick Road. Jack leaned into her and moved his arms down further.

"Eh, that's not my back!" Marji shot.

"Relax honey,"

But Marjorie couldn't. She didn't feel comfortable and was all too aware of the hundreds of people around them. As Jack gripped her bum she started to feel a panic come over her. He leaned in and kissed her hard on the lips.

"Jack please don't!"

What am I doing? She thought. Here I am with the most popular boy in school and he wants to kiss me, oh Marji, don't screw this up!

Jack moved his hands again, this time to her small breasts. She could smell it off him then, the stench of alcohol.

"Jack please take your hands off me,"

She looked around for John but couldn't see him.

"Come on baby, relax,"

"I can't relax with your hands all over me!"

"Then maybe we could go somewhere more private?"

"No."

"Oh come on, don't be shy,"

Jack's hands were everywhere and Marji could feel herself trying to pull away.

"What's the problem baby? Come on I bet you're hot for me,"

"I said no!"

Then Marji did the first thing that came to her mind. Wallop!! Right across Jack's face.

"You bitch!" Jack shouted, cupping his cheek.

Marjorie looked around at all the faces staring at her in shock.

"You're a freak Marjorie Dawson!" Jack screamed.

Soon enough everyone was joining Jack in his taunts.

"Freak! Freak! Freak!"

Marjorie could feel the tears welling up in her eyes. Tough Marji, tomboy Marji, had been reduced to tears and in front of everyone at school.

She ran out of the dance hall, pushing her way passed Kate O'Hara and her friends. She could still hear them shout freak as she exited the hall.

"Marjorie wait!" John shouted after her. But it was too late, she was gone.

Marjorie sat back down to her laptop. Still no replies. She berated herself for reminding her about that incident at school. She was taunted for months after that. She was just about to call it a night when she heard the bing bong message of an email coming through. It was from someone called, 'just looking' and it was brief but sweet. Hi there, welcome to Lifes2short, you can call me 'J.' Marji never felt so nervous, she felt like her new email friend could see her and her reactions. What do I write back? She thought. Ok Marji, get a grip. She thought herself silly for using her real name, but it was too late now. 'Hi I'm Marji, I'm totally new to this, never done it before!' She clicked send and waited excitedly for a reply. A few minutes passed then came another message. 'Don't worry Marji, we're all new to something, tell me about yourself.' Marjorie came to a halt and wondered what to type, then her fingers did the talking. She told 'J' about her life working as a PR Executive, places she travelled, people she met, her interests and hobbies and before she knew it they'd been talking for an hour. She bid goodnight to 'J' and promised to stay in touch. She had taken the first step and was happy.

***

Brigid made her way to the doctor's office for a check-up, upon the insistence of her children. She thought it ridiculous, she'd never been sick in her life, she even tended to avoid the common cold. She put it down to an active life and a glass of sherry a day. Even her cane, that gathered dust on her coat rack never quite made it with her on her walks and today was no exception. Claire, her youngest, wanted to drive her there, but Brigid was adamant she'd make her own way. Her family doctor had long since passed and even though she would never admit it aloud, she felt she'd beat him by hanging on longer. Oh shameful, she thought to herself, but grinned inward. He was a nice doctor, practical and to the point, which Brigid liked, now his son had taken over the practise and at thirty-two, was too young to have such an important job in Brigid's eyes. Sure he was only a baby. So much so to Brigid that she insisted on calling him Ian. The title of doctor was saved for seasoned men and women who earned the title, not some paper—round handed down by Daddy. Brigid was never rude, she would die at the notion, but she felt that at this stage in her life, she knew her body better than any boy with a doctor's kit.

"Good morning dear, I have an appointment with Ian at 12.20."

The young girl on reception tried to salvage a professional demeanour, but in the end gave way to a little giggle at the mention of her superior's first name.

"Of course Mrs. Mannion, please take a seat."

Brigid didn't notice the giddiness in the receptionist and took her seat, perusing the worn out magazines in the waiting room. She didn't have to wait long as she heard the last patient leaving and was quickly ushered in by the giggling receptionist.

"Thank you dear."

"Mrs Mannion, how are you?" Doctor Wiggins—Ian, gave Brigid the biggest hello. He knew what kind of woman Brigid was and thought the whole Ian thing was hilarious. But true to herself Brigid shot back with her quickest answer.

"I don't know you tell me, you're the doctor!"

Ian laughed, then quickly composed himself as he knew that Brigid expected professionalism, even if he did get his licence through a distance learning course. He didn't of course.

"Well what can we do for you today then?" he asked, as he made his way around his desk with his stethoscope.

"Well apparently I am unwell," snapped Brigid, not directing her annoyance at him per say, more so at her fussing family. She felt bad for Ian then and offered a white flag.

"It's my children you see Ian, they make too much of a fuss over me and I'm as healthy as a horse! So I'm sorry to waste your time, but if I hadn't come here today there would be no end to the questions and the guilt trips you know?"

"Yes I understand," Ian replied as he warmed his stethoscope on his palm, breathing on it too.

Brigid continued on, saying how it was absolute poppycock to get sick this late in life for the very first time, but secretly she wanted the doctor to find her as healthy as she felt and send her on her way. The thoughts of a hospital visit scared Brigid, although she would never admit it to her family. Her husband had died in hospital, as did her mother and father, so she had no intention of ending up there herself—too many bad memories. She realised she was still talking as the doctor said um and ah as he examined her, asking her to take deep breaths. Brigid had good lungs, never smoked in her life, but at eighty-three, found herself short of breath climbing the stairs.

"Any shortness of breath?"

"None."

Ian laughed to himself, you can't lie to the doctor.

"That's fine Mrs Mannion all done,"

"All done? Great! Well I'll be off so..."

"Wait, just one moment please Mrs Mannion, I'd like to send you for some tests,"

"Tests?" Brigid's heart lurched.

"Yes just some routine tests, nothing to worry about," Ian smiled, but Brigid didn't trust his boyish grin.

"So I would have to go to the hospital?"

"Yes but only for a day trip, I'll set them up and send you out a letter of confirmation."

Ian could see she was worried and tried to inject some light heartedness into the consultation.

"Still taking your sherry?" he teased.

"Young man, if you're suggesting I have some sort of drink problem then..." Brigid was once again back in the room.

"Not at all Brig...Mrs Mannion, on the contrary, I'd love to know your secret," Ian said, still smiling. He was an attractive young man she thought.

"Wouldn't we all deary!" and she left, her stomach in knots. Tests. Tests! The word resounded in her ear. She made her way out of the surgery and was immediately met by Claire standing at her car.

"I was in the area, thought you might like a lift?"

Brigid saw how concerned Claire was and couldn't bring herself to chastise her.

"Thank you dear,"

Claire beamed as she opened the car door.

"So, doctors go ok?"

"Oh yes, fit as a fiddle! I told you all not to worry!"

"And that's it? He doesn't want to see you again?"

"No, no need, all ticking along nicely," Brigid lied, not mentioning the tests, "Now come on let's go and get a cuppa I'm parched."

Chapter Four

The women eased into their weekly coffee morning and Mary's nerves had long since subsided. She was surprised at how much she came to look forward to each weekly chat.

"Hi Mar!" all the women but Rosa greeted her as they sashayed into the room.

"So where's Rosa today then?"

"I don't know, said Mary, maybe she's been delayed. The other women paid no attention as they sat down with their cups and chocolate biscuits. It had become an unspoken rule that each of the women took turns to bring the biscuits, today was Marji's.

"Sorry girls," she said, "I'm not into the whole baking malarkey, so Dunnes best will have to do!"

"Oh they're fine Marji, I never say no to anything with chocolate," said Mary and the women agreed.

"Do you remember when you were younger and you got a Kit Kat with loads of chocolate at the end? said Alice, "you thought all your Christmases had come at once!"

"Oh I know," said Cathy, "although I had to stay away from all the 'bold things' when I was modelling, you wouldn't think it now though!"

"God Cathy, I would kill for your figure," said Alice.

Wish my husband did! Thought Cathy. Suddenly all the girls were very interested in Cathy's modelling background.

"So tell us about it Cathy," said Marji, "must have been very glamorous!"

"Oh believe me, there were days when it was anything but, do you know that one day I had to stand in the middle of Grafton Street in a bikini on a freezing cold day with a bowl of fruit on my head?!"

"A bowl of fruit?" said Brigid

"Yeah I was promoting a healthy eating regime for some company, I can't even remember the name of them now,"

"Still," said Mary, "I'd say it was a lot more glamorous than cleaning up after a husband and three children."

"Ah it had it's good days, I did model for John Rocha at one stage, that was quite cool,"

"Oh I love his stuff," said Alice, "but the closest I'd get to John Rocha would be the bed linen from his range that I bought last week,"

"Who in God's name is John Rocka?!" Brigid said, and the women laughed. Brigid didn't care for fashion labels and thought the whole 'who was wearing who' fascination sounded a bit rude. She was more of a Penney's than a Brown Thomas shopper.

"He's an Irish designer Bridg," offered Alice.

"Designers puh! Give me Penneys any day!" scoffed Brigid.

The women laughed again. Brigid was simply set in her ways and the other women loved her for it. She had a practical approach to life that they all admired. Mary had never envisaged that such a diverse group would grow to enjoy each other's company so much, a group that she had brought together. Her heart gave a tiny little flutter and a lovely warm feeling brushed over her. She smiled inwardly as the women regaled stories from their youth. The drinking, the smoking.

"My first drink was cider," Alice said contorting her face, "ugh, was disgusting."

"Pint of piss," Cathy returned.

"Speaking of em..piss," Mary giggled, "I remember one time when my old Dad was sick in bed, he had a bottle of lemonade beside his bed, of course I thought what a treat! But it turned out it wasn't lemonade..."

"Oh Mary! You serious?" said a disgusted looking Marji.

The other women's faces turned and they all mimicked vomiting, except for Alice.

"What was it Mary?" asked a baffled Alice.

The women broke into fits of giggles.

"What?" said Alice, which spurred their laughter on even further.

"Piss Alice!" shouted Marji.

"Piss what? Oh! Oh!" said Alice, the penny finally dropping, "Oh Mary, ugh, that's disgusting!"

"It was," said Mary laughing with the other women. They eventually calmed down, wiping their eyes as they did so.

"My first drink was red wine," said Marji, "my older brother made me drink it when I was fourteen, the pig, I puked it right back up!"

"I was never a big drinker," said Brigid and none of the women seemed surprised, "do like my nightly glass of sherry though," she smiled.

"Ugh sherry, reminds me of the trifle my Nan used to make, ugh," said Cathy.

"Your first drink was probably champagne was it?" Alice asked Cathy, getting slightly giddy.

"God no," said Cathy, "cheap vodka! Then came the harder stuff," she revealed casually.

The women became quiet, feeling out of their depth, knowing what Cathy meant, well most of them at least, Mary did have to mouth the word 'drugs' to Alice, whose face turned bright red. Cathy was oblivious to their reaction of course, sitting there, studying her nails.

"Hey, just a thought, but would anyone fancy a drink one night, just us girls and Rosa of course," Marji suggested.

"Yeah that'd be great Marj," all the girls said.

Mary felt her stomach lurch a bit, she wasn't a big drinker and never thought of herself as good enough company for a night out. Even when she and Frank went out she would just have a Baby Cham and listen in to what Frank's friends had to say. She never felt she brought much to the table in the way of interesting conversation. She agreed to meet the girls, nonetheless.

"Great!" said Marji, "I'll pop it into my diary,"

"Well ladies, that about wraps it up for today I'm afraid," said Mary, quite disappointedly.

"What? You serious Mar?" said Marji, "that time just flew in."

"I know," said Mary, "but you know what they say, time flies!"

"It certainly does," piped the girls.

Mary bid the girls farewell and began tidying up the cups. Alice had offered to help her but Mary was insistent. If she was honest, she actually enjoyed cleaning up after each coffee morning, it was a nice finish to an enjoyable morning. She was just about to lock up when she heard a knock on the door. She turned to find Rosa standing in the doorway.

"Em, hello Mary, I am so sorry for not being here today, I was at hospital,"

"Oh Rosa is everything ok?"

"Oh yes, I just burn myself with kettle, it is not bad I am ok,"

Rosa indicated to a small bandage on her arm.

"You poor thing, would you like a cup of coffee or tea?"

"Oh no thank you, I am better to get home now, Peter will be home soon."

"Ok, well, I'll walk out with you so."

Mary left Rosa at the door and told her to mind herself

and Rosa promised to try and make their impending night out.

***

Later that afternoon Mary sat in the house as she watched a cookery show and sipped her tea. She was delighted that today's episode focussed on cakes, not only did she like eating them, but watching them too. Her mind wandered to the night out with the girls. She was still apprehensive, but a part of her really wanted to go. She thought then of her daughter in Canada, of how she missed her, but was hesitant of calling her as she would have to tell her about the coffee morning. Was it time? She felt silly for keeping it such a big secret, but she wanted to get used to it herself first. She thought about Lily again and remembered the time difference, Lily would be at work, so she was slightly relieved. It was then that her phone started to ring, it was Marji.

"Hi Mar, it's Marj, how are you?"

"Fine Marji how are you?"

"Oh plodding along, you know yourself. I'm just ringing about drinks Saturday night, we're thinking of going to the Haven,"

Mary's stomach dropped. She knew that if she went to the Haven she would have to run into Frank, but if she told Marji this she would have to tell her about her situation.

"Erm...yeah that sounds...great,"

"Are you ok Mar?"

"What? Um yeah I'm fine, no, the Haven sounds fine."

The dread set into Mary like a tonne of bricks. The Haven, of all places! Mary was a very private woman and didn't like to divulge any of her woes, not nearly to a bunch of women who she hardly knew, but she was starting to think of the women as friends and hoped they felt the same. Where did all the confidence go that she had as a young girl? She remembered being this free spirited young woman going to dances every week. Oh how she loved to dance. She would get all spruced up and meet her cousins, who were all male and they would head to the local dance hall. Whether she knew it or not Mary was a catch and all the boys noticed her as she strode into the dancehall with her 'bodyguards.' One boy in particular noticed that night and he introduced himself as Francis. He was attractive, in his fitted suit and Beatles style haircut. They had a dance and talked for a while and despite his reputation for being somewhat of a gurrier Mary agreed to let him walk her home.

By the time Mary was eighteen herself and Francis had been dating for a year. Not the smoothest of years though, Mary spent many a night standing at the park waiting for Francis to show up and when he didn't she made the humiliating walk home. Still, he always managed to get around her and her Dad liked him so much that when they were both Twenty-one they married in the local church surrounded by family and friends. It wasn't long after that Lily was born and Mary thought that with a new baby in their lives Frank might stay in a bit more, she was wrong. Mary dismissed his behaviour, as most men Frank's age went for a few after work and as much as she loved her Dad it irritated her that Frank had become his new drinking buddy.

Mary thought back to the night out with the girls. So what if Frank would be there, she was entitled to her own life and it's not like they were even together anymore. Why was she making excuses? And why was she so anxious about a few drinks? Mary resigned herself to the fact that those were the times she lived in, the woman stayed at home, tended to the kids, kept the house tidy and had dinner on the table when the husband came home. But Mary always wanted more, sure there were happy times and she never regretted being a stay at home mother but listening to the women at the coffee morning she realised that she had missed out on so much—that burning desire to do something about it could no longer be ignored; she had all the time in the world now to pursue it.

***

"You're going boozing with your mates now?" Stephen Stafford teased Alice.

"Yeah, is that ok?" asked Alice with concern.

Stephen laughed, "love I was only messing with ye, of course it's alright, you know you don't have to ask me?!"

"I know but it's just, with the IVF coming up and that..."

"Listen don't be worrying about that, there'll be a time to quit the drink, now's not it, go out, enjoy yourself!"

"Really?"

"Of course love, come 'ere what are you like?" Stephen laughed, giving his wife a cuddle.

***

"Yes, so I must go to Filip's school for meeting," Rosa hated lying to her husband, but there was no way he'd agree to a night in the pub with a bunch of women, no way he'd allow her. But Rosa had made friends, something she'd almost given up on when she moved to Ireland and she wasn't about to lose her only lifeline to the world beyond their house.

"I will come with you," said Peter, with a slight

suspicion to his tone.

"Um no, you can mind Filip," Rosa lied again, her palms sweating. She did her best to convince Peter that he would be better off at home, as it was just for parents, or more to the point, one parent and she knew that Peter had no interest in conversing with these so called teachers about the welfare of his own son anyway. He of course, knew better. Eventually the subject changed, but Rosa needed a definite decision.

"So, I go?" she asked timidly.

"What? Yes yes, now quiet woman, football is on," Peter said with annoyance. Rosa was pleased and let out a sigh of relief, a faint smile appearing on her face. Peter shot her a look to which her expression changed immediately, as she went about tidying the house before he scuppered her plan.

**

Marji tapped on her laptop keys with gusto. The conversation was flowing with J and it turned out that they had a lot in common with each other. Namely movies.

- *Jaws was a great movie*
- *Oh definitely, great score too*
- *Genius*
- *Who'd have thought, 2 little notes..*
- *I know! He was laughed at when he wrote that*
- *Really? I didn't know that*
- *BRB*

BRB? Thought Marji, what's BRB? She started to panic slightly when it appeared that J was offline. Oh no thought Marji, I've messed up. What's BRB? Maybe it's some sexual shit! She was about to log off too when J appeared back online.

- *Sorry about that, someone was at the door*
- *Oh ok*
- *You ok?*
- *Yes fine, well actually....what's BRB?*
- *Be right back lol*
- *Oh! Lol!*

Marji laughed to herself. "Have to get with the lingo Jeeps," she said to her faithful friend. Her eyes were starting to droop as she bid J farewell. "Time for bed Jeepers."

***

Brigid had received the dreaded letter in the post. Her tests would take place in two weeks' time. That's fast she thought. She sank down in her chair for the moment, trying not to think of the worst and was delighted when the phone rang.

"Hello?"

"Mum hi it's David,"

"Oh hello son how are you?"

"I'm good thanks, listen, me and Alicia wanted to ask you out for dinner on Saturday?"

"Oh thank you love that's very nice of you, but I have plans on Saturday,"

The phone went quiet for a moment.

"Sorry Mum, did you say you have plans?"

"Yes dear," Brigid replied matter of fact.

"Oh."

"You ok dear?"

"Yeah it's just... where are you going?"

"Oh to a pub in the village with my new friends,"

"New friends?!" David sounded shocked.

"Well yes I am entitled to have friends you know," Brigid said, annoyance in her tone.

"Well yeah of course, I know it's just..."

"Yes?"

"Well, be careful Mum, ok?"

"Be careful?"

"Well yeah, I mean you're not twenty-one anymore,"

"Why does everyone feel the need to remind me of my age these days?"

"Mum I didn't mean..."

"I know I know, listen love I must dash, have a cake in the oven," Brigid lied.

"Oh, ok, well speak to you soon."

"Yes love, bye!"

Brigid slumped in her chair. She hadn't intended to lie to her son, but she just needed to get off the phone right then. The letter had shook her slightly and the last thing she needed was to be reminded that she hadn't got many years left. Whether she had or she hadn't, she wasn't about to waste one more day. She thought of the planned night out with the girls and she smiled. If there was one place where she wouldn't be judged or discriminated against, it was with these wonderful women that she had grown so fond of. She often tried to set herself a weekly goal and this week's was simply to let her hair down and have fun. She smiled triumphantly.

***

Mary got home from a grocery shopping trip and laid her bags on the floor. She just about made it to the phone when the machine picked it up and as she unpacked her shopping Helen's voice echoed around the room, 'hi Mum it's just me, was gonna pop round later if you're in, let me know, bye!'

I'm always in thought Mary sadly, but then reminded herself of her impending night out with the girls. God, 'the girls,' Mary laughed, she hadn't been out with anything that resembled 'the girls' in such a long time. It was time to tell her daughter what she'd been getting up to, her secret 'double life' she laughed nervously as she dialled Helen's number to invite her for tea.

"Oh I'd love to Mum, can I bring Gerry?"

"Yes of course love."

Mary felt the dread once again, it was bad enough telling Helen but Gerry would jibe her she knew it. She was very fond of her son in law, but he was the biggest joker she knew and took nothing serious, but in a good way. He took great care of Helen and she was forever grateful for that. She thought about the coffee morning then. It surprised her how much she had come to love it and love all the girls. It was the first time in a long time that she'd had something of her own that didn't involve her marriage, her children or taking care of the house. But being the overly cautious fool that Mary thought herself to be, she was afraid of the bubble bursting. Maybe it was because her childhood had been so fraught with uncertainty about where the next meal would come from, she was always careful not to count her chickens, so much so that at times she denied herself the guilty pleasures in life. Holidays, nights out, doing something wild for no apparent reason. She wondered if that was the reason why Frank drank so much? She wondered if she held him back in some way. She blamed herself for far too much for far too long and for the last time.

"A coffee morning?" Helen was trying to comprehend what her mother was saying.

"Yes a coffee morning,"

Immediately Helen went on the defensive, but in a caring way.

"Oh Mum, is it because I've been so busy lately? Did I make you feel lonely? Oh God I'm sorry Mum, I knew I should have come over more when you and Dad separated, I'm sorry…I.."

"Helen, Helen stop love! It's nothing to do with you," and then Mary felt guilty at what she had just said, she knew how soft Helen was and didn't want her to feel left out of the situation, nor did she want her to be a part of it.

Helen was upset now, Helen got upset easily and it wasn't because her mother had a new hobby, it was because she felt like her parents were slipping further and further apart and longed for them to reunite. Mary was aware of this and tried to be as sensitive as possible towards her hormonal daughter.

"It's just something for me love, you know? I can't rely on my children all the time, it's not fair on you,"

"I know, I mean it's just that I've been busy with Josh and getting the house ready for the baby and I should call around more…"

"Helen, it's ok," Mary took her daughter's hand.

"Mum I'm sorry, I'm really happy that you have something to do it's just, Dad and…"

Helen didn't finish. Mary wiped the tears away from her daughter's eyes and smiled.

"Look at me," Helen said, "I'm like a crying moron, it's these bloody hormones I can't control them."

Gerry, who had been sitting there in amazement at the two 'mad' women in his company finally spoke, "yous two are off yer rocker!! Your Mam tells you she has a new hobby and you start crying? I dunno women are mad..." Gerry shrugged and laughed as he walked into the kitchen to put the kettle on, then he turned to Mary, "here Mary, you should be making the brew you're the expert!"

Mary and Helen laughed and all was back to normal. Mary understood why Helen got upset. Anyone else would have thought it silly, but Mary knew the bond she had with her children and how they would feel left out of her life with something so out of character. They were all happy she was getting on with things, but sad that they were no longer a family unit as such, even though they were all grown up. Helen left the house that evening, excited for her mother at her new life, but with a nervousness that Mary would find a new man in her life and forget all about her Dad. She felt silly then and decided that life's goes on, even for her parents. And besides, in two months' time she wouldn't have the luxury of contending with her own thoughts with a baby and toddler to look after. Gerry sensed her worry and noticed how quiet she'd been on the drive home.

"Hey, you ok?"

"Sorry babe, just thinking,"

"About your Mum?"

Helen leaned back to check if Josh was awake but he was sparked out in his car seat.

"Actually about Dad, I hate the thoughts of him living above a pub and what if Mum meets someone?"

"Helen, they're your Mum and Dad, I know I joke a lot about them but they are the only partners each of them has ever known, do you really think either of them is interested in finding someone new at this stage?"

"Suppose"

"And besides, we have our own family to think about now," Gerry patted his wife's tummy and Helen couldn't help but smile.

"I know…..oh she's kicking feel…"

"She?"

"I'm telling you it's a girl!"

Gerry laughed, "Women's intuition again?"

"Don't joke about it, it was in one of those books I read,"

"Which book?"

"The one with the blue cover,"

"Helen, did you actually read that book?"

They both laughed.

"Ok, I read the back of it."

They laughed again and thought of their new arrival as they continued home.

***

It came to the Saturday night that Mary was dreading and she was momentarily distracted by the chore of deciding what to wear. An easy enough feat she thought, until she went to her wardrobe. She thought of Frank and although she was nervous of seeing him she also didn't want to rub his nose in it. Then she thought of meeting the girls and more panic surfaced. Mary hadn't had a night out with 'the girls' in, God ever! When she was a young girl her best friends were her male cousins. She felt protected while around them. Mary never thought of herself as the stunner that most young men saw and never discerned that this was the reason that most girls didn't give her a chance. She often turned the heads of the boys in the area, even the ones with pretty girls on their arms. But Mary's lack of confidence never let her see this and it made her even more attractive and appealing than any of the girls she knew. She loved her cousins dearly, but she longed for a girlfriend to share intimate secrets with. She came close once with a girl called Moira, who lived in the same flat complex as her. Moira seemed undeterred by Mary's 'reputation' and was kind and friendly. They remained good friends until Moira's family moved to England. Mary was devastated and the shy little girl in her returned along with the company of her cousins for want of 'real' friends. Moira would write, but Mary knew it wasn't the same.

Mary looked at her wardrobe. It wasn't that bad she

thought, for a woman of her age. Mary's looks had followed her into her sixties but the confidence to carry them off never materialised. She rummaged through her wardrobe, not sure what to select. It reminded her of her first coffee morning and how nervous she was. But surprisingly she felt at ease with the girls now and some part of her was actually looking forward to a night out with them. She came across a brown cammy top and crochet cardigan and matched it with a long brown crystal necklace which she had picked up in Penneys for €2. She wore beige trousers and brown shoes and had made a successful attempt at blow drying her own hair. She eyed herself in the mirror and smiled nervously. She had to admit, she looked quite decent. Not overdressed or underdressed, casual yet smart. She was pleased. She took out a light jacket and set off towards the park where she was meeting Alice. It was nearing April and the promise of Spring surpassed the mild chill in the air. She tried to put Frank to the back of her mind until she had to deal with seeing him. She had conflicting thoughts as she made the short walk. Should she have just told the girls the truth? That she was a sixty-five year old separated woman? Fate had dealt her a card tonight. Of all the bars in town, the girls had picked the one where her estranged husband worked. There was no doubt about it, the truth would unfold whether Mary was prepared for it or not.

She reached the park entrance where Alice was yet to arrive. She felt a bit silly, like she was waiting for a date. She quietly prayed for Alice to hurry up, even though she was ten minutes early. Mary was never late. Good old reliable Mary she thought to herself. After what felt like an eternity, Alice finally arrived. Stephen pulled up beside the park to let his wife out. Alice excitedly waved at Mary and Mary waved back. When they were close enough Alice opened the door of the car before the car had even stopped. Mary giggled.

"Mary! Hi!"

"Hi Alice, you look lovely," and she did Mary thought.

"Me? Would you stop, look at you! Swits swoo!"

Mary giggled again as Alice turned to introduce her husband.

"Stephen this is Mary who I was telling you about, she organised the coffee morning." Alice was like a kid on parent's day at school, showing off her paintings. Mary smiled.

"Hello Stephen it's very nice to meet you,"

"You too Mary," Stephen beamed "she wouldn't let me drive yous to the pub, said I was cramping her style,"

"Don't mind him Mary, he'd only make a show of me if I let him,"

"That's ok," Mary said, relieved that a young man wouldn't be dropping her off at a pub where her husband worked.

"So, you all set Mary?" asked an eager Alice.

"Yes let's go and meet the rest of the girls,"

Stephen revved the engine jokingly and shouted, "sexy ladies!"

Alice retorted, "piss off you and let me have a decent night out without ye!"

Stephen laughed, "you just make sure you come home with clean knickers on Alice Mulroney!!" and he was gone, still laughing at his joke. Mary could see that they were a perfect match, both with a great sense of humour.

"Sorry Mary, he's been slagging me all day about tonight, I haven't been out on a girlie night in ages,"

"That's ok, he seems quite funny,"

"Yeah, but the only person that laughs at his jokes is him unfortunately!"

Mary laughed, Alice linked her arm as they made their

way to the Haven. They had a nice chat along the way. Alice told her how long she and Stephen were married, about the children that she looked after and how she had finally finished her home improvements. Mary was happy to let Alice do all the talking, because she enjoyed listening to her and because she was avoiding questions about her own marriage.

They arrived at the Haven where Cathy was outside on her mobile, deep in loud conversation with who they had gathered was her husband. She waved at them and rolled her eyes up to heaven as she gestured to the phone. Mary and Alice didn't know whether to wait for her or head on in, so they paused. Then Cathy started yelling down the phone.

"She's gone out with her friends for god's sake she's eighteen years old...I don't know...eleven probably...what do you mean what time will I be back at? Whenever I feel like it....well get your own god damn dinner!..." then she hung up.

"Sorry girls, Thomas has just entered my world of daughters and dinners and an hour in and he can't cope! Men!...anyway how are you?" Cathy kissed them both, telling them how gorgeous they looked, even though she outshone them in her designer gear. She wore skinny white jeans which hugged her long legs, long tan boots, a white chiffon top and what looked like a real fur bolero. The Haven was in for a treat from their usual slacks and blouses clientele. Mary's stomach did a little flutter as they entered the bar and they saw Marji wave vigorously beckoning them over to where she had secured a table. The girls waved back and made their way over. Mary quickly scanned the bar for Frank but she couldn't see any sign of him.

"Hi girls, you all look fantastic," Marji exclaimed.

"Oh so do you Marji," said Alice as they all sat down.

"Any sign of Brigid or Rosa?" asked Mary.

"Not yet," said Marji as she sipped her drink.

Mary couldn't relax. She was about to excuse herself to go to the ladies when Brigid walked in with her daughter.

"Hello girls, my you all look beautiful,"

"Hi everyone," Brigid's daughter looked like she was dropping a toddler off at playschool for the first time.

"Hi Claire," they all responded.

"Claire insisted on walking in with me, thinks I've never been in a bar before! But she's not staying, are you Claire?" It was more of an order from Brigid than a question.

"No no, you girls enjoy yourself, Mum, ring me when you're ready to come home ok?"

Brigid shooed her out the door, "yes yes love now go on, go home to your family and stop fussing."

"Ok, see you later, bye everyone."

"Bye Claire," the women said as they waved her off.

"Honestly, you get mothered by your own children at this age," said Brigid.

"Ah she's probably just worried about you Brigid," said Marji.

Brigid didn't answer and just made a face. The girls giggled. Then Rosa entered, "I cannot stay long everybody, Filip, he is unwell,"

"Oh I'm sorry Rosa, hope it's nothing serious?" Mary asked

"Oh no, just a bit flu I think, he will be ok."

The bar was in full swing and the girls got ready to order a round of drinks. Mary saw this as a perfect opportunity to get to Frank before they did. She felt guilty that she couldn't trust them but she simply liked having people to talk to who didn't always enquire how her husband was.

"I'll get the drinks in, need to stretch my legs a bit," said Mary, standing up from her seat.

"Oh ok Mary, I'll give you a hand," offered Marji.

"Eh...no that's alright, won't be a tick."

Mary made her way to the bar, with an order of a gin and tonic for Brigid, a white wine for Cathy, somebody called Captain Morgan for Marji, a Heineken for Alice, a coke for Rosa who was driving and that just left herself. It had been so long since Mary was out that she had no idea what she liked to drink anymore. As she got to the bar, there was no sign of Frank, but she did see a familiar face in Paul, another bar man.

"Hello Paul,"

"Oh hiya Mary, God haven't seen you in here for a while, are you looking for Frank?"

"Eh...no.. I mean, is he here?"

"No he's off tonight, gone to see match out in Bray,"

"Oh right." Mary had never felt such relief. She knew her night out would get back to Frank, but at least she didn't have to deal with it tonight. She wondered why she was so worried about him finding out. It was a mixture of things. He would know about her coffee morning for one. Was that such a bad thing? Maybe not, but it was still new to Mary and she didn't know how she felt about it yet so wasn't prepared for questions. She realised how silly she sounded in her head, how she made her coffee morning sound like an affair. The sneaking around, the secrecy. It felt juvenile. But Mary knew that anything that resembled her getting on with her life away from Frank would hurt him. That was the only the reason she could think of to explain her behaviour anyway.

"Could I order a round of drinks Paul please?"

"Certainly, what can I get ye?"

Mary listed off the drinks order and then stumbled when she came to Marji's.

"..and eh...a captain Mor..."

Paul saw the confusion in her face and finished her sentence, "a Captain Morgan's?"

"Yes that's it, with ginger ale."

Then it came to her drink. She looked at the array of new beers and bottles of pink, yellow and even blue drinks and felt out of her depth. In her day it was Babycham and Advocaat and she remembered the last time she ordered one of them that the bar man had to go down to the cellar and dust one off. She thought better of it this time and ordered a vodka and diet coke. When she arrived back at the table with the drinks, escorted by Paul, the girls were in deep conversation. They hardly noticed Mary arrive back or notice that Paul had used her first name. She sat down and relaxed and for the first time that night; felt a night out with the girls was just what she needed. Everyone's attention was on Cathy as she bellowed out tales of her marriage with a reckless lack of concealment.

"He's a knob, I swear to God, I raise his child, cook his meals, clean the house and he can't even get excited about a holiday!"

"Don't you have a cleaner?" Alice asked.

"Well yeah, but..."

The girls started to laugh and Cathy, feeling a bit silly, couldn't help but laugh too.

"I don't know if I'd like a cleaner," said Alice, "what if she thought I was a messy bitch?"

"That's the whole point," said Cathy, "you're entitled to be as messy as you want!"

"Yeah I'm with Alice Cathy, wouldn't like the idea of someone seeing how messy I was and then telling all their friends about me," said Marji.

The girls quickly dispelled any snobbery that Cathy may have portrayed on the subject and Cathy was quickly and happily brought down to earth. Especially with what Brigid had to say, "well it vexes me how in this day and age a woman can't look after her own home." Cathy didn't take offence, she liked Brigid and respected her statement, even if she did think it was a bit old fashioned.

"Yeah I hear what you're saying Brigid," Cathy interjected, "but is it too much to ask for a bleeding ride at the end of the day?" The girls screamed in laughter. It seemed Cathy became quite loose lipped with a few chardonnays in her system. Only Brigid remained composed and answered Cathy in her former teacher demeanour, "my dear girl, the way to a man's heart is through his stomach."

"Yeah but I'm not exactly good in that department either,"

"Well then, it would seem you really are screwed after all," said Brigid.

The girls screamed again, they had never heard Brigid curse and the word screw didn't seem right coming out of her mouth. Before they knew it they were on round five of their drinks and the conversation flowed throughout the evening.

The subject moved onto kids and Mary was delighted to share stories of her children who she was very proud of.

"Yes Greg is travelling the world, been away for a year now,"

"Wow that is great Mary," said Rosa, who was also glad that the story had turned to something she could relate to and Mary always spoke slower for her, which she appreciated.

"Yes I get a postcard from him every so often, I believe he's in Australia now, I can't keep up with him,"

"Yeah I modelled in Australia," Cathy bragged, but the girls seemed more interested in Mary's story, not that

119

the now intoxicated Cathy even noticed.

"So Mary, you must miss him?" Alice asked.

"Oh God yeah, he's my baby,"

"And your husband, I'd say he misses the only other man in the house," Marji interjected.

"Hmm," was all Mary could say and the subject was quickly changed by Brigid who sensed Mary's discomfort.

"Well girls, will we have one for the road?"

The girls hadn't realised that the night had nearly come to an end and they were suddenly interrupted by a very big, angry looking Polish man.

"Rosa!"

"Peter," said a white-faced Rosa.

Peter didn't stay to exchange pleasantries and summoned his wife out to the hall in Polish. Rosa quickly jumped up and followed her husband. The girls, all looking startled, bent their heads in one long row out towards the hallway, where they saw a lot of gesturing by Peter to a very meek looking Rosa.

"Wonder what he's saying?" said Alice.

"I'll sort him out," said Cathy as she tried to get up off her chair until Brigid stopped her, "I think this is best left to them Cathy." Cathy quickly sat down at Brigid's calm tone. They continued to watch, unable to take their eyes of the warring couple and then quickly turned away as they saw Rosa approaching alone.

"I am sorry, I did not know the time, I must go...Filip...he is very sick." All the girls pretended that they hadn't been nosing out to the hallway at Rosa's conversation.

"Are you ok Rosa?" asked Mary.

"Um yes I am fine, I will see you on Wednesday at coffee morning, goodbye."

But Rosa wasn't fine and everyone knew it. They were

silent for a moment and then Mary spoke, "maybe we should call it a night too girls."

They all resounded with a yes and began finishing their drinks. It wasn't long before Brigid rang her daughter to pick her up and Marji being Marji, was on her way into town for a late drink.

"Bloody lightweights the lot of yis!" Marji joked as she jumped into a taxi. Cathy on the other hand was practically carried into a taxi, exclaiming that she wasn't drunk that she just a 'tit bipsy.' Mary was left with Alice as Alice offered her a lift home. She gladly accepted and was making her way out the door until she was met by a familiar face.

"Mary!"

"Frank!"

"What are you doing here?" He didn't seem angry, just taken aback, while Mary felt like she had been caught doing something she wasn't supposed to.

"Oh em I just came out for a drink with em...em," With that Alice came back from the ladies.

"Oh hi! I'm Alice, from Mary's coffee morning, you must be Frank?"

Frank, ever the gent, shook Alice's hand. Alice didn't notice the tension between Mary and Frank, nor the look of confusion on Frank's face.

"Are you ready Mary? Or are you staying with your husband?" asked Alice.

"Eh..no, I'll come with you now Alice thanks,"

"Ok well I'll just look outside and see if Stepho's there,"

Alice left the two of them in stunned silence.

"Mary, what's a coffee morning?" asked Frank quietly.

Mary felt like she was put on the spot and was a terrible liar so she just told Frank what she'd been up to the past few months.

"I see, so it's going well then?"

"Yes, very well," Frank went to say something but Mary stopped him in his tracks.

"Well I better go, have a lift waiting outside, I'll see you Frank."

"Yes, see you."

Mary's stomach twisted. She knew that she would have to explain herself to Alice, but Alice being Alice, never thought anything strange of the situation and Mary avoided the subject on their short journey home.

"So did you girls have a good night?" Stephen asked.

"Aw yeah it was deadly, Cathy got pissed and was telling us all about her husband and Rosa...." Alice went on. It was clear that Mary wasn't the only one who hadn't been out for a while. Mary wasn't really listening, she was too far away in her own thoughts. She bid Alice and Stephen farewell and made her way to her dark, two storey semi-detached house.

***

Cathy stumbled through the front door of her elegant house, making a clatter with heels and keys. She fumbled around the wall for the light switch and when she flicked it on she was met with her inebriated face staring back at her from her large silver frame mirror.

"Ugh, I look like crap," she said to her reflection as she pulled at her non-existent bags under her eyes. The only real flaw on her face was the running of her mascara and a slight blotch to her lipstick. Although Cathy hadn't felt flawless in quite some time and felt that she was losing her looks. She hadn't made love to Thomas in months and thought that the only reason for it was that

Thomas saw her as a model past her sell by date. Or that he had literally found himself a younger model.

She was surprised to admit to herself that she'd enjoyed tonight. She'd actually laughed, heartily, at the stories of the other women, although what was the deal with Rosa she thought? She brushed the thought out of her mind not wanting to add to the drama that already dominated her head. She looked at her watch, 12.50 am. Jesus she thought! Gone were the days when she was only heading out at this hour. Cathy decided that her night wasn't yet over and made her way to the fridge. Her eyes lit up at the sight of a bottle of chardonnay and as she grabbed a glass from the press she made her way to the living room, swaying and singing to herself.

"I can't get no!! Sat-is-faction!! Yeah!!"

She figured she was alone in the house but didn't really care and found the CD that played in her brain. She struggled a bit with the CD and then eventually inserted it into the CD player, pressing play and cranking it up full volume. Immediately, guitars riffs bellowed out from the speakers followed by Mick Jagger's famous sexy growl. Cathy danced around the room, taking slugs of wine, spilling most of it in the process. Boots were flung off and kicked to the far corner of the large room as she sang.

"watching my TV, man comes on an tells me, something you should be, get no...satis..."

With that Cathy was interrupted by the chandelier coming on, almost blinding her. She turned around to find Thomas, leaning against the doorway, arms folded, with a big smile on his face.

"Bit drunk are we?" he said smugly.

"S'what if I am, you're not boss of me...hic," Cathy answered, glass in one hand, bottle in the other. Thomas just laughed.

"Well when you're finished with Mick and the rest of

the Stones come to bed," he smiled.

"I not going to bed I'm part-y-ing," Cathy over pronounced, feeling very pleased with herself.

"Well you're gonna wake Jade babe,"

"So what?! She woke me when she was a baby, 's my turn now," Cathy guffawed.

"Come on babe, give me the bottle," Thomas said, a bit more serious now.

"No! 's my bottle, get yer own!"

"Come on love, I think you've had a bit too much to drink now come on,"

"No I'm dancing!"

"I can see that."

"Dance with me," said Cathy, doing her best seductive dance in her drunken state.

Thomas laughed again, "Come on that's not winning any prizes,"

"How dare you make fun of me!" Cathy's mood suddenly changed.

"Babe, I'm not making fun I'm just..."

"I'm a sexy woman I can have any man I want," shouted Cathy.

Thomas' face changed, the comment had hurt him, but Cathy was too drunk to notice and Thomas was too proud to show it. He simply said nothing, walked over to his wife and gently took the bottle and glass out of her hand. He knew she didn't mean what she'd said, but it cut him.

Cathy was too drunk to stop him and suddenly lost her balance, falling into Thomas' arms. Then, as always happened, her emotions erratically changed and she felt like a lost teenager in her father's arms.

"Why don't you fancy me anymore?" she said, staring into her husband's eyes. Saddened eyes, that mirrored each other. They stared at each other, neither knowing what to say.

They were interrupted suddenly by a sleepy Jade standing in the doorway.

"What are you two up to?" said a disgusted looking Jade.

"It's nothing love, just go back to bed," said Thomas. Cathy just hung her head down.

"God is she drunk?" Jade asked rhetorically.

"Just go to bed love." said Thomas again.

"Fine." said Jade as she wiped her eyes and made her way up the stairs, mumbling 'weirdos' under her breath.

Thomas waited until Jade was back in her room and gently lifted his wife into his arms, carrying her dead weight body up the stairs. Cathy had started to drift off into a drunken slumber as she nuzzled into her husband's chest. When they got to their bedroom Thomas lay her on the giant bed, brushing her hair away from her face. He turned to get the light thinking Cathy was asleep when he heard her voice whisper.

"Make love to me,"

He turned back and faced his wife, who was now wide awake.

"Cathy.." Thomas said, apologetically.

"Thomas, please.."

"I think you should sleep off the wine babe,"

"Thomas, I'm fine. Jesus is it too much to ask to want to make love to my husband?"

Thomas didn't answer, he just shrugged as he sat at the end of the bed, not knowing what to do. Noticing his slumped shoulders, Cathy sat up.

"What's wrong Thomas?" Cathy asked, concern in every syllable.

"Nothing it's just..."

"Yes?"

For a moment Cathy thought that that was the moment he would tell all, maybe that he was leaving her, but whatever he meant to say didn't come out that night, he simply turned and said "I love you Cath.." and the couple made love for the first time in a long time. Cathy knew there was more to say, but at that moment she didn't care, because for that moment he was all hers and it filled part of the loneliness inside her, a temporary fix which was enough for now.

***

Rosa sat in the front seat of the car and stared front. Every five seconds she would check the rear view mirror to see if her son was still asleep. He was, thank God she thought. She still couldn't believe that Peter had taken their son out of his bed to demand his wife home. Ok maybe she should have told Peter where she was going, but she was afraid to. She stole a nervous glance at him as he drove. He too stared front, knuckles white as he grabbed the wheel, furiously swerving in and out of traffic, face stern and eyes narrowed. Part of Rosa couldn't wait until she reached her destination, wondering if they'd make it home safely, the other part of her wanted to drive forever. Maybe Peter had no intention of getting them home. The thought caused panic to rise in her throat, not for her, but for her son.

Rosa would later find that the note she scribbled on with the name of the pub where she'd met the women, the note she crumpled up into a ball and put in the bin, was discovered by Peter. Rosa had told him that she was at a parent/teacher meeting. She was amazed that Peter had even let her out the door, but she'd stocked the fridge with his favourite beer and made him his favourite dinner, not realising it would work and besides, she hadn't planned on staying long, or enjoying herself, which she did, but right now it didn't seem worth it.

It had started to rain heavily and the rain made it harder to see the road. Heavy drops pelted off the windscreen yet Peter continued to drive fast. Rosa opened her mouth to say something but quickly shut it as Peter threw her a vehement look.

It was so dark and blustery that Rosa hadn't even noticed that they'd arrived home. She was relieved they'd arrived in one piece, but her relief was quickly dispelled as she knew what was waiting for her once she got inside.

"Get inside," Peter ordered.

Rosa just nodded, took a deep breath and opened her seatbelt. She thanked the heavens above that Filip was still asleep and prayed that he would remain in his slumber for the car to bed exchange. Peter was inside already, slamming doors, banging presses. Rosa cringed as she carried Filip up the stairs. He never woke once and as she laid him in his bed she touched his cheek. How perfect, how innocent, she said aloud, a single tear prickling her cheek. It was time to face her punishment.

"Rosa!! Rosa!! Where are you woman?!!" Peter screamed at his wife as she made her way down the stairs. A wave of dread washed over her as she made her way into the cold, dark living room. Peter didn't wait for her to answer, he just stared at her with wide eyes, a can of beer in his right hand.

"So explain yourself woman!!" he shouted.

"I…I…I'm sorry Peter, I just go for drink with these women," said a timid Rosa.

"What women?! Who are these women?!" Peter growled.

"They…I meet them at coffee morning, they just…"

"What is a coffee morning?!"

"It is a meeting, no, a chat…"

"So while I'm out at work you are sitting around drinking coffee with these bitches?!"

"They are not bitches they are my friends," Rosa bravely exclaimed.

"You don't need friends! You are a mother, you must take care of my son, that is all!!" Peter was red faced with anger and Rosa was shaken and fearful, she berated herself for telling her husband about the coffee morning, as she knew he would react this way, he was very possessive of her, a trait he concealed until after they were married. But part of her thought enough was enough and she suddenly found her voice.

"I am grown woman Peter and these women are my friends, I will go to coffee morning if I want!"

Peter's face turned from anger to boiling point. Rosa could clearly see the disgust in his face and barely saw him raise his hand.

Whack!!

The pain was instant. It hit Rosa like a prickly heat to her cheek. She instinctively grabbed her face in her hands should it not end there. But to Peter, he had made his point.

"You will not see those women again and you will not disobey me!" Peter snarled, unrepentant and left the room.

Rosa fell to the floor in shock. The threat had always been there, but this was the first time that Peter had struck her. He had thrown things at her, been verbally abusive, made threats, but this was the first time they were carried through. She winced at the pain in her cheek and the hot tears came fast down her face. She sat there, for what felt like hours, on the cold linoleum floor, stunned, bruised and completely subjugated, alone and lost.

***

Marji got back to her apartment after a great night out

with the girls. She had really enjoyed herself and it was just what she needed. She thought against a late drink in town in the end, but then the realisation of being at home alone suddenly hit her and her mood changed. Jeepers jumped out of nowhere and startled her, but she was grateful for the company.

"Ah Jeepers hello to you too," she said affectionately to her cat.

It was just after one and knowing she wouldn't sleep yet, she looked around her apartment for something to occupy her mind. Hmmm she thought, book? TV? None appealed to her. She was in dire need of a new book to read, having reread all that she owned and she was never a big fan of the TV, ruined by years of working in public relations witnessing the so called news orchestrated by spin doctors.

She decided to pop open the laptop and waited for it to load as she made herself a coffee. Marji didn't know where she was getting her energy tonight, she even folded some clothes she'd taken from the dryer, trying to fit in countless tasks before the kettle clicked off, as most women did. She was relieved that she hadn't missed the 'buzzer' and even had her coffee cup ready, sugared and all! It was when she was stirring her coffee that she was jolted by the sound of an email on her computer. She recognised the sound, it was from lifestooshort.com and the thrill of a new message sent tingles up and down her spine. She stirred her coffee frantically and took a big sip, nearly burning her tongue and made her way over to the screen.

You have one new message it read.

Excited, Marji clicked into her inbox and read out the message. Hi I'm D I'm rarely on this so send me a text. The message included contact number, accompanied by a very provocative topless pose which was obviously taken in the mirror! Ugh she thought, is this what I've been reduced to? She was just about to give up when she saw J's avatar online and only then realised that if she could see J, then J could see her. Should she send a message? Was it needy? Am I still drunk she thought? To hell with it she thought, as the website states, life's too short and she started to type.

Hi J Marji here how are you? She typed nervously, slight bit of Dutch courage spurring her on. Marji waited for what felt like forever, sipping her coffee, tapping impatiently on the keyboard, then ping!

- *Hi Marji how are you?*

Marji replied immediately, not caring how eager she appeared.

- *I'm good thanks*

Marji realised her reply didn't leave much of an opening to respond, so typed another message.

- *You burning the midnight oil like me?*
- *Great thanks yes just finished work busy night!*

Marji hit a block, what next? I'm not used to this she thought! She remembered J worked as a chef and not a prostitute that her paranoid mind was telling her. Although, what if J was lying? For all Marji knew she was talking to a serial rapist! But then J sent another message.

I actually got to serve Gabriel Byrne tonight! What a gent, even thanked me personally for a lovely evening ☺

Marji typed back.

- *Wow that's great, fabulous actor.*
- *Indeed, although you must have met tonnes of celebrities in your line of work?*
- *Not tonnes but a few!*
- *Oh do tell all!* J was intrigued.
- *Well Mickey Jo Heart from Eurovision fame was*

a sweetie, Ryan Tubridy also, funny guy...

- *Wow impressive! I bet you got a few offers from handsome celebrities?*

- *Ha! Hardly* ☹

Was J fishing Marji thought? Marji was far from the young, skinny blondes that graced the PR world today, would J be disappointed? She was brought out of her daydream by another message.

- *You should pop into my restaurant sometime* ☺

Oh shit thought Marji, I'm not ready for a meet! But she was enjoying the flirting and just wrote back – maybe.

From then on Marji steered clear of any areas of conversation that lead towards a meet and herself and J chatted into the early hours of the morning. They covered everything from PR to culinary delights to authors and movies. By the time 3am came Marji had felt tired but exhilarated, her confidence growing with every tap of the keys. She was far from ready for a meet but couldn't help fantasising about the possibility of a new relationship. It had been so long since anyone had shown any interest in her and it was nice. She bid goodnight to J, promising to make it into the restaurant 'soon' and was relieved J wasn't the pushy sort, who in turn promised to check out the book Marji had recommended. All in all, it had been a good day and Marji was pleased.

***

"How was your night Mum?" Brigid's youngest daughter Claire asked as she drove her mother home.

"It was lovely dear," Brigid's mind was on other things.

"You ok Mum?"

"Fine dear just tired," Brigid lied. She wasn't feeling

well and knew it wasn't the drinks she'd had.

They arrived at Brigid's front door, an old Irish tenement house where Brigid had raised all of her children, where she'd spent many a happy memory. Memories she felt that were now somehow coming to an end.

"I could come in tonight if you'd like?" Claire sensed her mother needed keeping an eye on tonight and for once Brigid didn't argue but being Brigid she wouldn't admit the loneliness she felt, maybe not even aware of it.

"Well there was something I needed help with, Rita Finney from down the road wanted a loan of my cookbook, you know the one with the recipe for a Victoria sandwich? Honestly, you'd think the woman would know how to make a basic sponge! Anyway, it's on the top shelf in the kitchen so could you be a love and get it for me?"

"Of course Mum," Claire was delighted, it was rare her mother let her do anything for her without protest and she took full advantage of the gesture.

Once they were inside Claire immediately popped on the kettle, then set about climbing the presses to retrieve the infamous cook book.
"You make the tea while I'm up here Mum," Claire called down to Brigid. Claire noticed the tops of the presses were not as pristine as her Mum normally kept them, she was shocked even, this was not like her Mum at all, but she guessed that her mother wasn't able for the spring cleaning anymore. She said nothing, knowing full well it would turn into an argument, so she dusted off the book and jumped back down onto the floor. Brigid had the tea made, traditionally in a floral porcelain tea pot and matching cups and saucers. It was laid out on an equally elegant serving tray, accompanied by a plate of shortbread biscuits. Claire smiled. She loved these

sporadic moments with her mother. The rest of the family were equally as good to Brigid, but most lived a distance and with Claire living so close, admittedly by choice, she found it easy to take her mother places and pop round as often as she could. She was Brigid's baby and with her father having died when she was just twenty, all she had left was her mother.

The two women sat in the front living room in matching armchairs, at either side of the old fireplace. Brigid shivered in the late night chill and pulled her cardigan tightly around her shoulders.

"You cold Mum?"

"Just a bit chilly love."

Claire loved this room. It hadn't changed in all the years she'd seen it, lived in it. Brigid and her husband had Claire late in life, their little surprise her father would call her, but Claire never found having older parents than that of her school pals had any sort of a negative upbringing. Quite the contrary, her parents never missed a school play, camogie match or graduation. She kept them young, well until her father passed away.

They sat in silence for a few moments, sipping their strained tea, nibbling at the biscuits, until Brigid spoke.

"That's my favourite picture of your father," she said, nodding at an old print of her husband at a wedding.

Claire was surprised, her mother rarely instigated a conversation about her late father. She answered any and all questions put to her regarding him, but to bring him up was out of character. Still, Claire didn't show her emotion.

"Yes I love that picture, how old was he then?"

"About thirty-five. It was his brother Joseph's wedding, he was best man, very proud of himself he was," Brigid smiled, not taking her eyes off the picture.

"You must miss him?" Claire asked cautiously. But

133

Brigid didn't answer, Claire wasn't sure if she'd heard her, she just stared at the picture, still smiling.

"Mum?"

"Yes dear?"

"Do you...do you want more tea?"

"Yes love that would be nice."

Claire had wanted to ask her mother more about her father, she wanted to know how she felt when he died, how she coped with five children. But she decided against it. Instead she savoured the moment, knowing that at her mother's age, every moment was precious. They sat in silence for a little while longer, until the grandfather clock in the hall chimed.

"You best be getting home love," said Brigid

"I was thinking of staying the night, if that's ok? Don't want to drive home so late," Claire fibbed.

"Right so," Brigid answered, drifting off in her chair, hoping that the pain in her abdomen would fade and that Claire wouldn't notice.

Claire got up from her chair and not wanting to move her mother, covered her with an old mohair blanket and kissed her on the cheek. Brigid was already counting sheep while Claire made herself a bed on the sofa, drifting off herself.

***

Mary arrived home perplexed. On one hand, she'd had a great night with the girls, on the other, it was marred by her run in with Frank. She tried to put him out of her mind but didn't feel tired enough for bed. She decided to take a late night walk around the estate. Frank would do this from time to time and she could never understand it, once Mary was in she was in, ready for bed. But tonight she felt unsettled. She grabbed her winter coat from under the stairs, tied a scarf around her neck and set off. It was a fresh night and the rain had subsided. Mary would have loved to be able to name the constellations at that minute, like they do in the movies, but the only star she could pick out was the one you wish on. She walked down the road out of her estate and thought about heading towards the beach but instead passed the closed shops and busy pubs. A few underage locals were outside trying to stand up and Mary thanked God they weren't her own. She passed the park that was all locked up and pulled her coat in around her as the breeze took up speed. The trees made a magical sound as they blew in the air and Mary was happy to just be for a moment. She came along to the community centre and found a bench just outside in the open and sat down. There wasn't a sinner around and Mary was glad that she could be alone with her thoughts. She sat there for what felt like an eternity, enjoying the dark nature that surrounded her. She thought about everyone, her family, her new friends. Silly thoughts popped into her head. The broken beam on the banister in the house, her net curtains that were in need of a wash. She thought of her daughter in Canada, whom she must call. She had a dozen tiny thoughts buzzing around her head and before she knew it her watch said 1.57am. She jumped up, thinking how late it was and how someone would worry. But who? She was returning to an empty house. So she walked slowly home. She wasn't nervous being out so late on her own. She had grown up here and always felt safe. By the time she reached her estate most of the lights of the houses had gone out. On her road alone only her porch light remained on. She let out a small sigh as she turned the key and entered her home. But something wasn't right. Things on her hall table were moved, the broken beam on the staircase was protruding out. All the doors were open, even though she was adamant that she had closed them all before she left. Then she heard a noise. Mary felt panic rise inside her. She thought about heading straight back out the door but she was frozen to the spot. She heard the noise again, coming from upstairs. She grabbed the only thing that she could find in the hallway, an umbrella and stood brazen at the foot of the stairs. The noise became louder, like footsteps, which became closer and closer. Mary couldn't even speak. Terror encapsulated her. Then, she saw a tall dark figure at the top of the stairs. At that moment Mary forgot where the hall light switch was and wondered if this dark figure could see her too. The figure came towards her, slowly down the stairs until he was but a few feet away. Suddenly a light came on and Mary screamed! "Aaaaaaaaah" she was waving the umbrella wildly in the air. She didn't even hear the figure speak until he put his hand on her mouth.

"Mum! Mum!! Calm down! It's me!!"

Mary stopped, the sweat dripping down her neck. Then she opened her eyes.

"Greg!!?"

"Yes it's me!!"

"Oh Greg!!" she cried and flung her arms around him.

"It's great to see you too," her son laughed.

Then wallop! "You scared me half to death!!" Mary shouted as she clattered her son across the head.

"Ouw! Lay off I've just had an eighteen hour flight!"

"I'm sorry, it's just that I thought you were a murderer or something! What are you doing here? Why didn't you phone? Come here!" Mary flung her arms round her son again, "welcome home."

"Thanks Mum, I missed you, hey where's Dad?"

Mary's joy was quickly dashed as she ushered Greg into the living room. "Sit down hun," she said, as she began filling her son in on the bad news that he wasn't expecting.

***

Frank cleared the bar after what turned out to be a late night in the Haven, no one particularly wanting to go home. January and February were always slow months but when April hit and all the Christmas debts were cleared—people were sick of the sight of each and after the holidays they headed for the pub. He had planned to go for a late night stroll but by the time he cleared up it was near 2am. Jeff the owner had left him to it, so he decided to have a night cap before bed. He poured himself a single vodka and sat at the bar. Almost instantly Mary came to his mind. He hadn't been to the house in over a week and he knew why. He almost didn't recognise his wife that night in the bar, she looked so well. He felt stupid, like he was invading her space, even though she was at the bar where he worked and lived. But there was something different about her. She had an air about her, almost a confidence, that he didn't recognise. Part of him was happy for her, impressed even, but part of him felt excluded, pushed even further away. It made him angry, but he wasn't sure who with. Himself? Maybe. Mary? Maybe too. How did things come to this? He decided that he would make his way over to the house tomorrow and collect his post. But he was dreading it. What if she had a new man? He put the thought out of his mind, threw back the remains of the glass and headed to bed for a sleepless night.

Chapter Five

Mary woke early, suddenly having to remind herself that the snoring coming from the next room was normal. It was 9am and if her son hadn't changed she'd be lucky to see him before 12pm. He'd been home a week now and Mary was delighted to have some company in the house. She decided to tackle his bag which reeked of boy and some other smells that she couldn't place—nor wanted to. By 11am she had done two loads of washing, a nice homecoming present for her she thought sarcastically. She knew the only way she could entice her son up was with food so she set about making a fry up. It worked. The smell of pork sausages and maple cured bacon travelled up the stairs and she heard a stir.

"Morning Mum, ooh that for me?"

Mary laughed, feeling a flourish of warmth as Greg planted her with a big kiss.

"Yes love won't be long,"

"Aw you're the best!" Greg patted his stomach as he searched around for something.

"It's all on the line son," Mary said, referring to his washing.

"Aw do ye know what? You're the best Mammy in the world!" Greg exclaimed as he picked Mary up into his arms and swung her around, Mary still holding the egg lifter.

"Would you put me down you silly boy," Mary laughed as Greg settled himself down at the table.

"So, how long are you home for this time then?"

"Eh..dunno, a while probably,"

Mary didn't know where she got her son from, he was as clear as he was settled. She admired him for that, but he certainly didn't get it from her. She smiled as she placed his breakfast down on the table and she sat down with her mug of tea, emblazoned with 'World's Best Mum' on the front, a present from Australia, or the airport knowing her son.

Greg tucked in like he hadn't eaten in a week, which he probably hadn't Mary thought worryingly.

"You not having any?" he asked with a mouthful of sausage.

"No, had my porridge this morning,"

"Right, porridge," Greg guffawed, shuddering at the very thought of it. Mary wondered where he put all he ate, there wasn't a pick on him. Although he was only thirty-one. His father was the same up until his thirties and Mary noticed how much her son looked like Frank. Frank hmmm, she would expect him over soon and then it was as if Greg read her mind.

"Might pop over to see Dad later,"

"Mmm he'd like that," Mary answered.

"That is...if it's ok with you?" Greg asked timidly.

"Of course darling! You don't have to check with me silly." Mary felt a pang of guilt, had she painted Frank as the monster in the break up? She hoped not. It was still very important that neither her nor Frank show any animosity towards each other where the kids were concerned.

"Great! Don't suppose you could loan me a score for a pint?" Greg asked his Mammy with doe eyes. But Mary could never say no to her baby.

"Oh go on here you go, I knew that mug would come back to bite me!" Mary teased and Greg went for a shower excitedly at the prospect of seeing his old man for the first time in over a year.

***

Frank was washing glasses behind the bar when Greg walked in. He didn't look up, not noticing his son at the door. It was a Thursday afternoon so there were a few punters in who had just got their pay check. Greg walked over to the bar and sat down on one of the stools facing Frank, who still hadn't noticed him. Without looking up Frank said, "what can I get ye?"

Greg could hardly contain his laughter, "eh pina colada please,"

"A wha?" with that Frank looked up at the unusual order, especially for the Haven.

"Greg!!"

"Heya Da!"

"Jesus Christ is it really you?" Frank practically ran around to the other side of the bar with open arms.

"My God son welcome home!"

The two hugged each other, smiles beaming.

"Let me look at you," Frank stepped back and then wallop! "No phone calls for a year??"

"Ow that hurt!" Greg screamed rubbing his head. "I sent postcards," he offered in his defence.

"Ah postcards me arse," Frank was unimpressed.

"Jesus why is everyone hitting me," Greg said quietly, then Frank laughed again and hugged his son tightly.

"I missed you too," Greg laughed.

"So how long are you home for?" Frank asked his only son.

"I dunno, a while, maybe longer, who knows?"

"Well you haven't changed son, quick, what do you want to drink?"

"Eh...pint of the black stuff would be great,"

"Right ye be, Jeff, can someone cover for me? Me son's home!"

Jeff just nodded and said, "Welcome home Greg."

Frank and Greg grabbed two pints of Guinness and sat down at a table away from the bar.

"So, how was Australia? Or Canada or wherever you were?"

"Actually spent a bit of time in New Zealand recently,"

"God, you sure got around didn't you?"

"Yeah suppose I did,"

"You're not in any trouble are you? Coz God help me I'll punch the life out of…"

"Dad Dad calm down," Greg laughed at Frank, he hadn't changed either. "No I'm not in any trouble, just decided I needed to see a bit of green for a change,"

"Plenty of that here son!"

The two men downed their pints as Greg regaled stories from his travels, Frank hanging on his every word. He had missed his son, he had missed anyone to really talk to but acted like loneliness was the last thing on his mind.

"Did you get something to eat? I could whip you up a sambo?"

"Nah thanks Da but Mum made me a fry up,"

"Oh right," Frank put his head down, not knowing if Greg knew about the situation at home.

Greg spoke quieter then, "Da, Mum told me,"

"Oh, I see," said Frank, slowly panicking.

"Dad what happened? I mean, I know you two used to fight but every couple fights! I didn't think that you'd break up,"

Frank didn't know what to say. He found it hard enough explaining it to himself let alone anyone else and Greg wasn't just anyone.

"It's a long story son, we just….I don't know, things ended."

Greg was despondent, his homecoming had met him

with a reality he just couldn't face.

"But it's you two, Mum and Dad!"

"I know son, we're still your parents we're just not…"
Frank couldn't bring himself to say it and decided that the
conversation should change.

"Here, plenty of time to talk about that, it's your
homecoming, let's treat it like one! Jeff! One and one
please?"

Jeff nodded again and the conversation went back to
stories of Greg bungee jumping off bridges, finding a
snake in his bathroom and meeting several ladies along
the way. Frank was relieved as Greg succumbed to the
effects of a cool, creamy pint.

***

Stephen Stafford started his usual day at work at his
landscape gardening business by loading up the truck and
grabbing his paper work. His assistant Gary, a young lad
who he'd become fond of and who had taken to the work
quite well, sat in the passenger seat eating a breakfast
roll.

"How do you stay so skinny Gar?"

"Me? Good metabolism!" Gary said with a full mouth
as they set off for a new job.

"Metabolism me arse, wait until you hit your thirties!"

They made their way to a leafy street on the Southside
of Dublin and parked outside number 26. Stephen got out
first and made his way up the huge garden path, crammed
with oversized trees, hedges and wild neglected plants.
This is going to be a long job he thought. He rang the
doorbell once. No answer. He rang again. No answer.
He'd spoken to the lady of the house on the phone, she
sounded like an elderly woman and lived alone. He rang
once more and knocked and was just about to give up

when he heard a loud rustling in the trees that led to the back of the house. Suddenly out of nowhere a four legged, brown lump, shot out from the trees and lunged at Stephen! And before he knew it he was lying on his back being licked to death by some ungodly creature.

"Bebe NO!!" screamed a woman hot on the dog's tail, struggling to run after this wild thing that had literally landed on her new gardener.

Stephen stood up, eventually, still in shock at being knocked to the ground. He wasn't afraid, just taken by surprise. When he finally got his bearings back he looked at the creature, who looked a lot lighter than it felt and saw these big brown eyes staring at him wagging its tail rapidly.

"I'm so sorry!" said the woman. "She gets a bit excited when she meets new people."

With that, the dog leapt at Stephen once again and it was only then that Stephen noticed how young she was. Perched up on his knee was a two foot tall brown Doberman, with floppy ears that were nearly as big as her legs and a big brown snout that burrowed into his crotch.

"Very friendly isn't she?" Stephen laughed.

"Friendly?!" the woman snapped, "she's out of control at three months old!"

"Well I think she's gorgeous, hello little girl, how are you?" Stephen greeted the dog in his babiest voice that even he didn't know he had.

"Well you can have her! Has my place upside down and I'm getting too old!"

"You mean you'd give this little precious thing away?!"

"Precious? Ha! And she won't be little for long!"

"What did you say her name was?"

"Bebe"

"Bebe?"

"Yes it's Spanish for baby," the woman snorted.

"You don't say?" said Stephen, as he began to daydream.

***

Several pints later Frank and Greg had forgotten the time, having too much fun, with Greg's €20 having been stretched along with the help of Frank's pay packet. They talked, played darts, sifted through the locals coming and going and before they knew it was closing time. Frank was looking worse for wear and Greg hardly knew his own name.

Mary paced the floor as 1am turned to 2am; she worried for her youngest. But as it crept to 2am worry turned to anger and it reminded her of how much she hated waiting up for Frank all those nights. It annoyed her that here she was once again waiting for her son in the same way. Finally, just after 3am she heard a ruckus outside and went to see what state her son was in. When she opened the door she met Frank, looking a bit dishevelled, but it was the sight of Greg, vomiting on her lawn that sent her over the edge and Frank would be on the receiving end of her backlash.

"Well I hope you're proud of yourself Frank Bannick, it was bad enough when you came home in this state but to put your son up to it as well!!"

"Hang on a second, he's a grown lad he makes his own decisions!" Frank shouted.

"And do you think puking in the garden was his plan tonight??"

"Look I brought the lad home, he'll be fine and anyway, it's my business what I do with my own son!" Frank stormed off, suddenly feeling sober.

Mary didn't say anymore, she hated to admit it but

Frank was right, what business of hers was it what Frank did? She just hated to see Greg in such a state and wanted someone to blame and it terrified her that Greg might pick up his Dad's drinking habits. She brought Greg into the house and somehow managed to get him up the stairs to bed. She didn't say anything to him but he kept mumbling, "don't fight with Dad Mum, 's not his fault" then he was out cold.

Mary sat down and cried with temper. It all came back to her, the drunken nights, the fights, the smashed dishes. Frank had never actually hit Mary but there were plenty of badly filled holes in the wall that took the brunt of Frank's temper. The worst part was the moods the next day. The snapping, the insults, how it was all Mary's fault because she loved the kids more than her husband. Did she? She did fuss over her children, especially Greg being the baby, but what mother didn't? She decided she was tired then and went off to bed. She knew that Greg would be back to himself the next day, he had traits of his father, but she tried to realise that he was also a young man with his own mind. Maybe he didn't need his Mammy anymore, maybe no one needed her anymore.

***

It had been a couple of weeks since the night out in the Haven and the women felt that they all knew each other so much better. Rosa was noticeably absent and Cathy was still suffering with the 'beer fear' and a forty plus conscience. Alice was running late. Mary hadn't seen nor spoken to Frank since their heated words and Greg knew better than to bring it up. Mary needed today's coffee morning to take her mind off her troubles.

"Was I really that bad?" asked a concerned looking Cathy.

"Don't worry Cathy we all get hammered at some point!" offered Marji.

"Yes don't be worrying Cathy," said Mary.

"None of you said no, thanks!" said Cathy jokingly, still feeling nauseous, "Jesus when did hangovers last two bloody weeks, I still feel like shit?!"

"Since we got older I'm afraid!" said Mary.

"I've never been drunk," Brigid exclaimed.

"Really Brigid?" asked Marji.

"What never??" asked an astonished Cathy.

"No, never saw the point,"

"Well you're missing out Brigid!" said a pale faced Cathy.

"Clearly," laughed Brigid, the comment lost on Cathy who was heaving. The conversation continued on until they were joined by a very excited Alice who'd brought along a friend.

"Hey!!!!" beamed Alice, barely making it through the door with her new best friend.

"Alice! What on earth?" asked Marji as they all gazed wide eyed at this enormous dog that pulled Alice along, taking chairs with him.

"I got a dog!" said a thrilled Alice.

"Yes we can see that love," said Brigid, giggling at the childlike innocence of Alice.

"What the hell is that?" asked an unimpressed Cathy

"It's a dog! My dog! Her name is Bebe," beamed Alice, "I hope you don't mind Mary, I asked them at the desk they said it was ok, I just had to bring her in to meet you all."

"No of course not," said Mary, watching Alice's face light up with glee.

All were impressed, except Cathy, who wasn't an animal person, well unless it was dead, skinned and draped around her body. The women were full of questions, where did she get her? How old was she? They all huddled around the excited pet, who was clearly loving the attention. Cathy kept her distance, then noticed the dog getting into a strange position.

"Eh, Alice, what the hell is your dog doing?"

"Oh shit!" said Alice, scrambling for a bag. But it was too late and oh shit was right, because that's exactly what the dog did, all over the floor.

"Oh Bebe no no no!!" Alice scolded the confused looking animal, "she's not quite trained yet," said Alice apologetically as she cleaned up the mess. But suddenly Bebe wasn't the problem anymore as they all turned to look at Cathy, who was making ferocious heaving sounds. Like a shot Cathy was straight out the door, cupping her mouth and shouting shit! shit! shit! as she bolted out the door to the ladies. The women stopped and stared, open mouthed, then looked at each other and then broke into fits of laughter.

***

After a wet April, May brought Spring along to its fruition. Daffodils lined the manicured gardens on Mary's road. Even the road seemed more alive. People were out pruning their hedges, children played in shirt sleeves, excited at the prospect of the summer holidays, car radios boomed as neighbours hosed their cars and the general buzz in the air with the arrival of the sun was hard not to succumb to. It was a glorious Saturday afternoon and Mary took pride in her newly washed windows. Greg, of course was still in bed, which Mary took some comfort in, although she got the feeling that her son was getting itchy feet again and would be leaving her soon. She dreaded the thought. She'd gotten so used to having someone in the house again, someone to look after and soon she would be back on her own again. Alone again, naturally, she sang to herself.

"Who's singing?" Greg had appeared in the doorway.

"Oh just a car radio son," Mary thought on her feet, not wanting Greg to know how she was feeling.

"Any brew on?"

"Cooker," Mary answered, as Gregg sleepily headed back into the house, rubbing his eyes, seeking a strong cup of tea to wake him up.

It had been a while since she'd seen Frank. They hadn't really spoken since the night he and Gregg came home from their night of drunken debauchery. He'd gotten his post from Greg, obviously avoiding Mary. She thought of when she would next see him, most likely at Helen's baby's christening, but that was a few months away. Helen had less than two months to go and Mary was very excited at the prospect of becoming a Granny once again. She adored all of her grandchildren, although found it harder and harder to understand her grandchildren in Canada and them her. She thought of her eldest then, all the way across the world. Canada fascinated Mary. The sites, the people, the traditions. Maybe she would make it there one day, what's to stop me? She asked silently. She decided she would call Lily tonight.

Greg was indeed on his next adventure.

"Latvia?!" asked a surprised Frank, so much so that he put his pint down.

"Yeah," said Greg, taking a sip, "why not?!"

"I dunno," said Frank, "I don't know where you get your ideas from! What, do you just open a map, close your eyes and point?!"

"Pretty much yeah," Greg said, laughing, but Frank knew his son only too well.

"There wouldn't be a girl involved in this little trip

would there?" Frank asked with a quizzical eyebrow.

"Maybe," winked Greg, as Frank shook his head, repeating 'Latvia' 'Latvia.'

***

"It's not another night out I need it's a holiday!" said Cathy, in the small room that had come to be the women's place of refuge over the months, Cathy, whose composure had slipped somewhat.

"Cathy you're a genius!" said Marji.

"I am?" Cathy looked like the cat that got the cream but had no idea why.

"Yes, best idea you've had yet,"

"Why thank you!...eh what idea was that?"

"A holiday! We should all go on holiday!"

Marji's suggestion was met with whoops and cheers and Mary felt a slight panic rise in her gut.

"Oh yes! Where will we go? Oh wait till I tell Stephen!" beamed Alice.

"Yes a holiday would be nice," said Brigid, "but not to Ibiza or anything, I'm not into those smoke machines and bubble parties."

The girls laughed, all but Rosa, who had no clue what Brigid was on about. They decided not to jeer her about it and Mary saved her blushes, "don't worry Brigid, I'm not into Ibiza either." Brigid seemed unfazed and no one seemed to notice Rosa's lack of enthusiasm. They spoke for the next hour about where to go, somewhere in Ireland, Spain, Alice even suggested Poland to get Rosa on board and then Marji suggested somewhere they had never even thought of. With all the talk Mary surprisingly found herself warming to the idea.

"Amsterdam?" asked Alice.

Everyone seemed a little taken aback, fearing that

Amsterdam was a little out of their depth when they considered their age and the notoriety that Amsterdam was famous for. Mary immediately thought she was too old and wondered what her children would think of her swanning off to such a place. She was more suited to the Gleneagles Hotel at this stage in her life, but then thought to herself that this stage had taken a definitive U-turn that she'd never expected. Suddenly Amsterdam became alluring.

"I think Amsterdam would be wonderful," said Brigid, "I've never been and I'm a bit long in the tooth to refuse somewhere I might never get to!"

"You're right Brigid, could be what we all need," said Mary. The girls all agreed and before they knew it their time was up and they were saying their goodbyes and already looking forward to next week's coffee morning.

Mary headed home, with a slight spring in her step about the prospect of a holiday. Money would be tight but she would make it work. Greg was off in Latvia so she had no excuse to stay home and honestly, felt like she needed this holiday as much as the rest of the girls.

***

Marji was over the moon at the prospect of a holiday.

"I'm glad it's not a beach holiday Jeepers, don't fancy casting a shadow on the ladies with my fat rolls!" Marji laughed out loud to her cat, who she could have sworn threw her a filthy look. It'd been a long time since Marji had been away for her own pleasure. She travelled a lot with work but did just that, work! She never got a chance to see the sights and explore. She looked forward to a few days in a foreign country with the women who had become her friends these past months, but she still longed for some companionship. Someone to read the papers in bed with on a Sunday morning, someone who loved her just the way she was, someone to come home to each night. She was surprised that J came into her mind and thought who better to share her news with?

- *Hi J*
- *Hi Marji how are you?*
- *In great form thanks! You?*
- *Good thanks, any news?*
- *Actually yes, I'm going to Amsterdam!*
- *Wow great, to live???*
- *God no, just for a few days* ☺
- *Oh..*
- *Oh?*
- *Sorry, thought you were leaving me already* ☹
- *Now would I do that???*

Marji had been aware of the flirting between her and J for quite some time and today she felt bold, brand new, like she had a new lease of life.

- *Well you have made excuses about meeting up..."*

Shit! Thought Marji, what do I do?? "Do you know what Jeepers? I'm tired of hiding myself away!"

- *How about when I get back?* Typed Marji boldly.
- *Really?*
- *Yes of course*
- *Great well I'll send you my number, so get in touch when you get back and we'll arrange a date*, J replied.
- *Sounds good to me*
- *I'll look forward to it* ☺
- *Me too*

"Oh my God Jeepers I've got a date!!" Marji sang out, not caring who heard her.

***

151

Cathy got home from the coffee morning and noticed the message light flashing on her answering machine. When she pressed the button she heard a voice from her past.

"Cathy darling! How are you? Lucinda Harley Price here. I got your message."

Oh shit Cathy thought, the message I sent when I'd had one too many glasses of vino.

"Anyway would loooove to meet up, I've called the rest of the girls and they're all up for it too, where have you beeeeen?? Can't wait to hear what you've been up to! Shall we say The Orchid, tomorrow at 2? Wonderful, see you there! Ciao."

Ciao? Cathy thought. Lucinda was from the south inner city for Christ's sake, but now lived in a plush five bedroom semi-detached house on the beach. Also a former model, Lucinda married into money, no kids and no longer had the need to work. Cathy had always liked working but Thomas was earning enough to provide for the three of them and insisted his new wife enjoy her life of leisure. Cathy didn't argue, Thomas wasn't controlling, but he was masterful and Cathy was impressed by that.

Cathy thought about the lunch and felt an odd sensation in her stomach, nerves maybe? She pushed them aside and thought about what she would wear. Truth was she hadn't been shopping for a while and wanted to keep up appearances for her old friends. Yet Thomas wasn't as free with her 'allowance' as he once was. God, that was all she had. Jade never wanted to spend time with her and Thomas. Well Thomas wasn't home much these days. To hell with it she thought, she would take a shopping trip, maybe even get her hair and nails done. Why not? I've nothing else to do she thought.

***

Cathy arrived at The Orchid restaurant and was greeted by Karl, the doorman of twenty years who still remembered her.

"Cathy Malone hello stranger! God it's been a long time!"

"Hi Karl!" Cathy beamed, feeling proud that she hadn't lost her looks after all these years.

"Well you're looking fabulous as usual!"

"Thanks Karl, you old charmer!"

"Well your friends are already inside."

"Thanks." smiled Cathy as she headed inside to their usual table.

She could hear the girls before she could see them. Talking loudly hoping everyone could hear them. Lucinda spotted Cathy and nearly choked on her cosmopolitan trying to shout her name.

"Cathy!!! Darling come here and let me look at you!!"

Cathy made her way to the table, excitement replacing nerves as she started to look forward to having lunch with her old friends.

"Wow you look amazing!" Lucinda said, as she air kissed Cathy.

Cathy had to admit, she did look well. She wore a grey wrap-around dress that hugged her tiny waist, with thigh-high grey suede boots. Her hair shone from the conditioning treatment she'd had at the salon and her freshly cut golden blonde bob looked like something from a L'Oréal ad.

Cathy kissed her hellos to Lucinda and the other girls, Stephanie Treacy, a former air hostess slash model who'd married a doctor, Davinia Taylor, stunning Davinia, whose mother was Mexican and it showed in Davinia's sultry dark looks and Rebecca Collins, the youngest of the former models who married the director of a very exclusive golf club. Cathy had to admit, they all looked fabulous and was glad she'd decided to visit the salon prior to their lunch. The women ordered a bottle of red wine, which was obviously a top up thought Cathy, judging by their loud banter and flushed cheeks.

"Merlot ok for you Cathy? What am I saying—of course it is, sure when have you ever refused a drink?!" Lucinda exclaimed, laughing at her own joke, which Cathy didn't find particularly funny, but laughed along all the same.

"So Cathy, what have you been up to?" Stephanie asked, not waiting for a reply, "probably flitting off to this party and that, tell me how's that delicious husband of yours?!"

"Em..he's good, busy," Cathy answered, taking a sip of her water.

"Oh yes I remember Thomas Ryan!" screeched Davinia, "what a looker and money to burn, sure even if he didn't have the looks who cares with all that expendable cash?!"

Cathy was taken aback, "well it wasn't the money that enticed me..." but she never got a chance to finish.

"Right! Sure it wasn't!" snorted Davinia.

Bitch thought Cathy.

"Now tell us Cath, how is your little girl, Jane isn't it?" asked Rebecca

"Uh Jade"

"Right Jade,"

"Yes she's good, although not my little girl anymore, she's eighteen now," Cathy mused.

"Wow eighteen!" the women screeched again, "Imagine one of us having an eighteen year old!" and they erupted into laughter. Cathy could feel herself getting bored already, but salvation came in the form of a glass of wine and she downed it in seconds. She tried to take the limelight away from herself for a moment, while she got a chance to slip back into her 'ladies who lunch' mode.

"Don't you have children now Rebecca?"

"Children? Spawn of the devil more like! Three boys, who take after their father of course, lazy shits!" said Rebecca, not caring who heard her.

Cathy was horrified.

"Oh but at least you don't have to bring them to the park and that Beccs, you've got Carla for that," said Stephanie.

"Oh yes, don't know what I'd do without my Carla, sure the kids prefer her to me."

"Oh mine are the same," said Davinia, "they cry every time the nanny goes home!"

Cathy couldn't believe her ears, none of the women worked, yet they all had full time nannies, so that they could get pissed at 2pm on a weekday. She thought about Jade. Ok she wasn't mother of the year and she did have a nanny once herself, but she worked at the time and she savoured those moments when Jade was a baby. It was her confidence which took a nose dive, she never thought she'd be cut out to be a mother and Jade wasn't exactly planned, but the love she felt and received from this little chubby bundle made her feel like she had finally made something in her life to be proud of. She snapped out of her daydream only to find the women were still bitching about their kids.

"That's why I never had any brats," piped Lucinda, "late night bottle feeds and terrible twos, sure I never had the time!"

Time? Thought Cathy. Time? The bitching didn't end there and soon it turned to the husbands.

"I mean he wants to go skiing again," rambled

Stephanie, "for Christ's sake we've been twice this year, I need some sun on my face! So I just took his credit card and booked Madrid for myself, Carla can take the kids," said Stephanie.

"Oh don't taaalk to me Steph," said Rebecca, "John expects me to wear off the rack for this charity ball, I was like, excuuuuse me I want couture or I'm not going and I'm not donating a penny of MY money until I get it! Of course he caved!"

"Good for you Beccs you let him know whose boss!" resounded the women, all but Cathy who just couldn't believe that she was once friends with these people. God, was she like this at one stage? She couldn't have been, could she? The women finished their starters and with mouths still full went on to complain about everything wrong in their lives, the upheaval marriage and children caused, how their husbands were never home, how they worked all the hours God sent. But there was no mention of the plush houses they lived in, the expensive cars, the clothes and anything else they only had to bat their eyelashes for and more importantly, no talk of love. The main course arrived and Cathy was counting down the minutes until it was acceptable to leave.

"Tell me Cathy," asked Lucinda, "do you ever hear of Maeve Ryan? All the women stopped chewing and waited for the reply.

"Em no, not for a long time,"

Maeve Ryan was Thomas' first wife, the woman he left for Cathy. It was a sore subject for Cathy, she was never proud of the fact that she broke up a marriage, but that feeling of guilt took a long time to surface. She was young and simply got caught up in the excitement of love and lust. After that, it was the guilt of not feeling the guilt that caused her stomach to turn.

"I remember you doing it in their bed!" screeched

Stephanie

"Yes well that was a long time ago," said a meek Cathy.

"Oh I remember that!" said Davinia.

"She was an awful ugly cow anyway," said Rebecca.

"Oh Beccs you're so bad!" said Lucinda and the women broke into giggles once again, as usual, at someone else's expense.

"Yes well you landed him in the end!" said Stephanie.

Cathy had had enough at this stage.

"I didn't land him Stephanie I fell in love with him."

"Love huh!"

"Yes love."

But Stephanie wasn't backing down.

"Well maybe it's time for a new model Cath," said Stephanie

"Em, you mean like Davinia's?!" said Rebecca.

"Shhhhhhh!!!" said Davinia, "that's supposed to be a secret you bitches!"

"Yeah right!" the women said.

Cathy had had a wakeup call, she thought by meeting up with her old friends she might get a piece back of the life she was missing, but she didn't want any part of this life. A bottle of wine per day, thinking of your kids as some sort of hindrance, cheating on your husband. It wasn't her anymore, maybe it never was, she loved her husband, she loved Jade and came to prefer having coffee in a community centre with a bunch of housewives than the superficial playdates that these women hadn't seem to have grown out of. She stood up and asked for her coat.

"You're leaving? But we're heading to the Shelbourne for cocktails?" said Lucinda.

"I'm sorry Lucinda, I'm sorry to all of you, but I've a family to get home to."

"Just ring your nanny and get her to take them!"

"Eh I don't have a nanny."

The women gasped in horror.

"What? No nanny?! How do you cope?" asked a visibly shocked Rebecca.

"Pretty well considering I actually like my child and want to spend time with her!" Cathy couldn't help herself.

"Oh you think you're better than us or something?" asked a disgusted Davinia.

"Yes I do actually," answered a smug Cathy.

"Well that peroxide is obviously gone to your head Cathy Malone," snapped Lucinda.

"And obviously the elitist suburbs have gotten to yours Lucinda and it's Cathy Ryan by the way."

"Well the nerve of some people! You were never one of us Cathy, even though you tried to be, you'll always be a dirty little nobody from bog land," said Lucinda.

"And you'll always be a gold-digging tramp Lucinda," Cathy retorted, as she threw €100 on the table and left.

On her way out she felt exhilarated, she never waited on a reply from Lucinda or any of the other girls, but the stunned silence from the table spoke volumes. She met Karl on the way out.

"Forget something love?"

"Yes Karl, I forgot my cop on!"

Karl smiled, "Won't find that in there I'm afraid!"

"You're dead right Karl," said Cathy as she bid him farewell.

***

Rosa was home ironing as she pondered the idea of a holiday with the women. There was no way in hell that she could go, she knew that, but she daydreamed nonetheless at the thought of some free time away from

"My name is Doctor Williams, but please call me Karen."

"Hello," they both answered in unison, still a bit nervous. Doctor Williams was used to this with so many couples coming through her door and adopted a professional, yet friendly approach.

"Please try to relax, I understand how stressful this can all be and the barrage of emotions it can raise, but we are here to help you both from beginning to end and will answer any questions and address any concerns you have at any time."

Alice and Stephen both relaxed at her words and their shoulders noticeably dropped. It was Alice that spoke first.

"Doctor...I mean Karen, sorry, all those thank you cards outside, are they really all success stories?"

"Yes they are indeed," she smiled.

"But not all are successful?"

"No, not all, but our success rate is very high and I think the best thing you can do is try to remain positive and hopeful throughout,"

Alice didn't seem convinced, assuming that she would be in the minority. The doctor sensed her doubt, while Stephen remained attentive to both Alice and the doctor, who had that day, fast become, the most important women in his life.

"Alice," the doctor spoke softly, "I understand your doubts and your fears and no I cannot guarantee that you will conceive, but we will do everything we can physically do possible and don't forget, modern medicine takes us so far and then in steps God."

"We haven't been to Mass in years doctor," Stephen offered, apologetically. The doctor laughed.

"That's ok Stephen, I wouldn't imagine you would be overlooked for that."

The doctor went on to talk about the various tests they would undergo, the types of treatments, injections, the after care and of course, the costs, which would take a substantial chunk from their savings.

"Sure who needs a conservatory anyway?" Alice remarked on the way home.

Stephen put his arm around his wife as they made the short walk to the nearest coffee shop, to take it all in, both feeling a little more hopeful than when they left the house that morning.

***

Brigid woke up from her afternoon nap and felt a chill as she pulled her cardigan around her shoulders. Even though the sun was shining through the window it wasn't a very warm day, typical of the Irish weather. She looked at the clock, 4.10pm.

"My God I've been asleep for two hours," she said to no one.

Brigid was used to dozing in the afternoon, but never for this long. Her doctor didn't seem too happy about her test results and she hated to admit it, but she was a bit worried. She decided to make herself a cup of tea and as she got up from her chair, she was stopped in her tracks by an unmerciful pain in her stomach. She automatically grabbed herself, hunched over and winced in pain. She'd had these pains recently, they came and went, but nothing like this.

Charlie jumped up from his basket and barked, sensing his owner's discomfort, pawing at Brigid.

"It's ok Charlie…" was all Brigid managed to say, before everything went black.

***

The weekend had finally arrived and the girls were buzzing at the thought of getting out of Dublin for three glorious days. Mary packed thoughtfully, prepared for cold and warm weather, not sure what to expect. Helen called her about ten times that morning already. Mum have you got your passport? Do you need a lift to the airport? Are you ok for cash? Seriously, Mary thought, when did I become the child in our relationship? She laughed to herself and then suddenly nerves took over her. Her biggest fear was that the girls would think she was dull, or that she'd run out of things to talk about. Still, she had to admit, her confidence was growing, something she'd never thought possible. Mary didn't even know what confidence felt like. When it came to her kids, Mary went to the ends of the earth for them. She had no problem challenging people that upset them, but when it came to herself she let things slide. Probably her Irish upbringing, the Irish always had a tendency to brush off the hard woes of life, always insisting they were 'grand.'

Alice pulled up outside Mary's house with Stephen behind the wheel. They insisted on picking Mary up as they lived the closest and Alice wouldn't take no for an answer. Claire was taking Brigid and Marji and Cathy were getting a taxi. Rosa, unfortunately couldn't make it and Mary had a vague suspicion of why.

Mary walked out to greet Alice at the door, who was waving vigorously through the window.

"Hi Mary!!!" Alice beamed.

"Hi Alice, hi Stephen," Mary waved into the car.

"God can you believe it Mary, three whole days in Amsterdam?!"

"I know," laughed Mary as she wheeled out her brand new suitcase.

"I'll help you with that Mary," offered a smiling

Stephen.

Alice was buzzing as they piled into the car.

"I've heard they have windows with naked women in them selling their bodies! Can you believe it?!"

"Yes I've heard, far cry from Dublin," said a bemused Mary.

"Watch out for them space cakes Alice Mulroney!" teased Stephen.

"Shut up you!" Alice replied, slapping her husband's head as he drove.

It was a beautiful day, summer had finally arrived in Dublin and Mary inhaled it's scent deeply through the open window. Alice was still yapping away like a giddy schoolgirl and Mary just smiled, enjoying her journey. It was a novelty to Mary to get out of Dublin, as she rarely did so. Even when she'd attend the regattas in Wicklow she felt a buzz of excitement being away from home, even if it was only for a day. But Amsterdam was right out of her comfort zone, but then so were a lot of things she'd done this year and maybe it was a good thing.

They arrived at Terminal 2 of Dublin airport, where they had arranged to meet the other women and Alice was hugging Stephen tightly.

"Look after Bebe won't you? And don't forget to turn the washing machine to D when you're doing a wash, and...."

"Alice! You're only going for three days I'll survive, now feck off and let me enjoy me freedom woman!" Stephen slapped Alice hard on her bum and she let out a little girlish yelp. Mary laughed.

"Ok, well I'll ring you tonight dude," Alice said as she kissed her husband for the umpteenth time.

"Go! Love ya!" Stephen blew a kiss out the window as he got ready to drive off and Alice reciprocated.

Mary and Alice grabbed their bags and headed over to

the check-in desk.

"Girl's mustn't be here yet," Mary observed, but then was quickly interrupted by a loud clatter at the entrance.

"Yes if you could just leave them there," she heard Cathy bellow, to a poor taxi driver laden down with three Burberry cases. Mary could hear the overweight and visibly sweating taxi driver mumble and curse under his breath 'snobby bitch.' Cathy of course was oblivious and Marji looked utterly mortified as Cathy flung the money at the poor taxi driver. They made their way over to the other women, Cathy cursing her journey en route.

"I mean, I know it's the longest avenue in the country but did he have to go so bloody slow?!"

"Ah sure we're here now," offered Marji as they spotted the women.

"Alice, Mary hi!!" bellowed Cathy. Cathy looked amazing thought Mary, a bit overdressed for the airport, but every hint of the former model. It was the first time Mary had seen designer luggage, she didn't even know it existed. Mary's pride in her new little wheeled suitcase from Dunnes suddenly took a nosedive, until she saw Marji produce a Mary Poppins style bag that had seen better days. Marji looked every bit the thrift shop scavenger, wearing a boho style skirt with beads on the end, she even had make up on, Mary smiled, each of the women had made their own effort to look their best and it was sort of humbling. Mary was always aware that women didn't dress to impress men, rather to impress their own sex. Women were more critical of each other, something that never dissipated with age.

After they all hugged each other excitedly, they saw Brigid making her way through the door with Claire, who insisted on accompanying her Mum all the way to the check in desk. The women laughed as they heard Brigid make her way over.

"Honestly Claire, I'm not going on a school trip I'm a grown woman!"

"I know Mum, just want to make sure you have everything you need,"

Brigid made her way over to the women, with Claire wheeling her bag behind.

"Hi Brigid, hi Claire," said Mary, followed by the rest of the women.

"Hello ladies, are we all set?"

"Yes all set!" answered the women in unison.

"Hi ladies, are you looking forward to your holiday?" asked a now embarrassed Claire.

"Just what I need," said Cathy.

"Oh can't wait!" said Alice.

"Just what the doctor ordered," said Marji.

Although their words tripped over each other as they all spoke together. Mary smiled. The women made their way to the check in desk as Claire said goodbye to her Mum.

"You will call me when you get there?" said Claire.

"Of course love, now you know you have to actually let me go so that I can come back?" said Brigid.

Claire giggled nervously, "I know I know, just..." Claire couldn't say anymore and suddenly grabbed Brigid tightly. Brigid was taken aback, standing there, arms still outstretched. But then she embraced her youngest daughter and whispered in her ear.

"I'll be fine love, try not to worry,"

"Ok," was all Claire could say, then she turned to leave.

Brigid joined the women on the queue and didn't notice Claire making a beeline for Mary. When no one was looking she gently grabbed Mary's arm.

"Mary, hi sorry, could you just keep an eye on Mum for me?" Claire whispered.

"Of course hun," Mary could see the worry in Claire's eyes, that stretched beyond the perils of a holiday.

"Thanks," said Claire, with glassy eyes.

"Claire, is everything ok?" asked Mary.

"Um...yes, fine fine," Claire smiled difficultly.

Mary knew there was something amiss, but it was obvious Claire wasn't going to divulge it today. Mary simply rubbed Claire's arm reassuringly.

"I'll look after your Mum ok?" whispered Mary kindly.

"Thank you," said Claire, then she quickly left.

Mary returned to the women, who were gaggling like flamingos and she took a sly look in Brigid's direction. But her face wasn't revealing anything out of the ordinary, so she put it out of her mind and focussed on the day at hand. Then suddenly Mary's stomach lurched. Shit, I'm going to bloody Amsterdam she thought and took a deep breath.

"You ok Mar?" asked Marji.

"Fine thanks," Mary smiled as she was brought back to the present.

After the women checked in they made their way to one of the coffee shops. Mary was starving, but her nerves prevented her from devouring the delicious looking fry up in front of her. Instead she opted for a fruit scone and a cup of tea. The women ordered their usual beverages and they all laughed at their 'international' coffee morning. The banter was in full flow as the women discussed previous holidays, what to expect from Amsterdam, who they were leaving behind that day and how much they needed the break. Mary's nerves subsided as she assessed the situation, thinking what a good start the holiday was off to.

***

Frank wasn't feeling well today and decided to take the day off. It was quiet in the Haven so he wasn't entirely missed, but rather than take to the bed to sleep it off, the four walls felt claustrophobic and he knew he needed to get out.

Frank found it hard to stay in bed these days, there was a time when that's all he did, all he could manage to do, having lost his job all those years ago. He was working in a factory on a temporary contract which lasted months at a time, with long shifts, sometimes through the night. It was hard work but Frank loved it. Many of his old school friends worked on the same contract which was always a bonus. Even the dinner lady in the canteen was an old friend and who was the reason for him putting on a few extra pounds with the second and sometimes third helpings she'd laden Frank down with. In total, the work lasted about fifteen years, but there was never an opportunity to be hired on a permanent basis, much to Frank's annoyance. He always seemed better in himself when he worked there, had more money in his pocket too. Money that sometimes Mary never knew about.

He always handed up his keep, but due to the drinking sessions that lasted sometimes three days, Mary kept a tight rein on his salary. This always infuriated Frank, making him feel like one of the children, with little or no respect to the fact that he was a man, who provided for his family. Back then there were no such people as alcoholics, they were simply men who liked a drink or someone who was 'fond' of his drink. It was never a drink 'problem.' All the conversations back then were the same, 'I heard there was murder in the pub the other night with so and so?' 'ah yeah he's a bit fond of his drink.'

Frank unfortunately was in that category, blinkered to the problem he had. He had all the excuses in the world not to stop. A man needs a pint after a hard day's work.

I'm just being sociable. I ran into an old school friend. Mary had heard them all. The kids were too young to notice, maybe Lily, being the oldest. But what was meant to be an exciting time as a newlywed for Mary, was her loneliest.

It was when Frank lost the job that things took a bad turn. Suddenly he wasn't the bread winner anymore, stripped of his provider role. Of course Mary just thought that the best thing to do was get back out there and apply for more jobs. Frank felt that she didn't or refused to get the fact that he wasn't as confident in other jobs. Frank didn't even know it himself and eventually, depression took hold. It was subtle at first, going back to bed after dropping the kids to school, not eating. But it was the mood swings that Mary struggled with. Mary maintained her cleaning job in the mornings and would get frustrated with Frank. Mary never had the luxury of a choice about whether to work or not. She worked since she was fourteen without a break and with five mouths to feed never stopped providing for her family.

Frank went from sitting idly in the kitchen, flicking through the TV channels, not uttering a word, to full blown outbursts of rage, leaving Mary feeling angry and alone. But Mary never let her feelings be known, she simply gave as good as she got and Frank saw this as being confrontational and having the tough exterior that Mary had, made her seem uncaring to Frank's emotions, which made him fall deeper and deeper into his black hole. He didn't see all that Mary had done for him, taking the kids out so he could sleep, always making sure he had a pack of cigarettes by his bedside, making excuses to people who he'd stopped saying hello to on the street and sending him on countless job interviews in the hope that they'd return him some self-respect and a reason to get up in the morning. It was hard on both of them, but Frank was too stubborn to admit defeat and Mary was too proud. In truth, depression had threatened Mary's life many times and scared her so much that she did everything she could to prevent it from encapsulating her. Frank didn't have such strength and relied heavily on Mary, without even realising it, to take on the role of wife and mother to them all. Their marriage was a constant battle for power that neither of them were even aware of—it manifested itself into constant arguments that eventually lead to their parting of ways. Textbook perhaps to the onlooker, but both were oblivious and given the times they lived in, there was no margin for dealing with the similar feelings they'd both had. Therapy and searching for oneself was an American concept, confined to those with 'serious' problems and those with little to do than spend their vast disposable income on.

Thankfully, the depression didn't last and Frank eventually got the job in the Haven, having spent so much time there, whether that was a good or a bad thing he wasn't sure, but he was happy enough. Today though, Frank felt that old tinge of depression creep up on him again and unknowingly taking a leaf out of Mary's book, was determined not to let it get the better of him. So he picked up the phone and start dialling.

"Helen? It's your Dad,"

"Dad hi! One second..." Frank could hear the ruckus in the background as Helen tried to calm down his grandson.

"Dad hi sorry...Josh no! Put that down! Sorry Dad how are you?"

Helen was more than pleased to hear from her Dad, he rarely rang her, never knowing what to say, but today he had a plan.

"I was just wondering if you had any plans today?"

"Josh no! No Nutella! Sorry Dad what did you say?"

"I..I was just wondering if you had any plans today? Greg is away and well..." Frank hit a block, he was never used to phones anyway, they made him uncomfortable, but he suddenly felt foolish, he somehow got it into his head that he was a hindrance on his daughters, Greg was a drinking buddy and a man, but his girls were different, they were strong, like their mother and it intimidated him slightly.

"I'm actually off today Dad why what's up?" Helen answered, breathless.

"Em, well, it's a nice day, so I thought maybe we could take Josh to feed the ducks?"

"Oh yes! I'd love that Dad, we'd love that!! Josh do you wanna go feed the ducks with Granddad?" Helen said excitedly. Frank was delighted, but his grandson had other ideas that made him chuckle.

"No I don't like Granddad!" he could hear in the background, Helen coming straight back on the phone.

"Sorry Dad he hates everyone today he's just tired he hasn't had a nap yet, I could do with one myself!!"

"No problem love," Frank chuckled again.

"Tell you what, if I don't leave the house now I never will so will I pick you up in a half an hour?"

"Sounds perfect love, I was thinking of Herbert Park?"

"Sounds lovely Dad, see you in a few..." Helen hung up without saying goodbye, obviously by mistake as the last thing Frank heard was Helen saying don't touch that button. Frank was ecstatic, he was glad he'd rang Helen and was looking forward to the day. Even his sinuses had cleared miraculously and he hurriedly grabbed his keys and jacket and headed downstairs. He met one of the barmen en route.

"Feeling better Frank?"

"Ah not great, gonna head the doctor—see if he'll give

me something, daughter's picking me up."

"Right ye be, hope it clears up!"

Frank thanked his colleague. It was a little white lie and Frank was confident he wouldn't burn for all eternity for it as he made his way out the front door. Helen had said a half hour but Frank couldn't wait. It was a gorgeous day out and Frank didn't want to waste it, so he sat down on one of the benches outside the pub and lit a cigarette. As he inhaled he took in the splendour of the day, birds singing loudly in the trees, cars flitting by with open windows and radio bellowing out summer tunes. He had presumptuously bought a sliced loaf for the ducks, but also a paper, just in case Helen hadn't been free. He was looking forward to seeing his daughter and his Grandson. Mary was off in God knows where doing God knows what and even though the thought etched at his emotions he wouldn't let it spoil his day. As Helen approached some forty minutes later he hopped up off his seat like he was sitting on a spring. He waved them into the car park and made his way over to the passenger seat, Josh in his car seat in the back, clutching a beaker of juice. He kissed his daughter on the cheek as they exchanged hellos and handed Josh a lollipop in the back, much to his delight and they set off.

***

The women arrived at their hotel overlooking the Prinsengracht Canal in the Jordaan district of Amsterdam City. The hotel was small but was tastefully decorated boasting chic and stylish furnishings. Mary had never stayed anywhere like this before and felt somewhat intimidated by its beauty. They were greeted by a very friendly young man behind the desk.

"Hallo, welcome to Amsterdam," he announced

warmly.

"Hello," said Mary.

"Oh wow," said Alice, "I totally understood everything you said."

The women erupted in laughter, giddy from the flight.

"What?" said Alice innocently, which made them laugh even more, then Cathy burst ahead of them.

"Excuse me, do you have Wi-Fi?" she asked curtly.

The poor guy was taken aback by her forwardness but remained smiling all the while.

"Um, yes we have Wi-Fi Madame," he answered, very professionally.

"Good, I need your pass code, also I need..."

"Ok! Let's get checked in," Marjorie interrupted Cathy, pulling her to one side. Cathy didn't argue, Marji was a big girl and Cathy reckoned she could wrestle her to the floor in a heartbeat. Marji apologised to the receptionist and gave all the details for their booking, including passports, booking forms and credit cards. Mary was delighted that someone else took the reigns as leadership wasn't her strong point. Marji was used to organising fundraisers, events, you name it, so Mary and indeed the rest of the women, were happy to take a backseat.

They were directed to their rooms, Mary bunking with Brigid and Alice, Cathy and Marji sharing a triple room. Brigid was quiet as they unpacked, each taking expert care in arranging their outfits for day and night time.

"You ok Brigid?" Mary asked.

"Sorry? Oh yes yes dear, happy to be here!" Brigid exclaimed, a bit over enthusiastically.

Mary thought about delving more into her mood, but Brigid interrupted her thoughts.

"I think a nice tipple is in order don't you?" she said.

"God, drinking in the afternoon, I'm not used to this!"

said Mary, her stomach a mix of nervous excitement.

"You'll be a long time dead Mary," said Brigid, her eyes piercing into Mary's. For some reason, Mary wanted to hug Brigid there and then, but thought it silly, so she grabbed her jacket and headed over to the phone, to alert the other women of their plans. They were all so excited at the idea. No kids, no work, no partners, no housework, five eager women on a trail of the unknown, the unfamiliar, they relished it like a snow day.

They met in the lobby bar, a stylish, quaint little saloon, decorated in plush purples and deep rose pinks. They found a little snug in the corner of the bar and waited for their drinks to arrive. They all decided to order a glass of Heineken, which seemed to be the beer of choice in Amsterdam. None of them, bar Marji, were used to drinking beer, but they thought when in Rome…

They enjoyed their drinks but enjoyed the banter even more.

"God I haven't had a beer since I was eighteen," said Brigid.

"This was my Dad's favourite drink," said Marji, toasting her late father.

"I hate beer, but it's alcohol so it'll do me," said Cathy.

"The last time I had a beer, Stephen had to carry me home," said Alice.

Mary was quiet, not knowing what to expect from the day. The nervous excitement still lingered on in her stomach and for a moment she thought of home. She always did, even if she was only an hour from Dublin. Oh God, what if Helen has the baby while I'm here? What if Greg comes back and burns the house down? She realised she was overreacting and scolded herself inside. Then she suddenly thought of Frank, what he was doing at that particular moment. She wondered why and almost felt guilty for leaving him at home, despite the fact that they were estranged. Old habits die hard I guess, she thought.

The women were still chattering at the speed of light and after two more beers, they decided they would take in a little sight-seeing, starting with the Anne Frank museum. Mary was delighted, she had always been fascinated by history and by Anne Frank, but never in her wildest dreams imagined she'd be entertaining her interests so far afield. The women raised their glasses in a toast to their impending adventure and as their glasses clinked, each were filled with anticipation of what the weekend had in store for them.

***

Helen parked the car just outside Herbert Park and the three made their way in. Josh was so excited and was making quack quack noises all the way there. Frank revelled in his time with his Grandson and wondered why he didn't do it more often.

"Can I have bread now Granddad?" he asked excitedly.

Frank smiled warmly, "of course you can kiddo, won't you be careful at the edge?"

"I will Granddad," Josh answered.

Frank showed Josh how to break up the bread as a very pregnant Helen wheeled the buggy over to one of the benches and sat down. It was a beautiful day, one to behold the work of mother nature. The sun glistened on the figure eight shaped pond, home to the best fed ducks in Dublin. Many rested in the centre bank of the pond, the small bushes and trees lending them shade, as they nursed their pregnant bellies. Trees outlined the pathways surrounding the pond and Helen remembered what a maze the park was as a child, although it seemed much bigger back then. The old bandstand still stood tall to the left, where children still played, which gave a perfect view to the overlooking hotel. The whole setting was so picture perfect Helen smiled, watching her Dad and son bonding so graciously. She leaned back and closing her eyes, she basked in the warm sun, the sounds of laughter hugging her tenderly. It was the first proper rest Helen had had in days and those ten minutes to herself served her better than a full night's sleep.

After the duck feeding the trio decided to take a walk up further to the football pitches, detouring along the Dodder river. Josh was in his buggy now and Helen knew it wouldn't be too long before he was asleep, as he always seemed to sleep better in it. As she walked Frank gestured to the buggy.

"Do you mind love?"

"No! Not at all."

Frank was now the driver, beaming with pride at wheeling along his now sleeping Grandson.

"Good for my back you know?" he lied foolishly.

"Course," Helen winked and they both laughed.

They decided to take advantage of the silence between them and sat down on a bench near where some school children were playing a football match. Frank leaned forward and watched intently as Helen adjusted herself to reach a comfortable position.

"Beautiful day," Helen noted.

"Tis love," answered Frank, lighting up a cigarette but not taking his eye of the match.

"Josh loved it, short lived as it was," Helen said, lovingly glancing at her sleeping son.

"He did," smiled Frank, looking into the buggy.

"Dad?"

"Yeah?" asked Frank, still staring into space.

"Why did you call today?" asked Helen.

Frank's let out a sigh, slumping his shoulders.

"Why did I call?" he said rhetorically.

"I mean, I'm so glad that you did, it's just that you rarely do and I thought that..."

"You thought there might be something wrong?" Frank finished her sentence, turning his head towards her.

"Well, yeah, sorry," Helen replied.

Frank took the final pull of his cigarette and tossed it away with ease, then clapped his hands together, rubbing palm on palm, like he was getting ready to get down to a day's work. Helen didn't know what he was going to say, was it bad news of some sort? Was he unwell? She waited for her Dad to speak and she was just about to ask him again when he spoke.

"I never did that when you were little," Frank said, gesturing to the buggy. Helen was confused.

"Did what?"

"Wheeled you around in your buggy, I never did that," Frank answered.

Helen was still confused, "what do you mean?"

"It wasn't a manly thing to do, wheel a buggy around, even for your own child,"

"O..k..?" Helen answered, not sure where the conversation was heading.

"Your Mum always did that, what do you call it, maternal stuff...me? Do you know I actually gave your mother the buggy with Lily in it one day because I saw a mate of mine and was embarrassed? Imagine that? I mean, I did other stuff, I taught you all how to tie your laces, ride your bikes, told you stories..."

"Yeah great stories," Helen said smiling, but with a feeling of concern for her father.

"I should've done more, with you, with Greg and Lily,"

Is he apologising? Helen suddenly thought, noticing

177

Frank's leg tapping rapidly.

"Dad, you were a great father, still are," she said, placing her hand on his thigh. Frank was back looking off into the distance.

"That's a penalty," he said, like it was the most important match of the season.

"Dad,"

"Or at least a corner," Frank was far away in thought.

"Dad?" Helen said again, a little more forcefully this time as she touched his arm, "you were a great Dad," she repeated.

He turned to look at her then, his face fixed with worry.

"Was I?" he asked earnestly.

"God yes! Of course! You're the best Dad anyone could have hoped for!" Helen couldn't believe that he doubted that.

"Really?"

"Yes really! Dad where is this coming from?"

"I dunno, just weighing up my life,"

"You're not sick are you?" Helen asked, suddenly panicked.

"No no no, nothing like that, just taking stock ye know, I'm nearly sixty-six, work in a pub, live in a bedsit, have a failed marriage, just don't want to have any failings to do with my kids too,"

"Well you don't and you never will."

Frank looked down at his feet.

"You listen to me, you didn't fail any of us do you hear?" Helen said adamantly.

"Failed your mother though," Frank said sadly.

"Oh Dad is that what this is about?"

"Oh I dunno love, shouldn't have even brought it up, sorry you don't need this love,"

"Hey, what are daughters for?" Helen said with

complete and utter love for her father, "and with Mum? I don't think either of you failed, no one was to blame, it would be a lot easier if there was and hey, maybe you don't work together, but you work apart, you're two very strong characters and we're all lucky to have you both as parents," Helen smiled.

"Jesus, when did you get to be so smart? Are you sure you're mine?" Frank joked.

"Actually think I'm adopted and my real parents will claim me any day now, filthy rich of course."

They both laughed and the jokes broke the tension. Helen put her arm around her Dad and they sat in silence for a few moments, head resting on head.

"Hey do you remember when you took us all to the Spring Show?" said Helen.

"I do indeed, you pissed your knickers," Frank teased.

"Oi" said Helen, giving Frank a playful thump in the ribs.

They stayed in their embrace, heads tilted into each other, looking out towards nothing in particular.

"I love ya kiddo," said Frank.

"I love you too Daddy," Helen answered, basking in the warm glow of her father's love and neither wanting the moment to end.

***

After an enjoyable day of sightseeing it had started to rain on the streets of Jordaan, so the women decided to head into one of the many cafes in Noordermarkt Square, whilst admiring the Noorderkerk Church which dominated the square. The square was busy—people hastily propping up umbrellas to avoid the light shower.

The women sat down wearily, having walked for three hours solid and ordered their usual non-alcoholic beverages. The coffee was superb as Cathy exclaimed and Alice excitedly displayed her little souvenir that she had bought at one of the stalls.

The women became nervous and they all shared the same concern as they sipped their teas and coffees.

"I wonder if this is one of those hash cafes," whispered Alice, who spoke what they were all thinking.

"In that case order me a large hash cake," bellowed Cathy, not caring who heard her.

"Shhhh, they'll hear us," said Alice, giggling.

"I don't think this is one of the smart shops," said Marji.

The women's faces were blank. Marji was a bit of a hippy by appearance, so they were all in awe of what she 'knew.'

"Sorry Marji, what's a smart shop?" asked Mary quietly.

"That's where you get joints, hash cakes etc., not all cafes sell it," said Marji.

"Oh, I see," said a bewildered Mary. Mary had never taken drugs in her life, wasn't even a big drinker, still, she was in Amsterdam, wasn't she required by law or something to try it? She hadn't a clue. They were all surprised by Alice, still giggling when she said, "I'd like to try it!" The women's eyes all lit up, they were all thinking it, but none of them had the guts to say it, for fear of being judged.

"To hell with it me too," said Cathy, none of the women particularly surprised.

"Well you're in the wrong place I'm afraid ladies," said Marji.

"I'd be afraid to try it," said a responsible Mary and all the women but Brigid nodded.

"Well I wouldn't!" exclaimed Brigid and the women looked at each other in shock.

"What? I'm eighty-three not dead!" she answered their faces.

"Look if you really wanna do it, we can go there," said Marji.

"You mean where the windows are? Stephen told me about them," Alice smiled like a cunning cat, very pleased with herself.

"No," Marji laughed, you don't have to go to the Red Light District to get some."

"Oh I don't know," said Mary, now a bit giddy.

"Suit yourselves," said Marji and the subject was quickly changed. The women decided they'd had enough excitement for one day and set off back to the hotel, all but Marji, who wanted to take some photos of the square and assuring them that she was a big girl, they left her to it.

***

The women decided to go for dinner that evening in the hotel and all congregated in Mary's room to get ready. It was like the scene of a teenage slumber party, bottles of hairspray, make up, hair straighteners, mostly Cathy's equipment. There was still no sign of Marji, but Mary had gotten a text from her to say that she had gotten delayed.

"Fair play to Marji, I wouldn't have the gall to explore a strange city on my own," said Alice as she brushed her hair in the long mirror.

"I know hope she's ok," said Mary, suddenly feeling concerned about her.

"It's a shame Rosa couldn't make the trip, what happened to her again?" Alice asked. "I told you, said Mary, she couldn't get a babysitter for the whole weekend." Mary hated telling lies, she was never good at it, but this time she made an exception, as she had to respect Rosa's wishes.

"She should get that lazy arse of a husband of hers to do it, it's his child too," said Cathy.

Mary tried to ignore Cathy. It had been an uncomfortable chat with Rosa. Rosa trying to convince Mary and herself, that she had been neglecting her home life of late and that she needed to spend more time with her family. It was a lie. Mary knew it and Rosa knew that she knew it, but Mary didn't want to pry, even though she felt like challenging Rosa about her situation. A situation that unknown to Mary, was rapidly worsening. The mother in her wanted to take Rosa in her arms, but the friend in her simply wished her well. Mary was afraid that even one look would give way to the truth, so she set about ironing her top that she was wearing to dinner. They weren't paying attention to Cathy, who was fiddling with something in the corner, then were met with a loud pop!

"Woo hoo let's get this party started," whooped Cathy as she raised a bottle of champagne above her head.

"Ooh is that real champagne Cathy?" asked an eager Alice.

"Honey I don't do Cava," winked Cathy as they searched for some glasses.

"I suppose it would be rude not to," smiled Brigid and Mary agreed.

They were all sipping their expensive champagne when they were interrupted by a banging on the door. They all looked at each other, wondering who it could be. Mary put down her glass and went to the door and when she opened it there was a flushed looking Marji standing there.

"Marji!, we were about to send out a search party for you!" said Mary, relieved she'd found her way back.

"I had to leg it up the stairs, lift was taking too long," Marji said, breathless.

"My dear girl, why are you in such a rush?" asked Brigid.

"Because I was smuggling in this!" she said, holding out a bag of marijuana.

The women stared at the bag with saucer like eyes.

"Oh! My! God!" screamed Alice.

"Is that what I think it is?" asked Mary.

"Sure is!" beamed Marji, "I know it's legal but wasn't sure of the hotel's policy so had to run up with it, nearly shit meself!"

"Well now it's a party!!" shouted Cathy, raising her glass.

Even Mary was excited. Still they all turned expectantly in the direction of Brigid, waiting for her reaction, like bold little school girls.

"Well bring it in for heaven's sake," said Brigid and it was met with whoops and cheers.

They sat round the room in a circle, all giggling excitedly and looking at each other for reassurance. Marji produced the bag she'd bought earlier that day and Alice folded out the Rizla papers, a bit too neatly. Cathy had 'undone' about ten cigarettes which were laid out on the floor. Then they all turned at looked at Marji.

"What? Why are you all looking at *me?*"

"Well...We just thought..." said Alice with a mousy voice... "that you would..."

"God ladies what do you all think I am a pusher?!"

The women laughed, for all Marji's worldly bravado, they unanimously assumed in their minds that she knew how to role a joint.

"Listen girls," Marji said, with a 'hate to disappoint you' look, "it was my idea to buy this that doesn't mean I know how to make it!"

The women eyed the bag of what now looked like a foreign object, if not illegal object back home and perplexed their minds as to what the hell they were going to do next. Then Alice piped up.

"We could make hash cakes!!"

Mary giggled a snort, "Alice I doubt if any of our suitcases carry a travel hash cake baking kit,"

The women erupted into laughter at Alice's ditsy remark. Then they all sat mouth open as Brigid got up from her seat.

"For Christ's sake girls, don't tell me that out of the lot of us I'm the only one who knows how to roll a joint."

On went Brigid, back in teacher mode, with her lesson in joint making. Mary laughed to herself as she pictured it. Brigid, back in her teaching days; looking pristine in her power suit and articulate accent, holding one of those long teaching canes from years back. 'Now class, today our lesson is rolling the perfect joint. Now there will be points deducted for unsealed ends and too much tobacco, and for heaven's sake Mr. Parker, try to remember the filter this time.'

Mary was brought back from her daydream by cheers and whoops from the women as Brigid licked and sealed the first joint they would share. Cathy took the first puff, she was ok as she used to smoke, then Marji, then Mary, back to Brigid and then Alice took the biggest drag from it and nearly puked.

"Oh my God Alice your face is green," said Marji, who couldn't help her giggles. Especially as she watched eighty-three year old Brigid puffing away.

"What? said Brigid, I wasn't always a strait-laced history teacher you know." The women went on to enjoy their guilty pleasure, as the room filled up with smoke. They all loosened up pretty fast.

"Oh God," said Cathy, "I haven't smoked a joint since

high school!"

"Me neither, well I never did actually, this is my first how cool am I hee hee hee?" said Alice.

"Ah an occasional one is ok," said Marji, "calms the nerves,"

Mary was surprised, "sure what would you have the nervous about Marji?"

"Oh lots of things," Marji said, her thoughts drifting.

"God I'd only kill for your confidence Marj, the most exciting thing I've done this year is mix the colours with the whites in the wash!" said Mary.

The women broke into hysterics and regaled stories about their boring day to day lives.

"I swear," said Cathy, "Thomas came in one night pissed a fart, could hardly stand. I had to undress him and put him into bed and what does he say to me? Thanks Silvia!"

The women stopped laughing for a minute and echoed a chorus "Silvia?"

"Yeah Silvia, that's his mother's name aha ha ha ha ha ha ha..."

"Oh things were a lot different in my day let me tell you," Brigid's voice sang out and the women surrounded her like a pack of wolves, waiting to hear more from Brigid's wild days, "you only did the nasty when you were married, not like now, I wish I'd known a few things about Mr Mannion before I married him let me tell you!"

"Why, did he have a small willy?"

"Alice!!"

"Sorry Mary, it just came out."

"Yeah that's what he said!" piped Cathy and they all fell around the room in laughter.

Brigid seemed unfazed and went on, "do you know, when Mr Mannion and I went to London for our honeymoon, his mother sent us off with a present,"

"That's nice," thought Mary aloud.

"Oh no, this woman took it hard that I was stealing her only boy away from her and she made it all too clear with her 'present.' She gave us two matching pairs of flannelette pyjamas with strict instructions that they were to be worn backwards!"

"Well that's the best contraceptive I've ever heard of!" said Alice, taking another drag from the fourth rolled joint of the night.

"Well Frank is the only man I've ever been with," said Mary, starting to loosen up, "don't think I'd know what to do in this day and age," she giggled.

"Belieeeeve me," said Cathy, "you're not missing much, it never changes for men, get in, get out, job done, whereas women..."

"I have a good sex life," said a giddy Alice, "Stephen is great!" she laughed, her face turning red, but Cathy, ever the cynic, couldn't accept this, "honey, if he ain't hitting the G spot, then it ain't worth it!" and the women laughed uncontrollably. Then Mary noticed that not all the women were sharing funny stories.

"Marji you're very quiet over there, don't you have any stories to share with us?!

"Oh yeah," said Alice, "I bet you have a sailor or two up your sleeve hee hee hee."

"Yeah come on tell us!!" shouted Cathy, clearly succumbing to the puff of hemp.

"There's nothing to tell really," said a suddenly shy Marji.

"Oh come on I bet you have wild Sex and the City stories to tell us," all the women itched for the gory details.

"Really there's nothing."

Even Brigid couldn't hide her curiosity, "Marji,

there's no man you've ever had that sticks out?"

"I bet they all stuck out!"

"Shut up Alice!" said Cathy.

"No hate to disappoint you but there's no one,"

"No one that made a lasting impression?" Mary asked.

"No, I mean there's no man, never has been."

Marjorie started to shift in her seat.

"You...you mean you're a virgin?" asked a puzzled Alice. But Mary could sense Marji's response before she said it.

"I'm gay ok?!!"

"Ha ha ha, very funny Marji, what do you think we are stupid??" Cathy said.

But Marji's face said it all and Mary thought she saw a faint tear fill up in her eye and quickly shot Alice a look so that she knew to keep quiet. Marji jumped up and headed for the loo. The sudden atmosphere in the room hit a lull. All the women just sat in shock, not knowing what to say. Then Mary got up, "I'll go and see if she's ok."

Mary knocked on the door and could hear Marji crying behind it.

"Marji, it's Mary can I come in?"

"I'm sorry Mary, I shouldn't have said what I did,"

"Don't be silly hun, we're glad you told us, aren't we girls?"

"Yeah, yes, yes of course we are," the women shouted across the room in unison.

"Come on out Marji," Mary pleaded, let's all have a drink and a good chat."

Marji opened the door, mascara drooping down from her eyes.

"Now wipe those panda eyes and come and have a drink."

Marji answered like a little girl, "ok."

The women all grabbed a drink from the mini bar and sat down on the floor propped up against the beds for support, waiting for Marji to sit down and compose herself. None of them really knew what to say, they had become so close to each other yet this revelation threw them, Alice of course was the first one to open her mouth.

"So does this mean you're a lesbian?"

"Alice for Christ's sake!" said Brigid.

"Well I'm just asking, I've never known a live one, well there was this one girl in school that always had facial hair and we thought she wanted to be a boy because she was always into sports and that..." Alice trailed off naively oblivious to the glares she was getting from the rest of the group.

"Alice!!"

"It's ok Mary," said Marji. "Suppose I had to tell you all sooner or later, I just hope it doesn't change our friendship?"

The women again spoke in unison, "not at all Marj, jeez now why would it?"

"Thanks girls."

"If you want to date women, hell if you want to date a horse we're all behind you and we're all still your friends, right ladies?" said Brigid.

"Right!" the women resounded.

"Thank you Brigid," said a now smiling Marji.

"As long as you don't slip the hand on us while we sleep," laughed Cathy.

All the women laughed, even Marji and the joke broke the tension.

"So how long have you known?" asked Mary.

"I guess I've always known, but never did anything about it, or told anyone. Well there is one other person, I met her online about six months ago. But look at me, I'm in my fifties, it's hard enough dating at this age, let alone trying to find a gay partner, I just don't think it's worth the hassle."

"Don't be silly," said Mary, "you have plenty of time to be happy, plus, you deserve to be."

"Oh I don't know, sometimes I wish I didn't feel this way, that I'd be better off married to a man and have kids, like you Mary,"

"Like me?"

"Yeah, I envy your set up of marriage and kids, sometimes I wish it was that simple for me,"

"Nothing's ever simple Marji, especially, my set up."

"Why, what do you mean?"

Mary hesitated, was this the time, or the place? What if the other women thought little of her for keeping up the pretence that she was still with Frank.

"Well, the thing is, Frank and I have been separated for nearly a year now, I just wear the wedding ring to avoid questions, and I suppose I was ashamed to admit it."

"Well I think you're very brave, to admit it," said Brigid, "marriage isn't easy, and just look what you've accomplished this year alone, we wouldn't all be sitting here, smoking joints like teenagers, swapping life changing stories, you've done us proud Mary."

Mary instantly felt at ease, like a weight had been lifted from her shoulders. The pretence of living with the lie she feared would cost her her new friendships—only strengthened them, and she felt a strong sense of pride for putting the group together.

Suddenly a voice shot out from the back of the room, "my husband's having an affair!"

Everyone turned to look at Cathy, ex-model, trophy wife Cathy, who's revelation had shook them to their very core, almost as bad as when Tom and Nicole split up. Cathy didn't wait for a response from any of the women, "about six months ago I noticed he'd been working late, ...said that more and more people wanted to view properties in the evening, as they had work commitments, all that crap. I just accepted it. But then some things just didn't add up, our sex life for one, or lack thereof...we always had a great sex life and I always thought that Tom should be the one to be glad of his younger wife. Now it's me questioning myself, and my marriage, wondering why and if I'm not good enough for him anymore." Cathy trailed off into a hysterical cry with Mary running across to her to lend a shoulder.

"There there, you're probably just being paranoid, us women have a knack for that, I'll bet he's at home right now wondering all sorts about what you're getting up to, not the other way around!"

"It's just that, I feel like I deserve it you know, Tom wasn't exactly single when we got together," said a feeble Cathy as she blew into a tissue.

"Take no heed of that my dear, announced Brigid, "karma is overrated, sure when myself and Mr Mannion got together, according to my parents, he wasn't exactly from the right side of town if you know what I mean. He came from the flats and we were from Haddington Road. We weren't rich or anything, but those days if you had any sort of steady income you were considered well to do. My father ran a shop and my mother, well she sat in the shop all day long, gossiping about customers and passers-by. I don't think she did a day's work in her life after she met my father."

The women were once again enthralled in Brigid's seemingly quiet life, even Cathy had stopped blowing her nose and her red swollen eyes were transfixed upon Brigid speaking.

"So what happened, did your mother forbid you to see

him like in that film?" asked an excited Alice.

"Well it was nothing like the films my dear, but he did sweep me off my feet,"

"Ooh like Clark Gable in Gone with the Wind?"

"Well, no, not exactly," Brigid giggled, "he was a road sweeper! And one day as my friends and I sat outside Daddy's shop he approached me, broom in hand and asked me out on a date. Well if you'd call a walk to Sandymount Strand for an ice cream a date—there was an ice cream shop there once. My friends made fun of him of course, a road sweeper and Thomas Rochford's daughter, it seemed farcical. But he made me laugh and kept on making me laugh until the day he died."

There was silence in the room and there wasn't just Cathy with tears in her eyes.

"When did he die Brigid?" asked Mary.

"Oh, seven years it would be now, the big 'C' took him in the end."

"I'm so sorry," chorused the girls.

"Oh don't be sorry for me ladies, I'll see my love again. You know the last thing he said to me before he died? 'Well Bridy' that's what he used to call me, much to my father's dismay, 'I used to sweep the streets for hours on end in the hope that I would find a penny, but when I swept outside your shop that day, I picked up a pound.' It was just like him to say something like that, something funny with a hidden compliment."

"You must miss him," said Alice.

"Yes I do love."

All the women were so engrossed in Brigid's story they said nothing for a while, each engrossed in their own thoughts. Mary thought of Frank and for the first in a long time, she missed him, their parting wasn't as cut clean as an affair or death, theirs was more complicated, but became less important as she listened to the hardship of her fellow 'coffee mourners' and what they had been through. She thought about being a little nicer to him the next time she saw him.

Alice of course broke the ice once again, "Aw I feel all left out, me and Stephen are fine."

"Don't look so disappointed," said Marji, back to her old self.

"No it's just that you all have fascinating stories and I feel so boring."

"Sometimes boring is nice," interjected Brigid, "do you love him?"

"Who Stephen? Oh yeah, actually I do have some news of sorts, we're trying for a baby!"

"Wow that's great," beamed Mary, this is your first isn't it?"

"Yeah, we're really excited, although we've been trying for a while now, hope nothing's wrong,"

"You'll be fine dear," encouraged Brigid.

"Ah I know, it's just that you spend your whole life trying not to get pregnant, then when you want to, it doesn't happen, God I hope I'm not pregnant now, the baby'd be born stoned!"

Another round of laughter and all the women were settled for bed finally, at 4am. It had been a long night.

***

Frank had had a good weekend and was feeling much better about himself. Maybe his symptoms were more of an emotional flu and his day with Helen and Josh had been his lemsip. He was back to work and ready to take on the world. Then he thought of Mary. What if she'd met someone in Amsterdam? He felt like a teenager, in pursuit once again of the best looking girl in town. The rational part of his brain told him that Mary could never just meet someone and 'click' it wasn't her style, nor Frank's, but paranoia took hold and before long it was all he could think about. Even the thought of Mary off travelling, with a bunch of women she hardly knew was unsettling, why? He thought. Am I not happy for her? Should I not be happy for her? Am I jealous? He laughed to himself at the ludicrous thought but stopped short when he considered it to be true.

The bar was busy, punters trying to postpone the dreaded Monday blues by topping up on their hangovers. Frank was pulling a pint, lost in thought, until he was snapped back to reality.

"Can I get a glass of ice with that? Sorry! Can I get...." a rude customer waved his hand at a bewildered Frank.

"Sorry mate? Oh oh yeah sure sorry," Frank answered, ignoring his tone and went to fetch the precious glass of ice. It didn't take long for Frank's thoughts to be put on the back burner, with the arrival of a local football team who'd just won a match. Here we go, said Frank to himself and once again he was ensconced in a revelry of clinking glasses and what would be several rounds of 'we are the champions.'

Chapter Six

Mary arrived back to the house after an eventful weekend. She had liked Amsterdam, although she didn't get to see much of it, due to the first night's revelations. Was she foolish to share her business with the girls? A knot twisted in her stomach. It wasn't like her to divulge such personal information, then again, she was carried away by one of the city's national past times. Oh my God she thought, I smoked a joint! What would her kids say? She wouldn't tell them she decided, they'd be shocked— Mary herself was shocked. Then again Mary had done a lot of things this year that would shock those who knew her. It was so out of character for her. But what is my character she pondered? I was once a wife and mother, who am I now? The thought made her shudder. Mary had lost her identity over the years, but then again did she ever really have one? The mother hen. First attending to her brothers and sisters, then to her husband and kids. She never resented it, never had the need to find herself, never had the time. That's all she had now though, time. Spatial gaps in her existence, to be filled with what? No one needed her anymore, the fact frightened her. Mary had come back to Dublin to a slap in the face of her reality, although she couldn't identify it, loneliness? Boredom? The incessant need to be needed? Wanted? It hit her like a tonne of bricks. No one would ever need her again.

She was pleasantly distracted by Greg's jeans that hung over a kitchen chair and rather than indulge in her feelings of hardship she did what she did best and started to load the washing machine.

***

"Now Brigid, tell me, how are you feeling today?" the

doctor asked.

"Oh I feel fine there's really no need to keep me here you know," Brigid was defiant that there was nothing wrong with her except for a few minor bruises.

"The thing is Mrs Mannion, your leg is not healing as well as I would like it to so I would prefer to keep you in for a few tests and observation,"

"Observation? I'm not an animal at the zoo remember?!"

"Yes of course not, I know, it's just that for a woman your age…"

Brigid interjected, "I'm in my eighties I'm not dead yet!"

"Oh Mum, please listen to Doctor Carroll," said Claire, knowing only too well how her mother would react to any implication that she couldn't cope.

Brigid softened to her worried daughter's words and this time gave respect to the man before her.

"Please go on Doctor Carroll."

"Thank you. It could be nothing, but I don't want to take the chance."

Brigid eyed up the doctor, searching for clues as to what he thought she had, but his gaze remained fixed to a reflection of concern and sympathy. Then she looked to Claire, who had an urgency in her eyes, praying that her independent mother would let Doctor Carroll do his job.

"Ok, if tests is what you want, tests we shall have."

Claire's shoulders shrank back down in a sigh of relief.

***

Marji woke up from a leisurely sleep, echoes of dreams still floating round her mind. She turned and looked at the clock, 12pm.

"Jesus! How did I sleep so late?" she said to herself aloud.

Jeepers jumped up onto her bed and meowed loudly, checking for signs of life from his owner.

"Morning Jeepers, or should I say, good afternoon," she said scratching her head— stretching out a yawn. It had been three days since the women were back from Amsterdam and Marji was feeling the effects of a fifty-year old's recovery.

"Oh when did I get so old Jeepers?" she said, dragging herself from her bed. She made her way to the kitchen to brew some much needed coffee and leaned against the counter, daydreaming, while she waited for her coffee to filter. Then she remembered her dream. She was at a party with hundreds of people, but didn't know a single soul, it was like they were faceless. She meandered through the crowds, not recognising where she was or who she was with as she bellowed excuse me, after excuse me. Suddenly she was compelled to look up and when she did that's when she saw him. Standing somehow above the crowd, drink in one hand, cigar in the other and with a luminous grin on his face. She hurried to get to him, but her legs wouldn't move. She looked again and he waved, blowing her a kiss, then he was gone.

"Oh Daddy," Marji cried aloud as she grabbed her face with her hands, "I remember now."

It didn't feel like a dream to Marji, more like a visitation from her beloved father. She smiled and felt a warmth come over her like a plush blanket. Dream or not Marji felt comforted.

"You always said you'd look after me Daddy," she said to the empty room and she smiled again, but her warm feeling soon dissipated with the arrival of a knot in her stomach. Her impending date with J gave way to feelings of panic.

"What was I thinking?!" she said to herself, "I can't go, I just can't." Then she spotted a picture of herself and her father on the fridge. It was the two of them on a boat trip to Ireland's Eye, on his last Father's Day. She calmed herself and smiled again. Somehow she got the feeling that her dream wasn't just a coincidence and that she had gotten the seal of approval from the most influential person she'd ever known.

"Ok Daddy, I'm doing this for you!" she said to the picture, kissing her fingers and planting them on her Dad's face. I can do this. I can do this, she kept repeating, like a mantra in her head.

***

Alice and Stephen arrived at the fertility clinic and were shown to the waiting room. They both sat in silence for a moment, then Stephen grabbed his wife's hand.

"You ok babe?" he asked tenderly.

"Yeah just a bit nervous," Alice smiled.

"It'll be ok," Stephen reassured his wife, kissing her hand still in his.

"Easy for you to say, you're not getting a turkey baster shoved up your fandora," Alice laughed.

Stephen laughed too at his wife's avoidance of the word 'vagina' and decided to lighten the mood.

"You think that's bad? Every time I'm near that room I get a hard on!" he whispered and it was too much for Alice to hold in and she let out a loud snort. The two of them sat there like giggling school kids on a trip to church, then a thought suddenly hit Alice.

"God hun, I never even thought of how hard that was for you, here I am worrying about myself and I'd forgotten all the awkward tests you had to go through!"

Alice was becoming stressed.

"Hey hey," Stephen put his arm around his wife, "it's ok, what's a few tests when we might have a little baby at the end of it?!"

"Might," said a sombre Alice.

"Look," said Stephen, "my sister has a rake of kids, if this doesn't work, we'll offer to babysit the youngest and then skip town with him!"

Alice laughed again, Stephen always made her laugh, even at times like this.

"Still though Ste, it could be a long shot, what will we do if it doesn't happen?"

"Then we'll cross that bridge when we come to it love."

Alice placed her head on Stephen's shoulder and not before long it was their turn.

***

Brigid sat in her hospital bed scanning the room. Sixteen beds in total lined the walls, with sixteen lost souls suffering different ailments. Brigid wouldn't allow herself to wonder what ailments they could be, as far as she was concerned she didn't belong in this waiting room for heaven, but Doctor Carroll insisted on her staying in. It never occurred to her that she might actually be sick, all she was concerned about was getting home. The beeping from various machines were starting to aggravate her and she was longing for a cup of strong tea, which she had sent Claire to get. Where on earth has she got to? Brigid was about to press the call button when she heard the clatter of a tea trolley come into the ward.

"Finally!" she said aloud.

"Are ye gasping Maam?" a kind faced lady wheeling the trolley asked her.

Brigid became embarrassed, she hadn't directed her

comment at anyone in particular and wasn't sure anyone had even heard her, but the lady was right, she was gasping. Although she couldn't hide her annoyance at how she was addressed and wasn't afraid to express her feelings on the subject.

"My dear girl I haven't been a teacher in over thirty years, my name is Brigid, now when you're ready I'll have a nice cup of 'strong' tea." Brigid overemphasised the word 'strong.'

The lady just smiled, she'd seen it all before; women in their twilight years, active, all their faculties, thinking there was no need for them to be with 'sick people.' Mostly, it came down to one thing, they were scared. Her twenty years in the job had taught her to be patient with these poor souls who didn't know what lay ahead, so she smiled at Brigid as she brought her over a cup of tea with the bag in.

"Now dear, sorry, Brigid, if it were any stronger they'd serve it in a bar."

Brigid felt ashamed of her behaviour for the first time in her life and sheepishly thanked the woman for her cuppa. She took a long sip of the brew and sank back in her bed, letting out a satisfied sigh.

"Nothing like it is there?" the tea lady winked. Brigid felt instantly at ease by this woman. Brigid reckoned she was in her mid-forties, a homely girl with dark cropped hair, thick north side Dublin accent, a true salt of the earth woman. She didn't seem fazed by Brigid's manner and Brigid once again felt abashed at her bossy demeanour, so offered this lovely woman a life line.

"Thank you my dear, I needed that," she said quietly.

"Me Ma always said you can cure any issue with a nice cup of scald!" the bubbly woman replied.

"Your mother's a very wise woman," said Brigid.

"Was I'm afraid, she passed away a year ago," the

woman said, still smiling.

"Oh I'm sorry," said Brigid.

"Why? You didn't kill her!" the woman laughed and Brigid laughed too. She went about serving tea to the other women in the ward and Brigid watched, cup in hand as she had something engaging to say to each and every one of the patients. Some seemed to know her well sadly—the ones she paid extra attention to, who had no 'get well soon' cards at their bedside. Brigid felt herself lucky at that point, to have such a loving family, even if the youngest had seemingly gotten herself lost. She was so busy watching this strong character doling out tea and sympathy that she almost missed Claire's arrival, flustered, with two paper cups in her hand.

"Oh Mum there you are!" Brigid quickly came back to herself.

"Where on earth were you? I'm sitting here like an idiot the last half an hour!" Brigid scolded, but quickly felt remorse when she saw the worry etched on her daughter's face.

"Sorry Mum I was ringing the others to let them know you were kept in and...."

"What?! Now what would you do that for? Your brothers and sisters have enough to be worrying about than me in here!"

"I know Mum but they should know, what if..."

But Brigid wouldn't let her daughter finish, whether Brigid realised it or not, it was the 'what if' that scared her more than she cared to admit. She was in the middle of a tirade when she suddenly noticed the tea lady at her bedside and realising how much attention she was attracting, stopped talking immediately.

"Hi, you must be Brigid's daughter, would you like some tea?"

"Um, yes, please," Claire answered wearily.

Brigid remained tight lipped, for some reason she wanted to have the appearance of composure around this woman.

As she topped up Brigid's cup she chatted to Claire, "trust me, it's better than that crap from the machine." Claire laughed and Brigid felt a stab of guilt. The woman continued on, sensing the tension, but tackling it discreetly.

"So have you got brothers and sisters?"

"Em, yes, two brothers and two sisters."

"Wow big family, same as meself, no telly in our house growing up," she winked again. Brigid softened as the conversation went on, the woman asked what Claire did, if she had hit much traffic on the way in, all avoiding pieces about Brigid, until Brigid finally spoke.

"Claire is my baby," Brigid smiled affectionately at Claire and Claire smiled back, a slight tear forming in her eye.

The woman knew that it was her time to leave them to it and started to load up her trolley.

"Well I'm off, I'll be back again later, I'm Janice by the way, so if there's anything you need just give me a shout!" she smiled.

"Thank you," said Brigid.

"Yes thank you so much and you were right about the tea," Claire beamed and without looking she grabbed her Mum's hand.

"Right ye be," said Janice, "I better go and put the kettle on again if the rest of your children are coming up Brigid," Janice winked once again to Brigid and Brigid smiled as Janice left the two, tenderly gripping hands.

***

Alice lay on the bed, feet up in stirrups, her modesty

covered by a gown and sheets as she clenched every muscle in her body like she was preparing for her annual 'lady garden' check-up as she put it. Stephen could see the tense look in her face as he grabbed her hand and rubbed her forehead.

"You ok?" he asked.

"Yeah, just a bit ugh you know?"

"Yeah."

Stephen smiled at Alice as the doctor went about preparing her equipment for the procedure. She had seen many anxious couples in the same situation, but not always with the same results.

"Now Alice," she began, "if you could just relax as best you can, we can start to insert the eggs."

"Eggs?" Alice asked, alarmed.

"Yes, for our best chance at a positive result we implant multiple eggs,"

"So, I could have like, six babies?" Alice hadn't considered the chance of multiple births.

The doctor giggled slightly, "well six would be a long shot, but yes it has been known to happen."

"Shit!" Alice shrieked, then quickly remembered herself, "oh sorry doctor," she said, embarrassed by her outburst.

The doctor giggled again, "that's quite alright, I'm used to it."

Alice looked at Stephen for reassurance and mouthed "six" to him. Stephen as always took it in his stride.

"Listen love, if it is six then we'll just start the new Von Trapp Family and enter the Eurovision," Stephen joked. Alice was less amused and started to panic a little. "Look if you want to back out of this hon we can, just say the word, the doc can just put her turkey baster away and we'll forget the whole thing," Stephen said.

"No no no I'm just, I don't know, it's just....it's just so

real now ye know?" Alice replied.

"I know." said Stephen.

"Feck it let's do it doctor!" Alice was more confident now, excited even, she smiled at the doctor, then at her husband, who never let go of her hand. As the doctor positioned herself Stephen mouthed to his wife, "I love you" to which Alice mouthed back, "I love you too."

***

Rosa busied herself with dinner, not hearing Peter come home.

"What's for dinner?" he asked grumpily.

"Uh...spaghetti with red sauce," Rosa answered, startled.

"It is Bolognese, why can't you learn more English?" Peter barked.

Rosa ignored the sly comment and returned to the stove, her eye checking on Filip as he played with his trucks on the floor.

"Is there no beer?" Peter asked, one hand on the open fridge door.

"Um yes Peter, I have bought beer today," with the last of my pennies thought Rosa, as she walked over to the fridge, distractedly leaving the handle of the frying pan facing outward.

Filip, sensing a brewing argument grabbed his trucks and as he made his quick exit, he caught the pan handle in his sleeve, sending the dinner crashing to the floor, the sauce making it look like the scene of a murder. Filip stood there in shock, the hot sauce thankfully missing him and before Rosa could react, Peter was straight across the room, grabbing his son.

"Look what you've done you stupid boy!!!" Peter screamed at a petrified Filip, shaking him roughly.

"It was accident, Peter please!" Rosa begged, fearful for what his next move might be. She tried to remove Filip from Peter's grasp but Peter pushed her away, sending her falling to the floor.

Peter continued to shout at his son, who was now crying and shaking—Rosa stared in disbelief as she saw Peter raise his hand and feeling like she was running in slow motion, ran to her son's aid. The closest thing to her was the frying pan. She grabbed it and with full force slammed it down on Peter's head. Peter crashed to the floor, covered in what was left of the sauce with a look of shock on his face. Rosa grabbed her son and held him tightly.

"Don't you ever, ever touch my son again!!!!" she screamed, hot tears running down her face. She felt sick with adrenalin, an unfamiliar feeling of rage swept over her, as she watched her now pitiful husband sitting on the floor. Peter still couldn't speak, stunned at what had just happened. Rosa didn't even wait to see if he was hurt, she didn't care. Whatever Peter could throw at her up until now she could handle, but not when it came to her son, it was the last straw and even Peter knew it. She ran upstairs, Filip still in her arms and rocked him gently as they both cried in each other's arms.

Peter went out that night and stayed out until the next morning. Rosa didn't want to know where he'd been, nor did she care.

***

It had been a while since Frank had seen Mary. He was still shocked that she had flitted off to Amsterdam with a group of strangers. It wasn't like Mary, the furthest she had ever gone was to Wexford for the weekend. Frank just couldn't get over the changes in his wife, it unnerved him, she was slipping further and further away from him and this trip was the final straw. Whether he wanted to admit it to himself or not, he was jealous. In his short walk to the house his mood had changed. He used to look forward to seeing Mary, but her latest antics left him feeling bitter, excluded. He wasn't intending on starting an argument with her, but that's just what happened.

"So, you're back from your trip then?" he said, with a slight tone.

"Yes I got back last week," Mary said, oblivious to Frank's hostility.

"Have fun?" he said coldly.

"Oh yes, such a great time," said Mary, grinning from ear to ear at the memories of her escapade with her new friends.

"And your 'friends' I suppose they had fun too?" Frank said sarcastically, no longer able to hide his disdain.

"Frank, is something wrong?" Mary asked.

"You tell me," he shot back.

"Look Frank I don't know what's with you but I really don't have time for..."

"Oh of course, your new life, no place for Frank,"

"What? What on earth are you talking about?"

"You! Flitting off to a strange country with strange people!"

"Hold on a minute, I didn't just 'flit' off and these people are not strangers they're..."

"What, your friends?"

"Yes, my FRIENDS!"

"Please..." Frank spat.

"I should've known you'd react like this Frank, I go away for a few days and you can't handle it."

"What do you mean?"

"You're JEALOUS Frank."

"I am NOT jealous, what have I got to be jealous about?"

"You always do this, I do something that doesn't involve you and you turn into a child who wasn't invited to a party...I can't believe I'm even having this conversation with you..."

"What because we're not together anymore? We're still married, or have you forgotten that?"

"Yes, I know we're still married Frank, but it doesn't give you the right to have a go at me just because I'm getting on with my life!"

"You call fecking off to Amsterdam getting on with your life?"

"Yes I do, I've finally made some decent friends and here you are trying to belittle it like you always do!"

"What's that supposed to mean?"

"You were always jealous when I went out by myself,"

"But you never went out by yourself, maybe if you had we wouldn't be in this mess!"

"What do you mean by that?"

"You never had a social life and begrudged mine,"

"That's ridiculous I never begrudged you having a social life, what I didn't like was when you'd forget to come home!"

"Sure what did I have to come to? Being treated like one of the kids?"

"What's that supposed to mean?"

"It's true Mary, you only had time for the kids and then started to treat me like one of them."

"That's a lie."

"No! It's not, I wanted a wife not another mother!"

"And you think I wanted a husband who needed to be mothered?"

"I didn't need to be mothered! I'm the man of the house!"

"Well you never acted like it Frank, one of us had to be the strong one."

"There's being strong Mary and there's being cold."

"I had to be that way,"

"Why? Why did you have to be that way?"

"Because my family needed me!"

"At the expense of your marriage?"

"Don't talk to me about marriage Frank, our first few years of marriage were hardly marital bliss, every chance you got you were in the pub!"

"I worked hard I deserved my time in the pub, that's what you did back then!"

"Oh don't give me that excuse Frank,"

"Maybe if you had let your hair down more and joined me the odd time,"

"I couldn't."

"Why not?"

"Because we had a family to look after, who needed food, clothes, I didn't have the luxury of running off to get drunk when I felt like it, bloody drink I hate it."

"Oh here we go..."

"I grew up with an alcoholic father Frank, do you think that was easy for me?"

"I don't know Mary, you never talked about it,"

"I didn't need to talk about it,"

"There you go, closing up again, as soon as we hit on a touchy subject about you, you close up, Jesus Mary can't you ever let your guard down?"

"I had to stay strong I had no choice,"

"No Mary, you had a choice and it wasn't me,"

"See, we're back to you again, I couldn't afford to give into my emotions when I had to look after you."

"I never wanted you to look after me!"

"But you still let me Frank, you fell into the pattern of being taken care of !"

"I can take care of myself."

"Oh really?"

"Well I've been doing a good job so far haven't I?"

"Oh you think so? You can't leave it a week without dropping in!"

"Well maybe I shouldn't drop in anymore!"

"Maybe you shouldn't!"

Frank turned on his heel and walked out, slamming the door behind him. Mary slumped down on the kitchen chair, her head dropping to her hands, tears quickly forming in her eyes. She could feel the temper rising in her like venom. She grabbed the nearest thing to her, a cup and smashed it off the ground. It broke into a hundred pieces. Mary wanted to curl up into a ball and sob her heart out, but she didn't. Instead she got up, went to fetch a dustpan and brush, cleared away the remains of the broken cup and threw them into the bin. She thanked God that Gregg wasn't home to witness the fight. She was so angry at Frank. Was he right? Was she that unfeeling? She needed to get out of the house, fast!

***

The women settled down in the small room that had become their haven for the past six months. Mary was still in awe of the fact that they still met, like clockwork, every Wednesday morning, for tea and biscuits.

"I'm telling you he's definitely having an affair, why else would he get so grumpy at the thought of going on holiday with me?" Cathy spewed.

"You don't know that for sure Cath," offered Alice.

"Oh do I not? He didn't come home until eleven the other night and he never stays out that late mid-week, well at least he never used to."

"Maybe things aren't so good at work, you know what men are like, they never talk about what's going on," said Mary, still reeling after her words with Frank. She thought about telling the girls, but in truth, she was still trying to get her head around it herself.

"Every time I ask him about work he just says fine, everything's fine, well I'm not fine!"

Cathy started to cry again, something she'd been doing a lot of lately. Rosa sat there quietly, not being able to comprehend why Cathy's marriage was so unhappy when she compared it with her own.

"I'm so sorry girls, we're supposed to be having a laugh and here I am blubbering about my stupid husband, sorry Mary."

"God hun don't apologise to me, sure that's what we're here for,"

"I know, but I just feel like my marriage is falling apart and I don't want to end up alone."

The girls didn't know where to look.

"Oh God I'm sorry Mary, I didn't mean..."

"I know you didn't don't worry about it."

"God here I am moaning about being alone and look at how well you're coping,"

Mary allowed herself an inward laugh; if they only knew how she felt inside.

"Yes I'm coping, just about,"

"Yeah it must be tough for you Mar, do you ever miss your husband?"

"I do yes, but it's just, it's very complicated, I doubt if you young girls would understand,"

Mary didn't mean to sound sarcastic, but she felt that the problems in her marriage were not as clean cut as an affair and also a bit boring.

"I dunno Mary, try us!" beamed Cathy.

"There's nothing to tell really,"

"Oh go on," said Alice, "we're always moaning to you about our other halves, it's about time we returned the favour."

"Well I suppose, it's just that, there's really nothing to tell. Frank has always been the life and soul of the party you know? Talk to anyone, always has something to say and I, well, I've always been the quiet one in the relationship,"

Mary paused, hoping that the girls would be happy enough with what they already got, but they were poised and ready for the next instalment of her story.

"Well then, I suppose at some point we started to drift apart, we no longer went out together and the kids were all looked after, so there was nothing really left for me to do. Frank started drinking then and I just couldn't face the nights alone wondering if he'd come home, so I thought it was best to separate."

"And he didn't like cheat on you or hit you or anything?"

"Alice!!" Marji shouted scoldingly.

"Sorry Mary."

Mary laughed, "it's ok Alice, no he never cheated or hit me, nothing like that, after a while he just seemed to prefer the company of his friends instead of me."

Mary couldn't believe what she'd just said. She'd always thought it, but never said it to anyone out loud. She also felt a knot in her stomach at the very thought of the rejection she felt concerning Frank. And she wouldn't dare admit it but she also felt a little jealous.

"It must be hard for him too," said Marji, always straight and to the point.

"Yes I suppose it is."

Mary had never really thought about it, she simply thought that she had made the decision the two of them were afraid to make.

The group was smaller today, Brigid had been missing quite a few mornings these past weeks and Mary wondered if her age was catching up with her, but it seemed unlikely as Brigid had an incredible taste for life. She wasn't the only one thinking about Brigid right then.

"Where's Brigid been Mary, have you heard from her?" asked Alice, reading her thoughts.

"I don't know, she called me last week to say that her arthritis had been acting up and her daughter was away so she couldn't drive her here,"

"Jeez, I could have picked her up on my way," said Marji.

"I know I said that to her, but you know Brigid, she's so proud, she even hates relying on her daughter,"

"She really is independent isn't she?" beamed Alice, "I hope I'm like her when I'm in my eighties,"

"Maybe we should visit her," suggested Cathy, "might cheer her up?"

Mary wasn't sure, she loved Brigid dearly, but knew that she liked her privacy.

"I don't know Cath, I wouldn't want to land on her like that,"

"Not at all, I bet she'd love it,"

"Maybe I'll ring her first," reasoned Mary.

The women settled into each of their stories from the past week, Marji was still in contact with her friend online and Cathy was still suspicious of her husband, "he bought me flowers last week, is that guilty or what? I swear I'm going to follow him one of these nights, see what he's up to."

"Yeah we should all go with you Cathy, some moral support," said an over excited Alice.

"You'd really do that for me?"

"Of course we go," said Rosa, as long as I be back by

early, Peter likes me to be home to make dinner."

The women eyeballed each other, this wasn't the first time Rosa had suggested that Peter was more than a bit controlling. Then they were relieved to be interrupted by Mary's phone ringing.

"Hello?"

"Hi Mary? This is Claire, Brigid's daughter,"

"Oh hi Claire, we were just talking about your Mum, how's her arthritis? Giving her hassle I hear?"

There were shouts from across the room, "tell her we said hi" "we miss you Brigid!"

"Sorry, sorry girls, can you pipe down a sec, I'm sorry Claire go on?"

The women saw the worried look on Mary's face and quickly quietened down, then they heard the words they were all dreading.

"Which hospital?"

***

The women all piled into Cathy and Alice's cars laden down with get well soon presents for Brigid. When they saw her in her bed she looked like her usual self. Pristinely presented in her nightie and matching dressing gown, hair styled and full make up on.

"Well, will you look at what the cat dragged in, I told Claire not to bother anyone about me, it was just a silly fall," Brigid said, trying to stifle a laugh.

The women felt like bold school girls but were glad to see their friend looking well.

"You gave us a scare there Brigid," started Mary.

"Yes we worry so much for you," added Rosa.

"Poppycock I'm fine. I tell you, if someone my age has a fall people act like you're about to pop your clogs! It is good to see you all though,"

Brigid couldn't help but smile. She hated a fuss but was glad to see her friends and hated to admit it.

"Well seeing as how you couldn't be bothered to drag your lazy bum out of hospital, we thought we'd bring the coffee morning to you!" Cathy said teasingly.

"That is sweet Cathy thank you, thank you all very much."

Brigid seemed sad to Mary, scared maybe. But she hid it well. Here she was the patient yet she was the one trying to put everyone else at ease. She supposed that Brigid had had a fright with her fall but was too proud to say so.

The women were gathered around Brigid's bed, sipping Lucozade and munching on Digestive biscuits and swapping their stories of the week. They became completely unawares with their excitement and soon they sounded like they were at a party. They were interrupted by a doctor who appeared at the foot of Brigid's bed. He seemed perplexed at first as to where they'd all come from so suddenly.

"Excuse me Mrs Mannion, I'm afraid I'll have to ask your daughters to leave, it's past visiting hours and we would like to get that leg looked at today."

The women howled with laughter at the thoughts of being Brigid's daughters.

"I beg your pardon, Doctor, these women are not my daughters!"

The women laughed even harder at Brigid's disdain with being labelled a 'baby machine.'

Brigid addressed the doctor again, but this time omitted his esteemed title, "Excuse me, Mr Gaffney, but my 'friends' were just leaving, and my leg has been here all morning for you to 'look at.'"

The women sniggered, especially when the doctor seemed to get all flustered at Brigid's announcement. He seemed to shift his approach somewhat and his face changed from stern to gentle. Quite uncommon for a doctor these days Mary thought. She also noticed how attractive he was. He had grey hair that had a prominent silver streak running up the centre and it quite suited him. She reckoned mid to late fifties. She quickly stopped herself for noticing this man or any man at all as she was a married woman, if at least still by name.

"Well Mrs Mannion, I will make you my priority if your friends would kindly let me," then he smiled and all the women blushed at the Tommy Lee Jones lookalike doctor.

They all waved Brigid goodbye and were no sooner out the door when they all started talking about the doctor.

"Did you see the way he just smiled and none of us knew what to say?!" said Cathy.

"Oh I know Cathy," said Alice, "I mean it wasn't just me, he was gorgeous wasn't he? Never thought I'd fancy a man of his age, but he just seemed to have that film star kind of charm about him, like...like...Tommy Lee Jones or something."

Alice was like a giddy schoolgirl, then again, that was nothing new.

Mary thought the same, but berated herself for even looking at another man, still, she couldn't stop thinking about Dr Gorgeous, her thoughts drifted.

"Mary! Are you with us?" shouted Cathy.

Mary got flustered, "er...yeah what were we talking about?"

"The doctor!" Marji reminded.

"Oh my God you fancy him don't you!"

"Alice please I'm a married woman and sixty-five years of age, I don't go around fancying doctors!"

"But your face is all red, oh you do you do!"

"Yeah Mary, and while we're on the subject, you're separated, so you could really go for it and I think you should, there was no wedding band on his finger," said Marji.

"Oh Marji, you don't miss a thing do you," said Alice.

"He is, um...dishy," said Rosa, with a big smile.

***

Mary got home that day and laughed to herself about what the girls were saying about the doctor. Mary hadn't even looked at another man since before she met Frank at seventeen. She did notice this man though, he was very attractive and nothing like her husband. She felt guilty then but didn't know why. How could she even contemplate a date with a new man at her age? True she was separated, but what would people say? Dating a fancy man so late in life! She just shrugged her shoulders and laughed out loud, thinking of how silly the mere thought of it was. Mary had had enough of men at this stage in her life.

***

Cathy arrived home from the hospital with a heavy heart. The house was empty as what seemed to be the norm lately and she decided to pour herself a glass of wine. She sat at the table and kept the bottle nearby. She looked up at the clock, 1pm. Lunchtime. She told herself that a lot of ladies of leisure had a drink at lunchtime, but she knew that she would be seeing the end of the bottle very soon. She glanced around the room and then noticed it, a note stuck on the fridge. It was from Thomas and read, *'came home for a bite, will be working late, don't wait up, T x.'* That was it, Cathy was fuming!! She could feel the anger rise in her like molten lava, bubbling through every limb. She grabbed the note and scrunched it into a little ball and got the glass and smashed it into the sink while she let out a bellow. 'Prrrrrrrick!!' She stood there for a moment and thought about calling him, but then she strangely calmed for a moment and cleaned up the broken glass. Even in her fragile state Cathy couldn't stand a mess. She sat back down at the table and with a fresh glass, polished off the rest of the wine. She quickly started to feel the numbing effects of the alcohol and drifted off for a moment in a drunken slumber. She was awoken by the phone some minutes later and not knowing where she was for a moment, lay there with the excruciating sound of the ringtone belting in her head. The machine picked up, it was Jade, 'Hi it's me, I'm staying in Shauna's tonight so I'll see you in the morning, bye!' Cathy peeled herself up off the sofa and felt that rage seep into her again. No wonder Jade never came home, it wasn't exactly a loving family environment she thought. She looked at herself in the mirror, great big panda eyes stared back at her as she tried to wipe away the smudged mascara from her cheeks. And then, coupled with a slight inebriation, decided to ring Thomas.

She tried his mobile first, but it went straight to voicemail, which made her even more angry. So she rang his office and tried to sound sober.

"Thomas Ryan please."

"May I ask who's calling?" the polite, professional voice answered, which irritated Cathy.

"It's his wife!" Cathy didn't mean to be so rude, but at that moment she didn't care.

"One moment please."

Cathy twisted the phone cord around her fingers as she imagined it was her husband's neck and waited on the line.

"I'm sorry but Mr. Ryan has left for the day," came the reply in what Cathy felt like a smug tone.

"What?! What do you mean he's gone for the day?! Is he showing a house?"

"Um, no, he said that he had a personal appointment to attend to."

"A personal appointment?!!"

The receptionist had no idea what to say.

"Would you like to leave a message?"

"Yes I'd like to leave a message! Tell him his wife said that he can have that little tramp he's sleeping with because this marriage is over!!"

The poor receptionist, who was only doing her job, tried to offer Cathy something of a consolation.

"Uh...he did leave an address of where his appointment is, would you like me to call it out?"

"Yes, give me the address!"

The receptionist did as she was told, desperately trying to get Cathy off the phone. She had always been intimidated by Thomas' wife and this didn't help matters any further. She gave Cathy the address and Cathy slammed down the phone. Later, the receptionist wondered if it were the right thing to do, but she had panicked and felt that she could explain it later.

Cathy ripped the page off the pad with the address on it, grabbed her keys and headed out the door. She felt sober as a judge now and didn't think twice about getting behind the wheel of her jeep. All she could see in her head was Thomas, in the arms of another woman, their two bodies writhing around in passion in a strange bed. Her tears made it hard for to see the road, or was she still drunk? At that moment she didn't care and she sped down the road, narrowly missing other cars. She expected to be pulled over at any minute, but amazingly, she made it to her destination, without a scratch to herself or the car.

She got to the front door and checked the address several times before heading in. To her surprise it wasn't a house, but a mission hall. Still in a rage she pushed pass two poor unfortunates at the entrance, who thought better than to challenge her behaviour, until she came to a corridor with several doors. Unsure what to do, she stood there for a moment, looking for any clue as to where her husband may be. She jumped when she heard a kind voice behind her.

"Can I help you?" a smiling lady asked.

Cathy eyed her up and down, was she the other woman? She was a bit old and not very attractive, but she had kind eyes. Cathy paused, then timid as a mouse she addressed the lady.

"I'm...I'm looking for my husband," she said, now staring down at the floor. Something didn't feel quite right and Cathy was afraid of making an even bigger fool of herself.

"Ok," said the woman, "is he a client of ours?"

"A what? Em...I don't know,"

The woman could see that Cathy was in distress and wanted to help her.

"Why don't you tell me his name and I'll see if I can locate him for you,"

Cathy couldn't help but be taken in by this stranger, who genuinely wanted to help her. Was this why Thomas liked her? Or worse, loved her?

"Thom...Thomas...Ryan."

"Ok, why don't you have a seat and I'll see what I can find out."

Cathy just smiled sheepishly and did as the woman told. She could feel the effects of an instant hangover as she cupped her head in her hands. She looked up when she heard her name.

"Cathy?" It was Thomas.

"Thomas!"

"What are you doing here?"

"Me? What the hell are you doing here?!!"

"What's wrong is it Jade?"

"No it's not about Jade, why does it always have to be about Jade?!"

"I don't know what's wrong hun?"

"Don't hun me you two timing bastard! I know what you're up to!"

"Two timing what?"

"You heard me!" Cathy was crying uncontrollably and was angry at herself when she couldn't get the words out.

"I rang your office, they told me you were here, why did you lie to me?"

"Cath Jesus, what's going on?"

"So you did lie to me?"

"Yes but..."

"So you admit it! When I think of all I gave up for you..."

"Whoa wait a minute, it's not what you think!"

"Oh don't tell me it's all in my head Thomas Ryan, you lying cheating bastard!"

Thomas tried to put his arm around his wife but she pushed him away.

"I'm leaving you, you pig!"

"Cathy listen to me, you've got it all wrong!"

"I don't have to listen to your shit! I'm leaving you, I hope you and that slut are happy together!"

"Cath wait!!"

Cathy stormed out of the building and fumbled for her keys. Thomas followed her out and tried to coax her back inside.

"Cath come on, you've been drinking, you can't drive,

please!"

"Go to hell there's nothing wrong with me, I got myself over here didn't I?!"

Cathy managed to get out of his grasp and got into the car, locking it behind her. Thomas pleaded with her to get out.

"Please Cath, we can talk about this, please, I love you!"

This sent Cathy over the edge and she sped off, the wrong way down a one way street. She didn't feel the bang when she swerved to avoid the oncoming traffic. The air bags deployed and Cathy was left unconscious at the wheel. Thomas ran to his wife screaming her name.

Cathy woke up in the hospital to an array of different noises. She thought she heard Thomas speaking outside her curtain, but then fell back into a deep sleep. She awoke again and looked down at her bed, where Thomas was hunched over, asleep at the end of it.

"Thomas?"

"Hey you're awake!" Thomas said, his face full of worry.

Cathy could remember the accident then and started to cry.

"Don't cry baby, it's ok, I'm here,"

"The car...the car..." was all Cathy could muster.

"Hey, to hell with the car, it was too big for you anyway,"

They both laughed. Then Thomas took her hand.

"I don't know what I'd have done if anything had happened to you,"

"Oh Thomas, but what about the other woman?"

Cathy was calm now, maybe with the effect of the accident, or maybe because she was ready to listen.

"Babe, I told you, there is no other woman, there's

only you."

"But I mean, how we got together, I was the other woman and now..." Cathy started to cry.

"Look, I cheated once yes, do I wish things had happened differently? Yes, but I met you, we fell in love and there's no one else for me."

They gripped hands and stared into each other eyes and in a strange way Cathy felt safer than she had felt in a long time, with Thomas by her side.

"So if there's no other woman, then what were you doing at that place?"

Thomas paused and took a deep breath.

"Work hasn't been great lately,"

"Work? What's work got to do with it?"

"Well, a lot as it turns out. Cath, I wasn't at that place meeting another woman, I was at a support group,"

"A support group?"

"Yes,"

"But...for what?"

"I've been depressed, more than a bit down in myself. Work has slowed down a lot and it started to get to me and before I knew it I started wondering if you and Jade were not better off without me,"

"Oh Thomas, you didn't try?"

"No no, but I was heading that way and without this group I most certainly would have ended up that way,"

"Oh Thomas, I'm so sorry."

"Hey it's not your fault,"

"But I've been so bitchy lately and...and"

"And you'd every right to be, I must have been a nightmare to live with these past few months,"

"No Thomas, you were a nightmare to live without,"

They smiled and gripped each other's hand tightly.

"Why didn't you tell me?"

"Oh I don't know, I suppose I felt like a failure. I was

a king when you met me, top of my game, I just wanted to be the same guy you fell in love with."

"But you are,"

"Am I?"

"Yes,"

"Cath?"

"Yes?"

"I love you,"

"I love you too, you big eejit!"

Thomas laughed and leant over and kissed his wife hard on the lips, like he hadn't seen her for years.

"And anyway, who's the eejit? I wasn't driving drunk like a mad woman across town!"

"Oh shit! What was I thinking? Am I in big trouble?"

"Probably, but it could have been worse,"

They were interrupted by the doctor and Cathy sat up to attention.

"Now, Ms Ryan."

"Mrs,"

"Sorry, Mrs Ryan. Hmmm, you were a very lucky woman today,"

"Yes I know doctor,"

"And I'm sure I don't need to tell you that driving under the influence is a serious offence,"

Cathy didn't answer, she just nodded.

"But we'll let the police deal with that, for now I want you to rest. Amazingly, you came out without a scratch,"

"Thank you doctor," they both said.

"Oh don't thank me, thank whoever was looking after you from above. Oh and I'm glad to say that your baby is fine too."

Cathy and Thomas stopped breathing for a moment.

"I'm sorry doctor, did you say baby?" a startled Thomas asked.

"Yes, you mean you didn't know?"

"Eh...no."

"Yes about eight weeks along,"

Cathy couldn't speak, they had never discussed having another baby, especially so late in life.

"A baby?" Cathy asked, as if the doctor was having a laugh with them.

"Yes Mrs. Ryan, a baby. Look I'll leave you two alone, but I'll be back to check on you later. And Mrs. Ryan? No more alcohol for the next seven months yes?"

"Um...yes...of course doctor!!"

***

Mary made her way down the long corridor to Brigid's ward alone. The community centre was closed for refurbishment for a couple of weeks so she and the women had to take an unwanted break from their coffee morning. Mary began to miss them, but didn't want to bother them during their break, so decided to visit Brigid and as it was the Christian thing to do, didn't feel guilty about monopolising her time. She had just made it to Brigid's ward, when she was politely stopped in her tracks.

"Excuse me, Ms Mannion?"

Mary was caught off guard as she turned to face the handsome doctor the girls had been drooling over for the past few weeks.

"Eh…yes...I mean no I'm Ms. Bannick." Shit Mary thought, why didn't I say Mrs.?!

"Oh I'm sorry I just assumed you were Mrs. Mannion's daughter."

Mary thought he was joking at first and laughed, but his face was solemn and quizzical.

"Um no I'm Brigid's friend,"

"My apologies,"

223

He was as polite as he was attractive thought Mary, unusual for a doctor, or at least the ones Mary had encountered. Cold, matter of fact people who treated their patients as impersonally as possible. This never bothered Mary though, she always thought that to do such a job, full of stress, sickness, death, meant that you had to separate anything that resembled feeling, otherwise all the doctors of Ireland would be in hospital themselves. This doctor however was different. He held a professional stance but his eyes suggested that he took more of an interest in his patients than was obligated.

"Hardly something you have to apologise for Doctor, I haven't been mistaken for someone's daughter in a long time," Mary replied wryly.

He seemed distracted, staring down at what Mary could only assume was Brigid's file, and without looking up he did raise a smile out of the corner of his mouth. Then it was back to business.

"I wanted to speak to you about Brigid,"

"Yes," said Mary like a tentative school girl.

"As you know I can't discuss her condition with you as you're not a family member..."

"Oh of course," said Mary.

"However I have noticed significant improvements in her wellbeing, she seems more upbeat when you and your...?"

"Friends?"

"Yes friends, visit,"

"Oh," said Mary feeling very pleased "that's great!"

"Yes I do believe it has done her the world of good,"

"Well that's great Doctor Gaffney, we'll keep it up so,"

"Please, call me Daniel," he smiled.

"Ok, Daniel, I'm Mary by the way,"

"Nice to have met you properly Mary,"

Mary smiled as Doctor Gaffney, 'Daniel' nodded and bid her farewell. Having giving up on any sort of feeling towards another man Mary knew she was blushing. She felt silly. She wasn't having feelings! Was she? Had she been flirting? Oh God I truly hope not she thought! She suddenly forgot why she was there until she heard Brigid's voice travelling down the hall and quickly made her way to her room.

"Young lady I couldn't eat another jelly dessert, see if you can do me a favour and try and sneak me some of that lovely apple crumble that my neighbour had yesterday."

Mary walked in just as Brigid was lecturing the poor young nurse, if she was even a nurse she was so young, maybe a trainee. The young girl was about to remind Brigid of her strict diet but thought better of it and just nodded.

"Now Brigid, this isn't the Ritz you know," smiled Mary, who was a little disheartened to see Brigid looking a little tired today.

"Mary! How good to see you!" Brigid's face instantly lit up and Mary again worried as Brigid would normally tell her that she shouldn't have come 'all that way' to see an old woman with a small case of gout. But today was different, Brigid seemed to be getting cabin fever and was adamant she would be home soon, despite what the doctors said.

"So how are you keeping Bridg?"

"Oh the usual, bored! Claire has been good to me of course and the rest of the family, but I just need to get home, I'm no use to anyone in here!"

"I know Bridg but the doctors know what they're doing and they only want you to get better, we all do,"

"I know Mary, I know and speaking of doctors don't think I didn't hear you both chatting earlier!"

Mary blushed again.

"Brigid Mannion were you eavesdropping?!" Mary jibed.

Brigid laughed, "no no dear I simply don't miss a trick, never have! So, he's nice hmm?"

"Yes very nice and he's taking great care of you,"

"That's not what I meant,"

"What do you mean then, go on enlighten me!"

"Mary, you're an attractive woman, he's an attractive man.."

"Would you stop Brigid I'm sixty-five years of age and besides..."

"Besides what? You're single why not?"

Mary's face dropped.

"Single? Me?" She thought about putting up the pretence but at this point found it exhausting.

"Well aren't you?" asked Brigid kindly.

"Oh I don't know Brigid, some days I feel separated and then other days? Who knows?! I'm sure most women don't still fight with their ex-husbands!"

Mary hadn't meant to blurt out the words, but they had been scratching at her head since it happened and before long she had regaled the whole story to Brigid, who listened compassionately.

"I don't know Brigid, maybe he is right," Mary said quietly to her friend.

"Do you think he's right?" asked Brigid.

"I don't know, maybe, I don't...times were hard you know? I was seventeen when I met Frank. I was still looking after my brothers and sisters. Yes it was hard for me, but you just got on with it, you know? Does that make me strong? I don't know, I guess I just didn't know any other way to be. Maybe I did alienate Frank at times, but it's not like I had someone around I could offload my problems on, someone who could look after me for a change."

"Did you ever give Frank the chance to?" Brigid asked.

"Frank? Ha Frank couldn't find his shoe laces without me,"

"Did you?" Brigid asked again.

"No, I suppose I didn't,"

"Why not?"

"I don't know. Frank had a hard time with his mother growing up, tough exterior but when it came to his own family? I think he panicked,"

"But he was a good father?"

"Oh yes, but he got to be the fun parent you know? Which left me to be the bad guy,"

"You didn't have to be," said Brigid.

"But if I didn't..."

"But if you didn't, your family would makes mistakes, get hurt, fail."

"Exactly."

Brigid laughed, "Mary, you can't avoid these facets, they're part of life,"

Mary nodded, suddenly realising that Brigid was right.

"You may have needed to do these things when your children were babies and being a mother I know that that sense of responsibility never leaves you, but at some point we have to let go and let them live their own lives, including Frank."

"It's hard though,"

"I know it's hard; if it was easy everyone would do it. You are a strong woman Mary, but the biggest sign of strength is asking someone for help. Frank may not have been the model husband, but it may have dented his masculinity when you didn't place any trust in him to succeed. Maybe he's guilty of letting you, but maybe..."

"...I'm guilty too." Mary finished.

"You're not on trial Mary," Brigid laughed, "but maybe it's time to let go."

"Of Frank?"

"Of the old Mary."

Chapter Seven

Marji was shaking as she got out of the taxi. She thought about turning back, but knew the only way forward was simply that, forward! It was too late anyway, the taxi had pulled away, leaving her standing outside J's restaurant. It was a Monday night, so it wasn't too busy. She caught her reflection in the glass and immediately regretted her outfit of long woollen green skirt, white blouse and tan suede boots. I look like a hippy, a homosexual hippy, she thought to herself. She was grateful that her hair decided to behave tonight though, probably because it took her two hours to blow dry it. She thought about getting it done professionally, but then didn't want to show up looking like it was done professionally. She'd seen a few photos of J online and the only similarity they shared was their bulging bellies. 'Never trust a skinny chef' J said once said and it made Marji laugh. Come to think of it, Marji laughed a lot when J spoke, she'd forgotten dating could be such fun. Although now here she was, on her first date with a woman ever, it was practically a first ever date. The knot came back to her stomach, then her thoughts were interrupted by a voice.

"Are you going in?" a young couple asked her, grabbing the door handle.

"Um, yes...I mean no, I mean..."

The couple laughed sympathetically, holding the large glass door open for Marji.

"I'm sorry, yes I'm going in, thank you," she finally said, feeling like a fool. The couple just nodded and smiled and made their way over to their friends who were beckoning them to their table. Marji envied them, a night out with friends, oh if that was all her night entailed she'd be much happier. She'd had such a good time away with the girls and was overwhelmed at how supportive they were with her big reveal, she felt lucky. If they thought she should get herself out there, then she must have something to offer.

She smiled at the maître d' who was waiting to seat her.

"Good evening madam, welcome to Julien, may I help you?" he asked in a severely posh accent.

"Um, yes, thank you...I'm um meeting, um.." Marji couldn't get the words out.

"Yes madam? Do you have a booking?"

"Um, no, I mean yes!"

The maître d' looked confused, until Marji leaned in and whispered.

"I'm meeting the chef for dinner,"

"Of course madam, right this way," he smiled knowingly, leading Marji through the aisles, passing tables of loved-up couples clinking glasses and feeding each other like toddlers. Marji was wondering when the tour would end, as they seemed to pass a lot of empty tables, then he took her through some heavy doors to an empty room, with one table and two chairs.

"But..." Marji was about to ask, but the maître d' beat her to it.

"Chef's table Madam, for special guests," he smiled, taking Marji's coat, then breezed out of sight astutely.

Marji surveyed the room. The walls were painted crimson red and on the floor lay thick black carpet. The table too was black, as were the high backed chairs. The table was set; dinner for two, with one single candle lighting. Marji could hear the hustle and bustle from the busy kitchen; plates clattering off each other, orders being clamoured, steam hissing from pots and pans. She suddenly felt excited. It had been so long since she'd dined somewhere so fancy and at the request of the chef?

Not too shabby for Marji she thought. She fidgeted with her hands for a bit and after a couple of minutes, a door from the kitchen opened and out walked J.

"Marji hi!" she beamed as she walked in, arms outstretched. The first thing Marji noticed was her height, J was tiny, but had a beautiful smiley face. Her short blonde hair framed her round face and she had dazzling blue eyes. She was so friendly and confident, not an awkward gesture in sight. Marji guessed she was close in age to her which was a relief. Everything on her profile, besides her height, was true. Far from a deal-breaker, Marji was just so relieved that the person she'd been talking to for weeks was actually real. J had a genuineness that drew you, like she was really happy to see you. Marji wondered why J was interested in her.

J flung her arm around Marji and gave her a sweet kiss on the cheek. Marji blushed.

"It's so great to finally meet you," said J, not taking her eyes off Marji.

"It's nice to finally meet you too," Marji smiled nervously, not used to the touchy-feeliness.

"Please, sit down," J said, gesturing to Marji's chair. She was wearing a white chef's jacket and black trousers. Marji felt overdressed and J must have sensed it.

"I know, I'm in my work skivvies, so sorry. I hadn't planned on working tonight but then got suckered in, never off the job you know?!"

"Oh that's ok, duty calls I suppose," Marji said politely.

"Well, thanks again for coming," beamed J, "you look as lovely as your pictures."

Marji blushed again, but thought quick, she must repay the compliment.

"You look good too," oh my God thought Marji, is that all I can say? Normally I'm the one people can't get a word in with. J wasn't sure how to read Marji but wasn't one for beating around the bush either.

"I know, fit in your pocket couldn't I?" she laughed.

"What? No! You're fine, you look...fine," Marji said embarrassed.

"Thank you," said a bemused J.

Marji felt like an idiot, maybe because the attraction was instant, well on her part at least. Her date could probably do better she thought. What am I doing? She said to herself. I need to rescue this conversation from singledom or I'll be dining with the cat for the rest of my days. Come on Marji, bit of effort, she cajoled herself.

"So, now I know what the J stands for," said Marji, offering J a lifeline.

"Oh no you've got it wrong sorry," J laughed, "I'm actually Jillian, I picked Julien because it sounded more upmarket, I feared Jillian's would have portrayed my cooking as some sort of little café,"

"Right, I get you," said Marji.

"Not that I have anything against your little greasy spoon, I just spent too long working my way through college to serve chips,"

"No of course," Marji had gone back to short answers, she felt intimidated by J, Jillian, not in a negative way, but in a way that made her feel vulnerable, yet fascinated.

"You know what this date needs?" asked J rhetorically.

"New faces?" Marji replied, taking blame for the lulls she kept injecting into the conversation.

"No," Jillian chuckled, "alcohol!"

"You've read my mind!" said Marji, a bit too eagerly.

"I'll be right back," said Jillian, hopping up from the table, but as she got to the door, she turned, "I'm really glad you're here Marji," she smiled.

Marji couldn't help it, her smile radiated, "I'm glad

I'm here too," and off Jillian went to get a bottle of Merlot, leaving Marji to gather her thoughts and finally relax into what would be a lovely evening.

***

Rosa was feeling homesick. She wanted so much to hear her parent's voices, it had been so long, but she was hesitant. They had never wanted her to leave Poland. Maybe they saw something in Peter that Rosa was blinded by. She felt guilty and foolish, for giving up everything for one man. She also felt too ashamed to go home, with her tail between her legs. She sat with the receiver in her hand, the dull tone creating pressure around her. What would she say? How could she hide her unhappiness from her mother? She couldn't. Her mother could always sense when something was wrong. By her tone, the way she carried herself, hunched over, like she had a physical weight on her back. Maybe I could talk about Filip? She wondered, as she searched her mind, trying to fake a seeming contentment with her life in Ireland. Life in Ireland she pondered. Was it really that bad? She liked the scenery, the little she managed to see and the people, the few she managed to meet. Then she thought of her coffee morning friends and smiled. She had become really fond of each of them and loved how each differed from one other, especially herself. She wondered if they realised how much she needed them? Wondered if they needed her the same? Probably not, she concluded. But suddenly, thoughts of the women spurred her to make the call. As she dialled she thought of Cathy, who was probably at some gala, Alice, cuddling her sweet husband. She began to see some light in her life, felt that all was not lost and moments later the phone began to ring.

"Hello Mama, hello Papa," she spoke to the answering machine, "It is your daughter. I am happy in Ireland, I make new friends, they are very funny," she said with a smile, "I miss you," but the last comment stung her and she quickly hung up the phone, hugging herself tightly.

***

Cathy sat in Jade's favourite restaurant, as she watched her daughter across the table rapidly typing on her phone. Cathy was nervous. Nervous of the reaction of her eighteen year old daughter. She made several attempts to start a conversation, but was met with non-committal grunts, Jade not taking her attention away from her precious phone.

"Maybe we could go shopping after lunch?" Cathy suggested, a bit over enthusiastically.

"Mmmm"

"Or see a movie?"

"Whatever."

Cathy's heart sank. Had she let it get this bad? She had one daughter. One. A daughter that was more interested in talking to her friends than to her own Mum. Cathy was about to ask her to put her phone away when their food arrived.

"Ooh yummy," said a gleeful Jade, tucking into her Piri Piri chicken. Cathy on the other hand, had lost her appetite.

"Jade," she said softly.

But Jade was too engrossed in both her food and her phone.

"Jade!"

"What?!" she said annoyingly, but finally looked up at her Mum, seeing the worry in her eyes. Cathy took a large gulp from her water and swallowed it uncomfortably.

"Mum what is it?" Jade said, suddenly worried.

"I need to talk to you about something," Cathy could barely get the words out. She was scared. Scared of Jade's reaction to her news, scared she'd reject her, scared she'd finally lost her baby girl.

"Well, the thing is, your father and I..."

"Oh here we go," Jade rolled her eyes to heaven.

"What?" asked Cathy.

"You're getting a divorce aren't you?"

"What? No!"

"Then what's with the girly lunch, offering to take me shopping and shit?"

"Don't swear"

"Ha! That's rich!"

"Right I know I swear a lot,"

"A lot? Every second word out of your mouth is shit!"

"Keep your voice down,"

Jade tutted and returned to her phone and Cathy couldn't take the pressure any longer.

"Jade!"

"What?!"

"Put the damn phone down for a minute will you!"

"Ok," Jade said, stunned.

"I'm trying to tell you, that your father and I are expecting a baby,"

"What?!"

"Yes," Cathy couldn't help but smile.

Jade sat, open mouthed, searching for words, until she finally let out a burst of laughter.

"What's so funny?" asked a pissed off Cathy.

"You," Jade pointed, "are pregnant?!" and the laughing started again.

"I'm not past it you know?!" said Cathy.

"I know I know, Mum I'm sorry," Jade said, calming

down, "it's just, I don't know, like, eeuw"

Then Cathy started to laugh, "It's not eeuw!"

"You mean, you're not upset?"

"Why would I be upset? A little sick at the fact that you and Dad still do it, but no I'm not upset!"

"Well great," Cathy said with relief.

"I would have been upset if..." said Jade quietly.

"Yes?"

"If you guys were splitting up."

Cathy felt awful. She'd forgotten how soft Jade could be and how much she noticed what went on in the house.

"Honey I'm so sorry, I know your Dad and I fight and I know I haven't been the best Mum,"

"What? You're a great Mum!"

"I am?!"

"Yeah, you don't hassle me and question me all the time about where I've been, or who I'm with, shows you trust me,"

"It does?"

"Well yeah, duh Mum,"

"But I don't take you out anywhere, we never do anything together?"

"It's fine Mum really, I'm eighteen I like doing my own thing."

"But..." Cathy began, scared again, of this beautiful, smart young lady before her, who hadn't checked her phone in several minutes, "I don't...like doing my own thing."

The women stared at each other, both shocked by Cathy's revelation.

"You mean like going for lunch and stuff?"

"Yeah," smiled Cathy.

"Really?" asked Jade.

"Well of course,"

"Didn't think you wanted to," said Jade, looking down

at her unfinished plate.

"I'm sorry for that," Cathy whispered, feeling ashamed.

"It's ok," said Jade quietly.

"No, it's not," said Cathy, grabbing Jade's arm.

"Mum stop," said Jade, mortified.

"I love you hon," Cathy said, getting misty eyed.

"Aw I love you too, ok?" Jade returned, faking annoyance, then she laughed, "a baby" she said to herself.

***

Alice and Stephen were playing the dreaded waiting game. Good news? Bad news? Who knew? It was 50/50 either way. Alice didn't share the process of the IVF treatment with her family, or Stephen's family for that matter, so there was no way Stephen's sister could have known that her news would cause upset.

'That's great news Alison' she could hear her husband say over the phone. Alice gestured to Stephen that she didn't want to talk, so he told Alison that she had popped out.

'Yep, I'll be sure to tell her, she'll be delighted, congrats again' Stephen said goodbye to his sister and hung up the phone, all the while watching a heartbroken Alice, sitting in their living room, with tears in her eyes.

"That's number three Stephen. Three! And we don't even have one!"

"I know love, but our time will come,"

"Will it?"

Stephen hugged his wife tenderly, as she blew her nose and wiped her eyes.

"I'm sorry hon, I should be happy for your sister and I am happy, it's just..."

"A slap in the face?"

"Yeah."

The two sat side by side, Stephen's arm around Alice, with their hopes slightly dashed, but they still prayed for a miracle, a tiny miracle.

***

Mary sat watching TV with Greg, who was outstretched on the sofa, his long legs hanging over the side. Although what he found interesting about what they were watching was beyond Mary.

"It's called Porn Stars?" said Mary aghast.

"No Mum," Greg chuckled, "it's Pawn Stars, as in stuff you don't want you pawn, get it?"

"I know what a pawn shop is love," only too well Mary thought to herself.

Greg was lapping up his programme, oohing and ahing, with the occasional 'fecking eejit' thrown in.

"Think I'll get my book," said Mary as she got up from her chair.

"One of your dirty romance books Mam?" Greg teased.

"They are not dirty books," said Mary in annoyance, standing in defence with her hands on her hips, "they're Mills and Boons."

"Like I said, dirty books," Greg winked and Mary gave him a playful slap on the head. Just as Mary was about to head upstairs to retrieve the tarnished book—the phone rang.

"Who could that be at this hour?" Mary wondered aloud as she made her way over to the phone. No fear of Greg getting up from the comfort of his chair to answer it.

"Hello?" Mary asked.

"Mum?" said Helen, breathless, "It's time!"

"It's time? What? Oh God!! I'll be right there," Mary shouted, panicked.

"No Mum it's fine," said Helen with a laugh, "could be hours yet,"

"I don't care I'm coming to the hospital!"

"Ok," Helen laughed, giving in.

"Oh Mum?"

"Yes love?"

"Em, could you call Dad?"

Mary went silent on the phone, she hadn't spoken to Frank in a while and was trying to avoid another argument, but at the end of the day it was his grandchild too.

"Mum? You there?"

"Oh sorry, yes love I'm here, yes I'll ring him don't worry."

Mary was dreading the phone call, dreading seeing Frank. What would they talk about? She hated the tension but told herself that she wasn't at fault.

"Was that Helen Mum?" Greg asked, finally peeling himself off the sofa.

"What?" Mary asked, lost in thoughts of Frank, "Oh yes, yes love, baby is on the way!"

"So, what do we do boil sheets and stuff?" Greg joked.

"Very funny," said Mary, unamused, the excitement of the arrival of her latest grandchild; marred by her impending meet with her ex-husband.

"Do I have to go?" Greg asked.

Typical man thought Mary, gets that from his father. Frank wasn't present for any of the births of his children, well it was unheard of back then Mary supposed.

"No love it's ok," she said to Greg, "could be hours anyway."

Greg was pleased and climbed straight back onto the sofa, the remote control not leaving his hand. Mary was glad he was distracted and wouldn't notice the tension in her tone. She started to dial the number of the Haven and after it rang for several minutes, someone finally picked up.

"Haven?" said a voice, short and to the point.

"Em, hello, is Frank there?"

"Frank!" she heard the voice say, before a clambering of the receiver.

"Hello?"

"Frank? It's Mary."

"Mary? Oh Mary!"

"You know another one?" shot Mary sarcastically, but immediately regretted her tone. Thankfully, Frank hadn't heard her, due to the noise in the bar.

"Sorry Mary, what did you say?"

"It's Helen,"

"Helen?" Frank shouted, shushing people around him.

"Helen!" Mary was shouting now, "is gone into labour,"

"Labour?! Shit, eh, I'll leave now, I'll get some cover..."

"Frank...Frank!!"

"Yes?"

"There's no rush, it could be hours,"

"Oh right you are yeah," Frank said, feeling slightly foolish.

"Anyway, I'll call you when we have news,"

"Oh ok."

The volume levels of the bar rose even further, until Frank was barely audible.

"Mary?!...Mary!" he shouted.

"Yes?" said Mary, finally making out her name.

"Thanks," Frank said and it sounded so solemn that Mary felt a bit guilty.

"Sure." was all she could say back and she hung up

the phone.

***

Mary cradled her first granddaughter in her arms.

"She's so beautiful," Mary said to Helen, who lay in her bed, moments away from sleep. Gerry kissed the top of his baby daughter's head and both he and Mary shared a smile. Frank was on his way and as much as Mary would have loved to make her excuses and leave, she knew she couldn't. Firstly, because her daughter had just made her a grandmother again and secondly, because she had to face Frank sooner or later. She heard him before she saw him.

"Where's my little granddaughter then?" Frank beamed as he walked through the doors, arms outstretched, holding a bunch of flowers in one hand and a pink teddy in the other.

"Hi Dad," said Helen yawning.

"Hiya Frank," Gerry said, holding out his hand for Frank to shake.

"Gerry, congratulations," Frank said, nearly taking Gerry's arm out of the socket. After the surge of merriment Frank was suddenly in front of Mary.

"Hello Mary."

"Hello Frank."

It was polite, but with no gaiety. Mary was still holding the baby when Frank gestured asking to hold her. Himself and Mary made the exchange without speaking or making eye contact. Gerry winked at Helen, giving her a 'that went well' look.

"Would you look at that, grabbing my finger already," Frank announced proudly.

"Yeah I reckon she'll be a good rugger bugger," Gerry teased.

"What?" shrieked Frank, "this young lady will play football, like her Granddad."

Gerry laughed. It shouldn't have, but it made Mary jealous. Frank had always gotten on well with Gerry and it wasn't uncommon for them to have a joke and a laugh together. Today though, it made Mary feel uncomfortable, like she didn't belong there with this family dynamic. Frank could always see an opportunity for fun, as he and Gerry mockingly argued about what team the new baby would follow, then again, Frank was the fun one, wasn't he? Thought Mary.

"What's her name?" asked a beaming Frank.

"Isobel," said Helen, who's eyes were starting to droop.

"Is-o-bel," mimicked Frank, "hello Isobel, I'm your Granddaddy," he said softly as he cuddled to the newest addition to the family.

"Well I'll head off," Mary said, kind of abruptly, the atmosphere smothering her slightly.

"Oh Mum, you sure?" Helen asked half-heartedly, thinking only of the rest she was in such dire need of.

"Yes love. I'll pop up tomorrow. Congratulations darling, you too Gerry."

"Bye Mum love you," waved Helen. "Yes bye Mary and thanks," Gerry said, planting a kiss on Mary's cheek. Mary avoided Frank's gaze, who was still holding the baby, in her attempt to make a quick exit, until she reached the door.

"Bye Mary," Frank's words drifted to her back as she turned. Mary turned back and smiled weakly, feeling as though she was about to cry.

***

Mary decided to visit Brigid alone again today. The

242

two of them had become very close in the past few weeks and Mary looked forward to their chats more and more. Not that the other women hadn't become her friends, they had, much to Mary's delight, but with Brigid it felt easier. Mary saw a lot of her mother in Brigid, the tough exterior, her unwavering sense of responsibility she felt towards her children, but Brigid had a soft warmness to her that Mary's mother lacked at times. She felt guilty for even comparing the two, Mary loved her mother dearly, but she secretly craved a hug from her from time to time. Mary's mother was not a 'huggy' person. Oh she made up for it in many other ways, gigantic dinners on the table each evening, even with the little means they had, new clothes, most of which her mother made from the leftover pieces of material from her clients whom she made dresses for. I suppose hugging wasn't the done thing back then. Mary thought. Life was hard, you lived day to day not knowing where the next shilling was coming from. Living in a two bed council flat with eight children, never gave much time for carefree abandon days. Although Mary always remembered a trip to the beach that they had when she and her siblings were little. Back when summers were summers; blistering heat, crisps and sandwiches, flasks of sugary tea and if they were really lucky, an ice cream on the way home. Mary and her family were lucky enough to live close to the beach, as should it have required a train ride this would have been out of the question. The warm memory in the summer air made her smile and drift into a reminiscent reverie.

"Mam can we get into the water now?" a ten year old Mary asked.

"Wait until the tide comes in closer love, it's on its way."

Mary watched the tide on Sandymount beach come around by the nature walk path, stopping at the strand and leaving a gap in the middle, a gap that would quickly fill in with the rushing tide. They sat, just beside the rocks at the Martello tower, on an old blanket, adorned in their swimming suits or togs as they were called back then, eagerly anticipating the subtle crash of the waves. Mary's father sat on a flat rock, slowly inhaling a drag of tobacco, staring out to sea. Even at ten Mary wondered if her Dad missed his drink that day. She stared at him, shirt sleeves rolled up to the elbows, trousers rolled up to the knees, his sockless feet dug into the sand and his nicotine stained fingers grasping his cigarette. He caught her gaze and smiled, "tide's nearly in pet." Mary smiled back. She watched her brothers playing together, kicking an old ball around, laughing and joking, her sisters made shapes in the sand with an empty shell and her youngest brother who lay sleeping in his pram. Little did Mary know at that moment, that this would be one of her favourite memories that she would always hold dear.

After what felt like forever, the tide came in that day and for that one day Mary and her family forgot about money worries, their cramped little flat, drinking in the pub, school and the rest of the world were shut out.

The dreaded sand had dried into Mary and the rough towel to brush it away felt like razor blades on her delicate skin. Seeing her struggle Mary's mother came to her eldest daughter's side, producing a bottle of Cusson's talcum powder.

"Here love, let me," said her mother, as she smoothed the powder all over her body. Mary watched the sand and powder fall to the ground in soft, swift motions and once again she was dry and clean. Her mother wrapped a big towel around her shoulders and rubbed her back to heat her up as the blazing sun set in the sky.

"Thanks Mam," she whispered.

Her mother smiled and as she touched her cheek she

said, "my girl."

Mary came back to the present, almost with a tear in her eye, as she reached the hospital grounds. She entered the main door and made her way to the gift shop. She decided to treat Brigid and herself today, to some iced caramels. As she was making her way out of the shop with her purse in her hand, she dropped her change into one of the pockets, but missed and a two euro coin rolled along the floor. It stopped at a pair of men's feet and as she knelt down to pick it up she heard a voice.

"Please, let me,"

Mary slowly looked up and standing there staring, was Doctor Gaffney. Mary was speechless at first, momentarily losing her tongue, but then said, "thank you,"

"Mrs Bannick hello," he beamed, "it's good to see you again,"

"Doctor Gaffney hello, yes you too,"

"Daniel please, are you here to see Brigid?"

Mary was blushing and silently prayed that it didn't show.

"Yes, I thought she could do with some company," that's a lie Mary thought, it's me who needs the company.

"That's very good of you,"

They both looked at each other without speaking for what felt like a very long time.

"Sweet tooth?"

"I'm sorry?" Mary asked, as Doctor Gaffney, Daniel, gestured to her iced caramels. Mary blushed again.

"Oh, these? Yes, I can't resist the old favourites unfortunately," Mary let out a slight giggle.

"The old ones are the best," he smiled and looked even more handsome today than usual Mary thought, different somehow.

"You look different," Mary blurted. What?! Where in God's name did that come from?! Mary was shocked at her sudden forwardness.

Daniel laughed, "I think you've caught me on one of my good days!"

"I'm sorry?" Mary asked, confused.

Daniel tapped his cheek with his finger, "clean shaven."

"Oh," was all Mary could manage, she was utterly mortified.

"Yes I don't get a lot of time to groom in the morning, hindrance of the profession I'm afraid,"

Mary just smiled nervously and was delighted to hear the ringing sound of Daniel's bleeper.

"My apologies," Daniel so courteously explained, "duty calls!" Mary continued to smile nervously.

"Well, I must dash Mary, it was nice to see you again, I hope you and Brigid enjoy your sweets," and off he went.

Mary said her goodbyes and let out a heavy sigh of relief that he was gone. Why had she felt so exposed just then? And why was she so brazen with her comment about how he looked? She brushed off the feelings, or whatever they were and realised she was late for her visit and quickly hurried up to Brigid's ward.

***

All the girls bar Brigid who was still in hospital, turned up for their usual coffee morning after their short break, but Mary was uncomfortable at the air they'd brought about with them. Probably the rain, Mary thought to herself. Although no one seemed to be their self today. The only person with a smile on her face was Marji.

"God you wouldn't put a bottle of milk out in that

246

weather! Hi Mary," Marji greeted Mary, shaking the wet from her umbrella. Mary smiled back and handed Marji her coffee. Next to the coffee station was Alice, who looked a little lost.

"You ok Alice?" asked Mary.

"What? Oh yeah fine, fine just tired."

Mary was concerned, it wasn't like Alice to be down in the dumps and just as she was about to follow Alice to her seat she was interrupted by Cathy's arrival.

"Stupid rain! When will it ever stop?!" Cathy bellowed, to no one in particular, although she seemed more wound up than usual. They were just about to sit down when they heard shouting coming from the corridor. It was Rosa, but she was not alone. The women peered out through the tiny circle shaped window of the door, like nosey curtain twitchers, but neither Rosa, nor her husband had noticed. The women couldn't understand what they were saying, as they were speaking in Polish, but by the volume of their voices and body language it was obvious they were having a full blown row. The exchange continued on for about five minutes when Rosa spotted the women and the mortified look on her face urged them to scarper back to their seats like giggly little school girls.

Marji whispered, "shit did they see us?" and Mary nodded.

The fight came to an abrupt end with Peter storming out of the community centre, leaving a visibly shaken Rosa standing alone, her head facing the floor.

"Should we go out to her?" Alice asked, but the words were no sooner out of her mouth when Rosa opened the door. The women all looked at each other, guilt etched on their faces. The room was silent.

"Hello everyone," Rosa said quietly, tears in her eyes.

"Oh hi Rosa!" Alice exclaimed, like she hadn't just

witnessed the mother of all arguments and like she wasn't expecting Rosa to walk through the door at that moment. Cathy rolled her eyes to heaven at Alice, but still, no one spoke.

"Hello Rosa," Mary said, making her way over to the door. Mary had seen this many times with her daughters. Panda-like mascara eyes, broken heart, the 'oh Mum I thought he liked me' line ready to tumble out of their mouth. But this wasn't just a silly teenage episode that could be soothed with tea and a shoulder. Still, Mary rose to her maternal instincts and placed her arm around Rosa. It wasn't something any of the group had indulged in as yet, touchy feely kind of comfort. She half expected Rosa to pull away, but she didn't.

"Are you ok?" Mary asked softly, head tilted down to Rosa's damp face.

Rosa just cried quietly, wiping each tear away like it would burn into her skin. Mary was quick to the rescue.

"Girls, tissues?"

The women scrambled through their bags looking for tissues and of course the only tool they could muster was some crumpled up pieces of make-up stained toilet paper that had been buried, scrunched up and now stretched out for emergencies just like this one.

"Thank you," Rosa said, wiping her face and blowing hard into her makeshift handkerchief.

Mary delicately walked Rosa over to a chair beside Cathy and gestured for her to sit down. Rosa did as she was told, like always, it had become second nature to her at this point, she just wasn't used to this motherly affection and suddenly wanted to cuddle up in Mary's arms like she did with her own mother as a child. God how she missed her family, missed home.

The women stayed silent, all waiting for Mary's cue to speak, letting her take the lead in the situation. Mary gave

Rosa the time she needed to wipe, blow and collect herself until she was ready to speak.

"I am so sorry ladies, I wish you did not see that." Rosa said.

"It's ok, there's no need to feel embarrassed," Mary said, rubbing Rosa's back. Rosa continued, the room remained quiet.

"He was not always like this, he was kind before, I don't know why, why...." Rosa began sobbing again; far too upset to finish her sentence, so Cathy did it for her.

"I'll tell you why," Cathy bellowed, "because all men are bastards!!" Rosa didn't challenge Cathy, if she was honest Cathy scared her, she knew not to get on her bad side, or maybe she'd become so submissive she didn't know how to stick up for herself anymore. Rosa felt she was the polar opposite of Cathy, she couldn't envisage someone like Cathy taking shit from her husband, or anyone else for that matter. Cathy was still rabbiting on.

"I mean, some of them think that us women were put on this earth just to serve them!! Cook, clean, bear their children!"

"Not all of them are bad," said Alice, in a barely audible voice. She too felt slightly intimidated by Cathy.

"Cook and clean?" said Marji with a raised eyebrow.

"Well, maybe not cook and clean but the children part," said Cathy.

"Well at least you're done with that part Cathy," Marji answered, not sure where the conversation was heading.

"Oh I wish I was!" Cathy said.

"What? What? What?" said Mary, Marji and Alice one after the other.

"Yeah nearly three months, little critter growing inside me, there goes my figure!"

Alice had had enough and thought it was time Cathy got a piece of her mind.

"Do you have to be so negative all the time?!" Alice practically screamed across the room. "Do you know I'd give my right arm to be in your position? Me, who has wanted a baby for so long and a spoilt, superficial cow like you gets there first and she doesn't even know how lucky she is?!!"

Cathy was stunned, lost for words, no one ever spoke to her like that, especially not someone like Alice. But Alice didn't stop there.

"And another thing, not all men are bastards, maybe if you acted like a wife every now and then your husband wouldn't look for excuses to stay out of the house!"

Cathy saw red, Alice had hit a nerve.

"Don't you dare speak to me like that you have no idea what goes on in my life!!"

"Oh do I not? Because you tell us every week about what a prick your husband is, how your daughter wrecks your head!"

"Well we can't always have it easy like you Alice can we?!"

"Easy? You think it's easy minding other people's kids and not my own? Having to go through test after test, IVF treatment? You haven't a clue!"

"Alice, we didn't know...." Marji couldn't finish her sentence, she was as stunned as everyone else at Alice's sudden outburst.

"Alice!" was all Mary could say, but it was too late, Alice was grabbing her things and heading for the door.

"I'm sorry Mary, but I can't listen to this shit anymore." She was gone.

"You had to open your big mouth didn't you Cathy?!" shouted Marji.

"Hold on a minute, it's not my fault I got pregnant first," retorted Cathy.

"It's not always about you Cathy," snapped Marji.

"Girls, girls calm down, this is not the time.." said Mary, cut off by Marji.

"No Mary it is, people need to be put in their place!"

"And you're going to put me in my place are you Marji?" said Cathy.

"Well someone has to!"

"Marji!" scolded Mary.

"No Mary I'm sorry, but I'm tired of the dynamics in this group, you've got little miss makeup moaning about her upmarket lifestyle, Rosa in a, let's face it, violent relationship," Rosa looked stunned, "and everyone's too scared to say anything!"

"Peter is not violent," Rosa said, with uncharacteristic conviction.

"We've all seen the bruises Rosa," said Marji

"Marji! That's enough!" shouted Mary.

"Oh sorry Mary," Marji said sarcastically, "just because the opinion's not yours I'm not allowed to have it?"

"What's that supposed to mean?" asked a shocked Mary.

"The mother hen routine? It's getting a bit tired," said Marji.

Mary was shocked, she had no idea Marji felt this way, she felt that her personality was being attacked, she didn't know what to say.

"Marji, leave Mary alone!" Rosa practically shouted, Cathy was still licking her wounds.

"Do you know what? I will, I'll leave you all alone, I'm outa here!" Marji stormed out, grabbing her things.

"Well I'm not sitting here listening to this, to hell with the lot of you!" Cathy said as she stormed out ahead of Marji, much to Marji's annoyance and within seconds, all that was left in the room were Mary and Rosa. It was all too much for Rosa, who burst into tears again. Mary was still stunned. What had just happened?

"Mary, I'm sorry, I go," said Rosa, tears trickling down her cheek.

"Rosa, no, it's ok, I..."

"No, I go, I did not want to cause upset," and she was gone. Mary was left in an empty room, alone again, naturally.

***

Marji was delighted that Jillian was free for a coffee. It had been a couple of days since the fight and she was more upset than she had expected to be. Jillian picked a small cafe in town and they sat outside, so Marji could enjoy a cigarette.

"Thanks for meeting me," said Marji sheepishly.

"Please, don't thank me," said Jillian with a smile, shooing her hand in the air.

"I just didn't know who else to call," said Marji, taking a big sip from her cappuccino.

"Well I'm glad you called me"

"Bit of a cheat though isn't it? I called you because something was wrong," Marji raised both eyebrows.

"It's ok," said Jillian warmly, tenderly placing her hand on Marji's.

"I know I shouldn't be getting so upset, I mean, it's just a coffee morning," Marji said, looking away whilst lighting her cigarette, begrudgingly letting go of Jillian's hand to use her lighter. But Jillian was attentive and quickly took Marji's hand again when it was free. Marji smiled and felt a tingle down her spine. She wondered if Jillian felt the same. They had spent quite some time together the past month and Marji had loved every minute of it. Jillian challenged Marji in her thinking and the two would talk for hours. Jillian was also a great listener, which worked well in Marji's favour, as she never shut up!

"Seems like more than a simple coffee morning to me," Jillian said, smiling.

Marji could feel tears growing in her eyes, so quickly took a long drag of her cigarette, avoiding Jillian's gaze.

"Hey, you still with me?" asked Jillian softly.

"Yes," Marji laughed, then she relaxed her shoulders, "Oh I suppose you're right, hell I know you're right. These women, they just, accepted me, you know?"

"Uh hmm," Jillian smiled knowingly.

"Fifty years it took me to make friends like this, I just don't want to lose them," Marji furiously inhaled the smoke, battling oncoming tears.

"And you won't," said Jillian.

"But the things I said..."

"Will be forgiven and forgotten,"

"You think so?"

"I know so."

Marji didn't seem convinced.

"You're a hard character to forget Marji," Jillian chuckled.

"I am?"

"Yes," Jillian laughed.

"In...a good way?" Marji asked nervously.

"In a fantastic way," Jillian smiled.

Marji couldn't wipe her own smile from her face then.

"Thank you for being such a good friend to me," said Marji.

"Friend? Thought I was more than that," said Jillian.

"Would you like to be?" asked Marji quietly.

"Isn't it obvious?"

"No?"

Jillian laughed.

"I love you Marjorie."

"You do?"

"Yes."

Marji suddenly came over all giddy, tears of joy now springing to her eyes.

"I love you too," she whispered back to Jillian and the two held hands tenderly, the other customers and passers by becoming distant hazes around them.

***

"Oh Ste, I was such a cow!" Alice cried, stuffing her mouth with Maltesers.

"I highly doubt that love," Stephen offered, rubbing his wife's thigh as he sat on his hunkers looking up at a teary Alice.

"I mean, I should be happy for Cathy that she's having a baby, it's just..."

"You want it to be you?"

"Yeah and I was a bit jealous," Alice sobbed as she gorged on chocolate, becoming less audible the wider her cheeks became.

"It's ok to be a bit jealous love, jaysis I'm a bit jealous meself,"

"You are?"

"Yeah, sure we're only human,"

"Spose," Alice mumbled.

"Look, this will all be sorted out at your next coffee morning, just wait, you'll see,"

"Do you really think so?"

"Of course I do, now Mrs. Stafford, feet up on that sofa and we'll watch that stupid programme of yours where everyone talks a mile a minute!"

"The Gilmore Girls?" Alice asked with childlike excitement.

"Yeah that's the one, come on," Stephen nudged Alice

to make room for him on the sofa.

"But you hate that programme?"

"I know, but I know that when you're upset you need your box sets and chocolate,"

"Oh Stephen!"

"Come on before I change my mind woman!" Stephen teased as Alice kicked off her shoes and did a little gleeful chair dance. It wouldn't be long before Alice was back to herself and it wouldn't be long before Stephen was asleep.

***

"I mean it's not my fault if I got pregnant first!" bellowed Cathy to Thomas as they sat eating pasta in their oversized kitchen.

"Course not," Thomas answered dutifully, lashing forkful after forkful into his mouth, keeping one eye on the television.

"I mean I didn't know she was doing IVF!"

"No."

"I mean, it's not like we planned it!"

"No."

"Thomas Ryan are you listening to me?"

"Oh come on ref! What? I mean yeah course I am,"

"No, you're watching the telly that's what you're doing!"

"Sorry babe, it's an important match and..."

Thomas couldn't finish as he'd turned to face Cathy and was shocked to see tears welling up in her eyes.

"You crying babe?" Thomas asked, with a big unintentional grin.

"Well you don't have to look so happy about it!"

"I'm not, sorry," Thomas laughed.

"And you're laughing at me!" Cathy shouted.

"No, sorry," Thomas couldn't fight the amusement, "right I am laughing, I am sorry, it's just, I'm not used to seeing you like this,"

"Like what?" Cathy spat.

"Well, emotional I suppose,"

"I do have feelings Thomas!"

"I know I know I'm not saying that it's just…"

"What?"

"Well I just thought that this, coffee morning, was to get you out of the house,"

"It is!" Cathy shouted, then Thomas put his fork down and turned to his wife.

"Babe, you like these women don't you?" he said quietly.

"Well…."

"It's ok to admit they're your friends and that you like them you know?"

"I know, it's just, I feel silly."

"Why?"

"Well it's like school isn't it? I had a falling out with my friends and I come home crying about it to you,"

"It's ok to cry you know, I'd get used to it if I were you."

"That's another thing!"

"What is?"

"This crying bullshit, my hormones changing, getting fat,"

"Sorry love but that's pregnancy for ya,"

Cathy went quiet and Thomas was half expecting a slap across the face.

"Cath?"

"I'm nervous Tom,"

"About the birth?"

"About everything! But most of all, about being a Mum again, what if the baby hates me?"

"What?"

"Alice is right I'm a spoilt cow! How is a baby gonna put up with that?"

"Cath Cath, the baby will love you."

"You reckon?"

"I'm sure of it! And you're not a spoilt cow."

Cathy raised an eyebrow at Thomas.

"Ok well you're a little spoilt,"

Cathy's face dropped again and Thomas cupped her face.

"But it's ok, because I love spoiling you,"

"Really?" Cathy asked with her tear stained face.

"Really really." Thomas kissed his wife tenderly on the lips and they held each other in a tight embrace. "And don't worry," said Thomas, "you'll be back talking to your friends in no time,"

"Promise?"

"Pinkie promise," Thomas laughed, linking his baby finger with hers, as she gave him a soft elbow in the ribs, tears turning to giggles as they clung to each other, pasta going cold, television ignored.

***

Rosa couldn't get the fight with the women out of her head. It's all my fault, she thought, wincing at the memory of each word that was said. It was bad enough being trapped in an abusive marriage, but for it to spill over into her friendships, that was the final straw. She said the word abusive in her head over and over, abusive, abusive, abusive. For a moment she got annoyed with the women. Who were they to judge her? What marriage didn't have its turmoil? But she quickly realised that it was wrong, easier even, to blame the women for their opinions and stares. She knew that Peter would put an end to her weekly meeting somehow and soon, but she wasn't ready to let go yet. She had found the friends she never had, finally, but her guilt at how their argument had snowballed made her wince again. Time, she needed time. But for what, she didn't know.

***

Mary felt sick, she had a knot in her stomach since the fight with the girls and it wouldn't go away. It had been two days since the argument and she hadn't heard from anyone. It worried her and it surprised her how much it worried her. It wasn't like she had fallen out with family or a close friend, so why was she so upset? It bothered her what Marji had said. Mother hen? Was she a mother hen? Did she try and mother the group? Was that such a bad thing? She decided to try and stop obsessing over it all and go and speak to the one person who would understand the whole mess.

"I don't know what to do Brigid, should I contact them?" Mary sat in the chair beside Brigid's bed. Brigid didn't seem quite as alert today, she'd lost weight, she looked smaller, but she still had that dazzling smile that drew Mary in, making her feel like the most important person in the world at that moment.

"Leave them for now Mary, it sounds like everyone needs a bit of space." Mary wasn't so sure, she'd put every effort into making the coffee morning such a success and now it was falling apart. She was amazed at how much she missed something that she didn't have less than a year ago. Brigid sensed her discomfort.

"They'll come round," Brigid reassured her, placing her hand on Mary's.

"I don't know Bridg, the things that were said, I know it shouldn't bother me, I feel silly getting upset at being called a 'mother hen.' I didn't think that was a bad thing, is it a bad thing?

"My dear, this is what happens when you bring a group of strong characters together, each playing their role, they've been comfortable starring in their own movies for the best part of their lives and now they're being challenged, taken out of their comfort zone.

"Am I included in that description?" asked Mary.

"The moment you decided to set up a coffee morning."

Mary looked worried and Brigid laughed.

"Don't look so worried, it's a good thing what you did, a very good thing, whether you realise it or not, you chose to break free of that what made you who you were. Subconsciously you sought out the freedom to be somebody, someone other than the wife and mother."

"It scares me,"

"I know it does, if it was easy everyone would do it,"

"I suppose I have changed, a year ago I had no friends to speak of and now I'm getting over my first fight with them," Mary forced a laugh.

"And I'm sure there'll be many more to come," said Brigid, smiling.

"Oh don't say that!"

"Sorry," Brigid giggled, "it's true though, but it's a good thing, heated arguments suggest fire in a relationship, passion."

"Well in that case there was a lot of passion in my marriage."

"We hurt the ones we love the most Mary."

Brigid smiled and Mary smiled back. Their short conversation had such depth to it that Mary hoped she'd never forget it. It was tinged with advice and revealed new facets to who Mary was, maybe who she had always been, but had forgotten. She thought about the chat all the way home. She thought about the women and started to see the underlying truth in each of them, the characters they played, defined by status, their place in society. Maybe they were just like her, maybe they wanted to break the mould, this exceptionally diverse group that she had brought together. I did that, she thought, me, little old me and she smiled to herself.

Mary was at a loss of how to fill her day today, so decided the fridge needed defrosting and clearing out. Spring cleaning, whatever time of year, always gave Mary an immense satisfaction, especially when her brain felt a little muddled. It was like opening the windows and airing her mind. She got everything out that she needed, rubber gloves, oven cleaner, cloths and sponges. She was about to get stuck in when her phone rang. Mary quickly grabbed her reading glasses, but when she looked at the screen, she didn't recognise the number. That's strange she thought, must be one of those surveys. When she finally found the answer key, she said hello to her mystery caller.

"Hello?"

"Hello, is this Mary Bannick?" the deep, well-spoken voice boomed down the phone.

"Um yes, this is Mary," Mary still couldn't make out who it was.

"Mary hello, this is Doctor Gaffney,"

Oh no! Mary thought, Brigid!

"Oh no is it Brigid?!" Mary asked, alarmed.

"No no, Mrs. Mannion is fine,"

"Oh, thank God..."

"Actually, this is more of a personal call," suddenly Doctor Gaffney sounded flummoxed and Mary had no idea why.

"Oh?" was all she could say, not knowing where the conversation was heading.

"Yes I was wondering if you were free for lunch today?"

Oh my God! Mary thought, did he just say what I think he said? Now Mary was the one who was stumped and silence ensued on the phone for what felt like hours.

"Mary? Are you still there?"

Oh crap Mary thought, how long have I been quiet? What do I say?

"Em, yes, sorry, I mean yes, I'm still here,"

This couldn't be a date could it? Mary thought to herself and she searched her brain for an excuse, any excuse to say no!

"So, lunch? Today?" Doctor Gaffney politely asked.

Mary started to panic, she could feel bile start to rise in her throat. Why was this man really asking her out? Didn't he know she was married? Well, technically. She'd gone quiet again, trying to conjure up a reason why she couldn't possibly meet him today, or ever!

"I have to clean the oven!" Mary blurted out and she heard the doctor stifle a giggle. She could hear him smiling down the phone and it sent shivers up and down her spine. But the good doctor remained confident and cool.

"Maybe the oven could be cleaned another day?"

"Well I've got my rubber gloves on and everything so..."

Oh God thought Mary, did I really just say that?

"Then that settles it, you really should see a doctor if you have rubber gloves surgically attached to your hands," the doctor teased and Mary just guffawed. But the doctor was relentless.

"So, tell you what, you do your best to remove the gloves, I'll give you say, an hour? Then I'll come and pick you up if you would so kindly text me your address?"

"Ok." said Mary, in shock.

"Ok?"

"Ok."

"Right, see you soon so," and he hung up.

Mary was paralysed, stuck to the floor.

"What the hell have I just agreed to?!" she said aloud, thanking God that Greg was away yet again. How am I going to manage this? Why on earth did I say yes? Mary's brain was bursting, her head hurt, her stomach lurched. She had to get out of it, simple as. She would call him back and cancel, yes, that's what she would do. The idea of a woman of her age going on a date was preposterous, absurd! And what would Frank say? What could Frank say? She was effectively single. Oh God, single! She thought. Single and ready to mingle? Ugh! No, just no. She was happy on her own, she had her kids, her house, her new friends, she was happy, I'm happy, she thought. Then why did I say yes? Her stomach dropped, there was no time to delve into that can of worms. She straightened herself up, composed herself and then desperately pressed the keys in her phone looking for the good doctor's number to call him back. But how do I do that? She thought. Oh crap I can't work this thing, how do I find his number? Mary was frantic and realised that twenty-five minutes had passed, he could be on his way and Mary was still stood there in her kitchen, adorned in her rubber gloves, hair pinned back, old scrubs on, bleach stained and not ready for company of any kind.

Without thinking she reefed off the rubber gloves and ran upstairs to change. Even though she wasn't actually going on the 'date' didn't mean he had to see her looking a state. She quickly threw on a pair of black trousers and a red jumper, brushed her hair and applied a little mascara. She looked at herself in the mirror. Ugh, Mary thought, what an eyesore. The last time Mary had a date the reflection had a lot less lines, weight and age. Then she thought of the poor doctor's face once she would tell him it wasn't going to happen. He seemed like a nice man and Mary hated letting anyone down, even a virtual stranger who played no significance in her life. I'll just tell him I forgot I had to be somewhere, she said to the mirror, or that Greg was coming home, or that I'm married, ha! He'd run for the hills! She was still talking to herself when the doorbell rang. She held her stomach as it lurched again and made her way down the stairs. She took one last deep breath and opened the door.

"Hello Mary," the doctor greeted her with a dazzling smile, one that made his eyes crinkle and even with his lines he looked a vision. He was staring at Mary, his eyes piercing through her. It made her feel intimidated, exposed and a little excited, though she dare not admit that to herself. She searched her brain for the words, 'I'm sorry I can't make lunch, I'm sorry you came all this way, I'm afraid I...'

"Do you like pizza?" he asked, a slight glint in his eye, interrupting Mary's thoughts.

Oh just say it! Said Mary to herself.

"Um, pizza? Eh...sure," Mary replied. The words came out of her mouth automatically, robot like. She couldn't understand why she couldn't get the words out that she had wanted to say. Why can't I say no to this man? There was something about him, it wasn't just his good looks, or the fact that he was a doctor, he was charming, he was confident and Mary felt intrigued by it.

They were still standing in the doorway and Mary hadn't thought to ask him in. But then the neighbours would see her asking a strange man in and tongues would start to wag. Then again, this man had been standing at her door for what seemed like a long period of time, was obviously not a salesman, so maybe she should invite him in and was just about to when he said, "shall we go?"

He seemed to read Mary's mind, he seemed to read the situation without words exchanged, it was annoyingly charming. Mary grabbed her coat that was thankfully just behind the door and walked like a timid schoolgirl to the doctor's car. Of course it wasn't just a typical get you from A to B car, it was a vintage maroon coloured Jaguar with leather interiors. Mary didn't want to admit it, but she was impressed, especially when he held the door open and suavely ushered her into the passenger seat. No doubt Phyllis from across the road was having a field day with the spectacle taking place on their sleepy road. I'll pay for that later thought Mary, as the doctor got into the driver's seat. Mary sat ashen faced beside him, nervously clutching her handbag which sat on her lap.

"Shall I beep for the curtain twitchers?" he joked and Mary couldn't help but laugh.

Oh my God she thought, where did that snort come from? She cut short her laugh with a cough, looking all around for nosey neighbours, as the doctor started up the car.

"Ready?" he asked.

Mary just nodded, not knowing what she had let herself in for and within moments, they had left the street and were on their way for the dreaded pizza that Mary abhorred.

***

They arrived at a small little restaurant called Millers, where they served 'gourmet pizzas' as the good doctor pointed out. Mary wasn't sure if she was over or underdressed, but as she walked through the doors she immediately liked the place. It was rustic; the original bare stone wall was the focal point, with maybe a dozen or so tables. It was quite busy, there were office types munching away on some sort of tiered bread, ladies who lunch and one or two couples with shopping bags. You could see the kitchen from everywhere in the restaurant, it was small but frantically busy. Mary loved hustle and bustle, this place suited her and for a moment she forgot who she was with and the reason she was here. A very friendly older lady with a beaming smile came towards them.

"Table for two?" she asked, pen and notebook in hand.

"Please," said the doctor.

The woman showed them to a small wooden table with green wooden chairs, which took all of three seconds. The place was anything but pretentious which Mary had dreaded and she felt slightly more at ease as she took her seat, still looking all around her. She spotted the big chalkboard on the wall which displayed today's desserts and her eyes danced, although the thought of food at that moment made her nauseous, her nerves taking over.

She could feel the doctor's eyes on her but couldn't bring herself to look at him. Those eyes, those intense eyes, watching her every move. She awkwardly removed her coat and hung it on the back of her chair and fidgeted with her hands. Oh my God he's still looking at me, she noticed and eventually she lifted her head and met his gaze. He just smiled, a knowing kind of grin and Mary just smiled back curtly. She was delighted when the waitress came back.

"So, how are you folks today? Are we having wine?"

"Just a glass for me, Mary?" the doctor asked politely.

"Oh no, not for me...thank you, just water."

The waitress left again, leaving them with two menus.

"Not a wine drinker?" the doctor asked.

"No, not really, I'm not much of a drinker to be honest," Mary answered, feeling like she had to explain herself. He looked at her again with fascination and Mary instantly felt uncomfortable. She grabbed her large menu and practically hid herself from view. As she studied the menu, with some difficulty as she'd forgotten her glasses, she was confused. Did that really say wild boar? The doctor read her mind once again.

"Having some trouble?" he asked with a grin. Mary didn't know if he was mocking her when he asked her questions, she felt so obtuse around him.

"Em, well, it's just...I thought we were having pizza?" Mary said, feeling foolish.

The doctor laughed. What's so funny? Thought Mary.

"It is pizza. I'm sorry I should have explained, it's hard to imagine a Miller's experience without having tried it. Basically, everything you see on the menu, is served on a pizza. Well, except for the one pasta dish of course,"

"Right, so this Cajun chicken with all the....bits, is on a pizza?"

"Yes. Exceptional pizza I might add, spicy," Mary didn't like the way he said 'spicy.'

"Right," said Mary, still none the wiser. The doctor just smiled, he'd obviously been here before and had had the same reaction from guests he brought with him. I wonder how many women he'd brought here, thought Mary worryingly.

"This..." started Mary.

"Yes?" the doctor asked attentively.

"Wild boar, is that on a pizza too?"

"Yes it is."

"Right, I've never had wild boar before,"

"You should try it, it's really good, like a sweet pork joint,"

"Oh I don't know, I'm not that adventurous," said Mary, apologetically.

"I doubt that," smirked the doctor and Mary blushed. Thankfully, the waitress came back to take their order. Mary ordered soup for starter, to be on the safe side and the recommended chicken club pizza. She felt safe with chicken, there wasn't much you could do to change the taste. The doctor ordered the crostini and the Mediterranean pizza with feta cheese. Mary wasn't feeling very courageous today so stuck to what she knew. But when the soup came out, it was nothing like she expected.

They talked about the weather, the hospital, Brigid, the restaurant, all very business-like. Mary was surprised at how easy the conversation flowed, although it was nothing too personal. She expected to be put on the spot about her failed marriage for some reason, but the doctor was kind and kept the atmosphere light and friendly.

"How was the soup?" he asked.

"Delicious, I didn't think I'd like it to be honest, but it was lovely, I've never had Thai soup before,"

"That's what this place does to people, they either love it or hate it, but most are surprised at how much they enjoy the idea of a meal on a pizza and Thai soup of course."

"So you've been here a few times?" asked Mary boldly. Oh shit, why did I ask that? She thought, feeling like she had just asked him was she the first?

"Yes a few times, it's nice to sit here alone and watch the world go by."

"Oh"

"You thought I brought a lot of dates here?"

"Oh no! No I didn't...I," yes I did thought Mary and you've read me perfectly again.

"It's ok, it must seem that way, but honestly, I don't

go on many dates, married to the job I suppose," he said, looking away, looking somewhat sad.

"Have you ever been married?" asked Mary, stunned at her boldness.

"No, I came close in my thirties, got engaged, but no, never took the plunge."

Mary knew that the conversation would turn to her.

"And you?" he asked automatically.

"Oh here's our food," said Mary, dodging a bullet. Why was it so hard to admit she was separated? And why did she feel so guilty for being there?

When the food arrived Mary's eyes widened. The chicken was meticulously laid out, embedded in a spicy sauce, with herbs piled high, vibrant with colour. The presentation was incredible, even though she didn't know what half the stuff was on her plate, Mary had to admit, she was impressed.

"Impressive isn't it?" the doctor said.

"Yes, I don't know where to start!"

Mary didn't want to admit it, but she was actually having a good time. They talked some more about food, fine wines, although Mary just nodded through that part, being somewhat uneducated on the subject. The doctor politely avoided the subject of Frank and took the focus off Mary, just as he sensed she'd prefer.

When it was time to leave, he gallantly held her coat out for her and gestured towards the door, "ladies first," he said smiling.

They got outside to his car and Mary fumbled with her hands, not knowing whether to open the car door herself or let the doctor take the lead. Of course ever the gentlemen, he opened her door with ease and gestured for her to climb inside. Mary belted up quickly, as he made his way round to the driver's seat and kept her handbag on her lap, clutching it like a bar on a rollercoaster. The first few minutes of the drive were travelled in silence, Mary looking out the window, evading his face, his hands, his company. She knew she was bordering on rude but couldn't bring herself to start a conversation. The close proximity of their bodies made her uneasy. She was relieved when he turned on some music.

"I like that music," said Mary, throwing him a line.

"It's Satie,"

"It's lovely, quite sad, but nice."

The doctor smiled at Mary, giving her a shot of his dazzling green eyes. Mary looked away, embarrassed. Even though he had been the perfect gentleman, she sensed a glint in those eyes, a desire, something that had lain dormant in her for such a long time.

When they got to Mary's house, he turned off the engine. Mary hated this part. The end of the date. The awkward silence before the kiss. There is no way I'm going to kiss him, Mary thought, I'm a grown woman not some silly teenager and what if the neighbours see? Mary located the handle on the door to literally jump when the moment came. He leaned into her and panic rose in Mary's body. She squirmed back in her seat as he got closer, but then his head moved and he grabbed the door handle.

"Here, it's a little tricky," he said, opening the door for her.

"Oh, thanks, thank you," Mary said, feeling foolish.

"Didn't think you'd want the neighbours gossiping," he grinned.

"Oh, yes…right…you're right,"

"I had a really nice time Mary, maybe we could do it again?"

"Em, yes...sure," Mary couldn't wait to get out of the car at that point. She felt like she'd been holding her breath for hours.

"Here's my card, my number's on there, feel free to give me a call anytime,"

"Ok, thank you, well I better get inside," Mary said, leaping very ungraciously from her seat.

"Getting back to that oven?" he teased and Mary had nearly forgotten all about the dreaded oven cleaning.

"Oh yes! Ha ha yes the oven!" Mary was laughing like a hyena, a stupid, giddy, nervous laugh. She rummaged for her keys and said goodbye to the doctor.

"Bye Mary, take care." and he was gone.

Mary finally got inside and let out the biggest sigh of relief.

"Sacred heart of Jesus!" she said aloud. She needed a cup of strong tea like an alcoholic needed a whiskey.

***

It had been almost a week since Mary's 'date' with the doctor, almost a week since the fight with the women. Before the doctor, all she could think about was the women, if she should call, why they hadn't called? The next scheduled coffee morning was impending and all would be revealed. Most importantly, whether she still had friends or not, but today, she could think of nothing else but her 'date.' She still wasn't sure how she felt about it, whether it was in fact an actual date, whether she wanted to repeat the experience. But something stirred in her that day, but she couldn't quite put her finger on it and it made her uneasy. Mostly because, as much as she hated to admit it, she'd enjoyed herself. An unexpectedly pleasant afternoon that wasn't spent; watching soaps, playing with her grandchild, or cooking for Greg, all her tiny little pleasures that made her heart sing, but this was different, this was bold, someone outside the secure realm of her family was actually interested in her and to be quite honest, it made her feel like she was the only person in the room. She hadn't had that kind of attention since...ever! It made her anxious and exhilarated all at the same time, although she was having trouble discerning the two.

Greg was back home again and she was delighted to have some activity in the house besides the TV. She was just about to wake him up, at this stage for lunch instead of breakfast, when her phone beeped. Before she even took her phone out from her apron pocket she knew exactly who it was.

'Mary hello, it's Daniel' the text read, 'hope you enjoyed lunch the other day? I was wondering if you were free this Saturday afternoon?'

Shit, Mary thought, he wants to see me again! What do I do? What do I say? She stood staring at her phone, perplexed and ashen faced. She hadn't even noticed Greg walk in.

"Mum?"

"What? Oh I mean, yes love?"

"Eh, are you ok?"

"Course I am why?" Mary said nervously, arm still outstretched, holding her phone.

"You look like you've seen a ghost, who's on the phone?"

"Eh, no one, it's nothing," Mary said, quickly shoving the phone back in her pocket, she would reply later, to say what she still didn't know.

"Well you look like my ex did when her pregnancy test results came back!"

"Oh it's noth...what??!!"

"Relax relax they were negative!"

"Tests??"

"Mum I'm joking," Greg chuckled, he could jibe Mary so easily.

"Don't give me a heart attack like that," Mary playfully slapped her son's head, taking her mind off the other thing.

"Any grub going?"

"Was going to see if you wanted to go to Joanne's cafe for lunch?"

"Depends, do they still serve those gorgeous deep fried chips?"

"Yes," said Mary laughing, Greg was so easily pleased.

"Right, I'll just grab a shower!"

"Greg?"

"Yeah?"

"Have you ever had wild boar?"

"Wild boar? Eh…don't think so, had kangaroo once, why?"

"Just wondering."

"Ok...you're weird today Mum," Greg shook his head and laughed, heading up the stairs, then he came back down and shouted, "I wouldn't rule it out, God loves a tryer eh?"

"I suppose." said Mary, smiling to herself.

She watched Greg walking up the stairs, God how he resembled his father, although he was a lot taller than Frank, but had the same large, misshapen nose, Frank's coming from the countless bar fights he'd gotten into when he was younger, Greg's from GAA. She remembered every line of him as a baby, blonde hair, big blue eyes. Long gone was the blonde hair, having grown out into a mousy brown. Though he would always be her little blue-eyed boy.

***

Mary woke up to an empty house. Greg had gone to a

festival with pals, Mary didn't even know who, but that was Greg, he'd make friends anywhere. She'd thought she heard him mention that he'd met them on his travels. It was so great having him back, even if she did spend most of her time picking up after him. She would moan to him that 'this wasn't a hotel' and 'she wasn't his maid' but secretly she enjoyed it. It was nice having someone to look after again, someone who needed her. An old familiar feeling washed over her and her body slumped. She'd thought that when she and Frank finally separated that she would finally have peace. But it turned out that the peace she once craved now felt more like loneliness. She thought about ringing one of the girls, but then thought against it, as things were still pretty raw between them since the fight. Thankfully, the centre had closed for repairs, so it was ample time for everyone to calm down. Not that they'd have much to listen to Mary thought, what would I say? As much as their friendships had grown Mary was still hesitant to call them friends, let alone rely on them in her hour of need. It wasn't that they wouldn't be there for her, she knew they would, it was just that Mary only ever relied on one person in her life, herself. That way she wouldn't be let down, wouldn't get hurt, disappointed. It was a lonely existence, but a safe one. Frank's words started to ring in her ears and the realisation struck Mary like a bolt. Without thinking, she grabbed a large notepad and pen from the drawer and started to write. And did so, for the next hour and a half, until her hand cramped and she could write no more. She sat and surveyed her words and as the tears ran down her face she started to laugh and with each deep breath she laughed harder and louder until she had no more air in her lungs and a pleasant exhaustion took hold. Then she straightened herself up, grabbed her bag and coat and headed for the door.

"You look different," said Brigid, with a shrewd smile.

"I feel different," beamed an exhilarated Mary, "when I started to write I just couldn't stop, it was like I'd been holding all this anger and frustration inside me for...for...too long. I wrote about my mother and how at times she didn't show me love, how my father sometimes drank our housekeeping money, how I had two jobs at fourteen, not able to finish school, having to practically raise my siblings, how I married into the same life, how I gave up on my hopes and dreams..."

"And why?"

"Because I was afraid."

"Afraid of what?"

"Of everything! Of losing it, hell there were times I wanted to leave everything behind and get the bloody hell out of here!"

Brigid stifled a laugh, as Mary grew louder and more expletive and started to gather attention from the other patients.

"So why didn't you? Why don't you?"

"Because there was always someone to look after, someone who needed me and after time I craved to be needed, it was all I knew, I was trying to keep myself on an even keel, in case I fell apart, that scared me, I suppose I was scared of my own emotions, I didn't want to end up like my father, my brothers, Frank—I wanted to be strong."

"Mary, do you know, that a good sign of strength is knowing when to ask for help?"

"I do now and even the notion scares me to death,"

"But that's when you need to go for it, when it scares the bejesus out of you, that's life Mary,"

"That's just it, up until now I thought I'd been living, but I haven't, I was afraid to cry, feel, I felt like if I started to talk about my problems that I wouldn't stop and the person listening on the other end would get tired of me," Mary slumped again, it was exhausting feeling this alive.

"Have you spoken to Frank about any of this?"

"Frank? Oh Frank, God, do you think he was right about me? Am I this unfeeling, closed off—cast iron bitch who treated him like a child? Is my marriage break up all my fault?" Mary started to panic again.

"No no Mary, calm down," Brigid offered Mary a drink of water and Mary took several sips.

"We calm?" Brigid asked.

"Yes, sorry."

"No need to apologise my dear," Brigid smiled and waited for Mary to catch her breath.

"I think it would be a good idea to talk to Frank, but not straight away, give yourself some time to absorb all this and when you feel ready, talk to him."

"It is all my fault isn't it?" Mary said quietly. Brigid smiled tenderly.

"Why does it have to be anyone's fault?"

Mary was at a loss for words.

"Look, what I see are two people, plucked from childhood, not knowing what to expect from life and not having the best teachers to learn from, who married young, raised a family and with no time to discover who they really were, who deflected their own fears and insecurities onto each other, because to look at oneself can be so terrifying, the easy option was to avoid that mirror of judgement."

"So we blamed each other for our shortcomings?"

"Subconsciously maybe,"

"Really made a pig's ear of our marriage then didn't we?"

"Hardly, you raised three wonderful children and made a beautiful home together, I'd say that's an achievement in itself,"

"But what if that wasn't enough for either of us?"

"Then you go out and find that girl, the young Mary, Mary Russell, who had hopes and dreams,"

"I'm sixty-five Brigid."

"And?"

"Well I'm...too old!"

"Am I too old?"

"Well no, sorry I didn't mean..."

"I know," Brigid laughed.

"Look, you've had an epiphany about your life, gained an insight into who you want to be, you've taken stock of where you've been, most people waste lifetimes without ever reaching that milestone, count yourself lucky."

"Lucky? It's not like I can do much about it now,"

"Oh but you're wrong Mary, you're so wrong, you see, that's the best thing about getting a second chance, it's never too late."

Brigid smiled and suddenly Mary was filled with an incredible urge to hug her friend.

"Ah to hell with it," she blurted and wrapped her two arms around Brigid. Brigid hugged her back tightly, the two rocking each other from side to side. After a few moments, they let go, each smiling broadly as they held hands.

"Thank you," said Mary, not taking her eyes off Brigid.

"For what?" asked Brigid, looking into Mary's eyes.

"For everything," Mary beamed, kissing Brigid's hand before heading for the door. She turned back and gave Brigid a tiny wave and Brigid waved back.

She left Brigid feeling bemused. Yes, she'd reached a realisation in her life, but what next? It wasn't like she felt the urge to run into Frank's arms and exclaim her undying love for him! It didn't suddenly make everything better. Hundreds of thoughts darted through her mind and as she wandered in her dream-like state towards the exit door—bang!

"Oh my God I'm so sorry I wasn't looking where I was going," Mary said, mortified as she tried to pick up files and papers from the floor, not even looking at the poor soul she had just slammed into. When she finally did look up she was met with familiar eyes.

"Daniel!" Mary exclaimed in shock.

"Well hello stranger," he replied, in his chocolaty smooth voice, those piercing smiley eyes staring back at Mary's.

Mary didn't know what to say, she'd clearly been avoiding his calls and in her haste to come and regale Brigid with her profound words she hadn't thought about running into the good doctor. Mary blushed and scattily tried to gather up the files she had knocked to the floor. She knew she'd been caught out and knew he'd interrogate her about it so she didn't give him the chance.

"I'm so sorry I'm so clumsy!" she kept saying, over and over.

Daniel grabbed her with one hand, whilst picking up the papers with the other, still not taking his eyes off her. Mary blushed again. She quickly escaped his clutch and stood up, composing herself, staring at the exit with wanton eyes. She literally could not think of anything to say to the man.

"So, I take it you've been busy?" he asked.

"Um, yes, busy! So busy," shit I feel like a fool Mary thought.

"How is Mrs Mannion?"

"Who? Oh ha ha ha ha ha oh Brigid, oh she's good, good, she's good," seriously? Thought Mary, where on earth did that ridiculous laugh come from and why am I so bloody nervous?!

"Good," Daniel smiled a cheeky grin. He was obviously aware of the affect he had on Mary, on all women probably thought Mary. Damn it woman this is supposed to be the first day of the rest of your life where's your confidence? Get a grip! She scolded herself.

"So, where are you running off to?" Daniel asked.

"Oh I'm not running! I'm just, um...em...running, I mean going home," shit why can't I think of somewhere more pressing?

"Oven need cleaning again?" Daniel teased.

"Oh no the oven's clean," why am I giving him an opening Mary thought?

"So, unless you have some sort of hygiene related emergency, am I to assume, that right now, you're free?"

Oh no Mary thought, he wants to take me somewhere! What do I say? Then Mary thought, hang on, I've just spent the last two hours talking to Brigid about taking control of my life, trying new things, why the hell can't I be free right now?

"Yes, Daniel, it would appear that I am!" Mary almost declared the sentence, like she was at some AA meeting or something. 'I'm Mary and I'm free.' She'd obviously taken Daniel by surprise as his eyes grew wide and he let out a little chuckle.

"Ok, good, I just need to drop these files to my assistant for, um, rearranging and then we can pop off," Daniel smiled, nodding jokingly to the files.

"Ok," was all Mary could say.

"Meet you here in five minutes?"

"Ok," Mary said again.

"Won't be long," said Daniel with a smile as he touched her arm. Mary just smiled back and as he turned to walk away Mary thought of dashing to the door, but then he turned back to her.

"Don't run off on me now won't you."

Mary just laughed nervously, how does he do that she thought?

The two set off in Daniel's car and Mary didn't know, nor did she care where they were headed. She surprised herself at how much she was enjoying the drive and in a bold move she let the window down and enjoyed the warm breeze on her face. Daniel looked across at her and smiled.

"Nice to get away from it all isn't it?" he asked Mary.

"Isn't it just," answered Mary, gazing out the window.

They stopped at a beach and Daniel turned off the engine. Mary could feel her nerves starting to get better of her again and once again Daniel was reading her mind.

"Do I make you nervous?" he asked bluntly. Mary's eyes widened, then she looked down at her hands, that she fiddled with anxiously.

"You know you do," she replied, not looking up.

"Mary please, it's not my intention to make you uncomfortable in any way and if I implied that I was in any way aware of this then I'm truly sorry."

Silence filled the car, until Mary started to laugh, softly at first then hysterically, just like she had that morning.

"What? What's so funny?" Daniel asked, baffled. But Mary couldn't answer, she didn't know why but she just couldn't stop laughing and it wasn't before long that Daniel joined in too. They must have looked strange to the other parked drivers, two idiots, laughing at absolutely nothing. Mary eventually stopped her giggles and wiped her eyes.

"I'm sorry," she said, "I'm just, I don't know why I'm laughing, it's just, been a funny day,"

"No need to apologise for laughing," Daniel smiled, bewildered at Mary.

"You do make me nervous," Mary blurted out, "I

don't know why, maybe I feel intimidated I don't know,"

"By me? Why?"

"Well, you're...you! you know? You're a doctor and you're polite and charming and attractive,"

"And that's a bad thing?"

"No, it's just...you're...all those things and I'm..."

"Yes?"

"Well I'm just me."

Suddenly Daniel's face changed, gone were the smiley crinkly eyes, he didn't look stern as much as hurt maybe.

"Mary, dear Mary, do you want to know what I see when I look at you?"

"I'm not sure."

"Well I'm going to tell you anyway. I see a beautiful, vibrant, humble woman who's not afraid to speak her mind. Every time I see you, you look different somehow, it surprises and amazes me and today, I don't know why but you seem to have this glint in your eye, that something in you has shifted."

"Have you always been able to do that?"

"Do what?"

"Read people, know what they're thinking,"

"Am I reading you?"

"Maybe. The truth is Daniel, I'm at a stage in my life where for the first time I'm actually finding out about me, does that sound silly?"

"Not at all."

"See? You get that, so many other men wouldn't, my husband....well, other men wouldn't and as much as I also find you utterly fascinating and the whole idea of...this...is scary, yet exciting, I just don't know..."

"If it's what you need right now?"

"Yes. I'm sorry,"

"That's ok Mary, there's no need to apologise,"

"You're doing it again,"

"What?"

"Being charming!"

"I know, annoying isn't it?"

The two just laughed again.

"Come on, I'll take you home,"

They drove home exchanging pleasantries, it felt like the end of a relationship for Mary, even though there was no relationship to speak of, but she didn't feel sad, angry or regretful, she felt calm and peaceful. Meeting another man was the last thing on her mind, especially a man like Daniel, but during their short time he had given her a gift. He wanted her for who she was and needed nothing in return. Mary didn't know if she would ever see Daniel again, but at that moment it didn't matter. She was thankful for knowing him right then and there and that was all that mattered.

They arrived back at Mary's house and as the car came to a stop they looked at each other and smiled.

"Thank you Daniel."

"For what?"

"I'm not sure really," Mary laughed, "but thank you."

Daniel smiled his most alluring smile and for the first time Mary welcomed it. She got out of the car and turned to walk into her garden, then Daniel called her.

"Mary!"

Mary walked back to him and he took her hand, kissed it gently and said, "until we meet again Mary Bannick."

Mary smiled and Daniel drove off, in fact she smiled all the way up the drive, a feeling of contentment nestled in her belly. She hadn't noticed it had gotten dark, hadn't cared which neighbours saw what and hadn't noticed Frank, standing at the corner, watching on in dismay.

Chapter Eight

Mary wasn't sure if anyone would turn up today. She'd sent a text out to everyone saying that it was tea as usual, but got no reply, still she hoped everyone had calmed down enough to forgive and forget. She missed Brigid today more than ever, her very presence would change the whole mood, maybe the argument would have been avoided had she been there. Who knows? She imagined Brigid taking control of the situation and no one daring to question her. But Brigid wasn't here today, it was just Mary and the four walls.

It was ten after eleven and Mary thought about sending out another text. The kettle had just clicked off when she felt someone behind her.

"Mary?"

Mary jumped out of her skin, not hearing the door. It was Alice, holding a bunch of flowers.

"Alice! God you startled me!"

"Sorry."

"That's ok love, it's good to see you," Mary was delighted. If it was to be just her and Alice sipping tea in a cold room so be it, she was just relieved that someone came.

"Mary, these are for you," Alice said as she handed Mary the flowers, "just to say, ye know, sorry I stormed out," Alice looked like one of Mary's children when they did something bad. Mary felt so sorry for her, the girl was obviously under a lot of pressure, she just never seemed to show it. Everyone has a button I suppose, Mary thought.

"Alice you didn't have to do that, honestly," Mary said as she hugged Alice, who was close to tears.

"No I do, I really am sorry I don't know what came over me," said Alice, blowing into a well-used handkerchief. Mary thanked Alice for the flowers and then the door opened, it was Cathy.

"Morning," Cathy said quietly to no one in particular and avoided eye contact with Mary and Alice.

"I think there's someone else you might need to talk to today too," Mary whispered to Alice, nodding over in Cathy's direction. Cathy was sitting in her usual seat, legs crossed, arms folded, pretending to read some posters on the wall. Alice nodded to Mary and grabbed two cups from the kitchen. The door opened again, it was Rosa. She too made no eye contact, feeling that everything was her fault. She made her way over to the kitchen and simply said "hello" to both Mary and Alice. She thought against trying to start up any kind of conversation with Cathy in case her worse fears came true and that she did in fact cause the whole argument. Last to arrive was Marji, who also bid everyone and no one a "morning" and made her way to the kitchen, where everyone lingered, albeit keeping their distance from each other. Each were avoiding sitting down, dreading the post-war conversation. It was becoming ridiculous, no one speaking, stirring their cups nearly wearing away the pattern.

Enough is enough thought Mary. "Right let's sit everyone shall we?" My God thought Mary, where in God's name did that voice come from? It sounded confident, aggressive even. Sure, over the years she had used 'the tone' on her family when they misbehaved. 'The tone' had become something of a joke in the Bannick household. 'Oh no it's the tone, shit what did we do' her kids would say. Mary never saw the need for such exaggeration and didn't believe she ever had a tone. Nor she or Frank ever slapped the children, so words were the only option. And accompanied with the tone, it got results. Mary never thought of it as something to be scared of, but after hearing it for herself and looking at the faces of the women, she started to see what her children were talking about. Oh my God was she a scary mother? Did she ever use it on Frank?

The women all sat down, everyone looking in different directions and shifting uncomfortably in their seats. Mary felt like it was the beginning of a school day, with her at the helm of the class. She looked at Alice, who gave her a sheepish smile, Cathy who now had her hands behind her head, slumped back in the chair, staring at the ceiling. Rosa was nervously fiddling with her hands and Marji just stared at the floor. The room was so silent that you could hear the old heating pipes clanging in a recurrent tapping sound. Tap, tap, tap. Mary was just about to speak when there was a knock at the door. Mary looked through the small window and saw that it was Claire. Mary leapt from her seat.

"Claire!" said Mary.

Claire gestured and mouthed 'can I come in?' through the window.

"Of course! Come in come in!" Mary leapt off her chair to welcome Claire in.

"Oh good you're all here," Claire said, not noticing the tension in the room.

"So, said Mary, "How's our Brigid?" Mary had no sooner said the words when she knew the answer.

"Oh," was all Mary could say, as she quickly covered her mouth her hands.

"What?" said Alice, oblivious to Claire's demeanour.

"Mum died yesterday."

"What?!" asked Alice rhetorically, "but she only had a broken leg, how, what happ...Mary?"

"Oh my God," said Marji, her too raising her hands to her face in shock.

"Shit," said Cathy, softly, she too in shock.

The news hit the women like a tonne of bricks and even though Mary expected it, she couldn't quite comprehend Claire's words. Mary had seen it in Brigid's eyes that last day they spoke, they'd had such a good chat, she'd had a chat like that with her own mother before she died. Even with her mother's Alzheimer's, she was completely lucid that day, clear about her feelings, definite about what she wanted, for herself and for her family. It was like she was preparing for a journey, packing up, turning off all the lights, making sure the cat had enough food, cancelling the milk order and saying her goodbyes. It was the same with Brigid. Something about that day felt final, even though neither wanted to admit it. And now, the reality had hit them, six had become five. All was quiet in the room, each in shock, each coming to terms with their feelings, then Rosa spoke.

"I am very sorry," she said to Claire.

"Thank you," said Claire, reaching for her tissues.

Mary gathered herself and looked at Alice, who was still waiting for an answer as to how this happened and Claire gave her the answer she didn't want to hear.

"Mum was diagnosed with an aggressive form of cancer six months ago. She made me promise not to say anything, didn't want anyone to worry and if you knew my Mum like I did you'd know not to argue with her!" Claire feigned a laugh and the women smiled.

"But we could have done something, I mean...if we'd known, said Alice, "I mean, done more....I don't know," Alice couldn't talk anymore, big puddles of tears blinding her eyes.

"Oh no," said Claire, "You did everything she wanted, she didn't want to be treated like a sick person, even though she was, you know Mum, hates a fuss, hated, she wanted you to remember her like she was, a fighter, stubborn old coot that she was," Claire smiled again, "Heck I think if she could, she'd have kept it from us! She hated being sick and thank God she didn't suffer too long."

Mary placed her arm around Claire, tears welling up in her eyes.

"I just can't believe it," said Marji, "Mary, did you have any idea?"

"No, no idea," Mary lied. She knew there was more to what Brigid was telling her and knew better not to ask.

"Listen I hope you don't mind, but I can't stay. Lots to do and I'm afraid I'll start crying again if I stay any longer," said Claire.

"Of course," said Mary, "and listen if there's anything we can do," "yes anything at all," said the rest of the women. They each hugged Claire, telling her how sorry they were, all still in disbelief.

"Thank you ladies, I appreciate that and thank you on behalf of my Mum for your friendship, it gave her a new lease of life, she loved coming here and loved meeting you all," Claire started to cry again and everyone just nodded and smiled as Claire wiped her eyes, making her way for the door, then she turned.

"Oh Mary, before I forget, Mum wanted me to give you this," Claire handed Mary an envelope, "I haven't read it, strict orders you know? Anyway she made me promise to give that to you and you've to read it out for all the group. I'll be in touch about the funeral etcetera so....ugh water works," Claire smiled again and gave Mary one last hug before she bid everyone farewell.

The women all slumped down in their chairs, stunned, upset and visibly shaken. Mary held the envelope tightly in her hand as she stared at the inscription, 'to my coffee mourners.' Mary laughed, then wondered when Brigid had wrote what was inside.

"What is it Mary?" Marji asked.

"A letter I think, to us," Mary answered, still staring down at the envelope.

"Read it," said Alice.

"Yes read please Mary," said Rosa. Cathy just nodded and Mary opened the envelope and began to read the last words of their dear friend.

'To my coffee mourners, '

Mary spelt out the word mourner and the girls exhaled with a grin, typical of Brigid to make light of the situation.

'You're reading my letter so I can only assume that I've passed on. First and foremost stop your blubbering immediately, there is no need for tears for me, do you hear me Alice?'

"What?" said Alice looking up, sniffling into a handkerchief, "oh" she giggled through tears.

Mary went on.

'I have had an exceptional life. Five wonderful children and six wonderful grandchildren. A fulfilling career and a beautiful home filled with warm memories. My only wish was that Mr. Mannion had been around longer to watch his family grow. When I reached my eighties, the doctors and my family warned me to slow down and boy am I glad I didn't listen to them. I have had many friendships over the years, many I outlived, but never gave up hope of making new ones. And on the day I walked into Mary's coffee morning, a new, (final unbeknownst to me) chapter of my life began. I expected to have coffee and biscuits one morning a week, with a bunch of nice women. What I found, were five of the most amazing women I have ever met.

Mary, thank you for organising the coffee morning, I'm sure it wasn't an easy thing to do and you deserve a pat on the back for it. Cathy, men are not perfect, they left that to us women, look out for the little things that your husband does for you.'

Cathy smiled and patted her stomach.

'Alice, if I meet a little baby in heaven looking for wonderful parents I will send him to you.'

Alice smiled, a tear trickling down her cheek.

'Rosa, you deserve the best life here in Ireland, don't stop until you get it. Marji, thank you, you are the first gay friend I ever had and that made me feel, what is the word, cool?'

The women laughed.

'Finally, I want you all to think about why you came to the coffee morning, what you wanted to get from it. Has it come yet? It came for me. It taught me that the world is like a carousel, it will always keep turning, we may jump off from time to time, but we can always get back on that horse, because regardless of how much we try to stop it, life goes on, live yours. Your friend, Brigid Mannion.'

Mary looked up from the page and there wasn't a dry eye in the room, including her own. She smiled affectionately at the girls.

"Wow, "said Alice.

"Yeah," was all Marji could manage.

"Fair play to you Brigid," Cathy said, wiping her eyes.

"She was lovely woman," said Rosa.

"God I feel like a right bitch now," said Cathy, looking sheepish for the first time in her life.

"Me too," said Alice nervously.

Then they both looked at each other and within seconds blurted out the same sentence.

"I'm sorry! No really, I'm sorry, no I'm sorry, no I'm sorry," they both went on and on.

"Girls! This could go on and on!" Marji teased and they laughed.

"I didn't mean to give you a hard time about being

pregnant I really am happy for you," said Alice, with the utmost sincerity.

"And I didn't mean to be so negative about it, I suppose I can be a bit cynical at times," said Cathy.

"You suppose?" laughed Marji and Cathy couldn't help but laugh too.

"Right I'm a self-centred cow! How's that?" laughed Cathy.

"That's better!" laughed Marji.

"I am sorry I caused argument," said Rosa.

"Oh no no Rosa, you didn't, honestly, you just brought a few things to a head for all of us," said Marji.

"Bring things to head?" Rosa asked, confused.

"She means we all have our troubles Rosa," said Mary, as Marji's shameful eyes gaped across to hers.

"Mary I'm so sorry at what I said, I shouldn't have turned on you, there was no need for it," said Marji.

"It's ok," said Mary kindly.

"No it's not," said Marji, "here you are having organised this coffee morning and I slag you off for it, it wasn't on."

"Marji, it's ok really, like you said, everyone has their problems," said Mary.

"I know, but it's no excuse and I'd no right bringing mine to the group. I guess I just...well with Cathy and her news, Alice and her wonderful husband, you with kids who adore you by the sounds of it, even Rosa with her, well...you know, you all have something to get out of bed for and me? Well, I know you all had your own reasons for coming to this coffee morning, but me? I came because, well because I was.."

"Lonely," Mary said, finishing Marji's sentence.

"Yeah," said Marji, surprised, "but how did you..."

"Because I came for the same reason," said Mary.

"Me too," said Rosa.

"Me too," said Alice. Everyone turned to look at Cathy, who just said, "yeah" in agreement.

Mary couldn't believe what she'd just said. Did she really utter the dreaded word? The word that made her weak, pathetic? It was hard to even admit it to herself, but to others was even harder. But she'd done it and she wasn't alone. That amazed her, that people she admired, was maybe even a little jealous of, actually shared her pain. Who'd have thought, that admitting her loneliness, instantly made her feel, well, less lonely. She was relieved, exhilarated, like a weight had been lifted from her chest. She looked around the room, each of the women looking astounded, thinking they knew each other so well, thinking they had little in common with each other. Alice was the first to speak.

"I feel really bad that it made me feel good to say that, with Brigid just having died."

"Me too," the women all answered.

"I'm shocked that you all feel the same as I do," said Marji.

"Well I didn't realise how lonely I was until I came here and met all of you. Don't get me wrong, Stephen is everything I ever wanted, everything I need in a husband, I just wanted a friend too. I've never had much confidence to make new friends and I was so young meeting Ste that he kind of became my friend ye know? And minding kids, well as much as I love it, I need to talk to adults too and need other songs on my iPod instead of I'm a big purple dinosaur!"

The women laughed.

"I'd been losing it a bit too much the past year," said Cathy, "Thomas and Jade didn't seem to want to spend any time with me and rather than admit that I wanted them around more I ended up pushing them away. His work's not so great either and I'll admit I got too caught up in living the high life that I forgot the importance of just having someone who loved me. When I looked at you Alice I saw how little you had compared to my old fat bank account, yet you were ten times happier than me. Have to say I was a little intimidated by it."

"Intimidated? By me?!" said Alice, dumbfounded.

"Yeah, you had what I wanted and I wasn't used to not getting what I wanted," said Cathy.

"Not everything," Alice smiled.

"I know and there was me pissed off that I was pregnant, I was a fool," said Cathy.

"Have to say Cathy, I was really intimidated by you and your glamorous life, I never had that" said Alice.

"Not all it's cracked up to be believe me, I've recently learned that" Cathy smiled.

"Money can't buy happiness," said Marji.

"True," said Mary and the girls agreed.

"I don't know," said Marji, "A year ago I'd have swapped lives with any of you, anything seemed better than being a fifty year old fat lesbian!"

"You are not fat," said Rosa and all the women laughed.

"Thanks Rosa," said Marji, laughing at her honesty.

"I was not lucky when I met Peter," said Rosa, not giving too much away, "I am lucky now. I will make good life for me and my son."

"Good for you," said Mary.

"What about you Mary? You've been quiet?" asked Marji.

"Avoiding the issue," Mary smiled, but then found her voice again, "You'll probably find it hard to understand"

"Try us," said Alice.

"I suppose I never really had a friend, not even in Frank. If times were different we may never have got married, I don't know. Back then you got married, had kids and that was it. No one tells you what to do after that, when everyone's gone, when there's nothing left but an empty house and nobody needs you anymore."

"But your children need you Mary," said Alice, "they will always need you, that never changes."

"Doesn't it?" asked Mary.

"No, look at poor Claire, you can't tell me that she wouldn't give anything to have her Mum back?"

"It's true Mary," said Cathy, "as much as I say that Jade hates me around, "she can't go to sleep at night without a kiss from me," Cathy's advice was like a sudden revelation to herself.

"She's right Mary," said Marji, "I don't even have kids and have never stopped needing my folks, even now that they're gone. The nappies and bottle feeding ends, but the need to be nurtured doesn't. I was still my Dad's little girl until he died four years ago."

"Yes Mary," said Rosa, "I too miss my parents, I wish I see them more."

"And besides Mary, there's a few people in this room who need you too," said Marji, "mother hen," she winked.

Mary smiled, she was so moved she was close to tears and felt guilty that they weren't for Brigid.

"Won't be the same without Brigid, sitting in the corner, giving us advice even when we don't want it," said Mary, despondent.

"Sure even in death she's still coaching us through life, look at us," said Marji.

"You're right," said Cathy.

"She'll never be far away," said Alice.

The women smiled and then turned to look at Rosa as she raised her cup.

"To Brigid," she said.

"To Brigid," the women clinked their cups together, in

honour of their special friend.

***

The phone rang just as Mary sat down to watch Corrie and she cursed to herself. Thoughts of her late friend trailed through her mind.

"Mum?"

"Helen?"

"Mum you have to come quick, Dad's had an accident."

"What?! What kind of accident?"

Helen was crying, she was very soft and the tears came easily and Mary tried not to panic.

"Calm down love it'll be alright, now where are you?"

"On our way to the hospital, Gerry's driving, will we pick you up?"

"Is he in Vincent's?"

"Yep."

"No love I'll get a taxi don't worry, it's too far out of your way,"

"Ok Mum, see you there."

Mary got off the phone and rummaged around for her bag and umbrella. The rain was teaming down. She had to compose herself for a minute as the news sank in. Frank, accident. Oh God she thought, this is my penance for leaving him, it's all my fault.

When she got to the hospital, Helen and Gerry were already there.

"Hi Gerry."

"Hi Mary."

"Mum oh Mum I hope he's ok, the doctor didn't tell us anything yet, oh God I hope he's alright," cried Helen.

Mary put her arms around her eldest child, "there, there love, it'll be ok."

A voice from behind startled them, "Mrs Bannick?"

"Yes doctor, I'm Mary Bannick, how is my husband?"

Mary felt silly for calling him her husband after she abandoned him after forty years of marriage. Then again, she was still his next of kin, she just realised.

"He's fine he's doing well, Mrs Bannick, does your husband work out a lot?"

Mary didn't know, but the sheer notion of Frank trying to get fit was preposterous.

"Erm, no doctor, he em, no he doesn't."

Mary felt like she was being quizzed on 'how well do you know your ex-husband' she also felt like she was being judged by this stranger in a white coat, who didn't even know her situation. She felt like every question she didn't know the answer to put her on the spot somehow.

"Well then maybe he should take it a bit easy from now on, I'm afraid your husband has suffered a hernia."

"A hernia?" Helen and Mary gaped open mouthed.

"Yes, it's when the intestine projects through his abdomen, it's likely he was under some physical strain when it happened."

"I'm sorry doctor I'm trying to follow,"

"Of course I'm sorry, a hernia can erupt in a male or a female due to several reasons, it's where a part of an organ protrudes through the cavity or space that contains it. It does tend to cause some pain, it can happen when doing anything strenuous or something that the body is not used to. Some minor surgery will fix it right up and recovery is very successful given rest."

"Surgery?" Mary could hear the words going in but couldn't comprehend what was being said as quickly as she was being told.

"Yes I am eager to proceed with this today, we have your husband on painkillers at the moment but I'd like to get the hernia sorted out to prevent any further complications."

"Can we see him doctor?" asked Helen.

Mary was eager to see him but felt in some way that she'd no right to be there. And what if Frank didn't want to see her? Her thoughts were distracted by Helen.

"Let's go Mum,"

"Yes love of course,"

Frank sat in the bed looking dishevelled, hooked up to a heart monitor with an annoying repetitious beeping sound. His face changed as he saw Mary and Helen come towards him.

"Mary!"

"Hello Frank,"

"Oh Dad, are you ok?!"

Helen flung her arms around her father.

Mary didn't know what to say, part of her felt like she shouldn't be here. She suddenly felt angry and she didn't know why. Maybe it was because Frank had given them all such a fright and here he was now, joking and laughing with Helen. Suddenly, out she came with it.

"You gave us a nasty scare Frank, a nasty scare, poor Helen was very worried!"

"Mum..." shot Helen.

"No it's ok love, why don't you go back out to Gerry and have a cup of tea," said Frank.

"But..." Helen attempted to argue.

"Go on, sure I have your Mum here."

Helen left in silent protest. Mary sat down beside her husband, not really knowing what to say or do. She tried to mask her worry.

"Frank what in God's name were you doing to get yourself into this state?!" She hadn't meant to, but it came out like she blamed Frank for his own misfortune.

"Ah you know me, I was trying to lift a barrel by myself there was no one around."

"But what about Paddy? Why didn't you ask him to help?"

"Ah he was busy and besides, I'm well capable of doing my job."

"Not at sixty-six you're not, you're not in your thirties anymore!"

With that the doctor came in and Mary was relieved.

"Well then Mr Bannick, how are you feeling?"

"Ah I'm fine, don't know what all the fuss is for."

"Still, you should be more careful when lifting weights, I recommend if you want to get in shape to contact your doctor before you attempt any rigorous exercise."

Mary couldn't believe her ears.

"Weights??!"

"Doctor this is my eh…wife Mary."

"Hello Mrs Bannick."

"I'm sorry doctor, but you said weights?"

"Yes I've been trying to explain to Frank that a man of his age needs to be more careful."

"Yes, indeed," Mary grimaced.

"Well Frank we'll get you prepped for surgery, I'll be back in a moment."

"Yes thank you doctor," they both said.

Frank could feel Mary's wrath coming.

"Frank Bannick, do you mean to tell me that you got yourself into this state by doing weights??!"

"Mary, I'm sorry, I just..."

"You're such a fool, you had Helen worried to bits and you had me...well, what if no one could get to you?"

"Mary please, look I only started the weights to look a bit, well you know.."

"No I don't know! A man of your age trying to be a Jack the lad, it's ridiculous!"

Suddenly Frank piped up in the bed.

"I did it for you woman!!"

"What?"

"I said I did it for you!"

"I heard you the first time!"

"Who is he Mary?"

"What? Who's who?"

"The man you were with, I saw the two of you together!"

"Oh my God, is that what this is all about?" "Where did you see us?"

"At the house."

"Are you spying on me Frank Bannick??!"

"No, I...who was he Mary? I'm still your husband you know, at least on paper I am, how do you think it makes me feel?"

"That man was just a friend."

"A friend?"

"Yes Frank, a friend."

"A friend is a female Mary and by the way you two were carrying on it didn't look like just friends to me."

"This is ridiculous!"

"How long has this been going on, does Greg know?"

"What do you mean 'going on' there's been nothing going on Frank, Daniel..."

"Oh it has a name!"

"Do you know what, I knew you wouldn't understand, that you'd jump the gun as you always do, here's me thinking I could have an adult conversation with you, but you're just behaving like a child! So I made a friend, who happens to be a man, I never had friends Frank, all those years, cooking and cleaning and raising your children, I never had anything for me, I never had a friend to call my own and now here you are being selfish again, thinking that everything revolves around you!"

Frank was shocked, he'd never heard Mary talk this

way.

"Mary!"

"Forget it Frank, with you it's just me, me, me, I'm sick of it—did you ever think that for once in my life I just wanted to be me? Not the wife, the mother, the cook, the housekeeper! You wanted me to let go Frank, well I'm letting go!"

Frank was gobsmacked. He'd asked for this, but it didn't make him as pleased with himself as he thought he would be. This was not the usual Mary, the Mary he'd known, who was scolding him for drinking, she was different, new. It scared him and even though he was the one lying in a hospital bed, he felt like the selfish one. He'd wanted some sort of closure on his marriage but couldn't bring himself to face the end. Mary was standing over him, eyes bulging, fists clenched, her breath quick and heavy. They stared at each other for a moment, then Frank admitted defeat.

"I've lost you haven't I?" Frank said quietly, staring down at his hands.

Mary wasn't expecting to hear this.

"What?" she asked.

"I thought I'd lost you before, when I moved out, but you still, I still, you were still....mine...to an extent, but now....you've finally left me."

Frank started to cry and Mary felt awful. She sat back down and reached for his hand, which he pulled away.

"Frank," she said softly, but Frank was lost in a sea of pain, the kind of pain he was in the wrong place for.

Mary whispered again, "Frank."

Frank wiped his eyes and sighed.

"Look at me, blubbering like a baby,"

Mary said nothing, it was Frank's moment, his time to let go.

"Oh Mary, you were right about me, I put you down

and worse I kept you down, but only out of fear of losing you."

"Frank..."

"Damn it woman you need to hear this! I always knew you could do better than me, I had nothing to offer you, when I drank, it wasn't confidence, I was hiding, all that brawn and bravado, it was a front, I was amazed that you ever married me and every day I worried that one day you'd realise you could do better, so I took advantage of you, you're right I let you take care of me, I didn't realise what I was doing, I'm sorry Mary, I am—I'm sorry."

Frank started to sob again.

"Frank....Frank," Mary reached for his hand again, but this time he didn't pull away. He grabbed her hand tightly as he wiped his eyes again.

"I'm sorry too," said Mary.

"What have you to be sorry for?" asked Frank.

"Oh a lot of things, you were right too."

"I was?"

"Yes," Mary laughed.

"Jesus, forty odd years of marriage and we have to break up for me to be right for the first time?"

They both laughed.

"Hmmm" said Mary

"What?" asked Frank.

"Us, pair of eejits," said Mary.

"Is this the new you?"

"The new me? Gosh, who knows?"

"And what of us?" Frank asked.

"I don't know Frank, I really don't."

Frank wasn't disappointed, he wasn't expecting anything from Mary at that point, but one of them had to ask.

"Just promise me one thing Frank."

Frank raised an eyebrow.

"No more weight lifting?"

Frank laughed, "Deal."

They both laughed again.

"I wouldn't mind, but you never did a day's exercise in your life!" Mary teased and they both laughed again, still holding hands. They sat then, in silence, a temporary clearance in the air, then they were interrupted by Helen walking through the door.

"Don't tell Helen about the weights will ye?" Frank whispered.

Mary just nodded.

***

The winter had crept up on the Dublin streets once again. Shops were bursting with Christmas shoppers, children were eagerly anticipating the arrival of the man in red and parents, at the end of their tether, were in constant use of the 'Santa is watching' threat! Mary loved taking a sneaky look into each window on her street, to see what theme their Christmas tree took this year. As she walked to the community centre, hands warming in her pockets from the icy breeze, she left behind her normal feelings of dread for the holiday and instead focussed on all she'd accomplished this year. Her thoughts continued into conversation with her fellow coffee 'mourners' each thankful for the year, thankful for each other, no longer mourning over their shortcomings, but hopeful for what the new year would bring, but not before reflecting on their eventful year together.

"Well I came to the coffee morning to learn English and make new friends, which I did," smiled Rosa.

"I came to get away from my family, I'm ashamed to admit it but it's true, now I'm running to them," said Cathy.

"I came because that little girl inside me still wants to be popular, but substance over size is more important to me now," beamed Marji.

"I came to have fun!" laughed Alice and the rest of the women joined in.

They all turned to Mary. Oh no Mary thought, here goes nothing.

"Well I got to my sixties and realised I had nothing for myself. No husband, no little kids to run around after, no hobbies. I never expected to actually make friends. I was scared out of my wits on the first day and about twenty days after that. I suppose I wanted to improve my confidence, or to gain some and in essence, to scupper the loneliness, but knowing that you all shared my biggest fear has made me feel, well, not so alone after all."

Mary had, for the first time in her life, admitted how she really felt, it was a trust, a trust that her friends had earned, for want of a better word. She had laid bare her feelings for the world to see, there was no going back or retracting what she'd said. She stared down at the floor with an old familiar feeling, waiting to be ridiculed and laughed at. But no one spoke, at first. For a moment Mary thought she'd revealed too much, but then a little voice piped up from the back.

"I don't mean to sound like a twonk," said Alice, laughing at the use of the word 'twonk' for the first time, "but....I love you all."

Mary suddenly realised why everyone was so quiet. It wasn't judgement or shock at her words, it was a flurry of emotion that had unleashed itself on everyone. Suddenly everyone but her was embarrassed. It took a year, but the rolls had reversed for Mary.

"Me too," said Mary, offering a teary-eyed Alice a comradery smile. Alice smiled back, her eyes alight with a thousand thank yous. Then another voice spoke, then another, until all eyes were on Cathy.

"What?" she asked with annoyance. The women just stared at her, urging her to agree with their sudden revelation. Maybe it was too much of a declaration for Cathy, maybe it wasn't true, or maybe it was.

"Ok yeah me too, alright? Happy now?" Cathy grimaced, as Alice touched her hand.

"Well I can safely say," piped a newly-confident Mary, "that thanks to you ladies and Brigid of course, that the loneliness I felt is long since gone, I thought I was being stupid, to admit that I just wasn't happy, but now? I'm excited! I'm looking forward to the next chapter of my life! Sorry, that sounds like I'm in a musical ha! I guess what I'm trying to say is, thank you, all of you, thank you."

Alice, Marji and Rosa all thanked Mary in return, but Cathy still had her guard up. They all turned to her once again.

"What?" she spat, but the women knew her too well at this stage and understood Cathy's incessant need to keep a hold on her emotions. But in the end, it all became too much for her to retain and she sprang up from her chair and shouted, "Oh hell group hug!" The woman were laughing in disbelief as they all hugged each other in a circle, tears flowing, mascara running.

"I feel like I'm in an episode of the Golden Girls!" said Alice.

"I feel like a lesbian," retorted Cathy and the women stopped, fell silent and looked at Marji.

"Oh shit Marji I'm sorry I didn't mean..." began Cathy.

"Oh would you shut up it's no big deal, you're not my type anyway!" Marji laughed and the women united themselves in a tight embrace. Mary escaped from the gang for a brief second, grabbed her cup, raised it and yelled, "to the coffee mourners!"

"To the coffee mourners!!" everyone resounded as they toasted each other.

When everyone had calmed down from their feel-good moment, Mary made a suggestion.

"I think we should do something for Brigid," she said.

"Like what?" asked Alice, stuffing her mouth with a mince pie.

"Like a benefit night, for cancer" said Mary.

"Like, in her honour?" Marji asked, as everyone pondered the idea.

"I think that is great idea," said Rosa.

"Yeah brill Mary!" said Alice.

"Yeah Mary count us in!" said Marji.

"Fair play Mary yeah count me in too," said Cathy.

Mary was delighted, she had wanted to honour her friend in some way and was delighted that the girls were on board.

"I was thinking of a poetry night," said Mary, suddenly shy, not knowing if her idea would be approved of and after a moment of silence, the women became ecstatic.

"Yeah Mary cool!"

"Brilliant idea!"

"Where should we have it?" asked Alice.

"Well, that's the thing," said Mary, "I think we're sitting in it," she smiled and all the women smiled back and in no time the women were throwing suggestions and ideas Mary's way.

"I can donate spot prizes for a raffle," Cathy said.

"I can bake?" suggested Alice.

"I can get us a few words in the local papers," said Marji, adopting her PR approach.

"I can make, um, invite?" said Rosa.

"That's great!" said Mary, suddenly buzzing, "thank

you all so much!"

"God Mary, it's the least we can do," said Marji.

"Yeah, what are friends for?" said Alice.

Mary's heart was full, "we will do her proud," she said.

"I miss her," said Alice, slightly teary-eyed.

"Me too," said Mary solemnly and the rest of the women nodded their heads quietly.

***

The benefit night had come around quickly. Mary had arrived early, just had she had done at the coffee morning, just over a year before. The room looked beautiful. It was dimly lit, with star shaped lights hanging on the walls. There was a table with spot prizes for the raffle that Mary and her friends had collected. Everything from wine to bath salts and restaurant vouchers. Mary couldn't get over the generosity of local businesses who donated prizes. Helen had compiled a glorious feast of smoked salmon roulettes, cheeses and cold meats and the Haven had donated a few cases of wine for refreshments. Cathy had organised a harpist to play, to give the event some elegant ambiance and the local church choir had promised a performance later in the evening. Marji used her PR contacts to gain some press coverage in the local paper and Alice baked her favourite carrot cake cupcakes. Mary was overwhelmed at how easy it had come together, although at one mention of Brigid's name so many people were more than happy to donate and offer their time. Mary looked across the room to a photo of Brigid, that stood alone on a white clothed table, with a lighting candle and some flowers and she smiled. She missed her friend fiercely and for a moment thought she would cry, but when she heard the ruckus from behind her, she knew she didn't have the time to indulge her emotions. The first voice she heard was Marji's.

"Oh my God the room looks gorgeous!" she bellowed as she spotted Mary in the corner.

"Mary!" she shouted as she made her way across the room, accompanied by a friend.

"Marji hi!" Mary beamed as they hugged and kissed, Marji almost squeezing the life out of Mary.

"Mary, this is Jillian,"

"Lovely to meet you Jillian, I've heard so much about you," Mary said as she shook her hand.

"All good I hope," smiled Jillian. Marji was still looking around the room and commenting on each detail.

"Looks amazing Mary, Brigid would be proud!"

"Are you kidding Marji? She'd give out to me for making such a fuss!"

"Oh you're not wrong there," Marji laughed, then imitated their late friend's voice, "Mary, you could have picked a better picture of me!"

They both laughed and then felt guilty for doing so. Marji sensed Mary's sombre mood and wrapped her arms around Mary.

"I miss her too," she whispered. Mary could only manage a nod. The moment didn't last long with the arrival of Cathy.

"Christ it's warm in here!"

Mary and Marji laughed.

"Hi Cathy,"

"Oh hi girls," Cathy waved as she waddled into the room. Even at eight months pregnant she looked a million dollars. Thomas held her arm as he walked proudly into the room.

"This is Thomas."

"Hi ladies, Tom please, great spread, well done," he said as he popped a cube of cheese into his mouth.

"Oi!" said Cathy, "It hasn't started yet stop stuffing your face!" berated Cathy.

"You're one to talk fatso!" he shot back and turned to Mary, "she's not pregnant you know, she just can't get enough of those Big Macs," he winked. Cathy elbowed him in the ribs.

"He keeps telling everyone that—the pig," but Cathy couldn't help but giggle.

"He seems excited," said Mary as they both watched him stuff even more canapés into his mouth.

"He is," smiled Cathy.

"So do you," smiled Mary.

Cathy smiled shyly and nodded, patting her huge belly.

Alice arrived then with Stephen. She had a look on her face like a child in a sweet shop. She too had an exuberant glow about her. Mary hugged her tightly.

"Alice, you look beautiful," said Mary.

"Yeah a bit too well," teased Cathy, "you sure you're really pregnant?"

"Well, actually," said Alice shyly, "we got some news today,"

"More news?" said Mary excitedly.

Alice patted her belly and Mary knew exactly what she was going to say and before she even got the words out they were hugging again and cackling like schoolgirls.

"What?" asked Cathy, "what now?"

"Well," beamed Alice, "I'm having twins!"

"Get lost!" said Cathy, in her own sweet way, if it were possible to make an insult sound charming, "twins?! I knew you'd try and steal my thunder," Cathy finished, a serious look on her face. But it quickly changed to a smile and she hugged Alice tightly.

"Congratulations," she said, with a tear in her eye.

Marji had joined the group again and was dying to know what all the noise was.

"Whoa whoa what's all the noise? Cathy, you crying?" she asked.

"No I most certainly am not crying," Cathy protested in disgust as she wiped the tears away from her eyes. Thomas appeared behind her again, still with a full mouth.

"Hey baby, you crying again?" he teased, then he turned to the rest of the women, "caught her crying to the Notebook the other night," Thomas laughed and then received another elbow to the ribs.

"You promised you wouldn't tell anyone about that!" Cathy screamed. All the women laughed and Cathy had no choice but to join in.

"Damn hormones," she spat, laughing and wiping her tears at the same time. Marji was still perplexed as to what all the fuss was and Alice caught her gaze.

"Twins," she mouthed to Marji.

"Oh my God Alice that's brilliant!" Marji hugged her and planted a huge kiss on her cheek, while Jillian looked on and mouthed 'congratulations.'

More people started to arrive and Mary's butterflies turned to adrenalin. She literally buzzed, with excitement, nerves, but if felt good. As the room started to fill up with old friends and neighbours, new faces and new friends, Mary's eye was drawn to two figures out in the hall. Marji noticed Mary's demeanour change as she hurried out to the commotion. Thankfully, it was too busy inside to hear the screams, but when each of the women noticed the other moving, they quickly followed suit, sensing trouble in the air. The first person Mary noticed was Filip, hiding in a corner, while his parents argued. Like an angel Helen appeared out of nowhere and Mary quickly ran to her, asking her to take Filip inside.

"Come on little man, let's get you some chicken nuggets," Helen sang in an overcompensating voice. Rosa immediately stopped to look for her son.

"It's ok Rosa, he's gone inside with Helen," said Mary, not even realising that the rest of the women were standing behind her, like a pack of wolves, preparing to fight. Peter looked up to see the women standing there, his face like thunder, fists clenched. Rosa looked petrified. The voices in the hall had meshed into one vast mumble, but here in the hall, there was silence. Each hungry wolf examining each other. Mary knew that this would not end well, but it had to end, here and now.

"Rosa, come here to me," Mary reached out her hand.

Rosa looked at Peter, the man she had feared all these years, the pathetic bully that kept her a virtual prisoner in her own home. She hated him, with every ounce of her being, yet she still feared him. She looked across to the women and could almost see the heat rising from their bodies. Red, blistering embers, waiting to erupt. Peter, on one side, fighting to possess her and the women, her friends, fighting for her freedom. Mary spoke again.

"Rosa?"

Rosa looked at Mary and smiled, then back to Peter, with the same smile etched across her face and for a moment, she let Peter think he had won. Then she spoke.

"Peter, I am leaving you," she said with a vehemence she didn't even know she possessed. Of course Peter immediately exploded.

"How dare you! You cannot leave me! I own you, you bitch!" Peter screamed as he raised his hand. Rosa automatically flinched, knowing what was coming next. But his hand was stopped dead and a look of complete astonishment flashed across his face. Rosa looked up and was shocked to see Marji's hand holding Peter's.

"Now you listen here you bastard," she said to a

stunned Peter, "that is the absolute last time you will ever raise your hand to this woman, do you understand?!"

Peter was gobsmacked, as were the others. Marji wasn't the timid, impressionable, scared woman he saw his wife as. He'd never in his life have anyone, let alone a woman, stand up to him in this way. His anger reared its head again as he started to shout.

"You woman...."

"I'm not finished!" yelled Marji, stopping Peter in his tracks, "now Rosa is coming with us and if you try to stop us..."

Peter laughed, he would never admit it, but he was suddenly intimidated by these women, but he couldn't let it show.

"And what will you do? Fight me? Are you big strong woman?" he laughed sarcastically.

"Yes, as a matter of fact I am, but I'm not alone!" Marji shouted, still gripping Peter's hand. Peter laughed hysterically.

"So I am to leave my wife, because of her 'friends?'" Peter joked, looking around the women, "a pregnant woman, an old woman and her?"

"Yeah I may be pregnant but I'll pop you one you prick!" Cathy screamed, making an attempt to run at Peter, fists flailing with Alice holding her back.

"Cathy please!" Alice shouted.

"It's ok Alice" Marji said calmly, "Peter's going to leave now."

"Oh I am, am I?"

"Yes. Because you know what? These are my friends and Rosa's friends, but do you know what else we are?"

"What?" said a smug Peter.

"Witnesses!" Marji shot back.

Peter's face fell, with the sudden realisation that he had just played right into the women's hands. He lowered his arm in disbelief. He had been defeated and he knew it. The women stared on in amazement. Mary comforted Rosa, who was visibly shaken.

"Come on Rosa, let's go inside," said Mary, turning her back on Peter. Then the women followed, with only Marji holding Peter's gaze. As they got to the door, they heard Peter laugh again.

"You'll never last without me Rosa, you have no home, no money, nothing! You are nothing without me!"

Cathy had had enough and she turned around to face Peter. All the women stopped again, nervously awaiting Cathy's reaction.

"Oh I'm sorry," Cathy said, in her trademark, don't mess with me, I'm going to make you feel like you were never born tone, "Didn't you hear? Rosa is coming to live with me, so you can take your house and your money and shove it where the sun don't shine!"

Peter was shocked once again, as was Rosa, as was everyone.

"You'll be back Rosa!" Peter sniggered and Rosa turned to him. Mary was just about to drag her inside, but before she could, Rosa spoke.

"Never," Rosa announced, in a confident voice. That one word had unnerved Peter more than anything he had heard tonight. Rosa turned and her friends accompanied her into the hall, not looking back.

The women let out a collective sigh and smiled at each other.

"Whoop!" Marji shouted out and the women laughed, finally relaxing.

"Marji that was awesome!" screeched Alice.

"Yeah Marji," said Mary, "Remind me never to get on your bad side!"

"He's lucky I'm bleeding pregnant is all I can say," said Cathy.

The women laughed again.

Rosa looked at each of the women and smiled, "thank you all so much, I could not have done without you."

The women grabbed each other in a bear hug, each saying 'you're welcome' and 'what are friends for?' except for Cathy who was moaning that they'd crush her unborn child. They wiped tears from their faces and laughed.

"And thank you Cathy," said Rosa, "for pretending I am to live with you."

"What? I wasn't pretending I meant it!"

The women's jaws dropped open.

"What are you all looking at me like that for? I am capable of being nice you know?"

The women laughed again.

"Oh my God thank you Cathy, thank you so much," cried Rosa, hugging Cathy against her will.

"It's ok it's ok, stop getting soppy," said Cathy coolly.

"How can I repay you? I have no job, no money," said Rosa.

"Oh don't worry, you can mind the baby!" Cathy said, patting her belly, "I'll need all the help I can get!"

"Knew there was a catch," teased Marji.

"It's ok, I am happy to do it!" said Rosa, hugging Cathy again, then she pulled back and said, "but I am not doing your flipping ironing!"

The women erupted into fits of laughter, slapping each other on the back.

"Did I get right? Did I get right?" shouted a very excited Rosa.

"In one Rosa, in one!" shouted Marji.

When everyone had calmed down, they realised that the hall around them was full. Mary looked at her watch.

"Right ladies, showtime!" Mary sang.

The women took their seats and Mary grabbed her

notes to head for the stage. In all the upheaval Mary hadn't noticed him arrive. He looked more handsome than she ever remembered, wearing a beige suit and crisp white shirt and brown tie. His hair was slicked back and he wore a linen handkerchief in his left pocket. He made his way over to her and Mary was shocked to find that she was nervous and excited at the same time. Just like when she was a young girl in her courting years. She unnecessarily brushed herself down of imaginary dust and stood there, with a foolish eager grin on her face as he made his way over to her. He beamed when he saw her, it had been a while.

"Mary, you look sensational,"

"Oh I don't know about that,"

"No honestly you do,"

"So, you got my text then?" Mary asked.

"I did and I'm glad you got in touch, thank you for the invite,"

"Well thank you for coming,"

"Well I thought you could do with the extra support,"

Mary's cheeks flushed and she felt foolish, but she was glad he came, glad he was here. She quickly caught hold of herself but she knew that her obvious joy at his presence could not be wiped from her face.

"Would you like a drink?" he asked politely.

"I'd love one,"

They made their way over to the drinks table and helped themselves to two large Chardonnays.

"Cheers Mary,"

"Cheers,"

"Mary, I just want to say..."

"Please you don't have to…"

"I want to, I'm...I'm…I'm very proud of you."

Mary was flabbergasted, she never imagined what would come out of his mouth and never expected those words. She also couldn't believe that he knew exactly what she wanted to hear. Just then she was interrupted by Marji, "Mary! There you are, it's time, you're on girl go shine!"

As he watched her with pride Mary composed herself, cleared her throat and put down her drink.

"Well, this is it, I'd better go."

He looked disappointed that she was leaving, they had been enjoying so much seeing each other again.

"Well, the best of luck,"

"Thank you."

"Eh...Mary?"

"Yes?"

"I'd love to catch up later, if that's ok?"

"I'd like that."

"And Mary?"

"Yes Frank?"

"I love you."

Mary beamed. The man she had spent so much of her life with, the man she had three kids with, the man she left, suddenly was standing here telling her that he loved her and it felt so right. She didn't say anything, she didn't have to. She just smiled, a smile that belonged to no one else, but him.

Mary took to the stage and everyone clapped and then a hush came over the room.

"Hello everyone, my name is Mary Bannick and I'd like to thank you all for coming here tonight. As you all know, the reason we are here is to honour an amazing lady who has touched all our lives in such wonderful ways, Mrs Brigid Mannion. When we were trying to decide what to do in aid of the horrible illness that took Brigid from us, we looked back over the many passions Brigid shared with us over the past year at our coffee morning and thought it fitting that we read some of her many wonderful poems that she shared with us. I would like to start by reading a poem that she wrote for her late husband. It's called My Love and I."

You could hear a pin drop in the room as Mary emotionally read one of her friend's poems.

'My love and I walked through Merrion Row, passing street sellers and neighbours, chatting momentarily for the week's news

My love and I gathered meat and vegetables, for the weekend stew

My love and I listened quietly to the radio, as we cooked our lunch together

My love and I shared a wayward glance and suddenly it was forever

My love was taken from me, but I'll meet him again, my love, my only love, my one true friend.'

Rapturous applause followed, for the posthumous words from Brigid and the sensitivity at which Mary read them. More poems followed, some from Brigid and some from people who knew her. The night was a perfect homage to Brigid and Mary didn't realised how much she had achieved until Claire made a speech, thanking Mary for the best year of Brigid's life since her husband's passing. Tears filled Mary's eyes. The night had been very emotional, but she was glad she had put the effort in and as the night came to an end she gathered her bag and coat and headed for the door. She refused lift after lift, preferring to walk and as she made her way out the door she suddenly realised that the woman who had walked into the centre that first day, nervous and lacking in confidence had long since gone and what now stood in the doorway was a woman with an exciting new future ahead. She smiled and as she looked up one single flake of snow touched her cheek and she laughed. She didn't notice him come up behind her.

"Excuse me madam, but would you mind if I walked you home?"

Mary turned and smiled, "I'd be delighted."

"I'm Francis by the way."

"Mary."

Me, Mary.

The End

Epilogue

Dear girls, I made it! I'm finally here! Quebec has the quaintest feel to it. The small winding streets and cute little shops along the way make you want to soak up the warm atmosphere. We had dinner in La Stralle, a revolving restaurant at the top of a hotel, which boasts an impressive air top view of Quebec. A pianist captured the ambience of the restaurant with modern tracks including a haunting version of One Republic's Apologise.

My favourite part was the walk around the Old Town. Down to the boardwalk you can overlook the Saint Lawrence River. One shop that caught my eye was Geomania, on Rue de Notre Dame. It has an amazing selection of minerals and gems. I think I may take a trip there tomorrow to pick up something for the new me. I picked up a Christmas decoration from La Boutique Noel, an all year round Christmas shop. It was lovely and the decoration, a little angel, will be a constant reminder of how brave I was. It's never too early to soak up the magic of Christmas! It's so great to see Lily and the kids, even if we are having problems understanding each other! It's 10.30 now, 3.30 back home, so I think I'll climb into my enormous bed and watch fluff TV. Bon Soir!

Mary

www.blossomspringpublishing.com

Printed in Great Britain
by Amazon